Finding Waldo Within

A Journey Beyond Clarity

S. Bobby Alexander

Sweeter
MARKETING
LLC

First Printing, 2025

∿

Try not to resist the changes that come your way.
Instead, let life live through you.
—Rumi

∿

Author's Invitation

Before the journey begins, a quiet breath. Not to explain, but to welcome.

This is where it starts—with the willingness to listen. Even to the quietest part of yourself.

For the ones who are still tuning. Still searching. Still wondering if what they carry matters.

To those who have ever felt lost in the noise of life—this is for you.

∿

Dedication

∾

And to my wife and children,
Thank you for being my constant compass, guiding me when I've wandered off
course, reminding me of who I am and who I strive to be. You've been the
unwavering light that helps me find my way back, even in the darkest
moments.

May we all find the courage to embark on the journey within.

∾

Note from the Author

∼

Finding Waldo Within is a deeply personal story, shaped by the voices, ideas, and insights of many authors, creators, and artists whose works are thoughtfully woven throughout. Their words helped illuminate the path, and I am sincerely grateful for the ripple of wisdom they've offered me.

That said, the impressions, interpretations, and representations of these inspired works are entirely my own. They reflect my personal lens, how these ideas connect to Waldo's journey, and the broader themes of self-discovery, growth, and purpose. My aim has been to honor their influence while offering one possible way to see through the lens of Waldo's evolving inner world—not to impose a definitive understanding. For this reason, these understandings may differ from the original intent of the creators, as each work will speak uniquely to individual readers.

Thank you for choosing to begin this journey. I hope Finding Waldo Within sparks its own quiet ripple of inspiration, just as these works have done for me.
Sincerely,
S. Bobby

∼

Prologue

The first time Waldo Turner noticed himself fading, it wasn't dramatic. There was no sudden epiphany, no catastrophic unraveling. It was gradual, like the tide pulling away grains of sand, too subtle to recognize until most of him was already gone.

It started with a colleague giving him no more than a polite nod that barely acknowledged his presence. A waiter skipping past his table when he'd been waiting for over twenty minutes. A stranger cutting him in line at a café while the scent of coffee mingled with distant chatter. They were all small occasions. Forgettable moments. But still, they left him wondering, *Am I, in fact, that unremarkable? Or is something else at play?*

He had built the life he was supposed to want—a well-kept home filled with the sound of his children's laughter and where he could always find the warmth of his wife's embrace. By all accounts, he was a man of stability with a comfortable routine. It was a life that should have made him feel seen. Recognized. Valued. And yet, some days, Waldo questioned if he existed at all.

There would be moments where he caught glimpses of himself in passing reflections; storefront windows, the polished chrome of an elevator, but the guy staring back looked . . . remote. Detached. Like a person going through the motions of living rather than genuinely being alive. But when had it started? Was it the result of years spent catering to other's demands? The burden of expectations pressing down, shaping him into someone so safe, so predictable, that he had become invisible, even to himself? Or had he been fading for ages, with the courage to admit it only emerging during his quiet contemplations?

But the real question that haunted him wasn't just what he had evolved into. It was whether he had the strength to find his way back.

Chapter 1
The Invisible Man

It had been nearly two years since Waldo first realized he was drifting, and even though all this time had passed, it was still only steadily—a slow loosening, like a boat pulling away from its mooring.

Now, on a late-winter morning, as the last crusts of snow clung to the sidewalks, hesitant to release the season's grip, he sat once again at Cooper's Café, a sanctuary he visited every Saturday. His favorite corner booth had been his refuge for over a decade. Once, it had offered a momentary escape from the noise of daily life, but lately, it had become just another place to feel the silence inside of him. His coffee sat untouched, a thin film of cream gathering on its surface, while his fingers toyed absently with the edge of his napkin. Across from him, a small vase held a single daisy, its bright-yellow face the only color in his otherwise gray-scale world.

At forty-eight, he was a senior manager and trainer at a reputable mid-sized tech firm, valued for his stability and reliability. He had been married to his college sweetheart, Sara, for over twenty years; a beautiful, compassionate woman who'd stood by his side through every triumph and challenge. After mutual friends introduced them during a spring mixer, their relationship had unfolded in a way that almost felt scripted, as if they'd stepped into one of those classic love stories. She was everything he could have hoped for: warm, supportive, and steady, and together, they had raised two well-adjusted children who excelled in school, sports, and practically anything they set their minds to. They fulfilled every expectation of what a picture-perfect family should be.

They now lived in a cozy, two-story home on a tree-lined street in a respectable neighborhood—a place where the lawns were well-mani-cured and neighbors waved as they passed. Every entry way was deco-rated with a tasteful seasonal wreath with a "Welcome" mat lying neatly at the base of the front doors. Fresh paint gleamed on the mail-boxes. Picket fences framed the lawns, groomed like perfectly combed hair. And each December, the Turner's annual Christmas card featured them all in coordinated sweaters, framed by a backdrop of shimmering lights and festive décor. Their smiles beamed for all of their friends and relatives to see, radiating warmth and achievement.

But inside, beneath the glistening facade, Waldo noticed a hollow space growing deep within him, a sensation of being swallowed by the very life he had built. It was as if a ravenous beast lived inside of him now, and although it wasn't loud, it was constant, feeding slowly on the parts of him that used to feel alive. One day, one hour at a time. The home he'd worked so hard to secure had become a cage of sorts, each perfect detail only a reminder of the expectations he had to keep up. Even the emblems of his existence he should find fulfilling, such as the weekly lawn mowing, the annual fence painting, and the welcoming doormat, had grown oppressive. All he could do was continue to play his role as husband, father, and provider, even if that meant he was moving through life more like a placeholder than a person. Yesterday at work, he caught himself glaring at his computer screen, his fingers hovering over the keys. He was working yet, not fully engaged. This dazed state had become familiar, and whether he liked it or not, he'd grown proficient at functioning on autopilot. *Is this all there is to life?* he wondered, and not for the first time. In quiet moments, he would sit by the living room window and stare out at the street, watching cars pass, wondering if any of those drivers regularly felt the same hidden ache that no new gadget or family vacation could ever seem to fill. And if so, did they, too, sense themselves slowly fading away?

At the café, Waldo peered into his coffee, as if the swirling liquid would somehow reveal the answers that he couldn't quite reach.

"Dad?"

Just then, the voice of his son, Nathan, cut through the fog of his thoughts. The word was simple, but there was a gravity to it. Startled, Waldo looked up as his son approached the table. Nathan had a curious expression, a mixture of concern and quiet resolve that usually wasn't there during their normal father-son exchanges.

"Hey, Dad. Hope you haven't been waiting too long." Nathan smiled faintly as he slid into the seat across from him. Fresh out of college and in his early twenties, Nathan was still living at home, as his school had been nearby, but with a new job on the horizon, he was looking forward to finally being on his own. The sight of him, tall, young, and radiating the energy of someone standing at the edge of possibility, brought a grin to Waldo's face, filling him with a strange blend of pride and unease. Nathan had always been thoughtful, but today his gaze held a new depth, as if an unspoken question had long been gathering beneath the surface.

"No, no, not at all," Waldo replied, trying to shake off his haze. He gestured to the coffee cup in front of him. "Just . . . thinking."

"Still adding too much cream?" Nathan asked, eyeing the swirl in Waldo's mug.

Waldo smirked. "Only when I'm freezing on the sidelines of your soccer games."

"You brought a thermos and a folding chair like it was a camping trip," Nathan said, laughing.

"It always felt like one. Saturday mornings. Cold wet grass. Parents pretending to know the rules."

A flicker of warmth passed between them, momentarily softening the distance—although it didn't last long. Nathan went back to searching his dad's face, looking for reassurance, or a hint that he—and things in general—were going to be alright. Lately, he'd sensed a shift between his parents, an undercurrent of tension he couldn't quite name but felt deeply. His mom didn't say much about it, but he'd noticed her lingering at the kitchen sink a little longer lately, her gaze distant, like she was waiting for someone to come back who was still in the house. She didn't seem angry. Not exactly. It was a quieter emotion. Like she was grieving a version of his father only she remembered. Moments like these—breakfast with just his dad—helped to settle his mind, even if only for the time being. He didn't know what kind of conversation this would be, but something told him it needed to happen, for both of them.

"So, Dad," Nathan began, his eyes steady. "I was hoping you could help me make sense of a few things . . . but not in the way you used to." Nathan paused, brow furrowed, seeking that familiar fatherly guidance. It was simpler when he was younger, when his father's advice was like a compass, steering him in directions that required no questioning. The lessons were clear, delivered with authority and certainty, and he embraced his father's words as indisputable truths. But now, as Nathan stepped further into adulthood and found himself in the complexity of early maturity, with more responsibilities, independence, and the constant need to pivot, adapt, and balance, the straightforwardness of those instructions was slipping away. He realized that shaping a life true to himself meant moving beyond the framework of others, starting with changing the old dynamic of how much he relied on his dad for the answers.

Waldo knew this was happening too. He needed to learn a different kind of wisdom—one that neither did the work for him nor handed him the answers, but instead stirred the questions. The challenge now was not in providing guidance but in offering the kind of advice that resonated deeply enough with Nathan to invite him into his own reflections, nudging him toward his own truths rather than dictating them.

"My first question is, how did you know you were on the right path? Like, how did you realize you were doing what you were meant to do?" Nathan asked.

Not expecting such a profound question, a jolt of panic struck Waldo, making his mind go blank. Even though it had been a while since his son came to him, his colleagues, friends, and even strangers often sought his guidance, assuming he had it all figured out. It was as if having a stable job, a loving family, and a cozy home in a good neighborhood somehow symbolized a sense of inner peace and certainty. How could he ever admit that this couldn't be further from the truth?

The question continued to hang in the air, louder than any answer he could give, not that Waldo had an answer in the first place. Not the clear, confident one Nathan needed, anyway. He could have given an easy explanation, something like, "To achieve the goal of a picture-perfect life, you need to follow your passions," or, "Hard work, discipline, and adherence to the rules will allow you to grab the brass ring." Yet, in that moment, those answers felt strangely empty. Nathan's question hit a raw nerve, and that same unease from before rose within him, a feeling that had become a constant companion lately, whispering the question, *"What is the right path?"*

At some point, they must have ordered—Waldo couldn't even recall saying the words—but the food had arrived before he could reply, the waitress gently placing the plates between them. Ignoring his breakfast, Waldo pretended to ponder the question, staring at the bustling cafe scenery, hoping for a tick of space, the faintest pause to gather a reply for Nathan. Waldo's father's voice floated back into his mind, stirring memories of a time when life was simpler and the future seemed distant. It was an era marked by freedom from responsibilities, unburdened by the worries and complexities of adulthood. One day in particular stood out to him—the day when his twelve-year-old self was faced with the fork in the road.

It was a hot summer afternoon, the dusty road winding through a sun-soaked field, with his father walking beside him. They had been out walking for what felt like hours when they came to a literal fork in the road. Waldo, tired and impatient, wanted to take the path that led directly home. But his father stood still, looking down both roads thoughtfully, and for a moment, Waldo thought his father had forgotten which way to go. *"What's the holdup, Dad?"* he had asked, wiping sweat from his forehead. He pointed to the road on the left, which cut straight through the field. *"That one's faster."*

His father had smiled, but it wasn't a smile of agreement. It was the kind of smile that seemed to acknowledge a truth hidden beneath the obvious. *"The easy road isn't always the right road,"* his father finally said, kneeling down beside him. *"Sometimes, the straight path takes you home, you learning nothing new along the way. And other times, the longer one shows you what you're made of."*

Waldo looked at him, confused. *"But we know where the straight path goes."*

"That's the thing about life." His father stood and brushed off his hands. *"You'll come to a lot of forks in the road. Some will seem easy, like that one. But sometimes, it's not about knowing the destination. It's about who you become along the way. If you're not careful, you'll pick the easiest path and never discover what you're really capable of."* He paused, then added with a wry grin, *"And don't forget, you can't have your cake and eat it too."*

He blinked, trying to connect the dots. *What does cake have to do with forks in the road?* For a moment, he wasn't sure if his father had slipped in a joke or was testing him again with one of his cryptic lessons. But his father's face betrayed nothing, leaving Waldo to puzzle it out, as he often had to. It wasn't until many years later that he realized his father's wisdom often came wrapped in humor, a way of making the lesson stick. Regardless of if *cake* matched the metaphor, the message about choices and growth remained, leaving a sweet and lasting impression for years, resurfacing unexpectedly at distinct moments such as this one.

"Dad, other than work, what's your thing?" Nathan added, as if he could sense the perplexed suspension.

"My thing?" Waldo mindlessly repeated as he finally picked up his fork, coming out of the memory of his father.

"Yeah, you know, like, what makes you, you? All my friends' parents have something. Steve's dad is really into fishing, and Kyle's mom writes poetry. What do you do?"

Waldo stared at his son, fork suspended mid-air. What did he do? He had a job, a family. He paid the bills, drove carpool . . . but none of that was a 'thing,' was it? None of it defined who he was or made him unique. So, in order to figure out who he was, did that mean he also needed to figure out a thing, too? The idea just added another layer to the confusion already churning in his mind. "Well, I . . . I guess I don't have a thing." The admission tumbled out, each syllable adding another stone to the already overburdened basket of perceived failures, as though his life had been a series of near-misses and not-quites.

Nathan studied his father carefully, torn between letting the silence linger or breaking it open. He chose the latter. "Okay, so, what do you think I should do?"

His son's appeal for advice wasn't just a simple question; it was a mirror, held up unintentionally, forcing Waldo to confront his own uncertainties. *What if I can't provide the right answers, ask the right questions, to inspire him to create his own path?* Waldo's heart tightened with self-doubt as he looked across the table at Nathan. The booth seat creaked as Waldo shifted, uncomfortable not just from the question but from the unsettling realization that the bond between father and son was now anchored in shared uncertainty rather than wisdom—and only Waldo knew it. He wanted to be the guide his son needed, but how could he when his own internal compass had long ago faltered?

Waldo traded his fork for his mug, the coffee stone cold. He took a sip anyway. He looked at his son, and against his own wishes, spoke the hollow words he tried not to say earlier. "You'll figure it out," he said softly. "Sometimes . . . it just takes time." As the words left his mouth, Waldo felt the weight of them press back against his chest. Each recycled phrase felt forced. If he really believed it, wouldn't he feel more *found* by now? But looking at his son now— older, yes, but still searching—Waldo knew Nathan wasn't just asking for guidance. He was asking to be seen. To be known well enough where Waldo could push him in the right direction without having to walk the entire road with him, but Waldo wasn't sure if he'd earned the right to be that sounding board anymore.

Eventually, they gathered their things, stepping out into the morning light. The conversation wasn't over, not really. It would continue in its own way, in small moments, in future talks, in the quiet understanding between them, but for now, it was put to rest.

As they parted ways, Waldo settled a hand on Nathan's shoulder. "See you at home."

Nathan smiled, nodding. "Yeah, see you later, Dad."

Later that night, everyone but Waldo had retired to their bedrooms. Instead, he sat in his den home office, staring at the blank computer screen in front of him, the glow illuminating his face. The family photos on the wall seemed to watch him, a reminder that even when his family was asleep, they were still expecting something from him.

He could hear the faint creaks and murmurs of the house settling into night—a door clicking shut, the soft patter of Grace's footsteps, the low hum of Sara's voice followed by a quiet laugh. Likely at one of the videos she watched every night before bed. He yearned to join her, to lie beside her, and let that laughter soften the edge of the day. But he stayed still.

Something tugged at him. Was it sadness? No, not exactly. It was something older. A pull he couldn't name, like a memory stirring in the bones. *When did I start feeling so far away from all this?* The thought passed like a flicker—easy to ignore, but not so easy to forget. He turned back toward the screen, pretending he hadn't noticed.

Nathan's innocent question from earlier made Waldo accept the truth that he could no longer hide: when it came to himself, he didn't have a clue as to what any of the answers were. What was his thing? Who was he, beneath the mask, hiding behind his daily chores and commitments? Questions about his lost identity, entombed under layers built by years of expectation, duty, and routine, haunting him, resurfacing time and again, capturing the tension between his outward wakefulness and a deep inner disengagement he'd tried to ignore. Yet, no matter how often he buried it, the question kept pushing through, demanding to be faced.

Waldo picked up a pen and opened a notebook he kept on his desk to a blank page. His hand hovered above the paper, trembling slightly. After what felt like an eternity, he finally scribbled a single word at the top:

Lost.

He frowned at it. The letters, simple and unassuming, seemed to carry the entire burden of his existence. It wasn't just a word. It was a declaration. A confession. But it wasn't in the literal sense of being without direction, but in a metaphorical way—lost in the belief that success equated to fulfillment. Lost in the naïveté that the more he achieved, the more answers he would find.

But when had it started? When had the path he'd carefully laid out for himself began to disappear beneath his feet? Was it when the promotions he'd once dreamed of suddenly felt insignificant, just another notch on an already too-long belt of accomplishments? Or was it when the house, the accolades, and the respect of his peers became nothing more than window dressing, a meticulously constructed façade hiding the emptiness inside? Although he couldn't pinpoint the exact moment, he knew somewhere along the way, he'd stopped being Waldo, the person he had imagined he'd become, and instead, had morphed into someone who was just playing the part. The true Waldo, the one who once had fire in his belly and stars in his eyes, had vanished into the fog of expectations and obligations, leaving behind this husk of a man.

An old Pink Floyd song drifted through his mind, "Comfortably Numb." Then another surfaced, sharp and familiar: "Another Brick in the Wall." He hadn't thought about those titles in years, but now they landed differently. Like echoes from a script that he had never meant to follow. But that's exactly how he felt. Numb. Disconnected. Compartmentalized. Not just part of someone else's design but estranged from his own.

Nathan's query had been simple—too simple, perhaps—and yet, it had pulled a thread loose in Waldo that he hadn't realized was holding so much together. Not a web, he realized now, but a mask that he had worn for so long that it had fused to his skin.

He glanced down at the notebook again.

Lost.

He wasn't sure how, but this single word contained an entire breadcrumb trail, leading back through the years spent chasing validation, as if wholeness could be earned by climbing high enough or producing more. And yet, here he was. Not higher. Not fuller. Just . . . further.

Further from himself.

Further from Sara, who had once known him by heart.

And further from his children, Nathan and Grace, whose eyes searched for certainty he no longer believed he could offer.

I've been pretending, he thought. *Trying to outrun confusion by staying busy.* But the façade hadn't brought clarity. It had only deepened the fog.

He considered crossing the word out. Convincing himself, even now, that it hadn't meant anything. That if he just moved past it, the ache would lift. But he didn't. The truth, once named, had undeniable weight—and it wouldn't be dismissed so easily.

His hand stayed hovering above the page, but nothing new came. Readiness, it seemed, wasn't the same as willingness. He tapped the pen lightly on the page, the sound echoing the emptiness inside him. *Lost.* Maybe the word wasn't just a summary of where he stood. Maybe it was an invitation—a starting point. He had to admit he was lost before he could find his way again, didn't he? Maybe this was the moment he had to stop pretending and start searching for something real.

But now, a new question loomed: *where do I even begin?*

As the thought settled, Waldo accepted that he had spent all this time waiting for something, or someone, to reignite the spark that had long ago gone out. But deep down, a quieter voice asked, "Am I the one who needs to light that fire?"

He knew that walking the same road would never lead to a new destination. If he wanted real change, if he honestly wanted to ignite something within himself, he had to alter his course, step off the familiar path, and embrace the unknown. The same path would always lead to the same dead ends, after all. And he didn't want to keep circling the same thoughts, repeating the same lessons, telling himself the same stories. Something had to shift; it couldn't be about finding long-lost answers. It was about changing the questions. Perseverance alone wasn't enough to do this. He needed a radical adjustment, something bold enough to challenge everything he thought he knew.

He pictured his father again, kneeling beside him on a dusty road, pointing down the forked paths ahead. *"The easy road isn't always the right road. Sometimes, the straight path takes you home, you learning nothing new along the way. And other times, the longer one shows you what you're made of."* Had he been walking the easy road all along? He had always held onto the heat of that summer day, the feeling of his father's hand on his shoulder, but it was the warmth of his father's voice that lingered the longest. And now, it seemed, that warmth had been replaced by the icy sting of self-doubt.

The truth was stark: real growth required discomfort. It demanded vulnerability, honesty, and the courage to dismantle the comfortable life he had built.

He swallowed hard. Could he face it?

Chapter 2
The Awakening

Ten days later, on a Friday afternoon, Waldo sat in the muted stillness of a therapist's waiting room for the first time. Beige walls. A humming clock. The hush of someone else's breath behind a magazine. His own breath sounded too loud, like it hadn't quite adjusted to the quiet. He didn't exactly tell Sara where he was going—just that he'd be home around dinner. His office had announced an early closure for system maintenance, which wasn't unusual. He often used the extra time to run errands or decompress, but something in the way he'd said it that morning, too casual, too rehearsed, had caught Sara's attention.

The day had started like any other. Waldo, bag slung over one shoulder, grabbed his keys from the counter. Sara, finishing her tea, looked up as he passed. "Only a half day of work. A nice little break," she offered, leaving space for a reply that didn't come. "You okay?" Her voice was light, but her eyes lingered.

He looked away, thumb grazing his phone like he needed to check something. "Yeah . . . just figured I'd get a little space before diving back in." Too smooth. Too practiced. Like something he'd said to himself in a mirror, hoping it would hold.

She nodded, but there was a hesitation. The early closure was no secret; the IT shutdown had been on both of their calendars. She likely expected him home by mid-afternoon, maybe early enough to help Grace with schoolwork. "Early start to the weekend, at least," she said, a small smile flickering across her face. "Maybe we can do something later. All of us."

He smiled back, too quickly. "Yeah. Sounds good."

Then came the pause—that small catch of air where wondering lives. "But you said you're not coming home till dinner?" Not accusatory. Just... a thread of curiosity, tugging.

The moment hovered between them like a held breath. "Yeah, just thought I'd take the long way home today." He suddenly didn't know where to look, so he settled for the floor.

Sara continued to study him, the corners of her mouth pressing in, debating whether to ask more. "Okay," she said finally. Her tone was even, reminding him that she was there for him. Constantly present and ready.

And that—her willingness to trust what he wasn't saying—made the guilt flare sharper than if she'd challenged him outright. A scene stirred up from someplace deeper, the two of them, years ago, sitting cross-legged on the kitchen floor with mugs of cocoa, talking until the dishwasher finished its final sigh. Back when no thought stayed unspoken. But now, even as he stepped onto the porch, feeling her eyes linger, he didn't look back. He told himself it was space he was taking, just a little room to breathe. But her eyes had given him something harder to carry: permission. And it made him wonder if he was slipping away in ways that even he hadn't meant to.

He closed the door more gently than usual, as if trying not to wake something fragile—in her, or in himself. He hadn't meant to shut her out, but the truth was, he didn't understand it himself. At least, not enough to explain it, not enough to name it. It could've been the slow erosion, the steady toll of twenty-some years of marriage, the constant weather of raising kids. Or perhaps, he'd simply lost enough of himself that she finally felt it too. Even if Sara had noticed the way he'd defaulted to going through the motions, he couldn't explain that the man she married now felt like a ghost of who he used to be. He hadn't wanted to leave her in the dark. But in truth, he wasn't sure he could light the way anymore.

It was the same night he wrote *Lost* in his notebook that he finally set it aside and switched to his laptop. Opening a new browser, he typed, *Therapist near me.* He didn't know what he was hoping to find, only that he couldn't keep circling the same questions anymore. He stared at the search results for a long time before finally clicking one.

A name. A time. A beginning.

And now, here he was, stiff in a leather chair across from a woman named Dr. Benson, unsure where his story even began. She looked to be in her fifties, gray hair pulled into a loose bun, with the kind of calm that made pretending impossible. "So, what brings you here today, Waldo?" she asked, her voice gentle but direct.

Waldo took a deep breath. "I don't know who I am anymore. I know my name, my job, my family . . . but myself? I'm not so sure." He looked down, then back up, his voice thinner as he said, "It feels like I've been living someone else's life."

Dr. Benson didn't look surprised as she nodded. "It sounds like you've lost touch with your sense of self. That happens to many people, especially when they've spent years focused on responsibilities that live outside of them. Our identity gets absorbed in the roles we play: husband, father, employee . . . caretaker of everyone else."

Waldo sighed, relieved she understood. "Exactly. It's like I'm just part of the crowd, you know? I'm there, but no one really sees me. And the worst part is, I don't even see me."

Dr. Benson leaned forward. "Tell me more about this crowd. What does it feel like to be in it?"

Waldo hesitated. The silence stretched as he tried to find the right shape for what he felt. "It's . . . overwhelming. Everyone around me seems to have found their thing, their purpose. Even my son sees this. They're chasing their dreams, doing what lights them up. And I'm just . . . here. Background noise in other people's lives. Watching them thrive while I fade into the blur. I feel like I'm disappearing into this sea of people who know where they're going, and I'm still trying to remember what direction even feels like mine." His words hung in the air, worn and real. A muted confession from a man who feared his presence had become too easy to forget.

Dr. Benson gave it space before saying, "Waldo, what would it truly mean for you to stand out? To stop blending in? To carve space that's yours, even if you're still figuring out what belongs there?"

He blinked. What would it mean to stand out? Not to just be seen, but to risk taking up space? He didn't know. He couldn't even picture it because deep down, some part of him didn't believe he had anything worth carving. His fingers curled around the edge of the armrest, searching for something to hold onto, but all he found was the soft press of the leather and the echo of his own uncertainty. His throat tightened, just as it had when Nathan asked him the same question a few weeks back. *What if I have nothing to offer? No space that belongs to me?* Saying that aloud would make it real, and he wasn't sure he could handle that. "I . . . I don't know." His voice was low, his face unreadable. He looked down again. "I don't know what it would mean to stand out. What if I'm not meant to?" Even the idea of standing out felt presumptuous, like asking too much from a world that barely noticed he was there. The words landed hard. Bitter in his mouth. Heavy in the air. He didn't say it to be dramatic. He said it because it felt true. Because the doubt had become more familiar than any kind of certainty.

"Waldo, have you ever heard the phrase, *'Be the change you want to see in the world?'*"

He furrowed his brow, something sparking in the quiet. "Yeah, Gandhi, right?"

She smiled. "It's often attributed to him, yes. But let's not worry about the author. Let's talk about what it might mean for you. You said you feel invisible. That you don't know who you are anymore. What if, instead of waiting for clarity to arrive, you chose to become the source of that clarity?"

"What do you mean?" he asked, a rawness in his voice. The question had touched a place he rarely let anyone see.

Dr. Benson slid her chair forward, meeting him where he was. "You're feeling lost because you've been searching outward, for direction, reflection, permission. But what if the first step isn't out there? What if it starts with choosing to turn inward? What if it starts with choosing to reconnect with the version of yourself you've pushed aside? The one that matters most. The one that doesn't need permission."

Waldo's eyes narrowed, as if trying to clear space in a room long left cluttered. "But how?" he asked, his voice hushed. "How do I . . . actually become the change?"

"You don't have to become it all at once," she said. "This isn't a destination. It's a process—more unfolding than arriving. So, start small. What brings you joy? What makes you forget time exists? What's one value you believe in but haven't lived out lately? You don't have to know everything right now. You just have to start asking."

Waldo swallowed, the words landing more like an invitation than advice. "But what if I don't know what they are anymore?" His voice cracked. "What if I don't even know what I want?"

Dr. Benson nodded, affirming the sacredness of not knowing. "That's okay. Not knowing isn't failure. It's a beginning. You don't need a full map. Just a question. What stirs you, even faintly? What have you abandoned, not because it didn't matter, but because you did? Start there, with one small, unfinished thought that tugs, and follow it."

Waldo was quiet for a long moment. Her words didn't fix anything, but they named something. They reached down into the part of him that had gone quiet, the one the crowd had silenced. Waldo closed his eyes for a breath. The ache was still there, but it had a shape now. "Be the change," he repeated slowly. It seemed simple. Almost too simple. But maybe that was the point. Maybe this wasn't about finding some prewritten identity. Maybe it was about becoming, one honest step at a time.

Dr. Benson leaned back, her expression soft. "Exactly. Change doesn't have to roar. It begins quietly, with intention. And over time, the small shifts you make will internally ripple outward into your life. The goal isn't to be someone new. It's to remember who you are and to start living from that place."

Waldo nodded. He had spent so much time searching for validation — job titles, roles, routines—trying to prove his worth by molding himself into what others needed most. But now, he could feel the pieces of the cracked mold slipping through his fingers. That mold was never his. Maybe it was finally okay to stop holding it together and let something new begin.

"You don't need to find yourself all at once," Dr. Benson added. "You just need to take one step toward becoming the person you want to be. That's how transformation begins; not with answers, but with the courage to start."

Waldo exhaled. For the first time in a long while, being lost didn't feel like failure. Instead, it felt like a beckoning, an inaudible urge to break away from the crowd—not by seeking approval or direction from others, but by creating it for himself.

Waldo stepped out of Dr. Benson's office into the street's soft commotion, the glass door clicking shut behind him. He paused, letting the late afternoon hum of traffic and distant horns settle around him. The air felt clearer than when he'd arrived, a breeze wandering down the block, tugging at the edge of his jacket, while above, a heavy cloud shifted just enough to let a sliver of sunlight break through. It fell across the sidewalk like a quiet awakening. It wasn't blinding or not grand. Just a flicker of light, barely there, but enough to notice.

Waldo glanced up at the uneven sky, feeling that he was at the beginning of something important.

As he moved through the downtown streets, Dr. Benson's words replayed in his mind like a song stuck on a loop. What stuck with him most was her reminder: he didn't need to have all the answers right now. Maybe it was enough to just start, to make the smallest changes that felt right, even if he couldn't see where they were leading.

The rhythmic pattern of his footsteps matched the quiet pace of his thoughts. As he walked, the scent of fresh coffee drifted from Cooper's Café, just down the street, cutting through the cool air. It tugged at something familiar—mornings half-finished, cups left on the counter, and those rare slow weekends when he and Sara would linger in each other's company before the kids woke up. Waldo glanced at his watch. He had time; just enough to spare a few minutes before heading home. He hadn't planned to stop, but the scent of roasted coffee beans drew him in. Just a quick stop. Then, the car. Then, home.

He shifted course, angling toward Cooper's Café. He dodged tourists bent over a glowing digital map and a delivery worker maneuvering a box-laden dolly, waiting at the crosswalk as traffic zipped by in both directions. Two blocks ahead on the corner, Cooper's Café waited, and he could already picture the warm light, the clatter of ceramic cups, and the undercurrent of soft conversation. As he walked, memories unspooled—old film reels flashing through his mind. He saw himself as a boy, barefoot in summer grass, the laughter of old friends echoing from a time when life still felt wide open. Something from that session had unlocked more than just her words, and now, it was as if his mind had begun to stir, drawing on these fragments of his younger self to ignite something he hadn't felt in years. Not just nostalgia, but momentum.

Dr. Benson had said small, intentional shifts would ripple outward. But the phrase didn't feel new, just long forgotten, though the last time he'd heard someone talk about ripples like that, it hadn't been in a therapist's office. It had been at a lake, years ago, his father's voice echoing over still water. *"Even a small rock makes ripples in a quiet pond."*

Waldo smiled. The image rose unbidden: a noiseless lake, cool morning air on his skin, and the feeling of the fishing line in his hand. The water was still but waiting. He remembered the frustration, so many casts with nothing on the line. Eventually, he began tossing pebbles into the water, just to pass the time.

His father, ever patient, leaned back and said, *"You see those ripples, son? Even the smallest rock makes ripples."* Then came the knowing smile, the kind that always meant he was about to share one of his pearls of wisdom . . . or maybe drop a groan-worthy dad joke. *"It's not the size of the action that matters. It's what you choose to do with it. Even a minor effort can create a ripple bigger than you'd expect."*

Waldo could almost hear him chuckling, ready to follow it all up with,

"Or maybe the fish just really don't like rocks in their home, huh?" but that was his father's gift—finding meaning in the ordinary and then finding a way to weave humor in so it didn't feel so heavy. Whether it was a tossed rock or a creaky door hinge, life was always presenting a chance to teach something. The comment about ripples had seemed like just another one-liner at the time, but now, the ripples pressed into his chest with unexpected force. The memory didn't just surface, it resonated.

Waldo stood at the crosswalk, barely registering the red hand blinking across the street. His gaze drifted upward: Lexington & 5th. A corner he'd crossed a hundred times without thinking. Today, it felt marked, as if it had been waiting for him to arrive. When the light finally changed, he didn't notice right away. It wasn't until a cluster of people surged forward that someone brushed his shoulder. A firm nudge. Enough to shake him back into the present.

He stepped forward, catching his toe on an uneven stretch of side-walk. He stumbled, gaining his balance just in time, as an older woman walking beside him winked. "Gotta watch out for that one," she said. "Gets me every time."

Waldo laughed and kept moving, adjusting his pace. His thoughts looped back to the ripple. The shift. The lesson. It had always been the big, sweeping gestures that captivated him, the illusion that one major change could reset everything. But maybe it wasn't about that. Maybe, like his father had said, like Dr. Benson had echoed, it was the pebbles that mattered. The smallest acts. The overlooked moments. The gentle pivots no one saw coming but changed everything. The more he thought about it, the more it began to settle: maybe those were the stepping stones he'd been waiting for all along. Maybe they were enough.

Waldo continued his walk to Cooper's Café, caught in a spirited conversation with himself, his thoughts a mix of excitement and uncertainty. He turned the corner just past Elm Street when a gust of wind struck his face, sharp and bracing. A lingering edge of winter that refused to let go. But the chill jolted something loose, another memory, but this one was of the cold rinks, adrenaline rising as he laced up his skates, the sharp snap of the puck against his stick. He could almost feel the frozen sting against his cheeks, the cut of blades on ice, the electric rush that came with motion. At fifteen, he hadn't been the best player on the team. Not by a long shot. But the game made him feel alive, like if he just kept skating, kept moving, kept trying, anything was possible.

There had been an inspirational quote from that year that followed him from the ice into every uncertain corner of his life after: *You miss 100% of the shots you don't take.* Wayne Gretzky's words replayed in his mind whenever hesitation crept in. A soundbite, sure, but over time, they'd become something more. What began as a cliché, a banner hung in locker rooms, scribbled on notebooks, became a part of him. Especially during college, when life felt less like a hockey game and more like a complex enigma of choices; overlapping, contradicting, and without a scoreboard in sight. When he'd stare at course catalogs and career paths like they were riddles, Gretzky's words came back then— clear, almost taunting. *Success was impossible without risk. And maybe more than that: you couldn't win if you never played at all. Take the shot!*

He hadn't always taken the shot, far from it, and when he had, he hadn't always scored. But he'd come to understand that the biggest misses in life were the ones he never attempted.

A bus rumbled past, spraying a burst of water across the sidewalk. The splash hit his shoe, leaving just enough road grime to make him pause. He stepped aside and found a small bench near a restaurant entrance. As he sat, dabbing his shoe with a tissue from his pocket, the world moved on around him, people heading home, hurrying forward. He watched them, wondering how many were walking with purpose, and how many were just following the routine, like he had for so long. Had he been too careful? Too passive? Letting fear shape a life he never meant to build? There was that restless feeling again. Not just an itch. A hum—a knowing. The quiet ache of a man who might've waited too long.

He leaned back, letting the ache settle. Then, out of nowhere, his eyes snagged on a massive digital billboard overhead. A sneaker ad flickered to life: runners, climbers, and city dwellers all in motion, chasing something invisible. The rhythm of their movement was its own kind of language. The tagline: "One step at a time." The phrase latched onto his thoughts, and almost immediately, his mind supplied the melody, as if someone had turned on a radio. The lyrics to Jordin Sparks' "One Step at a Time" played in his head, the message reminding him of his own need for a journey of rediscovery.

Grace had first introduced him to that song. As the youngest, Grace wove music into everything, her room always echoing with songs that mirrored her carefree spirit—a characteristic that balanced with Nathan's ambitious, driven nature. Waldo liked to think she got that from him, or maybe from his mother, passed down like a worn heirloom. That thought stirred a combination of pride and recognition within him. Maybe he had preserved something that mattered.

Waldo stood, adjusted his jacket, and picked up the pace—the air felt colder by the minute. As he walked, his thoughts went back to Grace and her music. He hadn't always been this reflective, but now, he felt an urge to keep digging—to trace the invisible threads back to their source. Waldo grinned as a vivid reminder took hold, transporting him to a time when he was younger than Grace was now. It was choir practice, and Waldo's mother, her voice soft and melodic, had taken him along with her. He was reluctant at first, annoyed even. The hymns felt like a foreign language, slower, subdued, stretched with words that didn't land. A strange contrast to the world of cartoon theme songs and catchy radio hooks he knew by heart.

Sitting in the back pew, young Waldo fidgeted, crossing his arms, his brow knit in displeasure. And after an exceptionally long hymn, he muttered with a voice brimmed with the impatience of a child used to faster answers, "Mom, I don't like this music. It's boring. I don't get the words."

She had smiled with understanding. Then, kneeling beside him, she placed a compassionate hand on his shoulder. "Waldo," she had said gently, "you're trying too hard to hear the music with your ears, but you have to feel it with your heart."

"But I don't get it," he replied, frustration building.

"You don't always have to understand the words. Music is more than words. It's something you feel. Close your eyes for the next song, and don't worry about what the lyrics are saying. Let the sound move through you, like it's part of you."

Waldo hadn't entirely followed her at that moment, but something about the way she spoke calmed him. The next song the choir sang, he tried what she suggested—he closed his eyes and let the sound flood over him. Instead of focusing on the lyrics, he paid attention to the swell of the melody and the rise and fall of the surrounding voices, until finally, it clicked. He came to realize what his mother had meant; he didn't need to understand the words to feel the music. It was as if the sound itself was telling a story.

By the time choir practice concluded, Waldo's musical outlook had transformed; his mother had unlocked a broader appreciation in him for the way music could connect him to emotions beyond the surface. And from that moment on, Waldo carried a love for that art form, for the expressive, more soulful melodies that spoke to him in ways he couldn't always explain.

But despite the joy Grace's music brought to her, there had been nights when it overwhelmed him—the looping beats, the vibration in the air, the almost physical pressure behind his eyes. Too loud. Too constant. Too present. But still, he never told her to stop, telling himself that a minor discomfort was worth allowing her that freedom. She was fierce, vibrant, and alive in a way he hadn't felt in years, and maybe part of him envied that spark, even as it made him ache. So, he let her keep it. Let her be loud. Because what she had wasn't noise. It was identity. It was becoming. And now, thinking back to his mother's teachings, he realized he hadn't just passed down his love of music—he'd passed down her wisdom too: the quiet art of feeling what lie beyond the lyrics.

Waldo had spent so much time searching for answers in words and logic, but perhaps, as his mother had once hinted, the truth hid in the intangible; something you couldn't explain but only feel. Even though he had drifted from his own connection to music, he knew Grace wasn't just playing songs. She was translating her world. Where he searched for answers in logic, she found them in rhythm, and he wouldn't take that away from her. A gust swept down the block, sharp and pulsing, like the bass from Grace's room. It carried with it the faint trace of a pop melody, trailing through the air like something half-remembered. He could almost hear it again, Jordin Sparks' "One Step at a Time," playing softly from Grace's room, the rhythm filtering through drywall late one night. Back then, it was just another song in the house, barely noticed. But now, as the lyrics surfaced, they struck him differently. It wasn't just advice for Grace or a catchy line from a pop song—it was a quiet instruction for him. A whispered reminder that change didn't need to be dramatic. It could be slow, steady. Personal. The words echoed his mother's voice, too—life's journey, like a melody, had its own rhythm.

A rhythm he could walk to.

As he neared Cooper's Café, a group of college students spilled out, their laughter loud, unguarded. One had a guitar slung over his back, gesturing as he spoke with the kind of passionate energy Waldo once wore like a second skin. He had been that kid once, the one who believed anything was possible. Now, he stood still, hands pressed deep into his pockets, watching them vanish into the city's chorus. He didn't feel envy, not exactly. Just a strange pull—like a note played in a long-forgotten key. Had he really strayed that far?

When he stepped inside, the air was warm, the clatter of cups familiar. A couple occupied his usual booth, the one in the corner with the perfect view of the street. With a slight sigh, he pivoted and made his way to the counter, sliding onto one of the polished stools.

"Hey, Waldo," the barista warmly greeted him.

He returned her gesture with a shy grin. "I'll just have my usual order; coffee, light cream. Oh, and you know what, a slice of the lemon cake today too, please." He rarely ordered cake but today felt like a good day to say yes to something small and sweet and entirely his own.

It was late afternoon, an unusual time for him to visit, and the café was busier than he expected, filled with the *buzz* of conversation and the *hiss* of the espresso machine. As he waited, he let his eyes wander around the room, taking in the well-known scene from a strange vantage point. While he glanced around, his thoughts still lingered on the idea of being lost and how that may not necessarily be a bad thing. Perhaps it marked the beginning of something—not found, but forming.

He was still deep in thought when his coffee and cake arrived. He sipped, then traded the cup for a fork and a bite of lemon cake. The more he pondered, the more he realized that knowing more about life and about oneself didn't bring the certainty he had always assumed it would. In fact, the opposite seemed true. The more you know, the more you see how much you don't know. The world didn't offer answers wrapped neatly in understanding; it only offered more questions. *Maybe,* Waldo thought, *that isn't a flaw. Perhaps, it is the point. The whole idea.* Rephrasing it this way emerged both fear and freedom within him. Fear, because it meant he might never find the certainty he craved. And freedom, because it meant he didn't have to pretend he had the answers anymore.

Waldo exhaled slowly, letting the word *lost* settle over him once again. It still felt unfamiliar, yet there was something unexpectedly warm and inviting about it now, like sinking into an old, worn chair. The advice,"Be the change," followed closely behind, echoing in his mind, pushing him to keep going. It was such a simple concept but still managed to carry a force, a key to unlock something inside him—to a door that had always been there, waiting to be opened.

Waldo sat up tall on the counter stool, assuming a posture as if he was poised to hear his name announced for an award. His shoulders squared, and he clasped his hands on the counter, smirking faintly. He couldn't help but think about the progress he's made already. The steps he had taken to confront himself, to decide to break free from old patterns, and to start truly living with purpose felt significant.

For a fleeting moment, he imagined a spotlight turning to him, the world pausing as everyone took notice. It was a ridiculous thought, he knew, but it gave him a small boost of confidence, as if this unique vantage point stage at Cooper's Café might hold the potential for something extraordinary. But the applause would not be something the world would bestow upon him, but something he would bestow upon himself, celebrating even the minor triumphs. His being lost wouldn't solely influence him from finding his way back, especially because it wasn't about reaching a specific destination—it was about accepting there didn't need to be one. It was about preparing for a route that had no clear direction. He wondered what tools he would need for the next steps in his new exploration.

Maybe it was time to swap his old compass, not for something newer, but something truer. That thought sparked a memory, flickering in the corner of his mind; the old brass compass his father had given him as a boy. His father had reached into his pocket and pulled out a wooden box, its surface worn smooth from years of handling. Waldo, around ten years old, stood barefoot in their backyard, the summer air thick with the scent of freshly cut grass. He carefully took the box and lifted the lid to find a brass compass nestled inside, small and unassuming. Its needle wobbled unsteadily when he tilted it, a reminder that finding direction sometimes required stillness. He turned the compass over in his hand; a faint cross was etched on the back, shallow and faded, as if added by hand years ago. Tucked beneath it was a note in his mother's handwriting. He read it aloud: *For when you feel lost. Keep this close, but remember—not all directions can be found on a compass.*

His father had let out a low chuckle, his eyes gleaming with something unreadable. *"Sometimes, you've got to find your own way,"* he said, pausing just long enough for Waldo to consider the weight of his words. Then, he broke the moment with a playful grin. *"Why don't you try standing on your head, Waldo?"*

Waldo had hesitated, watching the slight upturn of his father's lips, the glint of mischief dancing behind his gaze. It wasn't just a smirk; it was that knowing expression, the one that always made Waldo wonder if his dad was giving him a lesson or just seeing if he'd take the bait.

In the end, it didn't matter. Whether it had been a lesson or just another of his dad's half-baked jokes, the words had stuck with him, lingering like a lyric he couldn't shake. Perched at the counter in Cooper's Café, amidst the constant rumble of people and motion, Waldo saw it differently. Maybe his dad was trying to say that wisdom doesn't always present itself in a clear, easy-to-understand way. Sometimes, it came disguised in humor, in passing remarks, or in fleeting minutes so ordinary that they seemed insignificant back then. He tapped his fingers on the counter, having just passed on the final refill offer for his coffee. As he gazed at the remaining swirls of liquid at the bottom of his cup, an awareness struck him: his father's greatest gift wasn't a tangible thing, but the ability to see beyond the obvious, to find meaning in the unexpected, and to embrace a change in perspective, even if it took a lifetime.

That compass had felt like an important gift, something to hold on to when the world felt confusing. But now, as he pondered his current journey, he realized it was the note that carried the deeper meaning. It wasn't about following a set direction or relying on tools to find his way. It was about trusting himself, learning to navigate through intuition, faith, and resilience, even when no direction was clear. Ultimately, it was the internal compass he needed—those were the lessons his parents had passed on. His mother often said, *"Difficult roads often lead to beautiful destinations,"* and his dad was quick to remind him, *"The harder I work, the luckier I get."* These weren't just sayings; they were guidance through the uncertainty, on how to trust the process, and how to find strength in the unknown.

Waldo wasn't as unprepared as he had thought. The tools he needed—patience, resilience, and vulnerability—were always there, subtly formed by his father's one-liner, made-you-think wisecracks. Each one, no matter how lighthearted or seemingly random, were intended by design to develop his critical thinking ability. His father's knack for wrapping wisdom in humor had taught him to see beyond the surface, to look for meaning even in the most unexpected places. These moments had all built something in him, tools he hadn't even realized he was carrying.

However, he now understood what they were and was nearly ready to use them. He was on the path to becoming the person he was always destined to be.

He carried that thought home with him, a quiet recognition settling in his chest.

Chapter 3
The Journey Begins

After that first Friday session, Waldo began seeing Dr. Benson regularly, agreeing on every Thursday during his lunch break. He could slip out of work with just enough time to make it there and back. He still hadn't mentioned it to Sara, even after he decided to keep going; not out of secrecy, but because he wanted time to feel the change before naming it. To let the sessions settle within him without the pressure of having to explain them too soon. But following the first couple of appointments, he finally felt ready, the words coming naturally.

One evening, they sat together in the serene comfort of their living room. "I've been seeing a therapist," he said, looking directly in her eyes. "Just a couple times so far. Thursdays, during lunch." He shared how he hadn't planned on pursuing therapy or had even given it much thought beforehand—the explanation for not telling her sooner—but that he also wasn't expecting clarity right away. But something shifted each time he sat in that office. The conversations didn't exactly give answers, but they still helped him start untangling the questions.

Sara had listened, her expression unreadable at first. But when he finished talking, her fingers brushed his hand as she nodded. "I think that's good, Waldo. I think that's great."

There had been no long discussions, no probing for details, just a shared unspoken understanding. Knowing he was really trying eased something in her, although the tension between them didn't magically disappear. It did, however, make it seem possible that it would one day. Especially because the weight between him and Sara continued to lighten over time, even if only in small ways, like the ease in their conversations and the way she didn't look at him with as much guarded concern.

Despite appearances, Waldo recognized this was just the beginning. The real work was still ahead.

Dr. Benson encouraged him to explore new hobbies and to try new things, anything that might stir joy, even in small flickers. She said doing this could reignite a spark he hadn't felt in years. He promptly took her suggestion and tried things he never would have considered before. So, this meant pottery, hiking, and even yoga made their way into his schedule. With a surge of courage, he even signed up for a beginner's guitar course. With this adjusted mindset, he was determined to leave behind the frustration and impatience of his childhood, no longer worrying about mastery; it was about the joy of learning, the simple act of reconnecting with something he had always loved.

At first, he was cautiously optimistic about Dr. Benson's advice, discussing how pushing himself out of his comfort zone felt and sharing stories of his clumsy attempts at forming a pot on the wheel or the surprising serenity he found in the woods during a hike. Each new attempt held promise—a glimmer of hope wrapped in unfamiliar terrain—but the results were mixed.

Pottery felt almost meditative, the cool texture of clay beneath his fingers, the slow shaping of something from nothing. His early attempts were laughably lopsided, drawing gentle encouragement from the instructor and a few self-deprecating chuckles from his classmates. "Embrace the imperfections," they'd said. But as the bowls stayed crooked, the imperfections began to feel less like freedom and more like failure. He saw each misshapen bowl less than an object and more like a mirror, showing there was something he couldn't quite fix inside himself. The laughter faded. The enthusiasm waned. What began as playful curiosity became a burden, heavy with the weight of expectations he couldn't even name.

Hiking was supposed to clear his head. Being alone on the trails, surrounded by the rhythm of his own breathing and the steady crunch of dirt beneath his boots, felt freeing at first. Until it wasn't. The stillness that had once comforted him turned into something else entirely—a silence that pressed in, reminding him of everything left unresolved. The trees offered no answers. The sky, no direction. One afternoon, he passed a group of hikers laughing, snapping photos, and lingering in that easy way people do when they're not carrying something invisible. He felt a deep longing he hadn't expected. He missed belonging. The shared language of companionship. The way things used to feel effortless.

And then yoga, stumbled upon during a bleary-eyed YouTube search, was another laugh. He tried to find stillness in the awkward shapes, to feel grounded in the breath, but mostly, he just wobbled. Not grace, not peace—just one long wobble. Sara had walked in once while he was mid-pose, trying (and failing) to balance on one leg. She had barely held back her laughter.

Even his beginner guitar lessons, which he'd once dreamed of, thinking it would be his way back to himself, began to feel like a duty. The strings bit at his fingers, the chords never quite settling. What he'd imagined as a joyful reconnection with a long-lost love felt more like a stilted reunion with someone who barely remembered his name. The music didn't rise up the way it used to. It stalled. Flattened. Refused to meet him where he was. "Is this a midlife crisis?" she asked, half-teasing.

He exhaled, bracing himself with one hand on the wall. "If it is, it's a very low-budget one."

She grinned but didn't press, the question staying unspoken between them: not *what* he was doing, but *why*.

The same one circling his own thoughts.

And though he wasn't ready to say it out loud, he was beginning to wonder if he'd been searching in the wrong places.

There were still brief moments of enjoyment in all these new activities, but the feeling of being a visitor in someone else's life, borrowing hobbies from a stranger's bucket list, was becoming harder to ignore. Most of them he picked because they were recommended to him by friends and coworkers, never stopping to ask himself if these were the right ones for him.

The previous instances where Waldo found comfort in the unknown and the seemingly endless opportunities was hard to hold onto. Back at Cooper's Café, he had accepted that change wouldn't happen overnight, but he'd still hoped that, by now, he'd see tangible progress. It had been nearly two months since that first session. Long enough, he thought, for something to shift. A small revelation. A ripple. Anything. But when that moment didn't come, his quiet optimism began to fray, unraveling into a single, unwelcome question: *What if there's nothing to discover?*

The following Thursday, during his usual session with Dr. Benson, something gave. Not with drama, but like a structure that had been quietly holding too much weight. Waldo sat stiffly across from her, his fingers tracing the shallow scratch marks along her desk's edge. His breath left him slow, more as a resignation than release. "I've tried everything; pottery, hiking, yoga, music . . . but none of it sticks. I keep hoping something will land, something will click. But it all just feels . . . diluted. Like I'm sampling someone else's life from a menu, not living my own."

Dr. Benson studied him for a moment, nodding. "What exactly were you hoping would happen?"

Waldo exhaled sharply, running a hand over his face. "I don't know. Some kind of realization? A hint of direction? Just . . . something to prove I'm not floundering."

She clasped her hands together and leaned in. "Waldo, change doesn't announce itself with a grand revelation. You're looking for a finish line, but what if that's not how this works? What if it's not about arriving?"

He frowned. "Then what's the point? If I keep trying and get nowhere, why keep going?"

"You are moving, just not in the way you expected. You're frustrated because progress doesn't *feel* like you thought it would. But sometimes, it's not loud. It's not fast. It's just . . . breaking the pattern. Quietly. Gradually."

Waldo sighed, crossing his arms. "So, what? I just keep throwing things at the wall and hope something eventually works?"

"No," Dr. Benson said, smiling. "You stop measuring every experience by whether it gives you an answer and start seeing it for what it is. Movement. Consider this: instead of chasing one defining moment, ask why you need one at all."

Waldo opened his mouth to argue, but no words came. Because deep down, she wasn't wrong. He'd spent years chasing clarity, waiting for the moment when everything would make sense. But what if clarity wasn't something you catch? What if it revealed itself slowly in movement? Not arrival, just continuing?

The same disquieting thoughts clung to him as he walked out of her office. He wasn't sure if he liked them. For now, though, liking it wasn't the point.

Some days, he could hold the lessons, remind himself that progress wasn't about milestones but momentum. Other days, doubt returned like smoke under the door: slow, invasive, and hard to push back. The familiar rhythm of self-doubt pulled him in before he even realized he was dancing to it. In those moments, when his steps felt aimless and even effort felt hollow, he struggled to reconcile the growth he'd made with the emptiness that still remained. The cycle wore him down; every glimmer of hope seemed to be followed by a low tide of disappointment.

His father's words, once a source of comfort, now reverberated empty in his mind as a cruel reminder of how aimless his life had become. *"Do not go where the path may lead; go instead where there is no path and leave a trail."* A trail? A path? Waldo felt like he was wandering in circles at this point, kicking up the same dust over and over. Every direction felt like a dead end.

What if this is all life has to offer, and there's no grand discovery or epiphany waiting for me? The thought lodged itself deep, pressing heavier with each passing day. Perhaps some people were just meant to exist quietly in the background, playing supporting roles in other people's lives. It was suffocating, but the stillness could pass for peace if you didn't look too closely.

Maybe chasing "more" was just another way of running from what was—a pointless attempt to outrun the mundane. And lately, even the chase felt impossible. Time, once something he longed to fill with new meaning, was no longer his to claim. Back then, he hadn't made time; he'd stolen it from things that eventually came calling.

The demands of daily life didn't pause to check on his emotional temperature. At work, deadlines loomed like storm clouds, paperwork piled up faster than he could clear it, and meetings stacked like dominos, each one draining more of what little focus he had left. Whenever he tried to carve out time for himself, something always intervened, like an urgent email, a last-minute scramble, or a fire only he could put out. Not because he was irreplaceable, but because he'd allowed himself to become indispensable to everything but his own wellbeing. Even therapy began to feel like a scheduling liability rather than a lifeline. He'd started checking the clock during sessions, mind drifting to deadlines, guilt humming beneath every minute he spent away.

At home, Grace's final year of high school had become a whirlwind —sports practices, choir concerts, late-night study sessions, and the mounting pressure of college applications. Only weeks ago, he'd been trying new hobbies, chasing sparks. Now, he couldn't even keep up with the calendar. Waldo wanted to be present for her, to hold onto these fleeting moments before she left, but it always felt like a trade-off. Every hour spent cheering from the bleachers or attending yet another college prep meeting came at the expense of something else—usually himself.

At first, he'd told himself he had the margin, that cutting pottery or hiking would buy back time. But the truth was, those hours had never been truly free. They'd just gone unspoken, scattered among the smaller demands he'd underestimated. Now, they loomed.

Through it all, Melody, Grace's sleek gray cat, was never far from her side. Whether curled on her bed while she studied or weaving around her ankles in the kitchen, Melody was her quiet companion. Waldo often saw Grace absently scratching behind the cat's ears while poring over college essays or whispering something to her in passing, as if the feline were her personal confidant. But the actual care for that companion? That always seemed to circle back to him. No matter how many times he reminded Grace, it was Waldo who grabbed the cat food, changed the litter, wiped the counters clean of paw prints. He had spent more time than he cared to admit muttering about fur-covered furniture, litter boxes, and the mysterious way Melody managed to clamor for attention at the most inconvenient times. A fuzzy force presence in his life too. This one by default, not by choice.

Nathan, on the other hand, was vanishing into his own orbit. Between his part-time job and late nights out with friends, he was hardly home anymore. When he did show up, it was normally long past midnight, quietly unlocking the door as the rest of the house slept. Waldo told himself it was normal. Part of growing up. But even so, he found himself staying up, listening for the creak of the door, the shuffle of shoes, and the soft *clang* of keys in the dish. Not because Nathan needed it, but because some part of Waldo still did. He still felt responsible for making sure everyone was home before resting.

And then there was Sara. For a while, things between them had started to soften; brief moments of ease, less guarded conversations, even laughter that didn't feel forced. But lately, that private progress had begun to slip. The distance he'd worked so hard to close was creeping back in with silence. With absence. She still tried to support him, but her patience had limits. Waldo couldn't say he blamed her. She was the one who always had to be steady, balancing her own commitments while picking up the slack he hadn't even realized he'd dropped. She never complained either. But some nights, as they sat shoulder to shoulder on the couch, both too tired to speak, he could feel the inevitable drift take shape again.

And that made it worse. Because now, he wasn't just disappointing himself. He was failing to hold onto the one relationship that had once anchored him. And in doing so, he was adding more weight to her shoulders, too—asking more of her without meaning to. Without even knowing how to stop.

Somewhere along the way, all the space he thought he had for change, for curiosity, had vanished. Frazzled and overextended, Waldo was now caught in a cycle that felt more like reaction than life. Each new demand was a pinball strike, ricocheting him from task to task. Work, family, and errands—each one a collision. He wasn't steering anymore. Just trying not to tilt the machine. And the weight of it all pressed heavier with each passing day.

One Wednesday evening, after a long and fracturing day at work, Waldo rushed to Grace's high school for her debate competition. He barely had time to park before running inside, mind still tangled in the training manual he was supposed to review for onboarding the new hire, the growing half-finished to-dos waiting at home, and the relentless tug of everything he'd left undone. But now, this needed his attention. As he stepped into the auditorium, scanning the crowd for a familiar face, he spotted Sara in the middle row, and next to her, to his surprise, was Nathan.

Nathan?

Waldo hesitated before making his way through the crowd. He hadn't expected his son to be here. Between his part-time job, college friends, and the slow fade of childhood routines, Nathan rarely showed up for family events anymore. But it was good to see him. It hadn't been long since he was the one on stage, the one Waldo and Sara had cheered for. Now Nathan sat in the audience, half here, half already gone. And Waldo . . . Waldo wasn't sure where that left him. Not as the center anymore. Not as the anchor. Just . . . watching them all step further into their own lives. And for reasons he couldn't quite name, that shift, Nathan choosing to be here, Grace standing tall on stage, mattered more than he expected.

Sara glanced up as he approached, smiling. "Hey, we saved you a seat."

Nathan glanced up, gave a brief smile, then tucked his phone away. It wasn't the kind of enthusiastic greeting Waldo remembered from years past, but it still carried something warm. He slid into the seat beside them, exhaling. Being here was supposed to count for something, and maybe, despite the static in his mind, it still did.

Grace was already on stage, standing confidently behind the podium. Just before she began, her gaze found theirs, and for a split second, it landed on Nathan. A flash of surprise flickered across her face, quickly tucked away. She reset her shoulders and started, voice crisp, words deliberate.

As the round ended, applause rippled through the auditorium. When Grace's eyes scanned the audience again, this time, her eyes met Waldo's. She gave him a small, uncertain smile. Her expression wavered, like she was asking something she didn't have words for. Could she tell that, despite sitting here, clapping in all the right places, his thoughts had been miles away?

Sara leaned over, her voice low. "He surprised me by coming."

Waldo nodded, glancing at Nathan. Although he had put his phone away during Grace's speech, he had it back out now, his thumb skimming the screen. It seemed he didn't waste a second after the applause faded and Grace stepped offstage. "Me too," Waldo murmured.

When the next round was called, Waldo clapped along, but he was still thinking about how tonight wasn't just about Grace's moment in the spotlight. It was also about what passed between the applause. The glance. The nod. The showing up. And maybe that's where the real shift began—not in the performance, but in the pause.

The following night, after Grace had gone to bed, Sara leaned against the kitchen counter, arms folded in a steady manner. She didn't raise her voice, but there was weight in her words. "Waldo, I know you've been trying. I see it. But you're stretched so thin. It's like we're losing you."

He looked up from the sink, unsure of what to say, his hands still wet from rinsing a plate.

She straightened, moving closer. "I don't need the perfect version of you. I don't need answers or clarity. I just need you to let me in."

Waldo felt the words hit deeper than anything he'd heard in therapy. She wasn't waiting for a better version of him, which he had convinced himself she was. Instead, she just needed the one who tried. Her words stayed with him long after the lights were out. He laid awake, staring at the ceiling, retracing the moments he'd let slip, the strained smiles from Grace, the quiet loneliness in Sara's eyes, the times he could have just . . . been with Nathan. Gone.

As sleep finally pulled at him, he made a private vow: to try again. To make time. To choose one small thing that might bring him back— maybe even to happiness, if he could manage it.

He had blown off his guitar lessons the last couple of times and had planned to do it again this week. *Well, guitar it is.* Tomorrow would be a better day. Hopefully.

The next morning, Waldo sat at the kitchen table with his coffee, watching the steam curl and disappear. Even though it was Friday, almost the weekend, the resolve he'd clung to the night before was already thinning. The day ahead felt impossible: a full workload, a meeting with Grace's college counselor, and the promise he'd made to himself to squeeze in a guitar practice. It was just a to-do list, but it swelled, dense and dragging, like a tide pulling him under.

"You're trying to force something that isn't meant to be forced, Waldo." Dr. Benson's voice returned, uninvited but timely. She had said that not long ago, after he'd rattled off every new hobby, each attempt to jolt himself back to life. At the time, he'd bristled at her words. He wasn't forcing it. He was trying, determined to figure out where he was supposed to go, to feel something, to care again. But even then, he'd known she'd hit something raw. *"You're looking for a finish line,"* she'd added, *"but what if that's not how this works?"* He'd hated that. Not because it wasn't true, but because it was. *"Maybe, instead of waiting for a defining moment, you ask yourself why you think you need one."* He hadn't had a response then, and now, walking the same tired mental loop, he still didn't. The thought hung, stubborn and quiet, like the last echo in an empty room.

But the question refused to leave him alone.

How do you stop chasing control when it feels like the only thing holding you together?

It felt like progress had slipped through his fingers—hours of reflection, carefully scheduled sessions, so-called breakthroughs. None of it felt like steps forward anymore. Just loops. He was tired of the effort. Tired of always being "in progress," excessive introspection overshadowing the joy he thought this journey would bring. Perhaps there was nothing waiting beyond the ordinary. Maybe giving up wasn't failure at all, just reality? The steam lifted again, delicate and fading, as if to underline the thought.

Waldo sighed. Why couldn't Dr. Benson leave his thoughts alone? Thinking back to his sessions caused the same irritation he'd felt sitting across from her. *"You're saying I'm overdoing it,"* he said at one point.

"I'm saying you're mistaking exhaustion for progress." That's all the explanation she gave.

He rubbed his face, frowning. *"I just thought if I did enough, if I threw myself into enough things, eventually, one of them would feel like... I don't know. An answer."*

Dr. Benson tilted her head. *"What's the outcome of this unchecked pace, layering on more and more, without stopping to re-assess? Where does it end? Think of your energy as a reservoir. If you constantly draw from it without refilling—through rest, enjoyable activities, or even just space to breathe— you'll eventually run dry."*

And she left it at that.

Waldo lifted his cup and huffed before taking a slow sip. The heat steadied him, settled him. But still, Dr. Benson's words stirred again. *"You need to focus on what actually matters, Let go of the things that don't."* She was probably right. But how? How could he step back when the whole world seemed to demand he keep moving forward?

As Waldo set his coffee cup down, the soft *clink* against the table brought back a sound from years ago—the sharp clatter of tools hitting the floor in frustration. Nathan had been nine, working on a model rocket project; something he had looked forward to for weeks. But that night, after hours of struggling, the parts wouldn't fit, and the launch refused to happen. Waldo could still picture it: Nathan's small hands clenched, his once bright eyes now dull with defeat. *"I give up! It's never going to work,"* he'd shouted, the wrench hitting the floor with a final clatter. Waldo could now sense that same level of defeat within himself. That same exhaustion. That same low thrum of effort unrewarded.

Nathan's struggle with the model rocket was Waldo's struggle too, a reminder of all the times he had felt ready to give up. But back then, when it wasn't his pain, Waldo had known what to do. He'd knelt beside his son and repeated the same line his own father had once told him: *"The harder I work, the luckier I get."*

Nathan had frowned, confused. Just like Waldo had, years ago. So, he'd softened his tone, adding, *"You're not giving up because it's impossible. You're giving up because you're tired. And I get that."* He explained what tired really meant—not just the need for rest, but the kind of weariness that settled deep in the bones. *"When every step forward feels like you're dragging the weight of everything behind you, when the journey feels endless and every setback seems like proof that you're not getting anywhere, that kind of tired makes you question everything—your strength, your purpose, even your reasons for starting. It's exhausting, physically, emotionally, even spiritually. And when that happens, giving up seems like relief. But rest . . . rest is different. You can pause. Breathe. Regroup. But don't walk away just because you're weary. Tired is temporary. But giving up makes it permanent."* Waldo paused to make sure Nathan was still listening. *"Giving up now closes the door on understanding why you started or discovering what might've been waiting just beyond the next step. Giving up now means never knowing what could have been."*

Nathan had sat in silence, still teary, but eventually picked up the tools again. The rocket hadn't flown perfectly that day, but it got off the ground, and that success, small but satisfying, was enough to reignite his determination.

Waldo had been proud of his son, but now, the moment lived in him for a different reason. It reminded him of the times he had wanted to give up, too, and how his father's quip had once given him the nudge he needed to keep going. Now watching his own son benefit from the lesson, he had felt a strange sense of continuity, as if he were passing on not just advice, but a piece of himself.

The chair creaked slightly as he shifted, the quiet sound pulling him back to the present. It occurred to him that there was a good chance he didn't need more effort; he just needed less noise. If only he could stop chasing and start focusing on what truly mattered. What mattered hadn't vanished. It had only gone still, waiting, buried under motion.

By the time he sat across from Dr. Benson that next Thursday, Waldo was exhausted—physically and emotionally. His mind churned with pressure, like the air just before a downpour. Dr. Benson waited to see if he wanted to begin their discussion, and when he remained silent, she gently said, "You seem heavy today."

He massaged his temples, letting out a long sigh. "Heavy is one way to put it. For months, I've been trying everything you suggested, but nothing's working. Even after we talked about realistic expectations last week." He shook his head. "It all just feels . . . hollow."

She nodded thoughtfully. "Tell me about that. What still feels hollow?"

"All of it," Waldo said, the irritation churning in his voice. How many times did he have to explain? "We're months into this "pushing myself out of my comfort zone," and I feel like I'm back where I started. Actually, I feel worse." He paused, his voice lowering. "Sara finally brought it up the other night, too. How I'm not present, not really there for her or Grace and Nathan."

"Do you think she's right?"

Waldo hesitated, feeling the sting of her question. "Yeah . . . I do. But I don't know how to fix it. I don't even know what's broken."

Instead of leaning forward, as she so often did, Dr. Benson uncrossed her legs and folded her hands in her lap. "Let me ask you something else. What if nothing is broken?"

Waldo blinked.

"What if the real work isn't fixing yourself, but facing where you are with curiosity instead of judgment?"

He slumped back in his chair, dragging a hand through his hair. "I don't even know where to start."

Dr. Benson's lips lifted slightly. "You already did. The question now isn't where you begin. It's whether you can keep going without needing the ending first. Let it unfold. Let it shape you as it comes. That's how change works—not with certainty, but with a shifting mindset that allows movement."

Waldo didn't respond. But something in him, that sliver that hadn't burned out yet, leaned in.

As he walked to his car after work that evening, replaying the session in his mind, Dr. Benson's words returned: *"Change your perspective, even*

in the smallest ways." They blurred with Sara's softer accusation: *"You're not here anymore."* He felt torn, caught between the weight of his doubts and the flicker of hope that maybe, just maybe, there was still a way through the storm.

He'd been reflecting—endlessly. But without direction, it had become a maze, not a path. What he hadn't given himself was space. Not to analyze, but to ask what was still worth holding onto. Learning to slow down didn't mean surrender. It meant *staying grounded*, even in small, deliberate ways. It meant letting himself breathe between the mental to-do lists, the emotional labor, and the pressure to always be moving forward. Rest and stillness weren't indulgences; they were necessities. As vital as any meeting. As essential as any deadline.

Waldo started the car and let it idle, as he always did. There was something about the soft hum of the engine, the stillness before motion, that helped him reset. He leaned back into the seat, the fabric worn to his shape. He closed his eyes, taking a deep breath. If only he could get a lucky break to give him a head start. But in this moment of reflection, he realized what his father had truly been talking when he said,*"The harder I work, the luckier I get."* He wasn't referring to luck, but persistence. Fulfillment wasn't about some cosmic force favoring you; it was about staying in the work long enough for your growth to catch up. Every small, seemingly insignificant step moved you forward, and you had to keep pushing on, especially when it felt like nothing was going right. Back when Nathan's model rocket refused to fly or one of his math tests ended in tears, he would say, *"You're not giving up because it's impossible. You're just tired."* Maybe it was time to say it to himself. *Tired* wasn't failure. *Tired* was part of the process.

Rest wasn't surrender. It was recovery.

Waldo reached over to the passenger seat and placed his hand warmly on the guitar he wanted so badly to master. Once he signed up for guitar lessons, it had been riding shotgun ever since. He thought it would provide a fun reminder of what he was working toward, but lately, it felt more like a hitchhiker he wished he had never picked up. But tonight, he saw it differently. Not as a reminder of what he hadn't mastered, but of what he was still willing to try. Of what he hadn't quit, even when he wanted to. He smiled, remembering how often his greatest perceived failures had actually been unexpected gifts. Each stumble, each moment of doubt, had pushed him in new directions, forcing him to grow in ways he never predicted.

He shifted the car into gear and pulled away from the curb, the headlights cutting through the dusk. Perhaps tomorrow would be the day something takes flight.

Several days later, Waldo left work feeling the strain of yet another long day. He had started his day by having an uncomfortable conversation with his boss, who wanted to discuss a project deadline that Waldo missed. He genuinely hadn't realized how close the deadline was. Time had blurred together, and what felt like plenty of time had vanished in an instant. But he knew this wasn't a good enough excuse. It wasn't a routine event, but still, he sat in his boss's office, taking the repercussions. It was then he noticed a plaque on Victor's desk it read:

**It's hard to remember that your goal
was to drain the swamp
when you're up to your ass in alligators**

Exactly! Waldo thought. It provided a good icebreaker for the conversation, giving him an opportunity to share a bit about the load he had been toting around. Although this didn't change the fact that he had dropped the ball, it at least provided his boss a little more understanding of why. And even though the meeting was brief and not too brutal, his briefcase felt heavier than usual as he walked out of the building now. He knew it wasn't the papers inside but his mind swirling through the past several weekly sessions with Dr. Benson, sifting through their conversations. Some were helpful, some frustrating, but all were meant to push him forward and give him the courage to embrace change. Normally, he would have jumped in his car and gone straight home, falling into the same routine, but tonight, he took Dr. Benson's advice. On a whim, he walked past the parking garage and continued the short distance to Cooper's Café. He didn't plan on settling into his usual booth, but just to grab a coffee to-go. A slight detour. A break from the familiar.

As he stepped inside, the warm scent of roasted coffee greeted him, wrapping around him like an old friend. He exhaled, placing his order at the counter, watching the rhythmic dance of the baristas behind the espresso machines. He wasn't sure what he was looking for in this moment, but at least, for now, he wasn't rushing past it. He paid then step aside, thinking about Sara while he waited for his coffee. He pulled out his phone, hesitating briefly before tapping out a quick text to her:

> Running a little late. Grabbing a coffee before heading home.

A few seconds later, his phone buzzed with a reply:

> Everything okay?

He exhaled, rubbing the back of his neck.

> Yeah. Just needed a minute.

Maybe tonight was about something as simple as that—taking a minute. There was a lull before her response came through.

> Okay. See you soon.

No questions. No concern. Just acknowledgment.

Coffee in hand less than ten minutes later, he stepped back out into the crisp evening air, taking a deep breath in to rejuvenate his mind. Next, he let his feet carry him in an unfamiliar direction, allowing himself the luxury of a few minutes to simply exist. As he strolled through the park near his office building, he noticed an old man sitting on a bench, sketching in a notebook. The man's concentration was absolute, his hand moving vigorously across the page as if the rest of the world didn't exist. Fascinated, Waldo felt compelled to stop, sitting beside him on the bench. The man offered a quick glance but said nothing.

Waldo watched intently as the man carefully shaded a section of the page, the charcoal pencil gliding smoothly over the surface to create the silhouette of a tree. At first, Waldo tried to be discreet, angling himself slightly, pretending to sip his coffee while stealing glances. Yet, the drawing's meticulous detail and the man's hand moving with such precision and purpose held his attention. He found himself leaning closer without realizing it, his curiosity outweighing his intent to stay subtle. Finally, unable to hold back, he blurted, "Excuse me, I'm Waldo." Even he could hear the mix of hesitation and intrigue in his voice. He gestured toward the sketchpad. "Are you an artist?"

The question hovered in the air, breaking the stillness of the moment as the man looked up, his pencil pausing mid-stroke. The man smiled faintly, startled but not annoyed. "No, I just like to draw," he replied. "It helps me see things more clearly."

Waldo grimaced, his brow curling as he repeated the words, almost as if he had misheard. "See things more clearly?" It was a simple idea, yet there was a deeper feeling to it. It was as if life was testing him, seeing if he could understand that clarity wasn't about deeper analysis or excessive overthinking. It was something else, something purer and more elusive. Was he missing the obvious while searching for the profound?

The man nodded, refocusing on his art. "When I'm drawing, I notice details I'd usually miss. The way the light hits the leaves, the texture of the bark. The world seems to slow down, and for a bit, every-thing is in focus."

Waldo looked at the man's sketch again. It was merely a tree in the park, but there was something captivating and real about it, as though the directness had allowed the truth of the scene to emerge. The lines were minimal, just enough to capture the essence, and yet, it felt full, alive in its own way. It reminded him of the gifts of life that Sara and the children had given him over the years, and how they'd taught him to appreciate simple, meaningful moments. Sara taught Waldo the power of accepting and enjoying things as they are. Like the sketch he just viewed, Sara's love was always pure and secure, never demanding or needing to be more. Her unique perspective found beauty in the ordinary, a struggle Waldo faced for years. Now, he understood that her gift to him went beyond love; it gave him clarity to grasp the true essence of things, free from distractions.

And then there was Grace, with her truth, vulnerability, and patience. She had a way of being present without forcing herself into the center, resembling the sketch's subtle lines. Grace's strength wasn't in grand gestures or loud proclamations, but in the way she moved through life with an openness that allowed her to fully experience the world around her. Just like the sketch, her presence in his life had taught him that simplicity didn't mean a lack of depth; it meant finding revelation in what was already there.

But Nathan—he had always been steady in his own way; not through sentimentality but through calm persistence. Whether it was balancing school, work, or the responsibilities he took on without complaint, his determination never wavered. Nathan didn't rely on external validation to guide him. His strength was in showing up, in pushing forward, even when things weren't comfortable or clear. His gift to Waldo was a reminder that progress wasn't always loud or immediate. Sometimes, it was simply the private, intentional act of continuing, even when the path ahead wasn't certain.

"I've been trying to figure out who I am," Waldo admitted, surprising himself with the confession.

The man didn't look up right away. His firm, deliberate pencil strokes showed he remained absorbed in his work. But when he finally glanced up, just briefly, Waldo caught it. An astute twinkle in his eye, something knowing, almost amused. "You won't find yourself by looking for answers," the man said, his voice as steady as his hand. "You'll find yourself by paying attention to the things you usually overlook."

The words washed over Waldo like warmth after a long chill. He hadn't expected clarity to sound so gentle. It was a message he and Dr. Benson had been through, so hearing it now from a stranger in the park was surprising. It only confirmed that he had been looking in the wrong place all this time. He had spent so much time searching for something grand, something definitive, that he had missed the subtler themes, the quieter revelations that were right in front of him. Even his father's cryptic sayings and dad jokes, his mother's soft wisdom, the memory of Nathan struggling with his model rocket—each of these moments had left something with him; benefits of resilience, patience, and courage that he hadn't realized he was carrying.

"So, you're saying that the lessons aren't out there, waiting to be found. They're already here, in the people I've met, the experiences I've had."

The man nodded. "Exactly. You're not lost, Waldo. You've been collecting these gifts all along. The trick is, most people never stop to see them for what they are."

"So, I haven't been wandering aimlessly, after all." Waldo sensed more to the emerging puzzle, specifically how important receiving, paying attention, and allowing himself to be shaped by people and moments were.

"Gifts, lessons, inspirations ...they're always there." The man paused both his words and his drawing, allowing what he said to sink in. "They're not hidden in grand events or distant dreams. They're delivered to you daily, in the most ordinary moments, randomly sprinkled through normal life transactions, in the offhand comments people make, in the way a stranger smiles, or how a barista remembers your order. It's in the way you pay attention to a child playing or the conversation you overhear while standing in line. Even in the frustrations, the delayed train, the difficult coworker, or the unexpected rainstorm, there's a message, a lesson, if you're willing to look for it. Every day, life drops you pieces, and although they may be barely noticeable at first, they matter." He went back to his art as if he hadn't just shared a piece of life-changing advice.

Waldo's mind raced through the scenarios. How many of those pieces had he overlooked? The subtle moments, the brief conversations, the things he had dismissed as frivolous. All the while, life had been offering him clues, guiding him toward something deeper, but he hadn't been paying attention.

The man glanced over again with a stillness that invited space. He leaned in, his expression staying open, quietly expectant, as if waiting for Waldo to recognize something that was already his. "The question is," he said, his voice low but clear, "are you ready to receive them?"

The words undeniably settled into the deepest parts of Waldo. It wasn't just about knowledge or understanding; it was about being open, willing to accept what life was offering, no matter how uncertain or uncomfortable. Waldo didn't need to look back to know—the man had seen enough. He remembered watching his father during those rare moments when words were few but carried the value of years. It was the look of someone who had walked the path Waldo was just beginning to understand, someone who knew the purpose of silence, of waiting for the right moment. It wasn't impatience or judgment; it was as if the man could see the struggle inside Waldo and knew exactly when to step in.

"I don't know. Am I ready?" Waldo asked, desperately wanting the man to give him the answer. Though, he knew it was one only he could decide for himself.

"It's up to you to decide," the man confirmed. "And it always will be. Are you ready to stop waiting for life to reveal its meaning, and instead, embrace the idea that you are the one who gives it meaning?"

The question loomed larger now, piercing and unrelenting. Was he ready to seize control, to abandon the endless search for external solutions, and trust the private guidance of his own inner compass? Wisdom didn't arrive in sweeping gestures; it lived in the stillness, in the seemingly insignificant events that carried the most profound lessons. The truth was everywhere, waiting to be noticed, ready to be received.

Chapter 4
The Value of Wandering

With his empty coffee cup in hand, Waldo thanked the stranger for letting him watch him draw just as much for the advice. Then, he headed back toward Cooper's Café to grab his car. As he did, Waldo reflected on the events of the day, understanding that each small decision, each private moment, held the key to clarity. The alligators, fierce and uncompromising, represented the challenges and fears that seemed insurmountable, yet essential to his journey. It was in facing them he could find strength he never knew he had. He was exhausted, yes—and surrounded by alligators, but perhaps this was no mere struggle; it was the crucible meant to test his resolve. Trusting the process, he knew the answers would come, bringing invaluable wisdom. The stillness, once overlooked, could now be his guide. And allowing that to happen was a different challenge altogether.

Two lessons in particular filled Waldo's thoughts: *I am the one who gives life meaning* and *I can move forward without needing all the answers first*. He appreciated the advice from both the man in the park and Dr. Benson, but he now considered what it meant to fully accept that he gave meaning to things and that he had to continue moving forward without all the answers. Was he ready to let go of the search for clarity and begin finding his own way?

As he reached his car and drove home, his mind was still trying to process everything he had learned and relearned recently when the vastness of the open sky caught his eye through the windshield. Between the glimpse of the beautiful sky and the message of finding his own way, a memory of his father's familiar wisdom intertwined with his thoughts. It was the story about a traveler, lost in the wilderness, who wandered aimlessly for days, unsure of which direction to take. At first, the traveler's steps were frenzied, driven by panic and desperation. But over time, his movements became slower, more deliberate. He noticed the changing landscapes, the way the stars shifted above him each night, and the trends of the wind through the trees. The traveler ultimately realized that what he thought was aimless wandering had been something else entirely—an occasion to observe, to learn, and to trust in the surrounding signs.

A compass could point north, sure, but it couldn't tell the traveler what may lie along the path—the obstacles he might face, the detours that would test his resolve, or the hidden opportunities he could stumble upon. It couldn't interpret the significance of what he encountered during his journey—the lessons tucked into the challenges, the meaning behind the seemingly insignificant moments, or the treasures disguised as trials. The journey required more than just direction; it demanded awareness, versatility, and the courage to navigate the unknown. A compass could guide you, but it was only *part* of the toolbox, not the entirety of it. Its power grew when paired with the mind of the operator, the discernment to decide when to follow, when to veer off course, and how to navigate the unseen.

Having always trusted his physical compass, he now needed to develop trust in his internal compass, supplementing his toolkit with mental clarity and flexibility for adaptation.

Alongside the compass, there were other tools Waldo had started to notice—not the kind you held, but the kind you carried inside:

resilience, intuition, experience, and adaptability. Each of these internal instruments had their counterpart:

1. A compass to reflect intuition—guiding, even when the destination was unclear.
2. A hammer for resilience—steadying, used to rebuild what's broken.
3. A sextant for experience—reading the stars of past moments to navigate what's ahead.
4. A rope for adaptability—not just for climbing, but for connecting, tying things together when the path fractures.

Waldo realized that success, in life and in change, wasn't just about having the right tools but about knowing how to use them and when. It was the atlas of his own awareness, his ability to understand his limitations and strengths, the very thing that turned the compass from a simple directional tool into something that could guide him through both the known and unknown with confidence.

Figuring out the right direction was only part of the equation; the other part was learning to read the terrain, to notice the details, the subtle shifts around him. The path wasn't pre-marked. It was something he'd have to shape as he walked, using every tool he had at his disposal. The more he learned to use those tools together, the closer he'd get to finding his own way forward, even when the destination wasn't entirely clear.

Waldo slowed as he approached a red light, his gaze drifting upward as the first faint stars emerged. With winter fading and spring approaching, the days were growing longer, yet he was usually home before he had the chance to witness the subtle shift. He was liking the idea of letting life lead him to where he should be, when he should be there. And just like his father's traveler story, which always closed with the same phrase—'Not all who wander are lost'—Waldo was beginning to see he wasn't lost either, only learning that the journey itself, the wandering, was the lesson.

As the light turned green and the cars ahead of him eased forward, he rolled down the window. The cool evening air rushed in, carrying with it the crisp scent, the renewed promise of spring. He inhaled deeply, holding onto the feeling before slowly exhaling. His attention drifted along with the low hum of tires on asphalt, the rhythmic passing of streetlights punctuating his scattered thoughts. The night had wrapped around him like a lullaby, the kind that made you forget, just for a moment, the restlessness inside. And then his phone buzzed. Glancing down, he saw Nathan's name illuminated on the screen. Surprised, he reached out and tapped the speakerphone button. "Nathan? Everything okay?"

"Hey, Dad," Nathan replied, sounding simultaneously rushed and hesitant. "Sorry if I caught you at a bad time. Are you driving?"

"Yeah, but it's fine. You're on speaker. What's going on?" Waldo adjusted his grip on the wheel, his shoulders slightly taut, alertness threading through him.

There was a pause, a quick, uneasy breath on Nathan's end. "I just remembered I have that interview tomorrow. The one at the software company. Anyway, they said it's casual attire. But like . . . does that mean actual casual, or is it some kind of test? Should I wear a tie, anyway? I feel like an idiot."

Waldo breathed a sigh of relief and chuckled, imagining Nathan pacing anxiously at home, probably staring blankly at his closet. A flash of tenderness warmed him, mingled with the weight of knowing how small these decisions felt in hindsight, but how massive they seemed in the moment. "You're right, it's tricky," Waldo began, his eyes checking the rearview mirror as he changed lanes. "Casual usually means they want you comfortable. But you still want to show respect. How about something you'd wear if you were meeting someone important but wanted to feel relaxed enough to be yourself?"

Nathan let out a breath, audible even over the slight crackle of the speaker. "Okay. Yeah. Makes sense. So, dress nice, but no tie."

Another silence slipped between them, lingering long enough for

Waldo to sense that something deeper simmered beneath Nathan's simple question. "You nervous?" he asked.

"A little," Nathan admitted. "Mostly just . . . unsure, I guess. You went through this stuff. Does figuring things out ever become easier?"

Waldo felt a gentle squeeze in his chest at Nathan's question, at the familiar echo of his own uncertainty. Headlights swept past, blurring briefly in his peripheral vision. He steadied his breath. "It does. Or maybe it just changes, where things stay the same but you're able to handle more. Eventually, you realize it's less about having a perfect plan and more about trusting yourself enough to keep moving forward, even when you don't have all the answers. Especially then."

Nathan was silent for a heartbeat, taking it in. "Yeah. Okay," he finally said, his voice calmer now. "Thanks, Dad. I'll let you get back to driving. See you later?"

"Of course," Waldo softly replied. "See you at home."

The call ended, quietness returning to the car except for the soft thrum of the engine. As Waldo guided the vehicle down the road, he felt lighter. Nathan's call, a simple practical question layered with vulnerability, reminded him of something vital: although he yearned to be Nathan's sounding board, even as young-adult life became more complex, his role wasn't always to supply neat answers, but to reassure, support, and walk alongside—even from a distance.

For once, Waldo didn't fight the stillness. Instead, he relaxed into the drive, letting the road ahead unfold, illuminated by headlights and a renewed certainty that each small moment of connection carried profound meaning. Wandering wasn't about losing oneself; it was intentional self-reflection, seeing the world and himself through fresh eyes. It was in the uncertainty that he discovered parts of himself previously hidden beneath layers of convention and expectation. Clarity emerged gradually, revealed through the very twists and turns encountered when he dared to stray from the familiar path. The road less traveled wasn't less traveled because it was wrong—it was less traveled because it required courage, a willingness to face uncertainty and trust in finding your genuine self along the way.

As he reflected, the cozy, sweet aroma of freshly baked bread drifted in through the open window, wrapping around him like a familiar embrace. The scent reminded him of his mother bustling in the kitchen, crooning as she worked. It was never a song he recognized, just a melody she carried, something instinctive and soothing, like the rhythm of her presence itself. He could almost hear her voice now, layered over the tune, offering the quiet wisdom she had always lived by: *"Sometimes, it's in the quiet moments, when you're not looking for anything, that you hear the music that's been there all along."*

As a young boy, he had believed she was simply talking about the notes she played on the piano. But as he got older, he saw that music was life itself; the small, unnoticed moments, the subtle rhythms hidden beneath the noise. His father had taught him to wander, his mother had taught him to listen. Together, they had given him everything he needed, and now he was certain he could make the most of those lessons.

Pulling into his driveway, his eyes fell on the guitar beside him again, its familiar shape patient as ever, waiting for all the melodies he had yet to play. Just like his mother's refrain— *there's always a message in the music*— life, too, needed to be noticed, recorded, and woven into something meaningful. Not grand revelations, but the little splashes of resonance scattered across an ordinary day. As he shut the engine off, Waldo made a promise to himself: *this time, I will pay attention.* He'd look for what was already there, recognizing the meaning hidden in the margins. He would even keep track of them.

"Oh, I've got just the thing!" he nearly shouted, leaning over to dig through the cluttered glovebox. His hand landed on an old notebook, its edges frayed, pages yellowed with time. Waldo thoughtfully flipped through it, seeing fragments of a past he barely remembered scrawled across the pages—half-finished to-do lists, long-forgotten appointments, and random doodles that had once seemed important. Many of the tasks were crossed out, but just as many were left undone, the artifacts of a life lived incompletely. He saw how much time he had spent managing the immediate while neglecting the meaningful. Maybe what he needed wasn't just a new notebook but a new way of writing his life.

For a minute, he hesitated. *This won't do.* He needed more than a place for hurried lists and forgotten plans. He needed a space for clarity. A journal of intention to capture the moments he'd been too busy to notice. He tucked the old one back into the glovebox and made a mental note to pick up a new one—blank, fresh, and ready for the journey ahead. Something that could carry the magnitude of his rediscovery without the baggage of his past distractions. And maybe this time, he'd start from the inside out; not with what needed to be done, but with what deserved to be remembered.

Chapter 5
Lost in the Maze

Waldo's perspective continued to shift a little more each day that followed. Life seemed to slow, revealing layers he had never noticed before. He wanted so badly to collect each inspiration, but he hadn't made time to buy a new notebook. As so often happened, life intervened, forcing him to prioritize other things. There was always another meeting, another errand, another reason to put it off. The days turned into weeks, and though the thought lingered at the edge of his mind, the promise to himself kept being postponed.

It wasn't until a quiet afternoon, when a rare pocket of time presented itself, that Waldo finally followed through. He found himself standing in the stationery aisle of a small bookstore, the soothing calm of classical music playing overhead. He ran his fingers along the rows of neatly stacked notebooks, each one a blank canvas, a promise of something fresh. After a moment, his hand hovered over a simple hardcover journal—unassuming, with a plain black cover. As he flipped through the thick cream-colored pages, a sense of anticipation stirred within him. This wasn't just a notebook; it was a vessel for everything he had missed, wanted to remember, and was trying to understand. It was sturdy but inviting, ready to hold whatever he poured into it.

Unlike the old one, cluttered with the remnants of a life spent rushing from one task to the next, skirting alligators, this was a clean start. A space for potential.

Leaving the store with the fresh notebook tucked securely under his arm, Waldo felt a modest satisfaction. It was a tiny step, but it was his —an intentional choice to take control of the narrative he was writing.

Later that evening, Waldo stepped onto the porch—not his usual spot, but one he found himself drawn to more and more. The hush of evening felt deserved somehow, offering a space apart from the day's noise. He opened the notebook once more. He had flipped through its pages at the bookstore, but now, under the soft glow of the porch light, it felt more than just inviting; it was personal, more real. It was solely up to him to face his thoughts, undistracted, and unfiltered.

In his hand, he held the same pen he had picked up during that restless evening in his home office. The one where he'd first dared to confront the void he felt, writing the word *"lost."* He could still see himself sitting there, hunched over the desk, staring at the page. Now, that same pen felt lighter in his hand, Waldo felt a strange sense of continuity. Back then, it had been heavy, weighted with the magnitude of his uncertainty. Tonight, it was imbued with something different— not answers, but the willingness to seek them.

With a steady hand, he lowered the pen to the page. The first sentence wasn't profound or poetic, but it also didn't carry the weight of despair. It was honest, and that was enough: *Today, I will begin to pay attention.* He paused, letting the words sit on the page, their simplicity grounding him. This wasn't about solving everything at once. It was about taking the first calculated, deliberate step, however slight, and trusting that each step would reveal the next. The surrounding porch seemed to hold its breath, the stillness of the evening amplifying the significance of this point in time.

The pen hovered again, and this time, Waldo smiled. He wasn't lost anymore, not entirely. He was still searching, still finding his way, but now he had a couple more tools to help him navigate. As he wrote, the words flowed not from a place of emptiness but from a serious, widening conclusion that the journey itself was the destination.

In the subsequent weeks, Waldo's vision of the world became more acute. His personal notebook became his constant companion, a repository for observations he would have once ignored. The rhythmic tapping of rain on a windowpane, the golden embrace of the sunset over the city skyline, the fluid waltz of shadows across the pavement as day faded into dusk. He even captured transitory interactions between strangers—the way an exhausted mother softened at the sound of her child's giggle, the minor shift in a weary commuter's posture as they caught sight of something familiar and comforting, a brief exchange with a cashier, the warm temporary connection in a stranger's eyes, or even the bubbling amusement of a child chasing a dog in the park.

In the margins of his notes, he underlined, highlighted, and annotated how certain moments stirred something within him, whether it was new feelings, subtle revelations, or the quiet confirmation of truths he had long ignored. But more and more, he found himself writing about Sara. Not in the way he used to, not in the effortless way that love had once spilled onto the page. Now, his notes carried a different strain. The way Sara moved through the house, absorbed in her own thoughts, never quite meeting his eyes like she used to before. Her brief pauses before speaking seemed to show she was measuring her words carefully. She instinctively reached for his hand, but her fingers no longer intertwined with his as naturally as before.

There was a distance between them, and he didn't know exactly when it had started or if she even felt it the same way he did. But he saw it, he felt it, and more than anything, he hated how much of it was his doing. Their story wasn't slipping away, not yet. But it had changed. Waldo wondered how he had been so caught up in finding himself that he hadn't realized he was losing them. He swore to himself he would change that. And the more he noticed, the more he realized how plugged in to the world he felt again. His days weren't just passing in a blur of obligations and routine. He was perfectly present, seeing, experiencing, and absorbing details he had once overlooked.

And yet . . .

Even as he embraced this newfound awareness, a subtle, almost imperceptible frustration simmered beneath the surface. At first, he dismissed it, chalked it up to old habits, the echo of unrest trying to find a new foothold. But as the weeks passed, it persisted. Not unhappiness; if anything, he was content in ways he hadn't been in years. But still, a sense of incompleteness hovered just below the surface. Like he was walking through life with the right tempo but missing a line of the melody underneath.

Still, his new awareness was deeply gratifying—catching life's quiet beauty in motion, noticing details he'd once passed over. Watching the evening light melt into the streets, soft and fleeting. Catching the precise dance of a barista's movements. The hush of the sleeping city before dawn. He even brought some of these reflections to Dr. Benson, who encouraged him to lean into them fully—to not just witness beauty but live within it.

And for a while, he did.

Despite unresolved issues, he felt lighter, more purposeful, and tethered in his relationships like never before. Conversations with Sara were still careful, like testing the weight of thin ice, but at least they were happening. Even when silence crept in, it no longer felt like an impassable wall. There were still missteps, still flickers of hesitation with Sara, where the distance between them remained just beneath the surface. But he was trying.

He also asked Grace more about school, understanding that his daughter didn't always need advice. Sometimes, she just needed her father to be there. So, he genuinely listened to her rants about how senioritis was hitting hard, making it nearly impossible to care about homework when graduation was so close she could almost taste it. But it seemed that all of the teachers had conspired to assign all major final projects at the same time, as if they enjoyed watching students suffer.

Nathan, immersed in his own expanding world, wasn't always around for long conversations, but Waldo no longer took it personally. Their interactions had a new rhythm: shorter exchanges, more space between them, but still marked by a quiet respect. In passing, Waldo asked about the interview. Nathan, distracted but not dismissive, answered with a shrug. "It went fine. They're hiring in waves over the next few months, so I probably won't hear anything right away." It was the kind of answer someone gave when they were juggling thoughts and trying not to overthink the outcome. Waldo nodded, sensing the subtext: *I'll talk when I'm ready.* And that was enough. He still made room for him. Left the porch light on. Sat a little longer at the dinner table when Nathan was home. He didn't press. Didn't fill the silence. He just stayed present, hoping Nathan would remember years from now, when he needed someone to lean on.

He also felt the difference at work. Tasks that once drained him now held a rhythm, small victories in steady succession. Change, he realized, wasn't about reinventing everything. It was about how you showed up to the same tasks with different viewpoints.

Even Melody, Grace's ever-watchful feline shadow, seemed to acknowledge the shift. Typically aloof toward anyone but Grace, she had taken to climbing into Waldo's lap in the evenings, curling up as if silently approving of his newfound presence at home. It became a small but oddly affirming ritual—one that Grace found endlessly amusing. "She senses when people need grounding," Grace had joked one night, watching Melody sprawl across his legs, declaring him her newest territory.

Waldo smirked, running a hand through the cat's fur. "So, now I need emotional support from a cat?"

Grace shrugged. "Hey, she's got good instincts."

But despite this new steadiness, something still tugged at him beneath the surface. It wasn't restlessness. Not anymore. It was more like building a puzzle and watching the border take shape—all while the center remained stubbornly blank. He wasn't chasing a destination now, and that was progress. But the walk still felt unfinished, like a trail that disappeared into fog, inviting him forward but offering no clear view of where it led.

The next Thursday arrived, predictable as ever. Waldo sat in the familiar chair, back straight this time, and although he wasn't tense, he wasn't fully at ease either. His hands fidgeted lightly in his lap, fingers threading and unthreading. He had grown used to this room: the quiet hum of the vents, the scent of polished wood and paper, the stillness that used to calm him. But today, that stillness pressed in differently.

It wasn't because he didn't want to be there—he did. In some ways, these sessions had become a refuge, a space where he could drop the performance. He had even started looking forward to them. But now that the early momentum had settled, now that he was noticing beauty in the ordinary and feeling more present with Sara and the kids, a new tension had crept in. He didn't want to say what he'd been thinking lately. Not to Dr. Benson. Not yet. Because saying it might sound like regression. Like failure. How do you admit incompleteness when you've been reporting progress?

He glanced at the floor, then at the bookshelf across from him. He knew the layout by heart now, as well as how long it would take for her to speak if he stayed quiet. He knew the gentle tilt of her head when she was waiting for him to find the words. He exhaled slowly and let his gaze fall again.

There it was; that flicker of skepticism.

Not about her. Not about the process. About himself. Maybe, despite the subtle shifts and fleeting wins, he was still circling something he hadn't named. It was the creeping sense that maybe he had been fooling himself all along, that this search for meaning, for purpose, was nothing more than a carefully crafted illusion. Despite all the talking and self-reflection, he still hadn't landed on anything that felt like clarity. He didn't feel like he was failing, but he didn't feel done either. And part of him wondered if she would be disappointed. He rubbed his palm over his knee to ground himself.

When Dr. Benson finally looked up, her voice was as steady as always. "You seem like you're holding something."

Waldo's jaw tightened, just slightly. He gave a faint nod, then swallowed. "I think I'm afraid to admit that I still feel incomplete. After everything. Even with the good stuff." There it was—said aloud. And suddenly, the silence in the room didn't feel heavy anymore. It felt earned.

Dr. Benson waited, never rushing him. She knew better.

Finally, he exhaled, shaking his head. "What if I've been the problem all along?"

"Tell me what you mean by that."

His voice dropped, a quiet resignation threading through. "I keep running in circles. I thought I was making progress, but I still feel stuck." Waldo now sat on the edge of his seat, unable to relax. "No matter what I do, I always end up back in the same place, asking the same questions.

Dr. Benson made a quick note in her book, then rested her elbows on her knees. "Let's say that's true," she said. "Let's say you're the problem. Then what?"

Waldo blinked. "What do you mean?"

She shrugged. "If the issue is you, if the common denominator in all of this is you, what are you going to do about it?"

His shoulders sank as he stared down at his hands. His fingers curled slightly, as if grasping for something just out of reach. His chest constricted with a low-grade ache that had no clear name. He shook his head again, staring at the floor. He let out a nervous laugh. "That's the problem, isn't it? I don't know how to fix it."

"Maybe that's because you're trying to fix the wrong thing." Her gaze stayed on him, unwavering.

Waldo's frown deepened. His head dropped, looking at nothing in particular, as if he were searching for an answer in the space between his feet. "Meaning?" he murmured. He felt drained, hollowed out by the realization that all his efforts—every step, every attempt to piece himself together—had only led him back to this same place. The same tangled knot of uncertainty. And now, here he was again, being told he might be chasing the wrong thing entirely.

She suddenly clapped her hands, a crack of sound that jolted Waldo from his thoughts. His head snapped up, stunned, as she leaned closer. "Waldo, let's step back for a second. Every time you come in here, you talk about what's missing, what you haven't found, what you don't know. You've built this narrative where you're incomplete, like there's some crucial piece of yourself still waiting to be uncovered." She let the words hang between them, watching as they struck. "What if that's untrue?"

His eyes narrowed. "What do you mean?"

"What if you're not lost?" she said plainly. "What if you're just unfinished?"

Waldo stilled. The word caught him off guard. He'd assumed he was fractured, not becoming.

"You keep searching for some grand revelation, expecting clarity to arrive like a neatly wrapped gift. But that's not how it works, Waldo. You don't find yourself. You build yourself."

"So, it's not about finding who I am, but building me?"

"Not quite." She studied him for a moment, then asked, "What are you waiting for?"

Waldo leaned back in his chair. "What?"

"It seems you're constantly looking for something to be given to you, as if a purpose is something you stumble upon." She shook her head. "Purpose is about more than simply finding what makes you happy. It's about giving something of yourself that feels meaningful."

He swallowed, his throat parched.

She straightened. "Perhaps the reason you feel empty isn't because you haven't found the right thing. Maybe it's because you haven't given enough of yourself to something that matters."

He wiped his hands on his pants, again, suddenly aware of the sweat on his skin. *"That's not fair,"* he almost said. But he knew she wasn't wrong. Not entirely.

She let the silence stretch for a moment before adding, "You've spent all this time asking, *'What am I supposed to do?'* Maybe it's time to ask, *'What do I want to give?'"*

He hadn't thought in those terms before. Not what he lacked, but what he might offer. The swirling thoughts in his mind didn't disappear completely, but they eased enough to remind him of the possibilities that awaited him.

It had only been two weeks since Waldo first began to wonder what he might give back, and he didn't mean in the grand gestures he once thought was needed. Instead, his focus was on the steady, unspoken gestures that reflected who he was becoming.

One evening, after returning home from work a bit later than usual, Waldo sat in the den, the mellow glow of a reading lamp casting long shadows across the room. Papers and books, the debris of a frantic attempt to prolong his tranquility, strewed the desk. He leaned back in his chair, feeling fatigue settling in again, not just physical exhaustion, but the kind that made him question his own abilities. He felt like he was in a never-ending maze, where each path ultimately led back to the same disheartening reality—that he was searching for a vital piece of understanding but never getting any closer.

The maze wasn't just external; it was internal, a web of self-doubt and uncertainty that wrapped tighter with every step he took. Perhaps something other than his inability to navigate the complicated path disoriented him. Maybe it was the need to name everything, to force every corner into a neat explanation, instead of just trusting himself to walk through it.

Desperate not to take more steps backward, he forced himself to look for meaning in every corner, every shadow, pressing so hard for those small moments that had once come so naturally. And now, standing at yet another dead end, he had to ask himself, *What if I'm looking for answers that don't exist? Or worse, what if I'm just too tired to recognize them when they do? And what use does my notebook have if the moments I recorded turn out to only be another question mark to my goal?* He stared at it now with suspicion. Once, it had been a lifeline, proof he was paying attention. But was it just another illusion? A way of recording without integrating? The thought stung.

Throughout his entire journey, there were brief, electrifying flashes when clarity felt within reach—glimpses where the lesson before him seemed to crystallize into something tangible and profound. It was in those moments that he felt as if a veil lifted, revealing the path ahead with startling precision, making him believe he had finally cracked the code to ending his own struggles. But just like every epiphany that came before, those revelations were short-lived. Inevitably, the comfort of his old habits would resurface, luring him back into the murky depths of doubt and uncertainty. Waldo wrestled with the dissonance. How could something that seemed so meaningful slip away so easily? It was as if his mind, desperate for resolution, clung to these lessons like lifelines, convincing him they were enough to stave off the deepening emptiness within. But the truth, he realized, was more complicated.

The lessons were real—sharp, fleeting, illuminating, and deeply important. The problem wasn't them. It was him. He could feel them pass through, unable to hold. Each insight fell like a drop into a bottomless bucket. Was he growing . . . or just gathering wisdom he couldn't use, deceiving himself into thinking he was closer to filling the void?

When the weight of these thoughts pressed down on him the most, when doubt whispered the loudest, he realized true transformation required more than insight; it demanded perseverance, action, and the courage to confront the discomfort that came with breaking free of deeply ingrained patterns. And yet, change wasn't linear. When exhaustion took hold, setbacks were unavoidable, making it easier to revert to old habits than to confront the work of genuine change.

And lately, that exhaustion had settled deep into his bones, following him into the quiet hours of the night. Not even sleep brought rest. Instead, it unraveled him. It was no longer a refuge, no longer a place of quiet retreat. The moment his head hit the pillow, the maze returned with its towering hedges and jagged, ruff walls. Initially, restless images existed in a disjointed way, but now, they were forming something more deliberate. More insistent. More real. The maze didn't just seem to trap him; it seemed to ask something of him. As if the walls themselves were waiting.

The deeper he fell into sleep, the heavier the sensation became—like being dragged beneath a tide, carried further and further from the waking world. Each night, the dreams stretched longer, their details more precise. He could feel the cold rocks beneath his fingertips, the scent of damp earth heavy in the air. They weren't passing thoughts or idle imaginings—these dreams were vivid, consuming. Each turn he made promised progress, but the walls reassembled taller, quieter, and more certain in their refusal, delivering only dead ends. In the dreams, his steps felt driven by an unnamed urgency. He was searching for something—or was it someone? The thought was obscure, unformed, like a shadow just out of grasp.

Was it Sara, woven into the silence? Her voice, her touch, her steady presence had always anchored him, and the maze seemed to linger with subtle remnants of her laughter, the warmth of her voice beckoning him forward. He was possibly searching for her, for the connection they had once shared before the chaos of life yanked them in diverse directions, but she was never there when he turned the corner. Or was it someone else entirely? Could it be his younger self? The boy who had dreamed fearlessly before the world layered expectations and self-doubt over his confidence?

The whispers, carried on the wind, teased him with their incompleteness, fragments of a voice that hinted at answers but never delivered. He would call out to the maze itself, as though it might have spirits or dwellers who held the truth, but all he received in return were echoes of his own cry.

Waldo pushed forward, desperate to decipher the cryptic carvings, to interpret the innuendos, to make sense of the scraps tossed in his direction, but each step deeper into the maze felt massive, like the air was thickening, weighing him down. The harder he pressed, the more the maze seemed to resist him, its paths twisting and looping until he couldn't tell if he was moving forward or backtracking. And yet, no matter how futile it felt, he couldn't stop.

His observations, the way he noticed every crack in the wall and every swish of wind, propelled him further into his mind. It wasn't just a tangle anymore. The corridors were his thoughts. The walls were his doubts and his unanswered questions.

The maze wasn't just around him.

It was him.

He was both the seeker and the obstruction.

Each wrong turn aggravated the shadows along the winding path. The cacophony of noise around him grew louder, drowning out his thoughts. Standing on the edge of losing hope, he called out to the maze again, cradling his head in his hands with defeat. The air hung dense with the mineral tang of stone and the wet rot of leaf-littered ground, while the isolated reverberation of his own voice disappeared into the vast emptiness.

A sudden eerie breeze swept over him, prickling his skin and sending a deep shiver down his spine. He closed his eyes as the wind roared through the corridors. When it stilled, when the shadows thinned, something else broke through: yeast—rosemary—warmth. He looked upward, and there it was—not a figment of his imagination, but a vision, dramatic in its sweep and haunting in its nearness, so vivid he could almost reach out and touch it.

He was sitting in the familiar sunlit kitchen of his childhood home, the scent of freshly baked bread wafting through the air. His mother was there too, her back turned as she hummed a favorite tune, her hands busily kneading more dough on the counter. She glanced over her shoulder and smiled, her expression comforting and knowing. *"Sometimes,"* she said, her voice gentle, *"when you're not searching, that's when the melody finds you — the one you didn't know you'd been humming all along."*

The words resonated through him, their lucidity startling, as though she was truly there. He'd remembered her saying that before, but now, it felt different, consequential. The image of her lingered, carrying the impression that she was alive and present and no time had passed, even though she'd been gone for several years. She filled the maze with a quiet glow, her presence not haunting, a pleasant reminder that the answers he sought might already be with him, hidden in the quiet.

His father, who had passed away four years before his mom, casually strolled into the kitchen, his voice blending naturally with his mother's, creating a harmonious chorus of profound wise words: *"Do not go where the path may lead; go instead where there is no path and leave a trail."* In a space where past and present overlapped, both his parents were there in the maze with him, not as ghosts but as something more enduring—portions of himself, advising him. Their voices intertwined, their foresight merging in a way he hadn't totally appreciated before.

Waldo had to catch his breath; the charged air around him had stolen it away. Frozen in place, the air held him. But despite this, he felt a strange lightness; the echoing parallels of his parents' voices pulsing over and through him created an almost sacred stillness in the maze. Then, unexpectedly, he stopped breathing entirely. The sheer magnitude of it all caught him off guard. He gasped, the air nudging him back to life. As an awareness hit him, he inhaled intensely; though his parents were long gone, this moment felt as real as any he'd lived. They weren't just memories—they were fused into the path he now walked, guiding him forward.

But when he awoke, the exhaustion and restlessness remained. But still, he pressed on. He continued documenting the small moments of his day, filling pages with quiet observations, tiny fragments of meaning he hoped would come together. The evidence that he was trying felt reassuring, proof that he was engaging with life, paying attention, that he was moving forward in some way. But the more he wrote, the more he saw a widening gap. Not between what he recorded and what he felt, but between what he understood and what was still too new to name. It wasn't discouraging like his prior frustrations. It wasn't the same agonizing near miss. It was more like standing at the edge of something vast and unknown, realizing the journey itself was far bigger than he had ever imagined.

One Thursday afternoon, after one of his usual therapy appointments, Waldo hadn't gone straight back to work. Instead, he'd stopped by Cooper's Café, needing a moment to process. He overheard someone at the next table say something that caught his attention. Although he didn't quite grasp it at the time, something about the phrasing lingered, so he jotted the quote on a napkin, folded it into his notebook, and forgot about it. Now, flipping through the pages, he spotted the napkin again. And this time, the message landed with unsettling precision: *"The more you know, the more you realize you don't know."* The line wasn't just a reflection. It was a challenge. An ultimatum. Not to solve everything. Not to rush toward an answer. But to release certainty's grip; embrace uncertainty fearlessly.

Later that night, Waldo's dream played out the shift in perspective from finding the napkin. Standing before the next turn in the maze, he understood it had no clear exit; it was constructed within his own mind to be disorganized and perplexing, forcing him to question every aspect of the situation, coming face to face with his own limitations. It regularly tested his resolve, and perhaps that was precisely the point.

Just as the feeling of being absorbed in the maze felt unbearable, Waldo looked down and saw he was holding his notebook. His eyes caught a note scribbled in the corner of the cover: *"Not all who wander are lost."* His father's wisdom about the wandering traveler, lost in the wilderness but finding clarity not through frantic searching but by slowing down and sincerely observing, floated in and out of his mind like a wave. Waldo realized that not having an escape was an invitation to learn how to see, to listen, and to trust the signs he'd been missing all along.

A sudden burst of clarity illuminated his mind, like a camera flash exposing a long-hidden truth. Was Waldo that frantic traveler now, constantly turning corners in his desperate quest for clarity amidst the chaos? Then it came back to him, a part of his dad's story that he had completely forgotten; before the traveler had his epiphany, he had been distressed trying to find his way, rushing wildly through the maze of trees, his mind clouded with fear and doubt. No matter how far he ran, the path forward only seemed to grow more tangled, the forest closing in tighter. Exhausted, he collapsed onto the forest floor, staring into space.

As he sat up, the sense of fluttering wings caught his attention. Right along the edge of his sight, he noticed a small clearing bathed in golden sunlight, and in its center, a group of butterflies danced in the air. For a moment, the traveler forgot his anxiety. He watched as the butterflies flitted gracefully, their movements calm and purposeful, untouched by the chaos surrounding him.

Overcome by their beauty, the traveler stood and carefully approached the clearing, reaching out, trying to catch one. But the harder he tried, the more the butterflies darted away, their delicate wings slipping through his grasp as he chased them back into the forest. Disheartened, he slumped back against a tree, letting out a weary sigh. As he sat there, worn out from the pursuit, he noticed a butterfly land on a nearby flower. The flower had done nothing but exist, yet it had received what he had struggled to grasp.

The traveler closed his eyes and took a deep breath, allowing the tension to leave his body. When he opened them again, a butterfly had landed on his outstretched hand, its fragile wings brushing against his skin. A quiet whisper reached him: *some things gravitate toward presence, not pursuit.* Catching the butterfly wasn't the point of the story. It was a lesson in relinquishing the urge to control, own, and possess. Waldo had spent his life grasping, convinced that only through relentless effort could he attain what he longed for. However, in the stillness, the answer arose effortlessly.

Waldo could see it now: the maze wasn't just an obstacle to over-come—it was a teacher, revealing lessons with every twist and turn. It wasn't about finding the exit; it was about understanding why he was there in the first place. Every dead end was a message, a lesson that would repeat until he absolutely grasped it. Each wrong turn was a signal that there was something more he needed to learn before he could move forward.

The maze wasn't blocking his path as he had thought for so long—it was showing him the gaps in his understanding, forcing him to pause, to reflect, to grow. He couldn't brute-force his way through it. Every misstep was an invitation to reclaim the tools he had neglected, the inner resources he had ignored. The answers wouldn't come through sheer determination alone. They required patience, awareness, and the willingness to learn what the maze was trying to teach him. Only when he stopped fighting it, when he embraced the lessons it offered, would the path forward reveal itself when he was ready.

And maybe he finally was. Maybe now, he was that traveler.

The next morning, Waldo carried the dream with him as he got ready for the day. The vividness had not left him, and he appreciated the new knowledge that the maze was like a master craftsman, only revealing the next piece of the blueprint when he had mastered the current phase. It wasn't about finding the quickest way out. It was about becoming the person who could handle whatever came next. And without learning how to apply all the tools at his disposal, the maze would keep teaching him, holding him there, until he learned. He needed to cultivate the ability to shift between work and rest, between pushing ahead and pulling back to reflect on where he had been.

As Waldo stood at the kitchen counter, waiting for the coffee to finish brewing, his gaze drifted to a small opened notebook pushed to the side, usually used for quick notes and the grocery list. Almost unconsciously, he reached for the pen beside it, tracing lines onto the page. Before long, the image took shape: a fork in the road, one path drawn smooth and straight, the other rough and winding, unfinished and uncertain. *"You'll come to a lot of forks in the road, Waldo,"* he heard his father say. *"Some paths look easy, tempting even, but it's not always about choosing what's smooth. It's about who you become along the way. Choose the easiest route every time, and you risk missing out on discovering what you're truly capable of."*

Waldo stared thoughtfully at the crude sketch before drawing small question marks beside each path, emphasizing the uncertainty they represented. He knew it was a reflection of the subtle tension he'd been feeling lately, the quiet restlessness he struggled to acknowledge. The smoother path seemed to promise security, predictability, and clarity— yet, there was something compelling about the unfinished route. It resonated with a deeper truth he was only beginning to grasp. Clarity wasn't always found in simplicity, after all. Sometimes, it emerged from embracing uncertainty itself.

Sara's voice startled him back to the present. "Coffee ready yet?"

He glanced up, pulling away from his sketch. "Just about," he said softly, setting down the pen. He left the notebook open, the forked paths exposed on the counter, unfinished but oddly meaningful.

An evening a few days later, Sara, Grace, Nathan, and Waldo sat together in the living room, something that felt increasingly rare these days. Though the vision of the maze stayed with him, like a faint melody waiting to be fully heard, Waldo was present in the opportunity he was being given with his family. Nathan, with a night off work, was sprawled across the couch, scrolling through his phone. Grace flipped through a music book, absentmindedly humming under her breath. Sara was curled up in the armchair, watching a show on the TV, glancing at Waldo over the rim of her mug every so often.

"So, Grace, do you have everything for the recital now?" Sara asked, breaking the comfortable silence.

Grace sighed, setting her book aside. "Almost. I still need to decide on shoes."

Nathan smirked. "You're stressing over shoes? You'll be standing behind a piano. Who's gonna see them?"

"It's about how they feel when I play," Grace said, shooting him a glare. "You wouldn't understand."

"You're right. I wouldn't." Nathan shrugged and went back to his phone.

Sara chuckled, shaking her head, while Waldo watched, soaking in the moment. The evening was unremarkable, filled with the everyday chatter that characterized their lives, but he couldn't imagine anything more important.

As the evening went on, one by one, they trickled away. Grace vanished upstairs, muttering something about practicing one more time before bed. Nathan yawned, stretched, and announced he had an early shift the next day. Sara stayed a little longer, but eventually, with a squeeze of Waldo's hand, she, too, headed for the bedroom. And, of course, Melody, who had been sleeping on the armrest near Waldo, hopped down and padded after Sara.

And just like that, he was alone.

Waldo rubbed the back of his neck, his eyes fixed on the darkened window. A heavy stillness replaced the warmth of family chatter. There was a deeper question at play, something unfinished, waiting to be faced in the moments he found himself without company, but as the traveler story reminded him, the answer wasn't in the reaching—it was in the allowing. So, he released a slow breath, allowing the quiet to settle around him. Fully awake, eyes closed, he summoned the maze with a kind of calm he didn't yet trust. He wasn't chasing escape this time. Instead, he was stepping back into the place he had once fled to understand it more clearly.

The image sharpened, and for the first time, Waldo didn't find himself trapped inside the maze. Instead, he stood just outside its entrance, staring at the towering walls that stretched endlessly in both directions. The familiar twisting pathways lay ahead, shrouded in shifting shadows, but unlike before, the sight didn't fill him with dread.

The jagged edges of fear and uncertainty had softened, no longer a threat. It was a choice.

Drawn forward, he lifted his hand to the wall. The cool stone beneath his fingertips was strong, real—a contrast to the restless unease that had followed him for so long. He listened to the faint rustling of unseen leaves, the distant hush of wind weaving through the corridors ahead. This wasn't just another passing dream, something ephemeral that would dissolve by morning. It was intentional presence, startling in its quiet precision. A message that unfolded the truth in pieces, refusing to be ignored. It felt imprinted, like something remembered, not invented. And tonight, there was a new detail to take in. At the entrance, carved faintly into the stone, was a word: *Begin.*

The dim glow of the maze light made the worn letters nearly imperceptible, yet they remained waiting for him, as a reminder. For so long, he had obsessed over the outcome. Where did the maze lead? Would he ever reach its end? How long would it take? But now, standing at the threshold, the questions that had once consumed him felt . . . irrelevant. He lifted his foot, hesitating only for a second before moving forward. The moment his sole met the stone path, the wind shifted—chilly, familiar, carrying something deeper than air. And then he walked.

It felt like only mere minutes had passed since he took a few tentative steps on his journey, but time inside the maze felt like elastic, as though the seconds stretched and compressed with each thought that flickered through his mind. Knowing from his dreams that he was meant to find someone, he was patiently calm until, finally, he saw the figure—a shadowy presence in the distance, standing still. It wasn't threatening, nor was it welcoming; it only existed, stoic and persistent, a sentinel in the maze's heart. Waldo's breath hitched, his heart pounding in his chest, its rhythm matching the weight of every unanswered question he carried. He couldn't tell if it was watching him or openly expecting, yet its stillness seemed to beckon him onward.

The labyrinth walls, tall and suffocating moments ago, seemed to draw back slightly, as though granting him a clearer path. Each step felt weighted with purpose now, the crunch of the unseen ground beneath him resonating in his chest like a distant drumbeat. The figure didn't move but its presence still grew stronger with every stride Waldo took. It seemed to anticipate his arrival, measuring the resolve behind each of his steps.

Doubts clawed at the edges of Waldo's mind. *Am I absolutely ready for whatever lay ahead? To know what this shadow represents?* Despite the questions, his feet carried him along. However, right when Waldo thought he was close enough to see the figure clearly, it slipped behind the next corner, dissolving into the shadows. He called out, but the figure didn't respond. Occasionally, it danced past his peripheral sight, elusive and indistinct, cloaked in a smoky haze, shrouded as a phantom in the fog. It was like a nasty game of hide-and-seek, where the seeker was always one step behind, the figure never appearing where expected, always slipping away before Waldo could get close enough to see its face. Sometimes, it loomed just at the edge of his vision, remaining emotionless. Yet, each appearance felt abundant with meaning, like a message wrapped in silence. Whose presence obsessed him?

Waldo's mind raced again, pulling up the possibilities he'd turned over before. Could it be Sara, her steady love tethering him back to who he was when they first met? Or his younger self, the wide-eyed boy with ink-stained fingers and wonder behind his questions, asking to be remembered? Maybe it was his father, offering another fragment of wisdom from somewhere beyond time. Or his mother, ever attuned to life's subtle rhythms, urging him to hear what hummed beneath the noise—the subtle rhythm most people missed. Or perhaps it was someone entirely unknown, a stranger bearing a message he hadn't yet learned to translate. Another frantic traveler, maybe. The uncertainty was maddening yet oddly exhilarating.

He hesitated, jaw tightening as a wave of frustration rose—a mounting tension that pulsed behind his eyes. Questions swirled, sharp and insistent. *Who are you? Why are you here? What are you trying to tell me?* The answers felt close, infuriatingly close, as though they were mocking him from just beyond reach, demanding one more step he wasn't sure how to take. Then, like a ripple building toward a wave, a new thought rolled through. *What if it's me?*

Not the man he was. Not the man he is. But the outline of who he could become. A future self; one refined by time, one who had wandered these same corridors of doubt and found a way to emerge changed, not broken. That version didn't chase certainty but walked beside the questions. He had learned how to move without needing to know what came next. Waldo's pulse quickened. The ambiguity didn't feel like failure anymore—it felt like permission.

Maybe he didn't need to know who the figure was. Maybe what mattered was that he was still following. Arrival wasn't a point on the map, but a decision to keep going, even when the path stayed unclear. "It's never too late," he said aloud, barely above a whisper, as though testing them. In a space where past and present overlapped, the maze itself might be listening. As the words left his lips, they rippled through him like a triumphant epiphany. They didn't echo back in mockery—they settled. *Maybe late isn't the same as lost,* he thought. *Perhaps it's not too late to change course, no matter how far I've wandered. Perhaps I'm perfectly on time.*

In that moment, something shifted deep within Waldo, like a stiff window finally nudged open, letting in air that had long been shut out. A slow, thrilling warmth spread through his chest; he had become so consumed by his quest for answers that he'd forgotten to notice the richness of his own passage.

He remembered what Dr. Benson had told him: *"You don't have to know everything right now. You just need to start somewhere. Be the change."* It wasn't about figuring it all out in one sweeping realization. It was about movement, about taking that first step, however uncertain. Nathan had reminded him of that, too—his determination to restart his rocket project no matter how much he struggled with it. With a little encouragement, his son hadn't let frustration stop him; he had simply begun again, piece by piece, failure by failure, until he made progress.

Sara, on the other hand, her gift had always been cutting through the noise, peeling back distractions to uncover what truly mattered. She didn't force clarity; she encouraged it. She didn't rush to fix things but had a quiet instinct for knowing what was worth holding on to, and what needed to be released. Waldo used to admire that about her, but somewhere along the way, he'd confused motion with meaning, tangling himself in the idea that if he wasn't doing, he wasn't enough. But Sara had always known that stillness could hold just as much truth, and now, he was beginning to understand it too.

And last but not least, there was Grace, with her openness that allowed her to experience life in a way he had once known but somehow lost. What she heard in music wasn't just sound, but feeling, a wave that moved through her, unfiltered and alive. He used to hear the world that way too—his mother had taught him that. But over time, deadlines and detours dulled that sensitivity. Grace reminded him what it looked like to let the moment unfold without trying to name it, to feel without explaining. She had a way of embracing the present without overthinking where it led, letting herself be in the moment without demanding it mean something bigger.

Surprisingly, Melody, too, had her own lessons to share, offering a kind of wisdom he hadn't appreciated until now. The way she could sit for hours, still and unbothered, watching the world with patient curiosity. She didn't chase every movement; she truly observed, letting the world come to her. Waldo had dismissed that kind of stillness for most of his life, mistaking it for passivity. But now, he saw the quiet authority in it—the way Melody met the world on her own terms, without chasing it. There was something powerful in that. A kind of presence he was only just learning to value again.

Opening his eyes, Waldo blinked, disoriented for a moment. He hadn't meant to fall asleep. He had been awake when the vision of the maze first formed, fully conscious as he traced its winding paths in his mind. And yet, at some point, without realizing it, he had drifted. The dream had claimed him, anyway.

Even as the details of his living room came into focus, the rhythmic ticking of the wall clock proving time was once again passing, something still felt off. He sat there for a long moment, the remnants of the vision still clinging to him like mist before the morning sun, knowing these fragments were just waiting patiently for him to understand. When he finally rose from the chair, he crossed the room to stand by the window, his gaze drifting over the street. Outside, the world appeared unchanged, with the same cars parked along the curb and porch lights flickering on as the night settled in. But inside, it was as if he had stepped onto a higher ledge, offering him a broader view of everything, not just around him, but within him. Maybe the person he had been chasing wasn't waiting at the end of some path. Maybe he was becoming that person with every step, every pause, every breath he finally allowed himself to take.

Chapter 6
The False Path

During the next two days, Waldo's life carried on much as it always had, but something about him was undeniably different. His step had a new bounce, and he moved with an ease he hadn't possessed before. Even the mundane became lighter. His morning commute, which had once felt like an endless cycle of brake lights and frustration, was no longer a burden. Instead of drumming his fingers against the steering wheel, impatiently counting down the minutes until he could escape the gridlock, he found himself appreciating these moments more deeply—the quiet rhythm of a jogger's feet hitting the pavement, the way the sunlight broke through the skyline, dappling the buildings with streaks of gold. It was subtle, but it was there.

Work, too, had shifted in ways that eluded his understanding. The endless spreadsheets, the predictable meetings, the emails that once felt like an avalanche burying him under their responsibility—they were still there, but they no longer crushed him. He moved through them with steadier focus, more engaged, sometimes finding a strange satisfaction in problem-solving rather than merely enduring the hours.

There were still short but powerful resurgences, where the pressure crept back in. A sudden influx of deadlines would remind him of the exhaustion that had once consumed him. And every so often, a message from his boss—the kind that seemed harmless on the surface —would send a familiar tension crawling up his spine, a ghost of the stress he used to carry like armor. These were reminders of how easily the old weight could return if he wasn't paying attention. The old feelings hadn't disappeared entirely, but at this point, they didn't drown him. Before, he had felt as if he were a man treading water, barely keeping himself afloat as the magnitude of his life pressed down on his shoulders. Now, he was learning to move with the current.

Sara noticed it too, though she tried not to allow her hopes to rise too quickly as she had the first time she saw his effort. Their last genuine conversation, the one where he had been distant, his answers clipped, his thoughts somewhere else, had been weeks ago, but she accepted he had to work through his problems alone. So, she let it go. And though the space separating them endured, something about him now felt easier. The guarded look in his eyes had softened, and he seemed more present, less consumed by whatever burden had once gripped him so tightly. It was the little things that gave it away: he asked more questions, his goodnights felt heartfelt rather than hollow, and he really listened when she talked.

That morning, three days after the vision of the maze in the living room, Waldo surprised Sara by staying in the kitchen long after Grace had left for school. No half-eaten toast, no distracted goodbye. Instead, he stood at the stove, flipping eggs, the scent of fresh coffee curling warmly into the air.

Sara leaned against the counter, mug in hand. "You're cooking?"

He glanced over with a smile, easy and unhurried. "Figured I'd go in late today."

She blinked, registering the shift, the intentional gesture. Waldo Turner—the man who once outran his own morning —choosing to linger? "Since when do you do that?" she asked, folding her arms with amused curiosity.

"Since now," he said simply, plating the eggs. "Thought I'd make some for Nathan, too."

Sara watched him for a moment, the scraping of utensils filling the quiet. There was something steady in his movements, but still, there was a faraway look behind his ease, like his mind was still walking through something she couldn't see. She'd seen him journaling, focused, curved in on himself. But this was different. For the first time, he seemed willing to bring that clarity into the room, to live it, not just seek it. Sara didn't press; not everything needed to be understood on cue. Some changes didn't come with explanations. Only presence. So, she didn't interrupt his progression. After all these years, she knew Waldo sometimes needed space to process aloud—and, sometimes, he just needed space. What mattered was that he wasn't drifting away. Still, she resolved to keep watch—not to stop him, but to gently guide him back if the weight returned and began to pull too hard.

They sat together, unhurried. Waldo asked about her day, listened without drifting, laughed softly at something she said—a sound that had been missing from their mornings far too long. And when breakfast was done and the dishes cleared, Waldo kissed her cheek and grabbed his keys. Sara stood by the window, watching him step into the car. She felt a flicker of recognition. Maybe the Waldo she missed wasn't lost. Maybe he was returning, piece by piece.

As Waldo pulled out of the driveway, the morning light cast a soft glow across the quiet street. The rhythm of the day awaited him—familiar tasks, the hum of work life, the structure he once clung to. But it all felt different now. Less like a duty, and more like a purpose.

He wasn't the type to shift schedules or take spontaneous time off. His days had long been constructed from habit and obligation, but Thursday's therapy had changed that. Thursday afternoons were his, work didn't own that hour anymore—he did. So, later that day, as he took his lunch break and drove toward the office, he also took time to appreciate the new feeling in his chest, the novel curiosity about what was unfolding.

As he settled into the chair across from Dr. Benson, the change showed, not just in his posture but in his presence. The familiar slump of exhaustion and doubt that had characterized so many of their sessions had given way to something more composed. Waldo leaned back in the chair, his hands resting lightly on the arms as though grounding him in this new sense of purpose. He didn't feel that he was bracing himself for another round of questions he couldn't answer as so many sessions before. "I've stopped treating the maze like a trap," Waldo said, relaxed but animated. "It's not about escaping anymore—it's about exploring what's inside."

Dr. Benson tilted her head, her pen resting on the notebook in her lap. "Tell me more about this maze, Waldo. You've not mentioned it before. What does it represent to you?"

"It started as a dream," Waldo admitted, his eyes brightening as he leaned into the memory. "At first, it was just flashes; brief, disjointed images that barely made sense. But over time, the same towering hedges, the same stone walls, the same twisting paths stretching endlessly in every direction became more vivid."

"So, what are you doing in your dreams?"

"I'm always searching," he said, slowly, his mind replaying the event. "For what, I don't know. My initial feeling was one of being enclosed and stifled. Regardless of direction, I remained trapped, unable to find my way out. Inscrutable symbols plastered the walls; the wind seemed to whisper secrets, elusive and tantalizing, like an unsolvable riddle."

"How often do these dreams happen?"

"Pretty often, but they don't feel random," Waldo said. "It seems they come to my rescue when I'm restless. Sometimes, I struggle to find the right words for what's on my mind. At first, I hated them. It felt like my subconscious was torturing me, confirming that I was stuck. But . . . something changed a couple of nights ago." His gaze flickered toward the window, as if he could see the maze forming beyond the glass. "I realized it isn't a prison. It's not a situation I need to escape. It's a place to learn."

"Tell me more." Dr. Benson leaned in.

"The dead ends, the twists and turns, even the strange emblems—they're not obstacles. They exist there for a reason. The symbols aren't mocking me; they're waiting to be understood. The whispers are more than noise; maybe they're my own thoughts, trying to tell me something I haven't been ready to hear." He ran his fingers through his hair, having a hard time sitting still. "The maze isn't just a metaphor or a setting anymore. It's me, my own mind showing me what I've been avoiding."

Dr. Benson glanced down at her notes. "That reframes everything, doesn't it?" she said, thoughtfully.

He let out a small, incredulous laugh. "I wasted too much time searching for the ideal life path, mistakenly believing a perfect route existed. But maybe that's not the actual issue. Perhaps the maze isn't a challenge to overcome, but an experience to be savored? Every wrong turn, each dead end . . . they aren't failures. They're lessons."

Dr. Benson's lips curled into a smile. "It seems you're starting to embrace the process, not as a puzzle to solve, but as something to live."

Waldo nodded, and this time, there was no doubt. "It feels different now. I don't feel trapped anymore. The maze hasn't changed, but my perspective has. It's almost freeing. Because I can finally breathe." He sat back in his chair, exhaling. With a path he didn't fully see, but finally trusted enough to follow, he felt a clearer sense of forward motion.

Dr. Benson's expression held both warmth and curiosity. "It's rare when a perspective shift feels that lived-in," she said. "And you're not just saying it. I can see it in how you're carrying it. It's not always easy to recognize when the change is already happening."

"I think I have felt it. And it started with something . . . unusual." He hesitated, the words catching in his throat. "It's going to sound strange, but I think I saw my parents in the maze."

Dr. Benson listened in careful interest. "In what ways did they appear?"

"It wasn't like seeing them standing there in front of me," Waldo clarified, shaking his head. "It was more like . . . feeling them. Their voices, their presence. My mom reminded me to find the music in quiet moments. My dad's words came back to me about making my own path. It didn't feel like I was just remembering them; it felt like they were guiding me."

She rested her hands in her lap, meeting his gaze. "Those moments tend to stay with us. I can see how much it's stirred in you. It's clear this impacted you, and I'm glad to see you feeling more connected to your journey." She paused before adding, "Just remember, although experiences like these can be transformative, they can also take space to fully process."

Waldo caught the subtle weight behind her calm. "Are you worried I'm reading too much into it?"

"Not worried," she said. "But I think it's important to stay grounded. These moments, whether dreams, memories, or something else, are significant. But they should also be explored in a way that keeps you balanced. Have you considered doing an immersive experience to deepen your understanding?"

"Immersive?"

"There's a three-day mindfulness retreat happening next week, just outside of town," she explained. "It's a quiet space to step away from distractions and really sit with your learning. They incorporate meditation, reflective exercises, and group discussions—tools that help people connect with themselves more profoundly. I think it could be a great way for you to explore the things you're going through while staying present in your everyday life."

Waldo absorbed her words, his fingers absently tracing the seam of the chair's armrest. "A retreat?" he echoed, uncertain. "I don't know . . . stepping away from everything feels a little out of my comfort zone."

Dr. Benson's lips quirked. "That's exactly why I'm suggesting it."

He let out a small chuckle, shaking his head. "You always push me when I think I've gotten comfortable with something."

"That's my job," she teased. "But this is different. Waldo, you've come so far, but insight alone is not enough. Insight is a door, but integration is how you walk through it. It's one thing to recognize that the maze isn't a trap, but another to fully integrate that realization into your life. I think this getaway could offer the space you need to do that."

"Okay, so what actually happens there?"

"It's less intimidating than it sounds," Dr. Benson assured him. "The retreat helps participants slow down and listen through meditation, creative exercises, and structured reflection; it's not about 'fixing' anything. It's about being present. The point is seeing what happens when you stop searching so hard and simply allow yourself to be."

He frowned. "I don't know. I mean, I have work and things at home—"

"And when did you last do something just for you?" Dr. Benson raised an eyebrow.

Waldo opened his mouth, but no words came.

She permitted the silence to settle before adding, "I'm not saying this retreat will give you all the answers, but I think it could be valuable. You've invested so much time into chasing clarity, and I think it's time to let it come to you."

She was right. He had spent his whole life obsessing over whether he was making the correct choices. But what if all of those choices didn't require a decision at all? But instead, they needed him to just embrace the experience? A slow breath escaped him, now entertaining the idea.

"Spots are limited, so if you're interested, let me know by tomorrow," Dr. Benson said. "It's still entirely your choice—just sleep on it."

But even as she said it, Waldo already knew: he was going. "Sign me up," he declared, a gradual smile forming, the hint of uncertainty fading from his expression.

Dr. Benson's own grin widened. "I'll send you the details. I have a feeling this could be another turning point for you."

He didn't know what the retreat would bring—only that he was ready to find out.

∼

Friday evening arrived slowly, heavy from an unexpectedly draining day at the office. He had spent most of the afternoon finalizing handover notes, fielding skeptical questions from colleagues who were unsure about why he'd suddenly taken three days off. Even after he'd explained the retreat—careful to omit details—his supervisor raised an eyebrow, commenting vaguely on the inconvenience. He was leaving behind unresolved projects, and even though he'd earned this time away, the guilt lingered stubbornly.

By the time he arrived home, Waldo's shoulders were tense, burdened by more than just the weight of his briefcase. But stepping through the front door, he felt some relief at seeing Sara's smile in the kitchen. With a gentle stir of something on the stove, she said, "You're home sooner than I thought. Did everything go well at work?"

"Just a lot of cynical looks and raised eyebrows about taking off next week. But it's done, everything's settled. I'm officially out of there for three days."

"Good," she reassured him, meeting his gaze warmly. "You deserve this."

Waldo set his briefcase aside, noticing Nathan sitting at the dining table, phone in hand, scrolling distractedly. Waldo paused mid-step, grateful to find Nathan home. Their schedules didn't often align, and tonight's overlap felt like a small gift. "Hey," Waldo said lightly, walking over to the table. "No shift tonight?"

Nathan looked up, shrugging slightly. "Got cancelled. Some kind of inventory problem at the store. They closed early. Figured I'd hang out here." There was no edge to his tone, just comfort.

Waldo lingered near the counter, hesitant for a moment, wondering how to bring up something that still felt a little new. "Since you're home, mind if I ask your opinion about something?"

Sara turned slightly at the request, hiding a soft smile. Waldo had always offered advice, not asked for it. Seeing him do so now caught her off guard.

Nathan set his phone down, visibly curious. "Sure?"

Waldo drew a breath. "I decided yesterday to take Dr. Benson up on an idea she mentioned in our last session—participating in a short retreat. I'll head out Monday. Taking three days away from everything."

"Like, completely off-grid?" Nathan asked.

"Sort of," Waldo admitted. "Limited phone use, no work stuff—just a break to think—or not think"

Nathan looked at him for a moment, weighing something silently before finally speaking. "That sounds good. I mean . . . You've been different lately, like more grounded. Maybe this will give you even more space to lean into that." He paused awkwardly, fingers tapping on the table. "It's probably the right call."

His son's subtle encouragement felt meaningful. Nathan wasn't usually one to weigh in, but tonight, his quiet vote of confidence landed with more weight than Waldo expected, cutting through his lingering uncertainty. "Thanks," Waldo said, genuinely touched. "I hope you're right."

Sara's spoon hovered as she turned, her smile edged with warmth. "It's nice having you both home tonight," she said. "Feels like a long time since we just . . . were."

Nathan grinned— quick and a little sheepish—before going back to his phone. Waldo didn't mind. The moment had landed.

Three days away wouldn't fix what time and intention were still shaping, but maybe it would offer more piece. Another space to listen. He looked around the kitchen, a trace of something new rising in the stillness. As it turned out, the benefits of the retreat hadn't waited to start on Monday. They had started the moment he allowed himself to arrive, wholly, honestly, and without rushing to understand.

The morning of the retreat, Waldo stood in the kitchen, nursing a cup of coffee as Sara set a plate of toast in front of him. "So, this is the big day."

Waldo nodded, swallowing a mouthful of coffee.

"And how do you feel about it?"

"I don't know," Waldo admitted. "Hopeful, yeah. But part of me keeps wondering . . . what if it's like before? The new hobbies—they felt big at first, and then just . . . faded. What if this ends up being just another thing that makes me feel like I'm chasing my tail?"

She placed the plate down and met his eyes. "Then it fades. Or it doesn't. But that doesn't mean it's not part of the journey. Sometimes, the thing that sticks isn't the biggest change. It's the one that happens after you stop expecting it."

"What if I don't come back with something profound to say?"

Sara placed a hand on his arm. "Then, you keep trying. You're doing the work, and that's what matters."

As he arrived at the retreat center, a converted bed-and-breakfast nestled deep in the woods on the outskirts of town, the sight of a large, unpretentious dwelling, its wooden exterior blending seamlessly with the elemental surroundings, greeted him. Pine and damp soil blended together, producing a fresh, earthy fragrance that permeated the air. Soft, organic sounds drifted through the atmosphere. The occasional bird chirp contributed to a tranquil, natural soundscape—subtle movements and quiet changes, as if woodland creatures were exchanging secrets. With each step toward the center, he could feel a sense of equanimity wash over him, like a gentle breeze caressing his skin.

That first day, Waldo approached each activity with high hopes. He followed instructions, joined the sessions, and tried to engage fully. But when the instructors encouraged the group to journal, something shifted. He wrote, yes, but it wasn't like the notebook he kept at home, full of raw fragments and stray observations that felt real. This was curated. Performed. As though the moment his pen touched the page, something unseen was watching. Expecting.

During a short break, Waldo wandered to the tea table and glanced around the gathering. That's when he noticed a younger man sitting apart from the others, shoulders hunched over a notebook, his pen moving furiously across the page. His name tag read Jamie. Waldo hadn't spoken to him yet, but there was something in the way Jamie gripped the pen—not expression, but escape—that intrigued him. As Waldo passed by to refill his tea, Jamie muttered, "I think the hardest part is not pretending you've figured it out just to belong." Waldo only nodded. But the line wouldn't leave him. It followed him like an echo down the corridors of his own mind, as if Jamie had named the thing he'd been unwilling to admit.

The hours passed, but a strange tension tugged at him, Jamie's comment continuing to loop in his head. What if that was exactly what he was doing here? Fitting in instead of sinking in? What if simplicity was the answer, and he'd been overcomplicating the path all along? He thought back to the artist in the park—how his steady, deliberate pencil strokes formed just enough to capture the essence, and yet somehow, it felt complete. Simple, but full. Maybe that was the answer, or at least, a contrast to all this noise.

That afternoon, the group was sent off to journal alone once again— forty-five minutes, no formal prompt. Just time. But even that carried its own unspoken pressure. Waldo wandered past the gravel path until he reached the forest's edge, where the trees thickened and the silence deepened. A weathered, crooked trunk waited at the bend of a clearing. He settled there, cross-legged beneath the trees, letting the notebook rest in his lap like a dare. The page he opened to was mostly blank, save for a few scratched-out lines. He'd been told to, "Let the pen move," but nothing felt honest. The words came out prepackaged, too polished, like borrowed insights he didn't believe enough to claim.

He couldn't stop missing his own notebook—the one back home, where fragments didn't have to impress or reveal anything on demand. But it hadn't even occurred to him to bring it. Those pages had felt like discovery specific to his home life and daily routine. But without it, with this new one, every line felt premeditated, like he was auditioning for clarity.

All around him, the retreat moved to its hushed rhythm—the soft murmur of voices, the gravel underfoot, the wind threading through pine. But inside, something twitched and skittered, restless as static in his chest. One of the facilitators, a woman named Elise with a voice like warm rain, had spoken earnestly about presence as permission earlier that day. He wanted to believe her. But the words floated past, like fog across glass. He wasn't rejecting them. He just couldn't reach them. He closed the journal and stared up through the trees, watching sunlight filter through the canopy like a Morse code he couldn't decipher. The wind shifted just enough to scatter the light, a momentary shimmer, like the forest was blinking at him, trying to get his attention. Was it an invitation? Or was it a warning?

He didn't know.

All he knew was it wasn't peace he needed. Or more insight. Or a circle of strangers nodding solemnly. It was impact. He needed something to break him open, to jolt him awake. The realization surprised him—not because it felt wrong, but because it felt true. Beneath the calm, there was a low hunger for contact. Something immersive that didn't ask permission, only presence.

Later that day, as others filtered toward their free reflection time, he heard quiet sobs coming from the bench near the meditation circle's edge. Jamie sat there, hunched, his notebook beside him like a shield that had failed. Waldo approached slowly. "Hey. Mind if I sit?" Jamie didn't answer, but he didn't say no either. Waldo took the silence as permission and sat down beside him.

For a long moment, neither spoke. Then, Jamie's voice broke the quiet. Everyone keeps saying to "breathe through it." But what if the breathing hurts too?"

Waldo exhaled, nodding once. "Then you breathe anyway. The pain means you're still here. As long as you're breathing, there's more right than wrong."

Jamie didn't reply, but his posture softened.

Waldo added, "What you resist . . . it doesn't leave. It waits. It circles back until you let it teach you what it came for." He looked out at the trees. "It's not about making it disappear. It's about staying long enough to see that it will pass—but only when you stop fighting it."

Jamie finally looked at him. "That sounds like something I need to hear more than once."

Waldo offered a half-smile. "Then keep it. It's yours now, too."

They exchanged numbers—not as a promise of friendship, but as a small bridge between two travelers crossing the same storm. Waldo didn't know if the words had truly landed as Jamie said, but sometimes, the smallest things stay with us longer than we think. Similar to Jamie, though, he wasn't absorbing this the way he thought he would. Instead of deepening his awakening, he felt himself thinning—his presence stretched across too many intentions. The more he tried to drop in, the more elusive the center felt. The workshop leaders spoke of releasing control and embracing the present, but their words sounded hollow, like an echo bouncing off a wall he couldn't break through. Not wanting to give up on the experience so soon, Waldo held on to the hope that perhaps a shared connection with others might be what was missing.

That evening at dinner, he cautiously revealed the vision he'd had of his parents guiding him through a maze with their wisdom with a few of the participants. He had counted on understanding, maybe even a similar story from someone else, that would make him feel less alone. Instead, the table fell uncomfortably silent. Finally, one participant awkwardly cleared her throat, while another offered a polite but dismissive, "Have you talked to a professional about that?" The words weren't cruel, just cleanly drawn, a subtle fence between his experience and theirs. Their expressions said what they didn't: they thought he was in the wrong place, that he needed therapy, not a workshop. Their responses stung in that private way rejection does when it's dressed in civility. Waldo nodded along with the rest of dinner, listening to their breakthroughs and borrowed mantras, but something had gone still in him. *Why is this resonating for them and not for me?*

By that night, Waldo felt utterly exhausted and discouraged. The rejection and self-doubt filled his mind as he walked to his room. He rehashed every moment of the workshop—the exercises, the discussions, the disappointing dinner conversation—searching for where he had gone wrong, for how he had missed the point entirely. When he reached his bedroom, he tossed his notebook on the floor and sank onto the edge of the bed, staring at the dimly lit walls. The unsettling silence of his quarters caused him to question the value of bunking alone. Lost in thought, he stayed there a long while, his mind whirling, until finally, he laid down, overcome by fatigue.

But as he closed his eyes, he thought of Dr. Benson. She had seemed genuinely excited for him when she suggested the retreat, her encouragement laced with an optimism he hadn't quite shared. She had believed this would be an important step, a chance for him to engage more deeply with his journey. Would she feel let down by the news of the first night's events?

Rather than feeling clear and at peace, he felt more uncertain than before. *Maybe that's what has been missing. Not clarity, but disruption. Something loud enough to break the silence inside of me.* Dr. Benson had said, "Insight is a door, Waldo. But embodiment is how you walk through it." Maybe this was what she meant. A door into something deeper. Or darker. He wasn't sure which, but he felt something stir.

He sighed, rubbing a hand over his face. He knew he was overthinking it. Perhaps tomorrow would be different.

When sleep finally took him, it didn't bring peace. It brought judgment. Last time, he'd entered the maze on his own terms—eyes closed, breath steady, intentions clear. But tonight, the dream came for him. Unbidden. Untimed. And the difference mattered.

He had followed the exercises, participated in the circles, written what he thought he was supposed to feel, but the maze could sense when he was faking it. It turned cold. Impenetrable. A consequence, not a cruelty. He no longer believed the maze was about escape anymore, but maybe, without realizing it, he'd started treating understanding like a destination. And still, somewhere in the haze, a steadier voice returned: *"The maze is a mirror. Don't chase clarity. Walk with it."* The dream had come to remind him that it hadn't darkened to punish him; only to prepare him for what he hadn't dared to look at yet.

It returned to being oppressive, its walls taller and more menacing, the narrow paths winding endlessly. The air felt thick, almost suffocating, and each step he took seemed to reverberate loudly in the heavy silence. He called out, desperate for guidance, for help, but his voice rebounded to him, distorted and mocking, as if the maze itself was snickering at his confusion. The symbols inscribed into the walls glistened harshly now, their edges sharper and more defined, but they were still incomprehensible. Waldo stared at them, willing them to reveal their meaning, but they remained frustratingly elusive, taunting him with their mystery. And then—movement. A trace of something just beyond his reach. Not a person, not a shadow, but a presence. Familiar and difficult to pin down, watching him from somewhere deep within. It moved swiftly, leaping through the maze with purpose, weaving effortlessly through the twists and turns, always remaining ahead of him.

Waldo's breath quickened as he tried to follow, his steps faltering on the uneven ground. With every turn, the figure seemed to tease him, its maneuvers fluid and assured, while he felt clumsy and insecure. He heard a *buzzing* fill the air next, low and faint at first, like the distant rumble of an approaching storm. But it grew, oscillating with an eerie rhythm that gave the impression of mimicking the figure's actions. He spun, his heart spiked. "Who's there?"

The sound wasn't neutral; it carried an insidious edge, rising and falling like a cruel laughter. It pressed against him, worming its way into his thoughts. The harder Waldo focused, the more the murmur seemed to take on a sinister cadence, each wave of sound mocking him, daring him to keep up. "Too slow," the chattering suggested, or perhaps it was his own fears projecting meaning onto the noise. He couldn't tell anymore. Every reverberation sliced through his resolve, making him question if the chase was worth it. Was this character leading him to an answer, or simply deeper into the maze of madness?

Waldo continued, his heart thumping in his chest as the *buzzing* intensified. It wasn't just noise; it was alive, drumming with an intent that felt both foreign and familiar. Another two steps toward the figure proved laden, as if the puzzle itself were conspiring to slow him down, to ambush him in his confusion. He continued to sprint, the narrow paths of the maze twisting and turning, but still, the shadowy figure darted ahead, close enough to keep him chasing, always slithering beyond his grasp. The next corner promised a glimpse of his elusive target, yet each time the figure disappeared just as he thought he was closing in. The more he pursued, the more illusory the vision became, until his chest felt like it was seizing with the exertion.

Suddenly, the image vanished completely, leaving Waldo alone in the eerie silence. He stopped, his breath coming in ragged gasps as he surveyed his surroundings. Only the towering embankments of the maze and looming shadows accompanied him. He found himself in a stretch of the maze that swallowed comfort but also provided the illusion that he was done unraveling. He had hit rock bottom. The weight of defeat pressed down on him, heavy and inescapable, like a sentence passed down with no appeal.

In the suffocating silence, the walls seemed to breathe, coming closer, as if the jumble itself was urging him to retreat. The message was undeniable. He was unprepared to confront the truth at the heart of the labyrinth.

Waldo jolted awake, drenched in sweat, his heart still racing. He sat bolt upright in bed, his head in his hands, pulling at his hair, as the reflections of the dream clung to him. The haunting visions that had invaded his sleep only amplified his doubt from the workshop.

He stayed on the edge of the mattress, the muted morning leaking through the curtain like a half-formed thought. But beneath the ache, beneath the noise, he remembered the voice that told him that the maze was a mirror and to not chase clarity. "Walk with it," it said. He believed it, still—even now, when belief felt harder to reach. But another part, temperate and sturdier, remembered what the maze had taught him: not all walls are meant to be escaped. *What if this isn't back-tracking? What if even this confusion is part of the process, just the next layer I haven't been ready to face?*

The silence in the room was absolute, broken only by the faint rattle of the heating system. The noise blurred into memory, translating into the distant hum from the maze. It started as a whisper, a barely percep-tible vibration at the edge of his mind, then swelled deeper, fuller—a primal force igniting a fire he couldn't fully grasp. It was enduring and steady, like Sara's voice gently guiding him through uncertainty. It was a sensation he couldn't shake, making it impossible for Waldo to ignore the feeling that the incident was meaningful. It was like he had just been handed a key to something vital but was left to search for the lock it belonged to. He didn't yet know what door it might open or where it would lead, but that whisper carried a promise, faintly undeniable, of metamorphosis. Somewhere in the fog of his thoughts, an alternative path waited, unstructured and raw.

A glimmer of hope returned to Waldo, like discovering another puzzle piece, despite the uncertainty. He knew the answers were there, within him, waiting to be uncovered; not through someone else's process but through his own. The reminder, although ambiguous, provided sufficient motivation for him to continue onward. He took a deep breath, steadying himself as he pushed himself to his feet. The fresh light of dawn crept through the curtains, softly dissolving the remnants of his unsettling dreams. He scratched his fingers through his hair, shaking off the lingering unease before rolling his shoulders and stretching out the stiffness in his limbs. A hot shower awaited—an opportunity to wash away the weight of the night's terrors and step forward into whatever the day had in store.

Day two of the retreat began much like the first: serene surroundings, tranquil disciplines, and instructions delivered in the leader's reassuring voice. But also similar to before, each guided meditation left him restless, his mind racing with thoughts he couldn't quiet. And when it was time, he didn't bother opening the journal. What was the point? Yesterday, he'd tried. Today, he couldn't pretend he wasn't bored with the exercise.

By mid-afternoon, his quiet thread of hope from that morning was raveling into something far more tangled. He wanted so badly to control the thread, keep the knots from forming, but the discord inside him had grown unbearable. It wasn't just that the exercises weren't helping—they appeared to pull him deeper into a state of turmoil. His thoughts spun like a whirlwind, a dizzying mix of frustration and panic. It reminded him of the spinning carnival rides from his child-hood; at first thrilling, the adrenaline rush almost exhilarating, but quickly disorienting, leaving him breathless and desperate for the ground beneath his feet. And before the afternoon session had even ended, Waldo couldn't bear to stay any longer. Demoralized and disen-gaged, he left. He didn't tell anyone he was leaving either. His journal stayed behind on the windowsill, the bag half-packed in the corner. Maybe he'd come back by dinner. Maybe he wouldn't. All he knew was that staying put felt impossible.

He wasn't entirely sure where he was heading, but a conversation overheard during the first dinner at the retreat had planted an idea. The mention of a mysterious, raw, and groundbreaking event promising a unique form of insight had stuck with him. It was located on the southern outskirts of town, and apparently, was a wild, boundary-pushing adventure that guaranteed enlightenment of a different kind. It was a place for liberation from everyday life.

The Edge—the name alone had intrigued him. He hadn't asked for details earlier, not wanting to make it obvious he had been eavesdrop-ping, but he couldn't resist his curiosity. So, that afternoon, he had discreetly searched for any mention of it online, but nothing concrete came up. The search results merely consisted of vague forum threads and cryptic references. No address, no advertisements, just word-of-mouth murmurs. So, now, as he drove south, he relied on fragments of what he had heard.

When he stopped for gas not too long after getting on the road, he took the chance and asked a gas station clerk if he had any information about The Edge, specifically an address. The clerk gave him a knowing smirk and nodded toward a stretch of road that veered past the town's limits. "Follow that until the pavement runs out," the man had instructed. "Then simply keep going. If you're meant to find it, you will."

Waldo was unsure of whether to take that as guidance or a warning, but either way, he kept driving.

When he reached a parking lot, just a few miles south of town, he leaned his head against the steering wheel. The retreat and Sara felt like a distant memory as he struggled with the storm of emotions brewing inside him. He needed to do something, *anything*, to break free from this spiral. *What if The Edge is the punch I need?*

Only a small, weathered sign marked the location, its faded letters narrowly visible. There were no big advertisements, no bright lights to guide the way—just this unassuming indicator, almost as if it were daring you to notice it. He approached the venue, which appeared to be an old abandoned warehouse cloaked in shadows. It was clear this wasn't some ordinary personal discovery event.

A man stood just inside the open doorway—not blocking it, but planted there with intention. His eyes were sharp and unreadable, scanning Waldo for a beat longer than comfort allowed. "You sure you're ready for this?" the man asked. His voice was low and gravelly. His presence, gravely serious.

Waldo didn't answer right away. Something in the man's gaze said he'd seen others turn back, that hesitation was common. That regret was, too.

"People come through here thinking they know what they're chasing," the man added. "But it only works if you stop pretending that you're ready when you're not."

Waldo nodded, not out of confidence, but because standing still would have felt word. "I need something real," he said.

The man held his gaze, then stepped aside. "Then go find it."

And with that, Waldo stepped inside.

A strobe light pulsed overhead, slicing through the dark like a signal. He squinted into the haze, and for a moment, it reminded him of the woods and how the sunlight danced through the trees at the retreat. But this was louder. Harsher. Not a whisper but a scream. And still, something in him leaned in.

The music was baffling, a throbbing force creating more sensation than sound, vibrating through the floor and pressing against his ribs. It wasn't just loud, though. It was hypnotic, a primal rhythm that seemed to synchronize with the very air around him. The atmosphere was dense with heat and bodies, but there was also a heavier element there —something unspoken.

People drifted through the space in a strange, liquid motion, their movements unhurried yet unsteady. Their faces were impassive, their eyes reflecting the neon light with a glassy sheen. Some whispered in hushed voices, others swayed as if caught in the music's undertow, their bodies lost in the rhythm that was deeper than sound.

The mismatched interior—murky lighting and flickers of firelight— made it hard to focus, but the shadows of individuals moved around him, some even in costumes, causing him to be unsure if they were participants or performers. The disruptive atmosphere seemed almost scripted, as if it was an orchestrated circus inside a cathedral.

Waldo moved farther into the room, and that's when he felt it—a sense of dread, like someone just out of sight was watching him. Even the smell was unrecognizable, being a strange mix of metallic and something decomposing, making his skin crawl. His breaths came in shallow gasps, and beads of sweat formed on his forehead, revealing the internal turmoil that rampaged within him. It was suffocating, as if the space itself was closing in, wrapping around him in an oppressive grip that tightened with every step. The pervasive evil appeared almost solid, as though intrinsically bound to the ecosystem's very being.

The genres and styles of music here didn't intend to comfort or uplift either. It felt like it was manipulating his psyche through sound associations to distort and disorient. Even the loud songs from Grace's room, with its overwhelming sonic immersion, paled compared to what he was experiencing at this juncture. This ghoulish noise and piercing tones twisted in his ears, corrupting familiar rhythms into something sinister, like a serpent slithering through a beautiful garden, injecting its venom into every flower and turning paradise into a haunting nightmare. Around him, people laughed and rocked like metronomes, synced to a beat that numbed rather than stirred, lost in their own worlds, oblivious to the oppressive feeling. *How can they not feel it?* he thought, watching in disbelief as they seemed to drown into the bedlam, their faces unnervingly relaxed. The further he ventured into the cyclone of sound and sensation, the more he realized he had made a terrible mistake. Forget exploration; this place would swallow you whole.

Suddenly, a woman approached him, her eyes glinting in the flashing lights, dressed all in red, her movements slow. She oozed open, inviting sexual appeal, her voice like velvet, promising pleasure and indulgence, offering treats and delights to be shared. Her influence was overwhelming, virtually bewildering. An intoxicating aroma filled the air around her, a tantalizing mix of enticing scents that heightened the senses. A charismatic energy emanated from her, creating a seductive pull that was almost palpable. Waldo experienced the magnetic force tugging at him, drawing him in, and for a moment, he faltered. The invitation, carried on by the sound of her words as it brushed against his ear, was exciting—a promise of release from the storm of confusion and tension coiled tightly within him. It was as if her words were molten, melting through the barriers he had built, attracting him closer to something he couldn't yet name but a gratification he desperately craved.

In the next instant, a memory from long ago shot through his mind. He was eight, maybe nine, standing in his childhood kitchen as the scent of dinner filled the air. His mother had warned him not to eat anything before supper, but then his best friend had come over, grinning, offering him a piece of candy that was wrapped in bright crinkling foil, gleaming like a tiny treasure in his palm. The temptation had been irresistible. The smell alone made his taste buds tingle, a burst of sweetness and a rush of joy awaiting him.

He had unwrapped it eagerly, popped it into his mouth—only for reality to betray him. The sourness hit first, a violent, stinging bitterness that burned his tongue and sent his eyes watering. He spit it out, but the damage had already been done. His lips and cheek remained raw for hours, a prolonged punishment for his moment of weakness. *No!* A surge of clarity pierced his clouded thoughts, like a spike cutting through fog. A knot twisted deep in his stomach, tightening with each breath. Nausea churned within him, clawing its way up as his body screamed in protest. The taste of bitterness filled his mouth—not from candy but from recognition. She was Pandora's box, the allure of a proposition that seemed unbelievably too good to be true. This was the same illusion. The same false promise wrapped in an attractive guise. *A prettier package hides the same poison; the same temptation whispers its invitation.*

Expectant, the woman lingered, the unspoken offer still between them. But the spell had shattered. Waldo took a step back. He knew what lay beyond that sweetness—an empty pleasure with a cost too steep to pay. Determined to avoid repeating the same mistake, he turned away from her, facing the heart of the room, which held a strange, altar-like structure, surrounded by people babbling incomprehensible words. Strobe lights pulsed erratically, seeming to penetrate deeper than just skin, reaching into their very essence, twisting, prodding, and unsettling. Laser shots hurled through the darkness, punching into each person's soul with relentless intensity.

Waldo stood there, frozen in time, adrenaline coursing through his body, his hands trembling uncontrollably. The physical effects of his turmoil were impossible to ignore, caught in the grip of his own emotions. It was less that something was drawing him in but that he was already there—already chosen, as if the maze had summoned him for a trial he didn't remember accepting. The spasming lights, warped beats, and savory smells created a disturbing harmony, intensifying the sense that something unnatural was at play, every incomprehensible background mutter an ominous warning.

For the first time since being a child, he felt genuine visceral terror. This wasn't just the disorientation of being lost; this was the sharp, gut-wrenching panic that something was closing in on him, a strange phenomenon far more dangerous than confusion. His body tensed, every instinct screaming at him to move, to escape before it was too late, but the paralysis of dread held him in place. His vision swam, a sting burning at the corners of his eyes, the threat of tears making everything waver like a mirage. And in this mirage, there was no means of escape. He wouldn't get out in time—not unless he moved. Right now.

Waldo turned to leave, but his legs felt awkward, like the floor was gripping him, holding him in place. Panic took control, and in that instant, something snapped inside of him, his fight-or-flight impulse surging. A raw, primal urge to survive overrode everything else. *Run . . . Run before whatever dark force lay behind that altar reaches you.* With a desperate burst of energy, Waldo pushed through the crowd, forcing his way toward the exit. He stumbled out into the frosty night air, gasping for breath, his heart still pounding. The cryptic, malevolent force he had endured inside seemed to have followed him, as if it had tried to latch on to him to escape as well. Its presence lingered just beyond the edge of a shadow, not quite touching him but not quite gone.

He stood in the parking lot, breathing in the night air like it might cleanse something internal, but the tension still coiled under his skin. Something was off. The trees around him, once backlit by late-afternoon gold, were now swallowed in deepening dusk. The sky had dimmed to a bruised violet. He blinked, confused—had it really gotten this late? Frowning, Waldo looked at his watch and his heart gave a small jolt. Three and a half hours had surreptitiously, silently vanished. It had felt like maybe twenty minutes had passed, an immersive blur of sensation and disorientation. But now, the heaviness made more sense. The tightness in his chest. The ache behind his eyes. The sudden drop in temperature. The smothering pulse of The Edge still drummed in his veins. It wasn't just the pounding music or the disorienting haze—it was its ability to consume.

His watch blinked back the time again—the same numbers. No mistake. A sharp pang of guilt flared in his gut. He hadn't told Sara he was leaving the retreat. She trusted he was still up in the woods, reflecting, meditating, becoming, and instead, he'd run off to a place no one would understand, least of all her. How was he supposed to explain that he left because he felt too alienated from everyone else, and instead of going home, he . . . ended up here? Sara had been the one in his life to remind him it was okay to walk away, to be different. Not long after they had met, when he had been grappling with the pressure to fit in, to belong to a crowd that appeared strange to him, she had said, *"You don't have to follow everyone else's path. You just have to discover your own."* She smiled, in that way she always did, gentle and sure. Sara's wisdom filled his mind again, calm and steady: *"There is no need for you to lose yourself to find yourself."*

And now, standing outside The Edge, his breath visible in the cold, all he wanted was to run straight to Sara, to tell her everything. The maze, the strange visions, the reckless plunge into the wild side of life in his desperate search for answers. He longed for her presence, the comfort of her understanding, her ability to make sense of his delirium. It was like she could see through the mess, and with just a few words, bring him back to solid perception. She had been his rock ever since they met in college. He could always rely on Sara when his anxiety about his future paralyzed him.

He smiled, thinking of how Sara had been the catalyst for those *"aha"* moments, those gentle but powerful shifts that had set him on a better path. She hadn't given him the answers, but she had always known how to guide him, to help him see what was already inside him. *"You already know the answer, Waldo,"* she would say, and now, even though the way forward still felt uncertain, Waldo could feel the wisdom of those past lessons guiding him. Sara had been right all along. Life isn't about finding the "perfect" direction, but about letting go of rigid expectations and allowing oneself to follow the paths that bring joy, even if they don't look like traditional success. Maybe, just like back then, he had been holding on too tightly to an idea of what his life was supposed to be, rather than letting it unfold naturally.

That was the lesson. And it hadn't been lost. Not entirely. However, this time, the consequences seemed to carry an enormous weight.

But as quickly as the reassurance hit him, a gripping fear took its place. What would happen if she didn't understand this time? What would she do if she believed he was unraveling, spiraling into a nervous breakdown, or worse, tumbling into a full-blown mid-life crisis cliché? What if she never again saw the man she had once known but a stranger who had changed beyond recognition, a person she could no longer reach? The dread of her rejection, of her seeing him as lost and irreparable, wrapped itself around him, winding tighter with each anxious thought.

This wasn't just another fork in the road where he could rely on her to steer him back. This felt like a massive cliff, a point of no return, with a cost far greater than he'd ever faced. There could be answers, but at what price? More than jeopardizing himself, he was risking her, their relationship, their family. As much as he craved her support, he knew in his core that this was something he had to confront alone. This journey was not solely about discovering simple solutions; it was a quest for self-discovery. It involved shedding illusions and failed attempts, ultimately transforming him into an individual capable of independence. Only after accomplishing this could he reunite with Sara, not as a man still engulfed in his search but as someone who had completely embraced the path he had chosen.

That night marked a turning point—deeper than the retreat could have ever been. Waldo no longer felt the need to drown in the noise to prove something to himself or anyone else. He didn't have to chase clarity in the chaos or wrestle for answers that had never lived outside of him. He'd learned something essential: fitting in wasn't worth losing yourself. And sometimes, the bravest thing you could do was step away, even if it meant walking alone for a while.

More than anything, Waldo was learning to trust his instincts, his voice, when he stood at a fork in the road. The tools had always been there; the lessons, the failures, the small victories, but it had taken time, and pain, to see that he didn't need anyone else's map. The path forward wasn't about proving his worth—it was about using what he'd gathered and believing he had what it took to begin. But that was still only the start. Answers wouldn't magically appear just because he finally knew where to look. They required action, effort, and intention. And the maze wouldn't solve itself. He had to walk it, take the turns, hit the dead ends, get it wrong—and grow through all of it.

He exhaled. *I already have the pieces. Now, it's up to me to assemble them.*

For years, people had tried to hand him those pieces—his parents, Sara, Dr. Benson, even strangers in passing conversations. Clues. Wisdom. Insights that might've guided him, if only he'd been ready to listen. He'd made progress, *real* progress, but he also knew how easily growth could coexist with avoidance. Even while stepping forward, he'd been scanning the horizon, still hoping clarity might arrive from somewhere else.

Maybe that was the heart of it—fear. Not just the fear of failure, but fear of change. He feared that finding what he sought would force him to become someone new. And maybe, in some strange way, it had felt safer to stay lost. But avoidance had a price. Like the sugar rush of the candy or the temptation of the woman in red, the comfort of distraction was temporary and would ultimately trap you. He'd spun a web of his own making, one strand at a time, until he couldn't see a way out. And now he had to ask himself the harder question: *are the walls of the maze even real? Or did I build them myself?*

The illusion had kept him caged, doubt woven from the very stories he told himself to avoid the work. The excuses, the distractions, the endless search for clarity elsewhere—they had all been part of the web. And now, the walls were crumbling. Could he let go of the search long enough to begin? Maybe, just maybe, stepping into the discomfort and embracing the mess would reveal not just answers but a version of himself that he hadn't met yet. Someone freer. Someone lighter. Someone ready.

Waldo stood still, the icy air brushing against his skin, but he didn't flinch. Instead, he reveled in the physical and spiritual clarity he gained. Yes, he had veered off course, chasing after something journaling alone hadn't provided, but now, he had the directions of how to get back on track. It had been ages since he last felt something stir within him. Perhaps it was faith—once dormant but now flickering back to life, offering an inner grounding. It reminded him that showing up might just be enough.

Above Waldo, who was still in the parking lot of The Edge, streetlights cast a dim glow, soft and steady. The wildness of the night—its noise, its temptations, its false clarity—was behind him now. And in its place, was conviction. His decision had taken root. As he walked toward his car, each step forward released a little more of the weight he had been carrying. Sliding into the driver's seat, Waldo closed the door behind him, shutting out the last echoes of the night.

Safe and secure, he leaned back into the comfort of his seat, closing his eyes, exhausted. With a long exhale, he drifted into sleep, his mind crashing into recharge mode. It wasn't by choice. When he woke, nearly two hours later, he was disoriented but felt reengaged enough to make the trip back to the retreat. He wiped his face with his hands, stimulating the rest of the sleep away, and put his key into the ignition. As the engine rumbled to life, he recalled the words from the man in the park: *"Every day, life drops you pieces, and although they may be barely noticeable at first, they matter."* And then, the echo of his father's voice—a fragment from the dream but clearer now, more certain: *"Do not go where the path may lead; go instead where there is no path and leave a trail."*

∿

By the time Waldo returned to the retreat, the night had stretched thin, dawn, closer than expected. The horizon, still cloaked in darkness, whispered of morning just beyond reach. The wind moved through the trees in gentle intervals, as if nature itself had witnessed his return.

He parked the car, turned off the engine, and sat for a long moment. His body was still too wired to go back to his bedroom, his mind still processing the chaos of The Edge. Instead, when he climbed out of the car, his feet carried him toward the garden, like a man coming home from war. Changed. Uncertain how to comprehend what he'd seen.

The garden was empty at this hour, untouched by the early risers who would soon fill it with sunrise meditations and hushed journaling. That suited him. He wasn't ready for conversation—not the polite curiosity or the searching glances. He didn't have answers. At least, not yet. He dropped onto a weathered bench tucked into a sheltered corner of the garden, hidden from view. The wood was cold beneath him, its solidity grounding. His breath left in a slow exhale, one that felt like it had been stuck in his chest for hours.

"So, I've been walking a false path," he said to himself. And the Edge hadn't just given him that clarity; it had stripped him down, exposed something raw inside—something he could no longer ignore. The retreat had sent him chasing enlightenment like it was a prize to be won. But hadn't he learned by now that transformation couldn't be forced? It wasn't hidden in external milestones. It lived inside the moments you stopped trying to control everything.

In the distance, an owl called, a lone sound cutting through the quiet. He looked over his shoulder, seeing the main building remained dark; the others were still asleep, nestled in their curated self-discovery, following a path that no longer fit him. He had been so obsessed with finding the right path, he hadn't realized the truth: there was nothing left to find. There was only the need to listen *to himself.*

He wasn't lost.

He was ready.

This place had offered all it could. And whatever it had awakened in him, he'd carry forward. As the thought occurred to him, a faint glint of headlights slipped through the trees from a road in the distance. It was only a flicker, soft and golden, catching on a dew-covered leaf, then vanishing as quietly as it came. But he watched it, unmoving. It reminded him of the first light at the retreat, when the sunrise cut through the canopy like a whispered invitation. Back then, he thought it meant he was headed for an awakening. Then, there was the light at The Edge, flashing like a warning. Loud. Demanding. Disorienting. But this, this was neither a beginning nor a collapse. It was a thread. A glimmer on the floor of the maze. Not a way out but a deeper way in.

He rose from the bench with a sense of direction and clarity blooming in his chest. The false path lay behind him now, but he didn't need a map to avoid it. Instead, he needed better questions—the kind that shaped a life, not escaped it. *Am I ready to forge my own trail? To meet the truest version of myself? To finally stop avoiding the questions that matter?* He wouldn't go back to The Edge. Like the retreat, he had gotten what he needed out of it. Now, it was time to go home. But since the fatigue of the last twenty-four hours clung to him like wet clothing, heavy and unavoidable, he would leave in the morning, when his mind was clearer and the road ahead less clouded by exhaustion.

Even though he felt an undeniable urge to go home, he would be careful not to treat it as an escape. It would be a recalibration, a return to center before stepping forward intentionally. The stakes were too high for shortcuts or half-hearted efforts. What came next would require focus, discipline, and a plan rooted not in reaction, but resolve. This time, it wouldn't be about survival. It would be about transformation.

As he walked back to his room, he made his decision; at sunrise, he would begin again. *I hadn't walked the false path out of apathy. I had followed it out of fear. And only now am I learning to trust the voice I'd spent years silencing beneath the noise.*

Chapter 7
The Edge and Beyond

Waldo stepped through the front door, the soft creak of the hinges breaking the early afternoon's quiet. Sara glanced up from the magazine she'd been reading, her gaze calm and questioning. It only took seconds of seeing him to recognize he looked different—a thoughtful weight pressed into his features, not mere fatigue but the presence of something deeper he'd carried home from the retreat. "You're back sooner than I expected," she said, closing the magazine and setting it aside.

"Yeah," Waldo replied, offering a small, tentative smile. He dropped his bag by the door and shrugged off his jacket, pausing as if taking solace in their familiar surroundings. Then, with a quiet thoughtfulness, he hung it on the wall hook, but not one of the usual pegs crowded with family coats, but the one just off to the side. A small gesture, almost unconscious, as if he was still unsure where he fit.

Sara stood, crossing the room to embrace him. "How was it?"

Waldo sighed, returning her hug, then ran a hand through his hair, considering how best to answer. "It was . . . hard," he admitted, his gaze drifting past her momentarily before returning to meet hers. "But good. Not in the way I thought it would be, though."

She stepped back, giving him the space she knew he needed to think. "Good, how?"

He reached into his pocket and pulled out a small, smooth stone, turning it over carefully in his palm before holding it up for her to see. "At the retreat, we did an exercise with these. They called it a touchstone—a reminder to ground yourself when things feel overwhelming." His thumb brushed the stone's cool surface. "When you hold it, it's supposed to bring you back to what really matters." He hesitated, fingers curling around the touchstone. "There's something else," he said quietly. "When I felt ready to leave the retreat . . . I didn't exactly go straight home."

Sara look visibly surprised, her eyebrows lifting above subtly widened eyes. But within a second, her expression returned to her neutral expression.

"I didn't tell you because . . . Well, I wasn't sure where I was going. Just that I couldn't stay. I ended up somewhere . . . different. Intense. I think I needed to see how far off the edge I was willing to go before I came back." He looked down, not in self-pity but in recognition. "I should've told you. I was scared to explain it. Or maybe scared you'd see it as a step backward."

Sara moved in closer, her voice calm. "But you came back."

"I did," he said, meeting her eyes. "Because I still want this. You. Us. But I needed to break something first, just to understand what was worth holding on to."

"And did it?" Sara asked, curiosity and cautious optimism softening her eyes.

"In a way." Waldo set the stone on the kitchen counter between them. "It made me realize that the answers aren't out there somewhere waiting for me to find them. They've always been right here." He positioned a hand lightly over his chest. "It's less about searching and more about remembering what matters—holding onto it."

She reached forward, carefully picking up the touchstone, running her fingers over it. After a moment, she placed it back into his palm. "And you feel okay about that?"

He nodded, closing his fingers around the stone. "I think I have to be. For a long time, I've been running, chasing clarity—some version of myself I thought existed elsewhere. Now, I know I need to build it from within. I guess the stone is my reminder that I've finally stepped onto the right path, even if I don't exactly know where it leads."

Sara set her hand on Waldo's shoulder, offering quiet reassurance. "Okay," she whispered simply, letting her presence communicate support more clearly than words. "I'm here, Waldo. Just . . . don't forget that."

"I won't," he promised.

She smiled, stepping back toward the kitchen counter. "Have you eaten? Let's make something."

He shook his head, feeling a wave of relief at the natural routine unfolding between them. "Lunch sounds good."

As he reached for two coffee mugs, Sara turned toward the stove, placing a pan on the burner. Waldo watched her move through the motions of preparing their meal, the quiet rhythm of home grounding him further. He slipped the touchstone back into his pocket, reassured by its gentle weight—knowing he'd reach for it again, as often as needed.

As the stove clicked on, Sara glanced over her shoulder. "Grace asked me earlier to remind you that her recital is next weekend."

"Of course. I wouldn't miss it."

"Good," she said, smiling with a small nod, turning back to the food. "Nathan's been scarce, as usual, but he actually came home before midnight yesterday, so that's something."

"Progress."

As they sat down at the table, the conversation moved gently—not into small talk but into the small anchors: what was left in the fridge, the couple pieces of mail that arrived for him since he left, whether the basil plant on the windowsill had survived the weekend since he was the only one who could remember to water it. Melody made an appearance too, rubbing against Waldo's leg before leaping onto a chair, tail flicking in casual disapproval of his absence.

"She's been sulking since you left. She made a point to sleep in your spot on the bed every night."

"So, I've been replaced."

"More like punished."

Waldo chuckled, scratching Melody's ears as she pretended to be indifferent.

Sara moved to the drawer, pulling out a small jar of fig jam. "I saved this," she said, smiling faintly. "It came in that farm box while you were gone. Figured you'd want to try it."

Waldo looked at the label, then at her. It wasn't about jam. It was about being seen. Remembered.

"What's next?" Sara asked.

He sipped his coffee, considering. "I've got an appointment with Dr. Benson next week. I think it's time to start talking about the plan forward, how to take what I've learned and actually apply it." He glanced across the table at her. "I know it'll take time, though."

Sara nodded. "That's alright."

He smiled. "I think so too. I'm not asking for everything to be okay overnight."

"I'm not either," she said. "Just don't disappear again without bringing back something worth sharing."

Lunch had barely ended when Waldo's phone vibrated against the counter, interrupting their peaceful connection. He frowned, looking apologetically at Sara as he picked it up. The caller ID flashed clearly— *Victor*. "Sorry," he murmured, stepping slightly away. "I should take this."

"Of course," Sara said, watching him walk out of the room.

"Hello, Victor?" Waldo answered, his tone carefully neutral.

"Waldo," Victor's authoritative voice cut straight through, tense and brisk. "I know you're technically still off today, but corporate has unex-pectedly moved up the quarterly review. We need your revised projections immediately. I wouldn't normally interrupt your time off, but this is non-negotiable. Can you log in and finalize them this afternoon?"

Waldo closed his eyes, irritation rising. The quiet optimism from the retreat frayed instantly under the sudden intrusion. "Victor, I had planned to finish those by tomorrow. This timing—"

"I'm aware it's inconvenient," Victor interjected, with the firm decisiveness that left little room for negotiation. "But this directive is straight from senior management. Trust me, I wouldn't ask if there were any alternatives."

Waldo inhaled deeply, sensing his boss's stress but struggling to suppress his own. He reached instinctively into his pocket, gripping his touchstone, slowly turning it in his fingers. The stone's cool weight steadied him enough to maintain his composure. "Alright," Waldo conceded finally, his voice steadier than he felt. "I'll see what I can do, Victor, but this is going to take some time."

"Understood," Victor replied, relief audible behind his curt reply. "Thanks, Waldo."

The call disconnected abruptly, leaving Waldo staring at the phone, his jaw tight as he continued turning the stone slowly in his palm. He walked back into the kitchen, where Sara hesitated mid-motion, setting dishes in the sink. "Everything okay?"

"Work emergency," he sighed, shaking his head slightly. He held up the touchstone with a resigned smile. "Guess I'm putting this to the test sooner than I expected."

She stepped closer. "Maybe that's exactly what it's meant for."

Waldo nodded, grateful for her quiet strength. Slipping the stone back into his pocket, he resolved inwardly not to let the stress derail him. These moments—unexpected disruptions and pressures—were precisely when the touchstone's symbolism mattered most.

He moved through the living room, into the den, his laptop waiting, ready to confront the disruption head-on. As he settled into the routine of logging in and opening files, he felt the stone's presence, reminding him of the lesson he was still learning. Life wouldn't pause just because he'd learned to breathe differently. But maybe that was the point.

Growth wasn't peace—it was presence. Especially when the noise returned.

Later that night, when the noise of work had faded but not disappeared, Waldo found himself moving through the motions—dishes, emails, half-watched television—but some deeper hum remained steady underneath. It wasn't certainty, but it wasn't dissonance either. He went to bed early. Not because everything was calm but because, for once, he didn't need chaos to feel alive.

The morning after Waldo returned, he stood by the kitchen window, the warm ceramic of his coffee mug pressing gently into his palms. Sleep had come fitfully—phases of tranquil clarity interspersed with uneasy dreams, echoes of the retreat still fresh in his mind. His phone *dinged* against the counter again, alerting him he had a new text message. Pulled from his reverie, he looked at the screen seeing that, this time, it was a number he didn't recognize—but something in it stirred faint recognition. He unlocked the screen.

> Hey Waldo, it's Jamie from the retreat. Heard you ducked out a bit early—hope everything's okay. That conversation stuck with me. I've been trying to hang onto the part about breathing through what hurts. Not easy. But thanks for saying it. You made more of a difference than you probably know.

Waldo read it again. A quiet beat passed.

He remembered that unexpected encounter, the soft tremble in Jamie's voice, the way the wind had hushed around them like it knew to stay out of the way. It was a small exchange that he hadn't realized would stay with someone else. He thumbed back a reply:

> Hey Jamie—good to hear from you. I didn't mean to vanish; just needed space to process some things. I'm glad something in that moment helped. You're right—holding onto it is the hard part. Keep breathing through it. That's still what I'm telling myself too.

He paused, then hit send.

That brief moment by the bench, he thought, had felt incidental. But maybe it was like the artist in the park had said: *"Sometimes, you don't know what you captured until someone else sees it."*

He set the phone down.

Even the smallest rock, he thought, hearing his father's voice across his memory, *still makes ripples.* Maybe that conversation had reached farther than he'd imagined. A smile ghosted across his face—not grand, just real.

Waldo stood by the coffee pot, straightening his tie with one hand, when a soft rustle from the hallway broke the morning stillness. Nathan emerged, yawning, his hair sticking up on one side. He blinked, caught off guard by the sight of Waldo already dressed. "Didn't expect you up yet," Waldo said, voice low but grinning. "Everything alright?"

Nathan rubbed his eyes and reached for a glass. "Couldn't really sleep. My manager called right after I got home last night. Said they're short this morning and asked if I could fill in." He poured some orange juice and added, "Kept thinking about it. My brain just wouldn't shut off, I guess."

"That's stepping up—not everyone would jump at an early shift." Waldo said. "I remember how it used to mess with my whole day."

Nathan nodded, then leaned his hip against the counter, still blinking himself awake. "Yeah. It's not ideal, but extra hours are good." He hesitated, then added, "Honestly, I don't know how you get used to these mornings." He fell quiet again, before thinking to ask, "How about you? First day back after the retreat, right? Feeling ready?"

"Ready enough," Waldo said. "Still sorting through the retreat, but yeah . . . it's time." He took a breath.

"You know, it feels good seeing you this morning. Glad you're home, even if it's just for a minute." Nathan gave a small, crooked smile—sleep-softened but genuine. "We barely see each other, so I didn't think it'd feel weird with you gone. But it kind of did."

Waldo let the words settle before replying. "Yeah. I felt it too."

Nathan glanced toward the clock, then back at his dad. "Guess we both adjust, right?"

"We do," Waldo said. "And I'm glad I saw you before you left."

Nathan picked up his glass and set it in the kitchen sink, then paused at the doorway. "You too. I'm glad you went—even if it's still kinda weird seeing you cook breakfast or smile before eight a.m."

That earned a laugh from Waldo. "Guess that makes two of us."

"Catch you later," Nathan said. "Good luck today."

The front door clicked closed, and Waldo stood alone in the quiet. The interaction was over in minutes, but it moved something—a small ripple, still unfolding after the moment passed. Nathan's subtle warmth, the open-ended nature of their exchange . . . it was a small but solid step forward.

Waldo glanced back down at the phone on the counter, Jamie's message illuminated softly on the screen. He felt newly determined. He'd taken the first step; now, he had to keep moving forward, navigating the delicate balance between the clarity he'd found at the retreat and the reality of home.

The days that followed blurred into a quiet routine. The clarity he'd carried home from the retreat still held, but it was being tested in new ways each day, competing with reality's steady pull. At work, Waldo found himself drifting now and then, his eyes glazing over spreadsheets, attention snagged by old habits. He noticed it quicker this time. Caught himself before the spiral deepened. Was this exhaustion? A lapse in discipline? Or something deeper—a persistent discontent that he couldn't quite name? He stared at the screen, rereading the email from his supervisor, irritation rising steadily. The request was abrupt and impersonal, filled with bureaucratic jargon:

```
Reconfigure  the  quarterly  projections  ahead  of
next week's meeting—senior management expects new
data-driven  targets  immediately.  I  realize  this
shortens  your  timeline,  but  there's  no  alterna-
tive. Thanks for understanding.
```

Waldo exhaled sharply, leaning back in his chair. The casual dismissal of his carefully prepared reports—and his time—felt like a step backward, a reminder of the very reason he had needed the retreat in the first place. It wasn't just the rushed timelines, it was the consistent disregard for balance, the unspoken expectation that personal time should always come second to work demands.

He reached into his pants pocket, his fingers closing around the small object, the smooth, palm-sized stone. He pulled it out, turning it slowly between his fingers, feeling its cool, comforting weight. Its surface was smooth but irregular, fitting perfectly into the hollow of his hand, a tangible symbol of everything he'd begun to understand. Not a cure, but a cue. *Presence. Breath. Choice.* All concepts easy to grasp in theory but difficult to hold onto in the messy reality of everyday life.

Holding the stone, Waldo closed his eyes, recalling the retreat facilitator's words: "*When stress starts to overwhelm you, stand still. Firmly grounded. Breathe. Remind yourself that you can't control the waves, but you can learn to ride them.*" He took a slow breath, letting the stone anchor him. Unable to alter the demands placed upon him today, he could, however, choose his response. He opened his eyes, feeling more in control. Resolutely, Waldo placed the stone on his desk, directly in his line of sight, a subtle but persistent reminder that he had the power to maintain his own equilibrium, even when the currents around him churned unpredictably.

And then, with clearer focus, he began to draft a response to his boss—measured, firm, and respectful of his own time. He outlined what could realistically be achieved within the given timeframe. It wouldn't solve everything, but it was aligned. A small act of integrity.

Mornings still began the same way. The hum of the coffee maker. Grace's footsteps. Sara's voice in the hallway. Nathan asleep behind a closed door. The rhythm of home had returned—familiar, steady. But Waldo didn't *feel* steady. He moved through the morning motions like someone trying to dance to a remembered song—one beat behind, just a little off-rhythm. It wasn't that he'd lost clarity. He *knew* the search had never been about chasing some grand, external truth; it had always been about confronting what was buried inside. But living with clarity? That was a different kind of work. The retreat had offered insight; this was the test of what came next.

Coming back from the retreat, he had returned hopeful. Certain, even. Determined to live with greater presence. And in many ways, he had. But some mornings, presence felt like pressure, like trying to hold every piece of meaning at once, and dropping half of them in the process. The more he tried stepping into this new understanding, the easier it became to slip back into old habits, especially at home.

Even the simplest chores, once automatic, now felt overwhelming. The dishwasher remained full longer than usual, laundry piled up untouched, and garbage lingered until its odor became impossible to ignore. Even yard work, a task he'd typically approach methodically, got postponed without reason. Responsibilities just eroded in front of him, and he didn't know how to stop it.

He wasn't spiraling, but he was slowing. And in that slowness came a new kind of discomfort—the realization that awareness wasn't enough. Saying he was "stuck" wasn't quite right either. He was just learning how challenging it was to embody each lesson every day. Change wasn't something he could achieve once and for all. It wasn't a sudden transformation. It was choosing, day after day, to keep going— even when progress felt invisible. It was leaning into a kind of psychic drag that came not from disinterest, but from *transition,* where you keep going, even when the breakthrough fades, and all you're left with is yourself. The kind you grind through. And that was the hardest part.

He glanced at the sink. It wasn't overflowing, but it was waiting. He rolled up his sleeves and reached for a plate—not to conquer the mess, just to meet it. That counted too.

The weekend arrived just over a week after Waldo had returned— enough time for his suitcase to be unpacked but not quite enough time for his inner footing to feel solid. By Friday, the household was shifting into a pace that felt faster than usual. Grace's recital was Saturday night, and in true fashion, she was balancing excitement with a hint of nervous energy that was not only impossible to ignore but contagious —for most of them.

In the living room, Sara stood by the window, fingertips absently tracing the curtain's edge as she watched Waldo unload grocery bags from the car. Afternoon sunlight portrayed a subtle difference in the way he carried himself. He moved differently now, less hurried, more present, and yet, a quiet uncertainty lingered. He seemed steadier and more deliberate, yes, even with everything going on, but he wasn't exactly closer. It was a shift she'd noticed ever since his return from the retreat, but even with so much time dedicated to thinking about it, she still couldn't quite articulate it. She hadn't fully understood the gravity of what Waldo had sought during those days away, and even now, she wasn't certain what he'd found.

She had grown used to the space between them, the way time can soften what once felt urgent. But since the retreat, that space felt more visible. As if she could finally trace its outline, feel the chill of its edges.

They had both learned to carefully navigate unspoken tensions, hesitant to disturb their fragile peace, and maybe that's what scared her most—not that he'd changed, but that she hadn't noticed how much until now, and she wasn't sure if she was still beside him.

Nathan's footsteps descending the stairs gently pulled her back into the present. She glanced toward the hallway, then back outside, catching Waldo's eye through the window. He offered her a warm wave, an easy gesture that brought relief despite persisting uncertainties. Sara returned his smile, a sudden commitment rising within her. Whatever Waldo had discovered, whatever internal journey he was on, she resolved patiently, openly, to walk alongside him. Despite their uncertainties, despite the changes, one thing remained clear: she would be ready, willing to navigate this new terrain step by careful step. With a quiet exhale, she stepped away from the window, ready to meet him halfway, just as Grace's voice rang out from upstairs, anxiously calling her name.

The recital preparations had begun.

As Friday evening wore on, the house buzzed with gearing up. Sara double-checked schedules, laid out outfits, and made sure Grace had everything she needed. Grace spent most of her time in her room, going over her songs one last time, humming under her breath while Melody curled up beside her, blinking leisurely, as if she didn't understand all the fuss.

Nathan, stopped by her room before heading out for the night, offering a quick thumbs-up and an encouraging, "You're gonna kill it, Gracie."

As for Waldo, he found himself caught in the motion of it all, standing in the kitchen with his coffee, watching the pieces fall into place around him. There was something unsettling about how easily life kept moving forward, how it offered no pause for integration. But for now, he was thankful just to feel tethered, even loosely, to the rhythm around him.

∼

By Saturday afternoon, Grace was pacing the house, her nerves getting the better of her. "I don't need a pep talk," she announced to no one in particular. "I just need to make sure I don't trip walking onto the stage."

Sara chuckled as she adjusted the straps on Grace's dress, smoothing a wrinkle near her shoulder. "Then, wear shoes you can actually walk in," she teased.

Waldo smirked. "It's an excellent strategy. Less drama that way."

Grace rolled her eyes but smiled. "Well, almost less drama."

Waldo appreciated the humor, but seeing her poised and determined, fully embracing the moment, evoked something profound within him. Lately, he had spent so much of his time caught up in his own struggles, but here was his daughter, standing on the threshold of an event that mattered to her, walking forward despite her nerves. And wasn't that one of the lessons he had been trying to learn all along?

When they arrived at the auditorium that evening, Grace had gone inside ahead of them, barely waiting for the car to stop before jumping out, offering a quick, confident wave before dashing through the side entrance to catch up with her ensemble group—no last-minute reassurances needed. Just forward momentum. And by the time Waldo and Sara made their way inside the venue and found their seats, the auditorium was already alive with anticipation, the energy nervous but warm, families all sharing the anticipation of seeing someone you love do something brave. The sound of families finding their seats, programs rustling, and the hum of tuning instruments echoing faintly from backstage set the background music as they waited, only building the excitement.

A few minutes before the lights dimmed, Nathan slipped into the row beside Sara, slightly out of breath but smiling. He gave a nod toward the stage. "Made it."

Waldo smiled, scooting his program aside to make room. "Good timing."

As the house lights lowered, Waldo reminded himself to be still—to stop analyzing, stop bracing. He let the murmur of the crowd fade. Tonight wasn't about him. Tonight was about Grace.

Ninety minutes later, the last note hung in the air for a beat before the audience erupted into applause. Grace stood center stage, her brilliance captivating him, her cheeks flushed with exhilaration, her eyes scanning the sea of faces before her. Watching her command the stage, clapping until his hands hurt, Waldo felt the weight of something deeper—how courageous it was to stand in your own light, nerves and all. Maybe that's all he'd been trying to do, too. He glanced at Sara, who was wiping a tear from the corner of her eye, then looked to Nathan, who gave a sharp whistle, smirking as Grace caught sight of them in the crowd.

She offered a subtle, proud tilt of her chin as the curtain fell and applause rang through the auditorium, the audience beginning to rise from their seats, the familiar scramble of coats, bags, and whispered praise filling the aisles. Along with a wave of other parents and siblings, Waldo, Sara, and Nathan joined the procession toward the backstage hallway. There, the corridor teemed with activity—students still buzzing from adrenaline, teachers offering last-minute praise, families weaving through the crowd in search of their loved-ones' faces.

Near the dressing room cluster, they spotted Grace, animatedly chatting with a few classmates. She stood tall, still in her performance attire, her gestures loose and vibrant, the thrill of the stage still coursing through her. When she saw them, she said goodbye to her friends with a bright smile, then stepped toward her family, her confidence faltering just slightly as she approached.

"Oh my God, that was so stressful," she groaned, covering her face with her hands before letting out an exaggerated breath. "Did my nervousness show? Please say no."

Sara laughed, pulling her into a hug. "You were incredible."

Nathan smirked, nudging her shoulder. "Yeah, Gracie—you crushed it. Only nodded off once or twice."

Grace shot him a playful glare, trying and failing to suppress her grin. "Ha ha. At least I wasn't the one snoring from row three."

"Excuse you, that was appreciation." He rolled his eyes dramatically. "Deep appreciation."

Grace shook her head, fighting back laughter. "You're literally the worst."

Waldo, watching their effortless interaction with warmth, smiled and pulled a bouquet of roses from behind his back. "You weren't just good—you were extraordinary."

Grace's face beamed with pride, her cheeks turning a rosy shade to match the flowers as she hugged the bouquet tightly. "Ugh. You guys are so much."

"Great, her ego's inflated," Nathan said in a theatrical voice. "Dad, quick—say something grounding."

Waldo chuckled, holding up his hands in mock surrender. "Don't look at me—I'm still applauding."

"Teenagers," Nathan muttered with an overstated sigh.

Grace elbowed him back. "You're barely older. And besides, I am the star tonight. I deserve this."

"See?" Nathan pointed at her. "This is exactly what I meant."

"Okay, you two. How about a celebration pizza before sibling rivalry ruins this lovely moment?" Sarah said, teasingly.

Nathan immediately perked up. "Now you're talking. Gracie?"

Grace pretended to consider carefully. "Pizza seems like an acceptable tribute."

"It's settled, then," Sara said, laughing.

As they moved toward the exit, their banter relaxed into conversation, the sounds from the evening drifting quietly behind them. Waldo lingered at the rear, savoring the comfort of the moment. Amid all his recent uncertainties, these simple exchanges acted as anchors; small but tangible reminders of the bonds that held them together. Sara waited near the exit, glancing back over her shoulder. She caught sight of Waldo behind them, hesitating near the auditorium doors. That familiar tug returned—a subtle ache she had become used to carrying without complaint. She drifted beside him, and together, they fell back into step behind Grace and Nathan, who were already halfway to the car, their laughter rising like steam in the cold night air.

Sara tucked her hands into her coat pockets as the door swung shut behind them. She wasn't sure when it had become so normal to feel uncertain—to sense that Waldo was there but not always fully. Still, something about tonight felt different. Closer. Delicate. Not fixed but inching toward honest. Not a breakthrough, but it stirred something. Maybe the retreat hadn't returned him to her exactly, but possibly, it had returned him to himself. And that mattered. She smiled faintly at the thought, matching his pace as they crossed the parking lot toward the car. *Maybe it isn't about returning to how things had been*, Sara pondered hopefully, *but finding a new way forward—not all at once, but steadily, like learning to walk through fog with your hand outstretched.*

Waldo reached for the car keys, but Sara was already unlocking the doors. Their eyes met briefly—not everything said but something understood.

With the comforting aroma of fresh pizza filling the car, and the dashboard clock reading 10:27 p.m., Nathan balanced the warm box carefully on his lap while they all settled into the gentle rhythm of the ride home. Grace, not being able to wait until they got home, eagerly claimed the first slice and devoured it between conversation, everyone recounting their favorite moments of the night.

"Did you see the look on Mr. Rainer's face during the finale? He totally wasn't expecting me to hold that last note for so long," she laughed, shifting the bouquet in her lap, keeping one hand free for her pizza. "I think he actually looked impressed."

Sara turned in the passenger seat, smiling. "He better have been. You worked hard for that moment."

"You truly were incredible, Grace," Waldo added, keeping his eyes on the road but meaning every word. Watching his daughter up on that stage had quieted everything in his mind, and, at least for the night, staying present came naturally.

Nathan leaned back with a crooked grin. "Not bad, kid. You might really have some talent after all."

Grace narrowed her eyes at him with mock offense, lips twitching with a smile she couldn't quite hide. "Might?"

Nathan chuckled. "Fine. You were amazing. There, I said it."

The rest of the short ride home hummed with easy laughter, the fresh pizza still steaming between them. The winding-down was happening naturally—Grace's words slowing, her voice softer as the energy of the night lightly faded. Sara exhaled, tilting her head against the window, and Nathan stifled a yawn. Even Waldo felt it; the transfer from the high of the evening to the inevitable tug of rest. The long day had definitely caught up to them.

As they pulled into the driveway, the glow from the porch light stretched across the front lawn, welcoming them home. Entering through the front door, they kicked off their shoes, tossed their jackets onto hooks, and continued their late-night chatter in the kitchen.

"I am so sleeping in tomorrow," Grace announced, setting her roses delicately on the counter before stretching her arms over her head.

Sara was already reaching for a vase, filling it at the sink. She arranged the blooms without fuss, her quiet care saying more than praise ever could.

"Good luck with that," Nathan teased, grabbing a bottle of water from the fridge. "Dad's probably gonna wake up at dawn like always."

Waldo chuckled, shaking his head. "Not making any promises."

Sara brushed a strand of hair behind Grace's ear. "Go get some rest, superstar."

Grace gave her a sleepy hug before heading upstairs, mumbling a final, "Night, guys."

Nathan followed soon after. "See ya in the morning," he said before disappearing into his room.

As Waldo loosened his tie and looked thoughtfully around the room, Sara walked back over to the sink, rinsing the few cups that were left out. The quiet *whirr* of the refrigerator and the running of the faucet felt strangely loud in the stillness between them. He leaned against the counter, watching her. "Tonight was special, wasn't it?"

Sara nodded, turning the sink off and drying her hands before meeting his gaze. "It really was. Grace looked so grown-up on that stage. It . . . It made me realize just how quickly everything changes."

Waldo understood her meaning beyond just tonight's event. "I've been feeling that too. Since coming home, things feel clearer, but also . . ."

"Fragile?" Sara offered, stepping closer.

"Exactly," he agreed, his eyes holding hers. "Like I found something important, but I'm still figuring out how to hold onto it."

Sara's fingertips lightly touched his forearm in reassurance. "Maybe you don't have to hold onto it so tightly. Maybe it just becomes part of you."

"I hope you're right."

They smiled at each other, both sensing the relief and ambiguity that reflected in their eyes. "We're both figuring it out," she whispered. "Together."

Waldo reached out, placing his hand on top of hers, a gentle acknowledgment of everything they weren't saying aloud. "Let's get some rest, Sara," he said finally, offering another genuine smile. "We both need it."

But as they climbed the stairs that night, Waldo felt it again—a subtle thread loosening, the clarity he'd fought hard to grasp slipping once more through his fingers, as elusive as the smooth stone he'd brought home from the retreat.

At the landing, he reached instinctively into his pocket, his fingers closing around the stone's cool surface, now warming in his palm. His grip tightened—not to hold it tightly, but to feel it become part of him. He didn't want to resist the unraveling but to learn how to thread it back into something truer. Not preventing the fraying, but continuing to stitch forward, even when the pattern disappeared.

With a slow breath, he continued upward into the quiet dark, willing himself to trust the uncertain path ahead.

Chapter 8
The Unraveling Thread

When Waldo woke the next morning, silence cocooned the house—a stark contrast to the noise and celebration just hours before. The post-recital energy had evaporated into stillness, leaving only a slow pull from sleep into wakefulness. He blinked into the faint sliver of morning light slicing through the curtain, pale and indifferent.

He had truly slept, deeply even, but it hadn't brought relief. Instead, he woke with a heaviness, like something had returned during the night and settled over him without asking. After a moment of considering, he decided it had to be the uneasy pause after clarity arrives but before courage kicks in. The silence of hesitation no one warned him about. He swung his legs over the side of the bed, stretching against the stiffness. Barefoot, he tiptoed quietly toward the kitchen. But questions pressed against the silence, trailing him with every step: *why this heaviness now? What is it trying to tell me? Has something shifted backward, or simply surfaced at last?*

The faint scent of coffee lingered in the air as Waldo entered the kitchen. He intuitively glanced toward the counter, expecting to see a fresh pot, but the machine was off, the carafe empty. Maybe it was yesterday's brew, the aroma still clinging to the space. Or perhaps he'd grown accustomed to it; Sara always had coffee waiting to start his day. He reached for the canister, intending to start a new pot, but something else caught his eye first—the guitar, resting in its new spot, just near the bookshelf. He had taken it out of his front seat so the family could ride together to Grace's event.

Now, his fingers flexed at the sight of it. He had a lesson scheduled for next week, but he had an urge to play now, and today felt like the perfect time. He would carve out space for something that truly felt like healing. He took a step toward it, then stopped, considering. "Maybe later," he murmured, letting the thought pass, something to return to once the morning fog lifted.

Another intention, quietly shelved. Like so many before it. Always with a reason. Always justified.

Back at the counter, he carefully measured the coffee, filling the coffee maker to the full pot level—today, he might need that extra cup. Everyone else was still asleep, and for a moment, the house felt like a sanctuary. Then came the sound—a low, impatient *mrrrow*. Melody, the only other early riser in the house, sat beside her empty dish, glaring at him, her tail flicking with ritual irritation.

Waldo laughed softly. "Yeah, I know. Coffee first, food second." He bent to fill her bowl, and as soon as the dish hit the floor, she dove in, all frustration forgotten the moment her need was met. Simple. Direct. No hesitation.

Waldo watched her eat for a long moment. Once she was satisfied, Melody curled beside the sun-warmed window. Somehow, she always knew how to settle. No search. No striving. No second-guessing. Maybe that's what presence really looked like.

He envied that.

A few days later, having skipped the last appointment by design, Waldo was sitting in Dr. Bensons office, but on this Thursday, the quiet didn't welcome him the way it usually did. Instead, it stretched, waiting, pressing down on him like something unfinished. It felt disappointingly similar to his earlier sessions with her.

Dr. Benson observed him from across the room, her expression expectant but patient. "So," she prompted, flipping to a fresh page in her notebook. "Tell me about the retreat."

Waldo sighed, rubbing the back of his neck. "Where do I start?"

"Wherever feels right."

A dry laugh escaped his lips. "That's just it. None of it felt right."

She didn't speak, just waited.

Waldo leaned back, fingers drumming anxiously on the chair's armrest. "I thought the retreat would offer some tremendous breakthrough, a clear direction or at least a better idea of where I'm headed. But the whole time, I felt out of place. Like everyone else was unlocking these life-changing truths, and I was just . . . chasing shadows."

She made a brief note but kept her attention on him. "Why do you think that is?"

"Because they were having those moments. Everyone around me seemed to get it. Meanwhile, I was going through the motions, waiting for something to click—and it never did."

"Do you think it was missing entirely? Or just not what you expected?"

He exhaled. "Maybe both."

She closed her notebook, setting it on her lap. "And now that you've had time to reflect, how do you feel about it?"

"It wasn't bad. Just . . . incomplete." He paused, fingers tightening slightly. "But . . . something else came up while I was there."

Dr. Benson observed him intently. "Did you leave the retreat?"

Waldo hesitated. "I did. Not right away, though. But I overheard some of the other attendees talking about this underground event. Something called The Edge. They were whispering about it like it was the real breakthrough. It sounded . . . like if the retreat didn't move you, this would."

Her brow lifted slightly, intrigued. "And did it?"

"No. It was the same as the retreat. It didn't offer the experience that I hoped it would. Instead, it was chaotic. Intense. People pushing themselves past emotional and physical limits. At first, I thought maybe that's what I needed. Something to crack me open. And maybe it did . . . but not in a good way. It got dark. I felt exposed. And then, I panicked."

"But you stepped away," she noted gently.

"I did. I left, knowing I had hit my limit." He met her eyes. "But I still wonder if going at all was a mistake."

Dr. Benson nodded slowly. "You sought clarity and ended up in chaos. That's not uncommon. But you recognized your boundary and honored it. You stepped back. That tells me something did change. That's growth."

"Then why does it still feel like I'm circling the same ground?"

"Because you're still hoping it all ties up neatly. We've talked about this—real growth rarely feels satisfying. Sometimes, it just means continuing to show up."

His jaw clenched. The truth stung.

Dr. Benson tapped her pen against her notebook, studying him a moment longer than usual. "Have you talked to Sara about any of this?"

Waldo remained silent.

"You haven't," she said. Not judgment—just fact.

He let out a slow breath. "I mean, I told her a little. About leaving the retreat." His gaze dropped, thumb running along the seam of the chair's arm. "But not where I went. Not what I felt. Not what it showed me." He paused, then added, "I wasn't hiding it. I just . . . didn't know how to bring it up. It felt messy. I wanted to understand it myself first."

"Or maybe, part of you isn't sure how it will sound aloud—with her."

He didn't deny it.

"You'd protect her from the mess."

Waldo nodded. "I would."

"But have you considered that the mess isn't the thing you need to shield her from?" She leaned forward. "Maybe it's the thing you need to let her witness."

He swallowed hard, the thought landing with discomfort. The silence felt deliberate, like space opening between thought and truth.

"You're not pulling her into the dark, Waldo. You're asking her to walk with you while you're learning to see."

Waldo was quiet for a long moment before saying, "Sara has always been my rock and someone I have relied on to ease my worries, but I'm just not used to needing someone in *this* way; when I don't have a fix to offer. It feels like . . . a kind of weakness."

Dr. Benson's voice was low, firm. "It's not weakness. It's intimacy."

That word hit different.

"You don't need to hand her a summary. You want a story you can tell her—something with a clean arc, a takeaway you've already lived through. But the truth isn't there yet. But that doesn't mean you have nothing to offer."

"What do I offer then?"

"Start with a sentence. A beginning. A door she can walk through." She paused. "Don't look at it as explaining. Reframe it as you're inviting her in."

Waldo ran his hand through his hair. It wasn't what he wanted to hear, but something in him accepted it, even as his chest tightened with resistance. Waldo exhaled, the tension loosening slightly despite himself.

Dr. Benson glanced down at her watch—a subtle signal. "Before we close today, how are things at home?"

"Better, I think. Sara's been . . . supportive. Patient. We've been talking more. But there's still a quiet between us. I wouldn't say it's peace or even distance— just something waiting."

She brought her finger up to her chin. "And what do you think she's waiting for?"

"I . . . don't know."

She gave him another moment to elaborate, but when he didn't, she gently said, "Is it possible she's not just waiting, but wondering? She may be on her own path, Waldo. You've been so focused on your journey that maybe you haven't realized she's on one, too."

The thought caught him off guard. Not because it hadn't occurred to him but because he hadn't let himself imagine what that might really mean. That she, too, might be changing—and without him. The weight of it landed deep, disorienting.

A silence settled, thicker this time. Then, Dr. Benson sat up a little straighter, her tone shifting. "Before we end, I also want to let you know that I'll be on hospital rotation for the next two weeks. Another doctor is out unexpectedly, so I've been asked to step in short-term. It means we'll need to pause our sessions for a bit."

Waldo sat back, absorbing the shift. "Okay . . ." he said softly. "Is everything alright?"

She smiled gently. "All's well. It's just one of those stretches where schedules get tight. But I'll be back after that. And if anything urgent comes up, you can always reach out by email."

He nodded, not quite sure about how he felt going a few weeks without seeing her, without even having the option to see her.

She closed her notebook carefully. "Use the time to sit with this. Don't rush to fix it. Let things unfold."

Waldo stood, murmured a goodbye, and stepped into the hallway. He felt more unsettled than he had going in. *Sara might be searching, too.* The truth of that statement made his stomach lurch. He had always imagined she was waiting, giving him space, holding the shape of them steady until he was ready to return. But what if she wasn't waiting anymore? What if she had stepped forward without him? And what would she think, if she knew where he'd really gone? What he still hadn't told her? It wasn't just the silence between them that scared him now. It was the part of that silence he was still choosing.

A flicker of fear bloomed in his chest, sharp and private. And this time, it didn't pass. He carried that anxiety back to work, through the evening, and into the next morning. He tried to dismiss it as overthinking, an unintended side effect of Dr. Benson's words, but by that following Friday, only a week later, the warmth Waldo had briefly regained while celebrating Grace's recital as a family felt distant. And by the time he stepped into his office that morning, the tension he'd been trying to rationalize snapped into something undeniable.

His phone *dinged*, a message from Sara appearing on the screen:

> Grace spent all evening sorting through graduation photos. She couldn't stop mentioning how much having you at the recital meant to her. Thought you should know how deeply you impacted her.

Waldo smiled weakly, Sara's message momentarily easing his anxiety. But the relief was short-lived as his gaze landed on a series of *urgent* email notifications, shattering the fragile calm. His inbox overflowed.

```
SUBJECT: URGENT
SUBJECT: FOLLOW-UP—URGENT
SUBJECT: Escalation Request — Immediate Attention
Required
```

His stomach dropped as he clicked the first thread, eyes darting over the contents. *Missed deadline. Client furious. Awaiting immediate response.* As he read further, his dread only deepened, with his pulse racing and the blood draining from his face. It was all about a presentation that was solely his responsibility—due three days ago. Distracted by his own turmoil, he had completely forgotten it.

A final email sat at the bottom, short and final:

```
Waldo, this is unacceptable. We need to talk ASAP.
Come see me the moment you're in. —Victor
```

. . .

Waldo swallowed hard, tension tightening along the back of his neck. He had told himself he was turning a corner—doing the work, moving forward. But here it was, plain and brutal: the old patterns hadn't disappeared. They had just waited for him to let his guard down. All the therapy. The reflection. The promises to do better, and still, he'd let something this important fall through the cracks. It wasn't just a slip. It was failure.

He stood frozen, heat rising in his face as the office door swung open. Victor Reese filled the doorway. "Conference room. *Now.*"

Waldo grabbed his laptop and followed, every step reverberating too loudly in the corridor. He could feel everyone's eyes tracking him. Were they glancing his way with concern or judgment? *Isn't that the guy who dropped the Miller file?* he imagined them saying. *Did you hear about the client backlash? He's been off since he got back. Everyone sees it.*

When the conference door shut behind them, the room was all glass and disapproval. Victor tossed a printout onto the sleek surface between them. "Explain why I woke up to this."

Waldo looked down, his stomach twisting at the paper. Emails. Escalations. His team trying to triage his mess. His throat was dry. "I . . . I missed it. It's on me."

"No kidding," Victor snapped. "Waldo, I gave you three days off. Because you said you needed the time, and I trusted you. But this." He gestured at the printout. "This isn't acceptable. This isn't someone who's back on point. Is everything okay?"

Waldo opened his mouth to explain, to say the retreat had been harder than expected, that he was still recalibrating, but the words sounded like excuses, even in his head. Had his team seen this coming? The recent hesitations, those careful check-ins, the tight-lipped smiles; they all took on new meaning now. So, he said nothing.

Victor's voice dropped. "Tell me the truth, Waldo. Can you still do this job?"

The question struck because it wasn't just about the job. It was the very thing Waldo had been asking himself. *Can I still do this life?* He straightened slowly. "Yes. I can fix this."

Victor didn't move. His gaze was long, searching. Skeptical. Then, he said, "You better. Because one more mistake, and I won't be able to justify keeping you."

The words were more than a reprimand—they were a reckoning. One more mistake. Waldo nodded stiffly, exiting the room without another word. The hallway was unbearably bright, the fluorescent lights reflecting off polished floors and anxious thoughts. And as much as he tried to ignore the hushed whispers of his coworkers, it was all he could hear as he passed, their comments only confirming what he knew they were thinking:

"How do you miss something that big?"

"He's been off for weeks."

"Maybe something personal. Isn't he married?"

Each step to his desk added weight to his shoulders.

When he finally returned to the privacy of his own space, his eyes landed on the touchstone beside his monitor—a symbol of stillness he hadn't earned. He touched it, then pulled his hand away. No more symbols. No more distractions. Just action. Taking a meaningful breath, he looked away, resolved. Only he could clean up his own mess. He opened the email thread again, trying to steady his trembling fingers.

Sara stood at the kitchen sink, hands immersed in warm water. Though the sponge was still in her grip, the dishes went untouched as her mind wandered somewhere else entirely. More often than not lately, she'd find herself in the quiet of the days, standing in a single spot, not doing anything, not really thinking, just . . . waiting. Not for Waldo to physically walk into the room, but for *something* in him to come back. The version of him who used to laugh at burnt toast, who once danced with her in the hallway just because a good song came on.

She wasn't angry, although anger would've been simpler—at least it had somewhere to go. Instead, she was grieving a version of her husband that only she seemed to remember, and even that memory was beginning to feel slippery. She had once found comfort in silence, in the stillness, after the kids ran off to school and Waldo left for work, but this silence felt different. It wasn't shared or restful. It was the kind that settled in the cracks of a marriage and slowly spread, unnoticed until it filled every corner.

She glanced toward the front door, unprompted—one of those reflexes built over years of timing someone's arrival without a clock. Waldo wasn't home yet. She never really knew what version of him would walk through the door these days. Sometimes, he'd be tired and distracted, and other times, he'd be present and tentative. It changed so often, even he didn't seem sure anymore.

Having dried most of the dishes, she noticed one of Waldo's favorite coffee cups sitting nearby. It wasn't freshly washed or used—it was just . . . there. Her thumb drifted along its rim as if noticing it for the first time. She hadn't set it out on purpose. But now that she saw it, she didn't move it either.

In that moment, Sara let herself feel something she rarely allowed: emptiness. She had spent so much of the last year adapting to Waldo's distance, to the changing needs of their kids, to the quiet ache of invisibility that threaded through her days, and though she did it believing it was her role as mother in wife, there were times, like these, where she just wanted to feel seen. She didn't resent Waldo for making her feel this way, not exactly, and it wasn't that she wanted grand gestures or perfectly articulated apologies. She just wanted him to notice her. Fully. Not as a reflection of his guilt or gratitude, but as herself. She missed him, and all the little things that came with him; the laughs they shared over nothing, a soft touch on her back while she cooked, their conversations that once drifted late into the night. Now, she barely recognized the shape of their days. And worse, she was unsure she still fit inside them.

There had been a time when she believed in waiting. In giving space. In trusting the process. But lately, the waiting felt like standing on a platform with no train in sight. How long was she supposed to stay in place, watching empty tracks, before admitting the train might never come?

The doorbell broke her thoughts. She dried her hands quickly, but the towel slipped from her grasp—like too many things lately. She scooped it from the floor and tossed it on the counter, rushing to the door. A familiar voice met her, an easy, steady, *unexpected* one. "Hey, stranger," he said.

Her smile came before she could stop it—reflexive, warm, and tinged with something she hadn't felt in a long time. Someone who saw her with intention. "Marcus." She hadn't seen Marcus in over a year, not since the school auction fundraiser. But when she ran into him at the grocery store earlier that week, it had felt easy to say, "Stop by if you're ever in the neighborhood." She didn't expect him to take her up on it. She certainly hadn't planned for him to show up today.

As Waldo drove home that evening, exhaustion filled his bones. He still had his job—for now. Yet, today had made one devastatingly clear truth undeniable: growth didn't grant immunity. Real progress wasn't just about breakthroughs; it was surviving the setbacks. And right now, one more could break everything.

When he pulled onto his street, he was physically arriving home but some part of him was still being left behind.

Chapter 9
The Fracture Line

Waldo's hand slowed as he held the key to the door. He hadn't just left a brutal day behind, he had carried it home, tucked in the space between his ribs. It wasn't just the threat of losing his job—it was what the mistakes revealed, fractures he thought he'd repaired now gaping wider. *What if the mistakes said something permanent about who I'm becoming?*

The front door opened to stillness—no clatter of dishes, no footsteps overhead. The den door was closed; dark and undisturbed. There was just the murmur of two voices coming from the kitchen. Nathan was at a friend's house tonight, so it couldn't be him, and it certainly didn't sound like Grace's voice. He hadn't noticed another car out front, but maybe he had been too preoccupied to notice. Waldo followed the sound instinctively, walking into the kitchen.

Sara stood by the counter, laughing. It only took a second to see it wasn't her polite laugh, the one she did out of habit. It was open, effortless, the kind of laugh he hadn't heard in months. Her shoulders were relaxed, her expression light. But what really caught his attention was the fact that this laugh wasn't for him. It was for the man leaning casually beside her, someone Waldo didn't recognize. The man was tall, easygoing, and mirroring her comfort, standing beside Sara like he belonged there. And the laugh, *Sara's* laugh, made the man's presence hit harder than anything he'd heard all day. Because in that moment, he saw something in Sara he hadn't seen in weeks, maybe months—happiness. Genuine. Unburdened. And it had nothing to do with him.

Sara's eyes met his, her smile dimming for a heartbeat, a flicker of uncertainty taking over, but when it returned, it was too bright. Too composed. "Hey," she said, her voice warm but oddly careful. "You're home. This is—"

"I've got work to finish upstairs," Waldo said, his voice sharp with more emotion than he meant to show. He turned before she could respond and climbed the stairs two at a time, like he was trying to outrun the sight of her easy joy in the midst of his absence.

He shut the bedroom door behind him, sealing in the dread. He stood still, breath caught in his chest. The silence was crushing. He tried to reason it away—maybe it was innocent, maybe he'd misread it. But something inside of him cracked. He had been focused on his own unraveling for so long, telling himself Sara was waiting, holding space for his return. But now, that fragile hope felt foolish.

Maybe she hasn't been waiting.

Maybe she's been deciding.

And maybe . . . she already has.

Downstairs in the kitchen, Sara stood frozen, her heart mixing with confusion and a pang of guilt as Waldo's footsteps faded rapidly upstairs. She exchanged an awkward glance with her guest, the warmth of their conversation now extinguished. Marcus was just an old friend, someone she hadn't seen in over a year until that unexpected grocery store run-in. She hadn't even thought much of her offhand, "Stop by sometime," comment until he actually did. Waldo had no reason to be concerned—there was nothing hidden or romantic. Marcus was just a familiar face from outside the walls of all this tension. Still, seeing the raw, wounded look in Waldo's eyes before he withdrew left her shaken.

She hadn't meant to hurt him or for this to feel like betrayal. She knew he'd misunderstood, but how could she explain, when every conversation lately felt breakable? She turned to Marcus. "I'm sorry . . . I didn't expect—'

"It's okay," he said gently, already stepping toward the door.

She sighed, turning toward the stairs, contemplating whether to follow or give Waldo space. The tension between those two choices felt immense, the thread between them stretching dangerously thin. More clearly than ever, she realized something essential: she wasn't just waiting anymore. She was trying to decide how far she was willing to go to save what they had left. And would Waldo meet her halfway?

The gray light of dawn spilled through the windows as Waldo stood in the backyard, rake in hand. Yard work had always been his refuge, a space where sweat replaced thought. But this morning, even the methodical scrape of metal against earth couldn't quiet the noise inside him.

Upstairs, Sara stirred in the bed they once shared. The space beside her was cold. Again. She listened for signs of him—the soft tread of footsteps, the click of the coffeepot—but heard only wind brushing against the house. Waking to an empty bed had become familiar but no less disappointing.

She padded to the kitchen, her eyes instinctively searching the window. There he was, alone again, retreating into labor. Avoiding everything that hurt instead of confronting whatever was truly wrong. She watched him for a long moment, arms folded against herself, witnessing his stiff and mechanical movements.

How long had they been like this? Perhaps she had waited too long for Waldo to find himself and return to her, now questioning again if she had been waiting in vain. The longer she stood there, the more it hurt—not because of what he was doing but because of everything he wasn't. No questions. No attempts. Just distance. And silence. She turned away from the window and busied herself with breakfast, determined to not let Waldo's isolation set the mood for the day.

Grace stumbled in first, rubbing sleep from her eyes, followed by Nathan seconds after, scrolling absently through his phone.

"Morning," Sara greeted, her tone bright but strained.

Grace yawned her reply, and Nathan nodded vaguely, his thumbs still dancing over the screen. "Where's Dad?" Grace asked, glancing toward the backyard.

"Outside," Sara said evenly.

Nathan finally looked up. "Again?"

Grace's brows pinched. "It's pretty early . . ."

Sara didn't answer. Instead, she walked to the sliding door, cracked it open, and called gently, "Waldo, breakfast is ready."

He paused mid-rake but didn't turn. "I'm good. I'll eat later."

She lingered briefly, a frustration constricting her jaw. The door clicked shut behind her, more final than she intended, and she silently returned to the table.

Nathan stirred his coffee. "He's been off lately."

Sara nodded. "Work's been . . . stressful." She tried to sound reassuring, but the words didn't land. Grace and Nathan exchanged a glance—they could feel it: Waldo's silence growing into absence.

After breakfast, the family scattered—Grace upstairs, Nathan out the door, Waldo disappearing into his den. Sara remained in the kitchen, caught up in the fog of silence, only the sound of her phone buzzing bringing her back to the present. The message appeared, simple and unassuming:

> Still good for this afternoon?

Sara stared at Marcus's message, her thumb hovering over the screen. She glanced toward the closed den door, the barrier Waldo had built between them. The plans had been made casually, nothing she would have hidden from Waldo, but he didn't exactly give her the opportunity to share anything going on in her life. With Marcus, there was no weight to carry. No cautious tiptoeing. Just space to breathe. She scanned the clock—still hours until they were supposed to meet. She typed her message and sent it:

> Yes. See you there.

She didn't need to leave just yet, but the house suddenly felt too still, too suffocating. She grabbed her coat and keys, stepped into the hallway, and paused at the foot of the stairs. "Grace, I'm heading out for a bit!" she called. "I'll be back before dinner."

There was a muffled acknowledgment from upstairs. Sara turned toward the front door, only glancing back once. She didn't owe anyone an explanation, but still, the silence from the den ached more than it should have by now. She slipped out the door before she could change her mind. The decision, and the relief that came with it, was easy, even freeing, as if she were stepping away from something that had become too heavy to bear.

Sara didn't drive anywhere in particular. No errands. No phone calls. Just a moment that belonged to her. A moment to breathe. Like locking the bathroom door and lighting a candle no one else would see. A pause between obligation and explanation—just to remember she still could.

In the den, Waldo sat motionless, his hands resting on the keyboard. His mind still looped through damage reports and apologies. Then, a sound; the click of the front door. He barely noticed it at first, but a beat later, the noise caught up to him. He stilled, leaning toward the door to listen. There were no voices, no footsteps. Just silence. He stood abruptly, leaving the den and moving down the hall. "Sara?"

Nothing.

The kitchen was empty. So was the living room. Sara was gone. The silence that followed wasn't just quiet; it was the absence of something. Or someone—who just slipped out the door before he could catch her.

Panic stirred, slow and cold. A sickening wave of uncertainty rose inside him. She never left without saying goodbye first. Had she mentioned plans? Or worse, had he just not been listening again? Instinctively, he pulled out his phone, expecting a text saying she was running late and couldn't find him. But no. No messages. No explanations.

A thought flashed—maybe the kids knew where she'd gone. Maybe she'd told them, assuming he was too checked out to tell. He went to the steps and almost called upstairs, but stopped. He didn't want to hear it. Not from them. Not like that. And if they didn't know, he didn't want to emphasize the gap between him and their mom. He forced himself back to the den and sat heavily, gripping the edge of the desk as if it might keep him anchored. He stared at the blinking cursor, but he wasn't working. He was unraveling.

He had been waiting for a moment to prove he'd turned a corner, to show her the version of himself he was still trying to become. But now, the moment she needed him to notice had already passed.

And he hadn't even looked up.

He didn't even know if she'd come back.

Hours later, when the front door clicked softly shut behind her, Sara stood quietly in the hallway, her coat still wrapped around her like a shield. Across town, sitting with Marcus in the gentle hum of a coffee shop, she had felt seen—not romantically but simply acknowledged and understood without effort. Yet, as she drove home afterward, the temporary ease had dissolved into an ache. Marcus had offered kindness, but he wasn't the one she needed that from. She wanted that feeling with Waldo, not borrowed moments of clarity that vanished the second she stepped back into their home. The contrast between Marcus's casual ease and the oppressive silence of their home made the quiet feel colder, emptier. She missed Waldo, the version of him who used to see her clearly, even when she couldn't see herself.

She glanced toward the den, seeing the door was still closed.

Still.

Unmoved. No questions asked.

She waited a breath longer, hoping for something, *anything,* from behind the door. She hovered in the hallway, listening for any sound—a chair shifting, footsteps, her name. Nothing. Not even the rustle of papers behind that door. She sighed and turned away, leaving him to the storm he still wouldn't share.

Slowly climbing the stairs, her footsteps became the only thing interrupting the soft hush of the house. As she passed Nathan's closed door and saw the sliver of light beneath Grace's, she paused between both rooms just long enough to say, "Goodnight."

No answer came—only more silence.

Waldo's thoughts had drifted too far from the screen to notice when Sara arrived home. But the silence had changed. It wasn't emptiness anymore. It was absence—and it stayed.

Sara woke early, another morning only confirming that Waldo had slept in the den again. Hearing faint movement downstairs, she could tell he was already awake. She wanted so badly to go downstairs, to go to him, both of them determined to figure out what they needed to do to mend the disconnect between them, but she couldn't summon the energy to reach out again. *Why should I always be the one bridging this gap?*

Downstairs, Waldo stood alone in the kitchen, staring at the coffee brewing. His thoughts churned louder than the machine. He knew he had to talk to Sara. Say something. Anything. But a half hour later, he sat at the table, staring at the bottom of his empty mug. He felt paralyzed by the weight of everything he wasn't saying. But before the rest of his courage slipped away entirely, he finally pushed himself up, chest tight, each step heavy as he climbed toward the bedroom. When he entered their room, Sara looked up, a book closing softly in her lap. "Hey," he offered, voice rough.

"Hey," she said, her expression tired.

"I know I've been distant," he began. "Work's been . . . hard. I've made mistakes. Big ones."

"I wouldn't know."

He swallowed. "I should've talked to you. I shut down, and in the process, shut you out. I know that."

"You did," she said, her tone steady. "And I was still here. I waited."

He took a step forward. "I don't know how to fix this."

Sara's eyes softened slightly, but she made no move toward him. "Maybe start by telling me what's really going on."

He opened his mouth. He wanted to say it—everything. The retreat. The Edge. The panic. The fear. But all that came out was, "I feel stuck. Like I'm waiting for something I can't name."

Sara studied him for a long moment. "What do you need from me, Waldo?"

The words stung. Not because they were cruel, but because they were neutral. Detached. Like she was preparing to let go. "I don't know," he whispered. "Just . . . don't give up on me."

After a minute, she slid her legs over the side of the bed, standing slowly. But she didn't come closer. She just stood there, arms wrapped around herself. Her posture said it all: she was present but protecting something fragile inside. She inhaled, then exhaled, her voice barely above a whisper. "I haven't." But the way her eyes dropped, the pause before she turned away, said what she didn't.

And when he left the room, it wasn't silence that followed. It was everything unsaid, pressing behind him like a shadow he couldn't outrun.

The following days blurred into quiet routines, but the silence in the house was no longer just fatigue; it was proof that something else had shifted.

Waldo buried himself in work, trying to prove he could still be relied on, even as he felt the personal threads of his life fraying further.

Sara and the kids moved around him like shadows, their interactions polite, cautious, as if too much honesty might cause the whole structure to collapse. Grace filled silence with stories about college prep, and Nathan drifted in and out, barely interacting except in passing. Even Melody, typically seeking attention, kept her distance, watching Waldo from afar.

The isolation felt complete.

Even when Sunday dinner arrived, it came without warmth or fanfare, with just Sara and the kids sitting around the table. Conversation was scattered, the energy muted. When Nathan dropped his fork with a frustrated sigh, it finally broke the silence, cracking the illusion completely. "Is Dad even coming?"

"He's . . . home, but in the den. Said he had to finish some things. He might—"

"Again?" Nathan interrupted sharply. "How long are we supposed to pretend this is normal?"

Grace stared at her plate. "Does he even care anymore?"

Sara's breath caught, recognizing her own buried fear in their words. She'd hoped their quiet strain had been subtle enough to remain hidden, but clearly, the kids had noticed. A pang of guilt surged as she steadied herself. "I know it's hard. He's just . . ."

Nathan shook his head bitterly. "If you're going to say he's going through something, please don't. We're all going through something. He just doesn't see it."

Grace glanced up, meeting Sara's gaze, sadness shadowing her young features, before she pushed back from the table and left the room without another word, Nathan following soon after. Sara knew she couldn't pretend this distance between them was sustainable anymore. The silence, the vigilant avoidance, it was costing them too much. She'd carried this weight quietly, hoping it would ease, but now she realized clearly: something had to change.

With determination, she strode to the den. Her steps were not impulsive—they were earned.

Waldo sat at his desk, thoughts spiraling. One crisis solved, another erupting. Work, his mistakes, his marriage—each fire burning hotter than the last. He knew he had to act before everything burned beyond saving. A chill went through him at that thought, just as sharp knocks on the door jolted him. Before he could respond, the door swung open. Sara stood there with piercing eyes. When she finally spoke, her voice was the fire Waldo had been avoiding, now fully ignited. "Are you ever going to ask?" she demanded.

"Ask . . . what?" Waldo said, caught off guard.

"About anything, Waldo. About who I was with in the kitchen or where I was last week. Or even how I felt about you just walking away like it meant nothing." Her frustration filled the room, pressing against him like a physical force.

His heart clenched. "I didn't think I needed to," he said weakly.

"Exactly," she snapped. "You didn't even think about it."

"I—Sara, I—"

"You saw another man in our kitchen and just walked away. Didn't you care at all? Didn't you wonder?"

His gut twisted. He hadn't considered her perspective, not fully.

Sara shook her head. "Do you even see me anymore?"

"Of course, I do." Desperation filled his voice.

"Then why does it feel like I could leave tomorrow and you wouldn't even notice?"

He opened his mouth, but the words dried out before they formed. This wasn't about the man in the kitchen. It wasn't even about the retreat. It was about her and the growing fear that she no longer felt visible in her own home. He'd been so consumed with where he fit in within the life he built that he hadn't even realized she'd started questioning whether or not she belonged here at all.

She stepped back, her voice low and flat. "I've been waiting for you, Waldo, but maybe I shouldn't be." With that, she turned away, slamming the door shut behind her.

Waldo was left there, stunned, breathless, the fear he'd hidden finally exposed. He wanted to follow her, explain everything, but instead, he remained frozen, heart hammering, drowning in indecision.

By the time he was able to force himself to move, the house had grown quiet. The dinner dishes were cleared, leftovers put away. But the tension still hung thick in the air. He passed Grace going up the steps and offered a quiet nod, but she barely glanced his way. *I deserved that*, he thought.

Upstairs, he found Sara in the bedroom, standing beside the bed, poised, but clearly worn down. "I don't know why I didn't ask," he admitted. "Maybe I was afraid of your answer."

Sara turned slowly, arms folded protectively across her chest. "His name is Marcus. He helped with a school fundraiser I volunteered for two years ago. I hadn't seen him since, not until we ran into each other at the grocery store a few weeks ago. It was just a quick conversation, but I said *'stop by if you're ever in the neighborhood'*—and he did. Then, last week, we ended up getting coffee. That's it." She uncrossed her arms. "But it wasn't about him. It was about me. About wanting to feel seen again, even if only for a few hours by a friend."

Waldo's throat tightened. "Sara—"

"You said you were afraid of my answer, but really, why didn't you care enough to ask?"

He stepped back, shame pooling in his chest. He hadn't just avoided Marcus, he'd avoided *her*. The silence had widened into a chasm, and now, neither of them knew how to bridge it—or how to stop falling through. "I've been trying to figure things out," he whispered, feeling small under her gaze. "I thought I needed to get my head right before I could fix us."

"I know." Her voice softened, but the sadness remained. "But you've locked me out. You let the distance feel normal. Whatever you're fighting, you haven't let me in. And I can't carry this alone forever." She paused, eyes holding his. "Eventually, I won't be able to keep doing this. And if that moment comes . . . I need to know you saw me before I left." She turned away from him and pulled back the covers so she could climb into bed. She climbed into bed without another word, her silence louder than anything she could've said.

Waldo stood by the doorway, watching her settle beneath the sheets, the room heavy with everything that had been left unsaid. Then, quietly, almost mechanically, he stepped out and pulled the door until it clicked shut behind him.

Back in the den, he sank into the darkness, his reflection staring at him from the darkened computer screen, mirroring a realization—the fear that had kept him distant wasn't of being lost. It was of losing the one person who had waited . . . for as long as she could. Knowing that she might not wait much longer was the truth he could no longer deny.

The next morning, Waldo sat at the kitchen table, staring into a mug gone cold before having to leave for work. Sara's words had replayed all night—he hadn't just failed her. He'd abandoned himself. Yet, beneath it all was a question that replicated his greatest fear: what if, in searching for himself, he discovered a man Sara no longer wanted? He'd forgotten how to live authentically, trapped by his own fears of inadequacy. Could she see that now, too? He couldn't keep circling. He had to confront the truth head-on, even if it meant risking everything. The alternative, living half-alive beneath regret, terrified him more than the unknown.

His fingers shook slightly as he reached for his phone. It had been two weeks since Dr. Benson left her office to be on hospital rotation, and he hadn't realized how much her absence would rattle him. But now, with everything unraveling, he couldn't afford another week without her. He tapped in the number, heart pounding.

"Dr. Benson's office," the receptionist answered.

"This is Waldo Turner. Just confirming my appointment with Dr. Benson in a few days, on Thursday."

There was a brief pause, the sound of her keyboard clicking filling the dead space. "Yes, Thursday at two o'clock. You're all set."

Relief washed over him, but as he set the phone down, glancing up toward the bedroom, so did dread. Three days was a long time. Would they survive three more days of this silence?

Finally, Thursday arrived. He entered Dr. Benson's office feeling far from the man he'd been at their last meeting. Waldo dropped into the chair across from Dr. Benson.

"You look like you've been carrying a lot," she observed.

He gave a tired laugh. "You have no idea." The rest spilled out of him—dropping the ball at work, the mounting fear that he was failing everywhere else too, letting Sara down, the weight of the silence . . .

"Do you think she's leaving?" Dr. Benson asked, her tone professionally considerate as much as it was genuinely empathetic.

He shook his head. "No . . . I don't think she is, or wants to. I think she's just trying to decide if I'm still someone she can wait for."

Dr. Benson was quiet for a moment. "Last time we spoke, I said maybe she wasn't just waiting but wondering. Wondering if she still belonged in your life. I still think that's true. But now, I think she's been watching, too. Watching to see if you'd notice her slipping. Watching to see if you'd choose her, before she has to choose herself."

Waldo looked down. "She said that too. She said she was hoping I'd finally see her before she had to decide not to stay." The truth pierced him.

"You've been waiting for clarity to save you," Dr. Benson said. "But clarity doesn't guarantee certainty. It simply opens your eyes to what's real—and that's where change begins."

Waldo nodded slowly. "Then, let's look at the truth. It's like I'm standing on the edge of something, and I can't move forward, but I can't go back either." He ran a hand over his face, his voice trembling. "What if, in trying to find myself, I destroy everything we've built along the way?"

"Waldo," she began, her tone measured and calm. "You're not alone in this. The fear you're describing, it's a normal part of growth. It's unsettling because you're stepping into the unknown. But let me ask you something: are you afraid of what Sara will see, or are you afraid of what you'll see when you look at yourself?"

Jolted by her question, he couldn't believe how obvious it seemed, though he had never thought of it that way. "Both," he blurted. "But mostly . . . what I see. Or what I don't see. I used to know who I was. Now, I don't even know where to start looking."

"Have you asked her how she feels?" Dr. Benson pressed.

"No," he whispered, voice tight. "Because I'm terrified that she's already decided."

"Is that what she told you?"

"She said that she can't do this forever. She's been patient, but now it feels like a countdown."

"You said earlier you don't think she wants to leave. So, do you believe she wants to stay but is afraid that you're not fighting for her to?"

Waldo's heart pounded as he realized Sara hadn't withdrawn to escape; she had waited desperately for him to finally approach her— and he hadn't. "But how do I explain something to Sara that I can't even explain to myself? And if I can't explain it to either of us, how do I let her in?"

Dr. Benson met his eyes earnestly. "Maybe your mistake isn't your confusion. Maybe your mistake is silence."

He leaned back in his chair, the weight creating a dull *thud*.

"You've avoided your feelings because they scare you. That's normal. But the more you avoid, the stronger they become. The answers won't come instantly. And until then, it's about learning to live with discomfort, not escaping it."

"So, what do I do now?" he asked desperately.

"Waldo, you know the answers are inside of you. But finding them doesn't happen overnight, and it doesn't happen without effort. It's a process—one that requires patience and a willingness to sit with discomfort."

He allowed her words to sink in. His gaze locked onto hers, hopeful for the possibility of some magical prescription of wisdom being offered.

"Are you ready to stop circling and take the first real step forward, even if it scares you?" She waited a beat and said, "To step into the discomfort and trust that the answers will come, not all at once, but piece by piece?"

He nodded, understanding her reminder to find patience in his life. No matter how often he reminded himself, he seemed to quickly lose sight of the importance. "I don't know if I'm ready," he admitted. "I keep thinking I am, but then I let myself down. But I think it's time to try again, for my own sake, for Sara, and for all of it."

Dr. Benson smiled. "That's all you need to start. The rest will come. The retreat gave you one thing that worked—uninterrupted space to reflect, even when it got uncomfortable. That space is worth recreating. A place where you can be alone with your thoughts, free from distractions. That's where you'll see your progress grow."

The silence that followed felt heavy but purposeful. Waldo absorbed her words, knowing their truth: he'd spent too long circling, afraid of what he might find inside himself. "So . . . what does the next step even look like? Because right now, it just feels like running in circles."

"Create intentional space. Now, don't confuse this with isolation. But make room for genuine reflection," she asserted. "Communicate openly with Sara, and include her in your journey so you can face this together. Find spaces where you can rebuild trust in yourself and ones that allow for reflection without pressure—not chaotic or overwhelming ones like The Edge. This might mean taking more time for yourself by stepping away from work routines and distractions to focus on what's truly going on inside." She watched his reaction for a moment. "But that kind of decision can't happen in isolation. You'll need to talk to Sara. Be honest with her. Share what you're wrestling with and work together to figure out what makes sense—not just for you but for her and your family, too."

Her words felt like both a challenge and a lifeline. His focus reignited, seeing the truth in what she was saying. He couldn't keep pretending everything would magically turn out fine, and he couldn't make progress if he kept trying to shoulder it all on his own. He thought he had been both sparing Sara and proving to himself he could do hard things, but maybe this hard thing wasn't meant for him to do it completely alone.

"It'll be tough," Dr. Benson added. "But sometimes, the hardest conversations are the ones that open the door to real progress. And it's not just about asking for time—it's about being clear with yourself and with Sara about why you need it and how you plan to use it."

"Clearly, it was never just my journey, but I didn't see that until now. I've been walking alone on a path that was meant to be shared. I still need to face this for me, but I need her to understand why. I can see all of that now. My struggle doesn't just stay with me. It spills over into Sara, into Grace and Nathan, and into everything we've built. I can't keep pretending it doesn't. If I don't address this, it's not just me who's affected; it's all of us." He swallowed. "I kept telling myself I was protecting her by staying quiet, but silence doesn't protect anything. It just leaves people alone with their own worst stories."

Dr. Benson nodded. "That's exactly why this conversation with Sara is so important. By bringing her into the process, you're not just asking for understanding—you're showing her that this journey, while yours to walk, is something you're willing to work through for the benefit of everyone."

Waldo leaned back, the enormity of the task ahead filling his chest, yet this time, it felt less paralyzing. He wasn't just doing this to fix himself; he was protecting and strengthening the life he and Sara had built together. He exhaled deeply, a blend of relief and vulnerability settling inside him. "I think it's finally time."

As Waldo stepped out of Dr. Benson's office and slid into his car, the heaviness in his chest began to ease, just enough to let him breathe freely again. This wasn't about mere survival anymore. It was about embracing uncertainty, confronting discomfort, and rebuilding trust with honesty. Sara's face flashed vividly in his mind; the frustration in her eyes, her patience stretched thin yet still holding. She needed to understand he wasn't running away this time. He was finally moving forward—for her, for Grace and Nathan, and for the man he was determined to become.

He sat in his seat, his hands firm on the steering wheel, feeling an unfamiliar yet empowering clarity. He didn't need armor or perfect answers—just the courage to speak honestly, no matter how raw. And for once, he knew he wouldn't have to face it alone. The dragons he'd feared weren't enemies at all—they were mirrors reflecting truths he'd long ignored. Facing them wouldn't destroy him; it would finally set him free. And the idea of breaking away from the chaos no longer terrified him. It felt necessary, essential even. He wanted to be more than someone merely getting by. He wanted to be a husband. A father. A defender.

Waldo's mind drifted back to when he was maybe eight or nine, invested heavily in stories of dragons and heroes—tales of knights battling dragons, defenders of the kingdom, their gleaming armor a symbol of courage and purpose. His father's voice rang out, steady and sure: *"Every man has his dragons. They're not just monsters to kill. They live in the shadows, where we avoid looking, until they threaten everything we've worked for."*

Back then, Waldo had loved the myths for the thrill, imagining himself as the knight, sword in hand, charging into battle, saving the day. But his father had always pointed deeper. *"They're not always the roaring, fire-breathing kind,"* he'd say. *"Sometimes, they're whispers. Hesitation. Procrastination. The fears we bury. The truths we avoid."* Now, Waldo finally understood. The dragons weren't enemies on the outside—they were the doubts and wounds he'd left unspoken. They were the shame he hadn't faced, the responsibilities he'd delayed. They weren't sacred to the journey, merely a convenient scapegoat for his own insecurities and shortcomings. They were the cost of refusing to look within.

Echoed like a prophecy, his father ended with, *"Dragons only grow bigger in the dark."* Waldo had let them grow. He had fed them with silence. And now, they towered over everything that mattered—his marriage, his kids, his sense of self.

But no more.

He knew it was finally his turn to walk into the story now, not as a child dreaming of heroics, but as a man brave enough to face his truths. There was the dragon of complacency, murmuring that "good enough" was fine. That drifting could pass for peace. Then, there was the dragon of fear, breathing fire into his deepest insecurities, telling him that he would fail, that he wasn't enough, that facing his truth would burn him to ash. And the most dangerous of them all—the dragon of hopelessness. The one that whispered his life was a maze with no exit. That the effort to fix things would never be worth the pain of trying.

He saw each one clearly now. They had power because he'd looked away. But he wasn't looking away anymore. He still wasn't a perfect knight, but he didn't need to be. He was a man who had lost his footing, and who now chose to stand.

Sara deserved more than good intentions and vague promises. She deserved a partner who would show up for the hard parts. A protector who wouldn't let fear make decisions for him. And his children—they needed to see what courage looked like up close. Not in fantasy, but in everyday actions. In honesty. In humility. In showing up, even when it was hard. His family was worth every battle he'd have to fight. Their life, the love, the hearts that had been waiting for him, hoping he'd finally show up—well, it was finally time he did. This wasn't a burden. This was a calling.

He wasn't just venturing into uncertainty. He was plunging into vulnerability. The next conversation with Sara wouldn't be easy, but it would be real. He was no longer interested in hiding. He was returning to himself, and hoping, desperately, she would still be there to see her patience was worth it.

A strategy began to form. No grand speeches, no sweeping declarations. Just this: he would start by telling Sara the truth—messy, incomplete, but real. He would explain why he needed time to face the dragons but that he wasn't doing it to pull away. He was doing it to come home

Chapter 10
The Decision Path

Waking up came later than usual that Saturday morning. By the time Waldo did, sunlight fell hard through the kitchen window—too bright, too clean. Waldo sat at the table, hands wrapped tightly around his coffee mug, though the warmth did nothing to steady the tremor beneath his skin. He'd spent the night rehearsing this conversation, rewriting and rephrasing his truth, but now, seated at the table, every version of it felt inadequate. Small. Unworthy of the truth he needed to speak.

The house was almost too still. Grace and Nathan had gone off with friends, leaving the space deceptively peaceful. But the quiet between him and Sara felt anything but. It was the silence of something waiting to fracture and all the unspoken strain between them. The silence felt like a verdict.

Sara stood at the sink, rinsing the last dish from breakfast, her back partially turned. She hadn't said much since he walked in. The tension between them wasn't new, but it had hardened into something with sharp corners. Something that could cut. Waldo cleared his throat. "Sara," he said carefully, not rushing it. "We need to talk."

She turned slightly, her eyes guarded as she dried her hands with a dishtowel. "I'm listening." Her tone wasn't cold, but it wasn't soft either.

"There's something I need to share with you." He didn't look up, not yet. "During the retreat, I metaphorically hit a wall. I reached a point . . . a breaking point. The structure, the process—it all helped at first, but it wasn't getting to the core. I left early, hoping to find something deeper, something more . . . real. And that's when I found The Edge."

Sara's brows creased faintly, but she said nothing.

"It was an underground event; it wasn't part of the program. But I was told it was a space where you're forced to face the version of yourself you spend your whole life avoiding. I chose to go. No one made me." He glanced at her then, just briefly. "And what I saw . . . was a man I didn't recognize. Angry. Disconnected. Hollowed out by pretending. I realized I've been performing so long that I forgot who I was beneath the act." He paused, his words catching in his throat. "That night broke something in me. But it also . . . opened something. I understood that if I ever wanted to find my way back—to you, to the kids, to myself—I couldn't keep dragging the same broken patterns forward. I had to stop. I had to step away. Rebuild. From the ground up."

Sara's eyes stayed on him, searching. "And why didn't you tell me this before?"

"Because I was afraid."

She tensed. "Afraid of what?"

"Of unraveling everything." His voice wavered. "Saying it out loud and making it real. Disrupting everything we've built. I kept telling myself I was protecting you, protecting all of us. But the truth is . . . I didn't want to face how far I'd drifted. I was scared you'd see it too. And maybe . . . you'd give up on me."

Sara blinked but her expression didn't soften. The silence stretched between them until, finally, Waldo spoke again, his words barely coming out in a whisper. "But when I saw Dr. Benson again, we talked about all of it. She thinks I need time. Not just to think, but to finally face what I've been running from."

She stepped back slightly, like the words had brushed too close. "Time?" Her voice was brittle. "What exactly does that mean?"

Waldo's shoulders rose and fell with a slow, deliberate breath. "Time away from work, from pressure, from pretending I'm fine when I'm not. A leave of absence. Intentional space to figure out who I am— not just who I've been trying to be."

"And what about us, Waldo? Where does that leave me? The kids? This family?"

Sara's facial expression tightened. "So, you're not leaving us . . . You're just leaving?"

"Not leaving," he said quickly. "Just stepping back."

She folded her arms. "And that's different how? Because it sounds a lot like walking out."

"It's not. It's about breaking the cycle I'm stuck in. The retreat made it clear; I can't keep pretending. If I don't step back now, I'm going to lose myself. And maybe . . . lose *us*." He forced himself to meet her eyes. "I need time—not to escape. To rebuild. To become the man you and the kids deserve."

Sara exhaled, like the air had turned thick around her. "And what am I supposed to tell Nathan and Grace?" Her voice shook. "That their father needed a break . . . from being their father?"

He winced. "No. That's not it. It's not about leaving you guys. It's about *returning*—as someone whole. I know I'm failing you and the kids by doing this, but staying and pretending fixes nothing."

Her jaw tightened. "You say that like it's noble, like it's brave. But I'm the one still here. Holding this together." She clutched her wedding ring, her eyes drifting toward Grace's senior photo on the fridge, her wide smile and bright eyes unmistakably hers. "And now you're asking me—no, you're *telling* me—that you're leaving to go find yourself. How is that fair?"

"I know how it sounds," he said, voice thinning. "And I hate it too. But if I keep going like this, I'll drown, and you'll be left with a hollow version of me anyway. I have to do this, Sara. Not just for me, but for us."

She stared at him with aching disbelief. "And what if you go," she whispered, "and realize you don't want to come back?"

His breath hitched. "Sara, don't—"

"What if you realize you don't want *me* anymore?"

Silence.

Then, Waldo stepped closer, gently taking her hand. Her fingers were cold, trembling slightly in his grasp. "That's not possible," he said. "I love you. That hasn't changed."

"I want to believe you . . ."

He squeezed her hand. "Then believe me. Please."

Her eyes searched his face—a mother, a wife, a woman trying to read the truth inside the man she wasn't sure she still knew. "You say you need to go . . . But what if you get lost out there?"

"I won't." His reply came fast, too fast. But then, slower, he said, "I won't. I can't. I'll come back. I promise." A beat. "This isn't about leaving you. It's about becoming someone who can stand beside you again. Someone the kids can be proud of. I need to face what I've buried for too long."

Sara's eyes glistened as she nodded, her lips pressed into a thin line. "I want you to find your way back, Waldo. Just promise me you'll come home."

"I promise," he whispered.

Her fingers curled around his briefly—a tether, a plea—and then she released her grip. She stepped back, steadying herself against the countertop. "You used to be my partner. The one who'd refill the coffee without asking, the one who sat next to me through the noise and the quiet. But lately, I've felt like a bystander.""

"I know. And that's why I *have* to do this. Now. Before it's too late."

She drew a breath, holding it like a question she wasn't ready to ask. "Then, go," she said. "Do what you need to do. But don't forget the way back home."

"I could never forget." And Waldo meant that with every fiber of his being.

She turned back to the sink, hands resting against its edge. She didn't feel angry. Just still, with acceptance, a fragile hope that maybe this wasn't the end. That it was just a painful step toward something better.

And as he watched her—strong, afraid, and unyielding—Waldo realized that they couldn't go back to what they'd been. And maybe, terrifyingly, that was exactly the point.

When the next morning came, Waldo felt as if he'd lived months in just a few hours. He replayed their conversation all night, adding to his motivation to take this leap.

When he went downstairs, he found the house empty. Grace and Sara had already left for the day, giving him space he wasn't sure he wanted but knew he needed. He sat at the table, coffee untouched, steam rising like silent questions he still couldn't answer. The quiet was interrupted by the sudden opening of the fridge. Nathan stood there, hair damp from the shower, drinking a sports drink in hurried gulps.

"Heading out?" Waldo asked.

Nathan nodded, setting down the empty bottle. "Gym, then break-fast with a friend. Probably won't be back till later." There was a beat between them, heavier than usual. Nathan's eyes searched his father's face before adding, "You holding up?"

Waldo's instinct was to dismiss it, to reassure him with a quick lie, but something in Nathan's quiet concern stopped him. He sighed instead, shaking his head. "Honestly? I don't know. But I'm working on it."

Nathan seemed unsurprised. With a thumbs up signal, he headed out. "See you later, Dad."

Then, the quiet returned, but it felt different now. Not isolating as all the mornings before but more like an invitation to face the things he'd spent too long avoiding. Sara's fears echoed within him again: running away, leaving them behind. Her words had cut deep because he understood the fear. He had been afraid she was getting close to leaving him too. But this wasn't running. This was stopping. He was certain of it.

For the first time, Waldo allowed himself to confront the truth he'd avoided: he wasn't just tangled. He'd deliberately tightened these knots himself—each unspoken fear, each avoided choice, adding another twist. He had spent years running through a maze he himself had constructed, blaming external circumstances for walls he'd built with his own hands. He ran a thumb along the coffee cup's rim; warm now, the heat fading.

His father's voice, his mother's quiet faith, Sara's steady patience, all had pointed toward the same truth he'd refused to acknowledge: the answer wasn't found by running faster. It was found by standing still and in turning inward. In finally facing the fears he'd buried at the center of his self-made labyrinth.

Something Dr. Benson said in one of their last sessions returned, clearer now. *"Some knots cannot be forced loose—they must be untangled gently, deliberately."* And this intentional leave was about unraveling those knots one painful thread at a time.

He didn't blame Sara for not fully understanding that yet; he hadn't told her anything until now, after all. He hadn't trusted himself to put this deeper truth into words, afraid she would see the depth of his uncertainty as weakness instead of courage. He had promised her he would return, but he planned to do more than that. He wouldn't just return physically—he would come home emotionally, mentally, and spiritually whole. The dragons of his father's stories grew stronger each day he pretended they didn't exist. They thrived in avoidance, fear, hesitation, and silence.

But no more.

～

Waldo entered the office Monday morning with a quiet but unmistakable sense of purpose. The fluorescent lights overhead buzzed faintly, an irritating symbol of everything that had worn him down over the years. As he passed his coworkers absorbed in screens, making small talk about meetings and deadlines, it struck him that nothing had truly changed here in a decade. The routine was relentless, the meaning elusive.

Earlier that morning, he'd emailed Victor, requesting a meeting to discuss his leave of absence. Sitting at his desk now, Waldo impatiently refreshed his inbox again—still nothing. He couldn't have been clearer about the importance of this meeting; the silence was unbearable. His message needed the weight of personal acknowledgment, especially after he'd fought so hard to regain his footing after his recent mistake. He glanced around the office once more, taking in the clicking keyboards, ringing phones, and the dull chatter of lives set on autopilot. He saw himself in every face—people who'd traded dreams for stability, creativity, for conformity. They were cogs in a system designed to suppress individuality, and suddenly, Waldo saw that he was no different. He'd become exactly what he never intended: complacent, robotic, existing rather than living. *No more,* he thought again.

He stood outside Victor's office for only a moment, then knocked twice and stepped inside. Victor looked up from his screen, mild surprise flickering across his expression. "Waldo," he said, setting aside his glasses. "Something wrong?"

Waldo closed the door behind him. "I emailed earlier, but after not receiving a reply, I decided this needed to be said face-to-face anyway."

Victor leaned back cautiously. "Go ahead."

"I'm formally requesting a leave of absence. Personal leave. I need to step away to rebuild myself."

Victor narrowed his eyes. "You're sure about this?"

"Yes," Waldo said, no hesitation in his voice. "If I don't do this now, I'll lose more than just momentum at work. I'll lose myself. I'll lose all the things I care about."

Victor tapped his pen on the desk. "You've just gotten yourself back on track. I need to know this isn't another spiral."

"It's the opposite of a spiral. I've spent years shrinking, second-guessing, putting off the inner work that matters most. I've been afraid to face the real problems, afraid to admit what needed to change. That fear has cost me too much already." He paused, exhaling slowly. "But I'm done letting fear set the terms. I've been standing at the edge for too long. This is me stepping forward—not away."

Victor regarded his words carefully. "How long are we talking?"

"A few weeks. Maybe a month," Waldo replied. "Enough time to untangle what needs to be untangled. To get it right."

Victor nodded. "I'll be honest, this puts us in a difficult spot. But I'd rather lose you for a month than burn you out for good. We'll cover the gap. But don't leave us hanging. I need updates. And I need your word you'll come back clearheaded."

"You have it," Waldo said firmly, extending a hand.

Victor shook it, already turning back toward his work. "Then, take the time. Just don't let me down. And Waldo," he said as Waldo placed his hand on the doorknob, "you're braver than most here. Just don't vanish on me."

Waldo felt relief ripple through him, unexpectedly powerful. "I appreciate this, Vic."

As Waldo stepped out of Victor's office, the hallway looked exactly the same, but he no longer felt like one of the many anonymous figures moving through it. He didn't carry this choice like a burden. He carried it like a sword; not to attack but to carve out space for healing."

He was no longer dodging dragons.

He was walking out to meet them, on his own terms.

Returning to his desk, he calmly shut his laptop, gathered his belongings, and took one last long look around. As he left the building, the air smelled different, like something was just beginning to break open. A gentle breeze touched his face, bringing both promise and uncertainty, quickening his pulse. Though the future was unclear, he knew it wasn't inside those walls.

Chapter 11
The Maze Narrows

In the days leading up to his departure, Waldo moved quietly through the house, each action purposeful. Bills were paid early, routines clearly outlined, and small reassurances carefully tucked away —little acts intended to comfort Sara and the kids while he was gone. He wasn't leaving forever, but he needed them to feel safe until he returned.

Standing in the kitchen, he ran through his mental checklist one last time. "I've set up auto-payments for the month," he explained, watching Sara's reaction closely. "But all the details are written down in case you need them."

"That's thoughtful, but we would've managed," she replied.

"I know," he said, stepping closer. "But it matters to me." A quiet beat passed before Waldo continued, "I haven't decided exactly where I'm headed yet, but I'll call as soon as I settle somewhere, and I'll check in regularly. You won't be left guessing."

"I appreciate that," she said, nodding.

"Sara," he started, his voice tentative. "I know how difficult this is for you, how uncertain this feels. But please trust that this isn't me leaving you—it's me trying to find a way back."

She hesitated, searching his face. Finally, softly, she said, "How can you be sure this will work?"

Waldo offered a sad, honest smile. "I'm not. But staying stuck isn't working either."

After a moment, she breathed quietly, her eyes holding his. "I haven't said it much lately, but I love you."

The sincerity in her voice caught him by surprise, pressing deep into his chest. "I love you too," he said, feeling the truth of it more deeply than he had in a long time.

They stood privately, not touching, yet something tender and fragile stirred between them—promising that maybe, just maybe, they'd find their way back.

Later that evening, he hovered in Grace's doorway, watching her sort through college paperwork, already half gone into a life beyond this house, building a future he admired.

She looked up. "Everything okay?"

"Just checking in," he replied, trying to sound casual. "You're good while I'm gone?"

She smiled faintly, reassuring him with her subtle strength. "Yeah, Dad. We'll be fine."

Pride and gratitude filled him. Maybe she understood more than he'd given her credit for.

His conversation with Nathan went similarly. As Nathan headed out, Waldo called after him, "You good with me taking some time?"

Nathan paused, adjusting his gym bag. "Yeah. Just . . . figure things out, okay?"

"That's the plan," Waldo said, appreciating his son's straightforwardness more than ever.

Nathan nodded once, and the door clicked closed behind him, leaving Waldo with a bittersweet ache. Nathan's words were few, but they landed with quiet power. There was something in his voice—a cautious respect, maybe—that told Waldo his son was watching, waiting to see if this version of his father would finally show up.

By Sunday morning, his duffle sat by the door, carefully packed. Clothes, his notebook, toiletries, essentials—and his guitar, a last-minute decision. He hadn't touched it much since abandoning lessons, but it had remained with him, leaning quietly in the corner, unplayed but never entirely forgotten.

Just before leaving, he made two quick calls—one to Dr. Benson's office voicemail, canceling appointments, and another text to his guitar instructor, thanking him for what he has taught him and then apologizing for not following through on the majority of their lessons. He only gave a brief explanation of why, but decided to leave it at that. The instructor's reply:

> Hope you find what you're looking for, Waldo

His well wishes settled in his chest, supportive yet sobering.

The aroma of coffee filled the kitchen as Waldo sat, reflecting one last time. Grace appeared unexpectedly sleepy-eyed but awake enough to share a hug. "Take care of yourself," she whispered against his shoulder.

"I will," he promised, holding her close.

At his feet, Melody appeared, purring while brushing affectionately against his leg. Grace laughed, breaking the tension. "Even Melody approves."

Waldo smiled, kneeling to scratch the cat's chin. "Or she's reminding me who's really in charge here."

As she stepped back, Grace gave a lopsided smile and raised two fingers in a peace sign—the same gesture she'd flashed backstage after her recital, when her nerves had finally melted into pride. Waldo mirrored the gesture, a grin tugging at the corner of his mouth. It wasn't just goodbye, it was their language now, a quiet reminder of a shared moment he'd carry with him. As she disappeared back to her room, Waldo turned, sensing Sara's presence before he saw her. Her gaze held a quiet resolve, her hands clasped, as though she were gathering strength for them both.

"Nathan's still asleep," she murmured, understanding his unspoken question.

He nodded. Nathan had said his goodbye last night already. He couldn't expect Nathan to alter his routine to say goodbye again.

Sara moved closer and reached out, touching his chest softly. Her fingertips lingered, warm and reassuring. Leaning in, she kissed his cheek, whispering delicately against his skin, "Find what you need, Waldo."

"I will," he whispered back, his voice thick with emotion.

When he climbed into the car only a few minutes later, the engine hummed as he glanced one last time toward the porch. Sara, Grace, and even Melody watched silently as he pulled away. In his rearview mirror, the house gradually faded yet their presence remained, anchoring him.

He didn't know what awaited him, but as the road unfolded under his tires, he knew one thing: wherever it led, it had to bring him home —not just for his sake but for the family he loved deeply and desperately wanted back. This decision hadn't meant the maze disappeared, but the walls didn't feel as tall anymore. And instead of walking in circles, he was moving forward—into the unknown, yes, but no longer lost.

Miles slipped past, each turn of the road emphasizing his determination. He was following an invisible thread, a pull toward something essential, and he was eager to see where it led him. There were no signs, no markers of progress, only the knowing that the farther he got from the familiar, the closer he came to something true. But that certainty thinned with distance, the rhythm of tires against asphalt not being able to fully silence the storm within. *"Find what you need."* Sara's word replayed in his mind over and over. She wasn't making a demand or even setting an expectation. It was more like she was expressing her trust in him. But what if he didn't even know where to start?

Dr. Benson's question pressed into his thoughts next: *"Or are you afraid of what you'll see when you look at yourself?"* She was right. Waldo knew the dragons he'd created—hesitation, insecurity, and fear—were now his responsibility to confront. Clarity wouldn't appear simply because he drove far enough away. It would require patience, stillness, and honest reflection—exactly what he'd avoided for far too long.

As daylight fell into dusk, a sanctuary emerged through a veil of mist, modest and weathered, tucked between dunes and pine. Waldo found himself slowing instinctively, drawn into Gull's Rest, a small coastal town, the name feeling like a breath exhaled after holding it in for too long. The sky darkened further as he entered Gull's Rest, as if the light itself knew to dim and hush. As if it had been waiting for this moment too. He rolled the window down, letting the salt air rush in, bracing and welcoming. It filled his lungs like a memory, clean and alive.

Waldo parked and sat still with his hands on the wheel. As the engine's hum faded, the quietest kind of welcome replaced it—wind through grass, the creak of wooden siding, the distant call of a bird. He had officially stepped into the center of the maze.

The town felt untouched by time: weathered storefronts lined quiet streets, boats rocked lightly in the harbor, and beyond them, the ocean stretched endlessly, rhythmic and patient. Waldo smiled as he checked into The Breakwater Inn, the irony of its name not lost on him. A break-water was something built to protect buildings, to buffer relentless waves. Perhaps this was the place where he, too, could find shelter from his own relentless thoughts.

Inside the modest room, he sat on the edge of the bed, phone in hand. It rang twice before Sara answered. "I wanted you to know where I ended up," he began. "It's a little town called Gull's Rest. It feels right, somehow."

"Okay," she said with relief, knowing he was safe. "And how are you?"

He exhaled deeply, choosing honesty. "I don't really know yet, but I think this is what I need."

The silence felt simultaneously full and unfinished. When Sara finally spoke, her voice still carried the warmth she answered with, but it now held an undeniable weight. "Just remember what's waiting for you here, Waldo."

"I won't forget, and I'll check in often like I promised. And don't forget, this—"

"I know, this isn't you running away. It's you finding your way back. Just be safe until you do."

Waldo felt a surge of gratitude, of longing. "I will. I love you, Sara." Before ending the call, he added, "Tell the kids I love them too, alright? Make sure they know."

"I will. Grace will pretend she's too independent for it, and Nathan will nod like it's no big deal, but they'll both hear you."

"Good," he whispered, his throat tightening. "Thank you, Sara."

"You're welcome," she replied, almost too softly. "Take care of yourself."

"You too."

When the line went quiet, Waldo sat motionless, absorbing their conversation, feeling its weight slowly settle into something steady within him.

The briny breeze beckoned him from the other side of the window. Stepping outside, Waldo breathed deeply, the cool, salty air washing through him. The ocean spread before him, an ancient and infinite mystery. Waves crashed and withdrew rhythmically, patient and endless. He listened, not demanding answers this time but accepting the steady rhythm that whispered softly beneath the noise in his mind.

He spent the following days walking along cliffs and across sand, feeling the sea breeze sweep through him. The vastness of the ocean made his problems feel smaller yet strangely more meaningful. The rhythm of the waves offered no quick resolution, only gentle reassurance that some things simply took time. Here, away from distractions, away from the weight of expectations, he finally stopped running.

When Waldo first decided to leave, he expected to see a battleground when he arrived at his destination—to face dragons, to have to win something back with fire and force. But he noticed how their power began to fade the moment he stopped fleeing and dared to look them in the eye. So, in the stillness of Gull's Rest, something gentler unfolded. Maybe some dragons weren't meant to be slain, only seen. Understood.

Here, by the sea, he realized: the war was never about conquering. It was about listening. *Maybe,* Waldo thought as he stared across the horizon, *this is how untangling begins—not with force but with patience. Not with desperate searching but with quiet acknowledgment of what I fear most.* And here, by the steady rhythm of the sea, he felt the first threads loosen.

On the fourth night, Waldo returned to his room, surprised by the late hour. Despite the exhaustion pulling at his limbs, his mind remained alert, the waves' cadence still echoing inside him. Without thinking, he picked up the phone and dialed home, waiting for Sara's voice to ground him once more. "Hey, Sara," he said gently when she answered. "Just wanted to check in. Everything okay?"

Her voice held the calm steadiness he'd always relied on. "We're fine. Nathan helped Grace finish up some college applications. She's getting excited about it."

A faint smile crossed his lips. He pictured Grace, focused at the dining table, navigating her future with a confidence that both amazed and humbled him. "Good. She deserves to feel excited." He paused briefly. "And Nathan? I miss them both."

"I know you do. He's staying busy but handling it. Working late, staying focused. What about you, Waldo? How are you?"

He glanced toward the window, where moonlight spilled across restless water. "Still figuring it out," he admitted.

The silence between their words stretched but didn't break. And

neither spoke about when he'd return. After hanging up, Waldo
lingered in the quiet, feeling the ache deepen but motivated to keep
going.

The following morning, dawn's pale light drew Waldo from bed
early. Coffee brewed in the inn's cozy breakfast nook, its aroma offering
comfort as he watched the town awaken. Conversations and the *clink* of
cutlery reminded him briefly of Cooper's Café, the sanctuary of home
where daily rituals felt grounding amid life's uncertainties. Coffee in
hand, he stepped into the cool morning air, curiosity guiding him
toward the town's pier. A small gallery caught his eyes, nestled incon-
spicuously between a seafood restaurant and a tourist shop. Drawn by
impulse, Waldo stepped inside, where paintings covered every wall—a
colorful chaos that felt oddly soothing.

An older woman, likely the gallery's owner, noticed his gaze and
approached. "Does it speak to you?"

Waldo considered the abstract painting before him, a swirl of blues,
greens, and flashes of yellow. "I'm not sure," he confessed. "It's . . .
confusing but compelling."

"Art is often like that," she said knowingly. "It doesn't ask to be
understood—only felt."

The words settled into him like a familiar rhythm. And then, unbidden, a memory of Grace returned, maybe thirteen, holding her sketch-
book up to him, her eyes shining. Her drawing had looked wild,
untamed, with bright streaks of purple and orange cutting through a
stormy gray swirl. He remembered trying to make sense of it, unsure
what it was meant to be. *"I know it looks messy,"* she'd said, half-laugh-
ing, half-defensive. *"But if you look closer . . . it makes sense."*

At the time, he'd nodded vaguely, too distracted to press further.
But now, standing before this painting, so much like her drawing, he
finally understood what she'd meant. Sometimes, clarity wasn't something you were handed. It was something you had to feel your way
into. And Grace had seen something he couldn't at the time. Her sketch
had been her way of saying that life doesn't have to be tidy to matter.
Chaos and beauty weren't opposites; they coexisted, waiting to be

experienced without judgment. A swell of affection rose in his chest. He wished he'd told her how proud he was then. He'd make sure to tell her when he got home.

He thought about a quote he hadn't in years: *"If you judge people, you have no time to love them."* Now, he saw it wasn't just about people—it was about perception itself. The painting. Grace's sketch. The music he'd dismissed. Even the unsolved parts of his own story. None of it needed to be explained to be felt. What mattered was being open. Still. Awake enough to witness it. And now, that felt possible.

"You see it now, don't you?" the gallery owner asked.

Waldo stared at the swirling colors, feeling their quiet pull. For a moment, he didn't respond. He just let the image speak for itself. "I think I do," he finally said, smiling. He nodded, not to her but to the part of himself that was starting to listen.

"Sometimes, being lost is exactly where you need to be," she continued. "Only then do you start to truly see."

As he stepped outside, appreciating the gallery owner's thoughtful take, the sunlight caught the edge of a narrow side street, one he hadn't noticed before. A tucked-away café sat nestled in the shade, ivy climbing the windows, faint music drifting from within. Waldo paused, appreciating its charm. He made a mental note to check this place out—not for today but for another time when he wasn't trying to unravel himself. For a time when he could simply . . . exist.

Turning to continue his walk, he slowed again, this time, outside a souvenir shop, inexplicably pulled toward a vibrant window display. Trinkets—shell keychains, sand-filled jars, delicate bracelets of polished sea glass—each one seemed ordinary yet meaningful; tiny vessels of memory, holding echoes of simpler joy and the power to reconnect, renew, and inspire. This made Waldo realize memories weren't only anchors to the past; they were fuel for the future.

Standing there, bathed in gentle sunlight, Waldo sensed another shift within. The journey ahead was still uncertain, but the frantic urgency had faded, replaced by cautious optimism. He didn't have every answer, but he had something better now: acceptance that he didn't need them immediately. He realized again that being lost wasn't failure—it was part of finding something deeper, something more authentic. Life's turbulence couldn't be controlled, only navigated with presence, openness, and trust. Taking a breath, Waldo felt ready to embrace the uncertainty ahead—not because he'd found absolute clarity but because he finally accepted that he didn't need it all at once. He no longer felt like he was unraveling. Instead, he felt like he was returning—not to who he had been, but to who he was finally becoming.

Chapter 12
From the Maze to the Music

In the days that followed, Waldo slowly adapted to the calming rhythm of the coastal town. Each morning, he awoke to the steady rush of waves, wrapped himself in a warm sweater, and headed out with his coffee in hand. His walks lengthened daily, tracing cliff paths, meandering through quiet streets lined with salt-weathered cottages, and wandering the open sands. He stopped pressing for answers, surrendering instead to the simplicity of each moment.

In his notebook, he recorded minor details that reminded him to appreciate the small moments—morning sunlight rippling in gold across the water, distant children's laughter echoing over sand dunes, the grounding sensation beneath his feet, as if the earth whispered, *"Stay present."* And each night, reflecting on these captured fragments, he noticed a growing clarity that emerged gently, organically.

The evenings ended the same way; with a phone call home. What had begun as periodic check-ins soon transformed into an anchor, a comforting ritual connecting him to Sara, Nathan, and Grace. Initially, Waldo convinced himself these calls were solely to reassure them he wasn't drifting away, but now, he recognized his own need for these conversations—moments that tethered him firmly to what mattered most. "How's Grace?" he asked Sara one evening, leaning against the balcony as a cool breeze brushed past.

"She had her final exams and college tours. She's buzzing about the future."

Grinning from ear to ear, Waldo exclaimed. "Tell her I'm waiting to hear all about those campus visits and to see her in that graduation dress. I'm still recovering from how perfect she looked on stage during her recital."

"Oh, she's counting on your input." The smile was evident in Sara's voice. Then, gently, she added, "Nathan got another interview scheduled. Still not saying much, though."

"That's great. I'm sure he'll be ready to share more when he has good news."

Sara paused. "He's been asking about you."

The simple phrase caught his attention. "He has?"

"Yeah," she whispered. "I think he misses you more than he admits."

Waldo drew a deep breath, touched by a wave of emotion. "Tell him I miss him, too. Please."

"I will," she promised.

After a thoughtful pause, Waldo said, "Sara . . . thank you. I know this hasn't been easy."

"We're okay. Just keep doing whatever you need. And don't forget, we're right here."

Each call became proof that, despite the physical distance, their bonds remained steadfast. He wasn't escaping; he was strengthening himself so he could return whole.

Days continued to pass, Waldo absorbing the town's familiar patterns—the salty breeze off the sea, the comforting aroma of fresh bread from the local bakery mingling with freshly brewed coffee, and the fragrance of blooms lining quiet streets. The town played the same song it always had—only now, he was finally learning how to hear it. The difference wasn't dramatic but incremental. Before, he'd collected insights like puzzle pieces he never quite assembled. Now, he acted upon them, testing and refining each revelation like chords on his guitar. That was it, he realized—the act of playing, practicing, and repeating—mirrored this internal transformation. His progress wasn't about mastering everything at once, but embracing incremental growth. Each new realization layered onto the last, creating depth he hadn't anticipated but hoped for. He could sense the importance of not merely living to survive but truly experiencing life.

One afternoon, the café owner had remarked casually how storms reshaped the coastline overnight. At first, it seemed like surface-level small talk, but now, Waldo could see hidden wisdom within: what appeared as destructive chaos was nature's way of reshaping itself, creating new possibilities. He let the thought settle, and for the first time since arriving, he picked up his guitar, the strings cool beneath his fingers, the wooden body familiar in his hands. He strummed gently— not perfectly but with greater ease, the notes resonating softly, echoing his inner calm.

One night, after a long evening spent wandering the cliffs, Waldo dreamed of the maze again. For weeks, it had been absent—perhaps hidden beneath exhaustion or the distractions of daily life. He'd hoped its silence meant he had finally learned enough from it, but now, as sleep claimed him, the familiar sensation returned, a creeping aware-ness, whispers curling around his consciousness. Yet, this time, it offered him something new.

The hedges loomed as high as ever, stones scattered along the path, but the shadowy figure he'd pursued for months felt closer, almost tangible. His pulse quickened, drawn forward by the conviction that answers waited just beyond the next corner. As he rounded the last bend, his breath caught. A figure stood waiting, silhouetted in the dim, uncertain light. Waldo froze, afraid a sudden movement might dispel the moment. He shielded his eyes from the glare as the shape stepped forward, illuminated by a burst of light.

Slowly, his vision adjusted—and shock surged through him. Standing before him, calm and composed, was himself; although unmistakably different. A younger sharper-eyed Waldo looked back, carrying a confidence he'd never known at that age, perhaps at all. A translucent haze clung to the figure, gently rippling like fog. Waldo reached out, fingertips brushing the veil, making it move delicately, like a spider's web—not simply obscuring but softening the truths he'd long avoided confronting.

As the mist dissolved, Waldo saw himself fully; the same face and frame but with a stillness in his stance and clarity in his gaze. It wasn't a look of arrogance but of the quiet confidence that only comes from walking through fire. Shaped by experience, his eyes had known failure, and still, his shoulders no longer carried shame. This wasn't a reflection. It was a glimpse of who he might have become. Who he still could be.

A memory surfaced, vivid and unexpected: his childhood obsession with the *Where's Waldo?* books his mother once gave him. He spent hours poring over crowded illustrations, determined to spot the tiny figure who shared his name. Back then, it had felt important, though he never knew why. But now, staring at this younger, idealized self, he understood: the game mirrored a deeper hunger—the need to prove himself, to decode the world, to earn his father's approval. *"Everything you've ever wanted is on the other side of fear. Sometimes, the dragons you're fighting aren't out there—they're the shadows of procrastination, confusion, fears you've avoided,"* he heard his father say yet again. He hadn't grasped the meaning then, but here, in the heart of the maze, it rang true. His father had been preparing him all along—not just for life's visible battles but for the ones waged quietly inside. The ones that only grew stronger the longer they were avoided.

In silent acknowledgment, the younger Waldo raised his hand and placed it firmly over his chest. The gesture reverberated through him, but not just as a symbol—as a reminder. Waldo mirrored the movement, his palm meeting steady rhythm, emphasizing his presence, his choice.

A voice, one felt, not spoken, emerged inside him: *"What you accept as true becomes the life you live."* And just beneath the voice, another memory came to him, of something he'd once said to someone else, spoken as if for them but meant for himself: *"What you resist . . . doesn't disappear. It waits, circling back until you're ready to let it teach you."* Hearing those words again, especially echoing from inside himself, surprised him. But maybe that was wisdom: something you give away before realizing how much you need it.

As the understanding took root, the vision dissolved, the younger self folded back into him, leaving only the quiet resolve he'd long sought. He'd spent a lifetime chasing answers, but the truth was simple: the maze wasn't something to escape—it was something to accept and then to walk. "You've always had the power," the voice whispered again. "It's time to choose it."

Within the dream, Waldo calmly opened his eyes, seeing the maze still surrounding him, unchanged yet it no longer loomed.

It waited.

Not as an obstacle but an offering. A path he could finally walk, step by step, at his own pace. Especially now that he knew clarity wasn't a noise to escape but a melody to follow. And for the first time, it sounded like something he could dance to.

Waldo blinked into the dim morning light, his heart steady, the rhythm of it like the first clean chord after silence. He lay still, the edges of the dream disappearing but the lesson remaining. He was no longer chasing shadows, and the emptiness he'd carried for so long had finally lifted. It wasn't replaced by easy answers but by something more powerful: the realization that his next steps would be shaped entirely by the belief he chose to carry forward. The journey he'd embarked upon—the wandering, the uncertainty, the restless quest for meaning— echoed those childhood hours spent hunched over pages of *Where's Waldo?* His younger self had endlessly sought a figure hidden among crowds, unaware he was rehearsing for life's greater search: finding himself within chaos. His mother had seen that in him early, handing him that book with a knowing smile. Even then, she seemed to understand: he wasn't just drawn to puzzles—he was built to search. And maybe the point was never to find something but to keep looking anyway. The answer had never been out there. The answer was *him.*

His father's words echoed again clearly: *"The two most important days in your life are the day you are born and the day you find out why."* His father had known life wasn't a straight path but a maze; full of misdirection, dead ends, and quiet traps, also warning him that, *"Not everything that looks right will get you there."* Waldo saw it now: every wrong turn taught resilience. Every wall, an invitation to adapt.

Waldo had waited too long for someone else to hand him all the answers he sought. But no external validation, achievement, or perfect pathway could define that. The "why" wasn't a riddle the world could solve for him—it was a purpose he had to forge himself, a reason he had to define from within.

Where's Waldo? had been the child's game of finding himself in the crowd. But "Who's Waldo?"—that was the grown-up question, a challenge of identity, authenticity, and self-belief; not as someone who had to be found but as someone who had always been becoming.

Chapter 13
Homecoming

Morning light arrived slowly, soft and full, as if the world itself had taken a breath with him. Waldo hadn't moved for some time. He wasn't asleep, just lying still, quietly changed.

He turned toward the window as the room brightened, the rhythm of the waves calling him to rise. Each crest and fall beyond the glass felt like punctuation to a deeper understanding: that clarity doesn't land like lightning—it arrives like music. And now, finally, he could hear it.

He sat up slowly, a quiet certainty in his limbs. Once dismissed as hollow, the phrase filled his mind again: *"Whether you think you can or think you can't, you're right."* It wasn't cliché anymore. It was his mantra.

He looked around the small, tranquil inn room. The rhythmic sound of waves filled the air, inviting him to the window. Standing there, Waldo watched morning sunlight dance across the ocean, each wave a gentle affirmation, each breath of salty air carrying quiet hope. The vastness didn't diminish him; it connected him to something greater, a reminder that there was space for him, exactly as he was. Turning from the window, Waldo reached for the notebook on the bedside table, filled with fragmented thoughts and scattered observations. Like musical notes he'd once struggled to master, each scribble, each sketch, and every hesitant thought now came together into a melody uniquely his own. They weren't random pieces anymore; they formed the music of a life reclaimed.

He recalled those early guitar lessons, clumsy and frustrating, and smiled at how closely they mirrored his recent journey. Music, like life, wasn't about instant perfection. It was about patience, consistent practice, and the courage to keep showing up, even when it felt hard. The waves outside echoed that lesson clearly: growth happened one note, one chord, one step at a time. His journey had been a crescendo and not because it was flawless but because he had persisted, learned, and evolved.

Now, he was ready. Ready to return home—not as the Waldo who had departed burdened by doubt and uncertainty, but as a man who finally knew himself. Who had learned to untangle his knots carefully, thread by thread, and confront his dragons—not with force but with understanding.

Waldo closed his notebook, running his fingers across the worn cover before slipping it into his bag—one final comforting action that marked the close of this chapter. With a sense of readiness that felt new yet deeply familiar, he picked up his guitar, slung it over his shoulder, and took one last look at the room. Nothing remained behind. He had safely packed everything essential—most importantly, within himself.

He stepped toward the door, where light traced the threshold just like it had shimmered and danced on the ocean in Gull's Rest. Not only was he returning to his family, but he carried the stillness of those waves, the rhythm of their patience. He was bringing himself home.

Waldo stood at the counter of the coastal inn, nodding politely as the clerk handed him his receipt. His eyes drifted toward a nearby rack of souvenirs, recalling the shop by the art gallery he'd visited. Among miniature lighthouses and postcards, one small keyring caught his eye —a delicate seahorse dangling from its chain. He picked one up, turning it thoughtfully between his fingers, the seahorse's graceful curves reminding him of a tiny dragon—harmless if tended but dangerous when allowed to grow unchecked. The symbolism resonated deeply.

He bought three keyrings.

As he returned to his car, Waldo held one keyring firmly in his hand, using it as a reminder to always keep his lessons close and accessible. The other two he placed carefully in his bag: gifts for Nathan and Grace. He'd wait for the right moment, ready to share the wisdom of recognizing their dragons, managing them early, and always keeping their keys organized and within reach, similar to the tools they'd wield when needed.

Sliding into the driver's seat, he transferred his keys onto the new keyring, feeling the gentle *clink* of metal—a reassuring sound that echoed the harmony he sought within. The seahorse charm caught the morning light, scattering a soft glow across the dashboard. It stirred a memory deep within him, recalling the sparkle in Sara's eyes the very first time they'd met—the quiet strength, patience, and unwavering love she had always embodied. His grip tightened briefly on the wheel. He had feared losing that love, yet now realized it wasn't something to clutch in desperation but to nurture with intention and care.

He reached for the ignition, then paused. Across the street, the small café he'd passed earlier in the week came into view, with its sun-striped awning, ivy curled along its brick façade, a hint of music drifting from inside. Back then, he hadn't been ready to sit still. But now, he found himself opening the car door again. Today, he stepped inside, not as a man searching but as someone learning how to stay.

The waitress greeted him with quiet ease, guiding him to a table near the window. He ordered without looking at the menu—something simple, warm—and let the world slow around him. Outside, the town moved gently: locals chatting over benches, seagulls looping in lazy arcs. No urgency. No chasing.

As he ate, Waldo found himself chewing slowly, savoring each bite without thinking ahead to what came next. It struck him how often he'd lived like that, sprinting toward the next goal, the next solution, as if happiness lived on the other side of accomplishment. But fulfillment, he realized, wasn't waiting at some milestone. It was already here, woven into the act of pausing, of noticing, of truly tasting what life had been offering all along. This, too, was part of the journey. Not just the breakthroughs but the stillness in between. The uncelebrated moments. The quiet lessons missed when life is lived in pursuit rather than presence.

As he glanced up, he noticed the subtle shift that hinted at summer's approach. In a few weeks, Gull's Rest would fill with vacationers: strangers hoping to trade noise for peace, burden for breath. Maybe some of them, like him, would find a magic touch of wisdom in their time here, a souvenir not bought in shops but carried quietly home in the heart. A wave of gratitude for the grace of having been given time rose within him. It was time to walk away. Time to listen. Time to return.

By early afternoon, the road stretched out before him, but he didn't feel pressed to conquer the distance. It wasn't about arrival anymore. It was about carrying what mattered with him—the rhythm of Gull's Rest, the stillness of its mornings, and the quiet courage he'd begun to recognize as his own. He considered calling to announce his return but decided against it. Sara deserved more than words; she deserved to feel the change in him, to see firsthand the clarity he'd discovered. With the decision made, Waldo started the engine and pulled away from the coastal town, the tiny seahorse swaying gently with each turn. The road ahead was more than just the path home—it was his journey toward becoming the partner, father, and man he now believed he could be.

He is ready.

~

When Waldo turned into his driveway, the house appeared exactly as he'd left it—warmly lit, quietly waiting. Yet, everything felt different, more vivid, as if he were truly seeing it for the first time. The dashboard clock read 9:52 p.m.—late enough for Grace to be asleep and for

Nathan to still be at work. So, for now, the house settled into its night-time hush.

He switched off the engine, fingers brushing the seahorse once more before stepping outside. He was halfway up the walk when the porch light snapped on. A second later, the front door creaked open, and Sara stepped into view—barefoot, holding a towel from the laundry, her eyes wide.

"Hey," Waldo said quietly, heart steady despite the moment's weight.

"You're home," Sara said, her voice carefully measured.

"I am."

A silence stretched between them, fragile and expectant, but neither moved, waiting for something intangible to settle.

"Come in," she finally offered, stepping aside.

Waldo crossed the threshold into the embrace of their home—taking in the lingering scent of cinnamon and vanilla, family photos along the hallway walls, and Melody watching from her shadowy corner. It was familiar yet entirely new.

Sara closed the door behind them. "Nathan's at work, and Grace turned in early—big week at school." She hesitated, then asked, "Should I wake her?"

He shook his head. "No. Morning's better. I'd rather she see me . . . when she's fully awake." He placed his duffel down, leaving the guitar slung reassuringly across his back.

Having laid the towel down over the back of a chair, Sara stood nearby, her arms loosely folded, assessing him, protective of herself and of the moment. Finally, she spoke. "Did you find what you were looking for?"

He met her gaze directly. "I found enough to start."

Sara's eyes softened, searching his face for confirmation of what her heart wanted to believe. Her posture relaxed, as if an unseen burden was lifting. "Are you okay?"

He nodded. "More than I was. And ready to figure out the rest—with you."

An understanding passed between them, a promise they both recognized but didn't yet voice. She hesitated, then turned toward the kitchen. "I'll put on some coffee," she offered, almost automatically, a gesture of return as much as warmth.

As Waldo followed Sara into the kitchen, his gaze settled briefly on the single mug placed neatly on the counter—hers alone. It was an insignificant detail, yet it revealed how subtly her life had adapted to his absence. He exhaled and slipped the guitar from his shoulder, setting it gently by the bookshelf. It wasn't just an instrument anymore, but a part of his voice. Melody padded quietly behind him, hopping onto a nearby chair.

Sara moved through the kitchen without a word, opening the cupboard and retrieving another mug, setting it beside her own—side by side—deliberate, unfussy. The scent of fresh coffee soon filled the kitchen, reminding him of intention. It wasn't habit. It was choice. It felt symbolic. She turned toward him, leaning against the counter. "I wasn't expecting you home tonight," she admitted, her voice cautious yet hopeful. "I wondered why you didn't call."

"I thought a surprise would be better," Waldo said, his thumb tracing the mug's edge. "I knew I wanted to come home, but part of me didn't know if you'd want me to, or if you were ready for me to."

Sara studied him for a long moment, the question forming behind her steady gaze. "Are you staying?" The vulnerability in her voice caught him off guard, and the words hovered, fragile as breath between them.

He met her eyes. "Yes. For good."

She nodded faintly, her fingers curling tighter around the mug, as if holding onto something more than her cup. "You said you found what you needed. But what did that actually mean, Waldo? What were you really looking for?"

Waldo paused, choosing his words with care, offering Sara the honesty she deserved. "When I left, I thought I was chasing answers. I didn't know what they'd look like—I just knew I felt broken." I kept hoping something out there would fix it, but there was nothing to find

—only something to finally face—the part of me that stopped trusting myself."

"Then what was it about?" she asked softly.

"I kept waiting for one clear moment . . . But it never came. And that's when I discovered that it wasn't a moment—it was a process. No magic fix. Just time. And honesty. And the decision to stop running." A breath passed. Then something else surfaced—something he hadn't expected to echo back at him. "There's a line I told someone once," he added. "That what we resist doesn't vanish—it waits. Circles back until we're willing to let it teach us." His voice lowered. "I thought I was helping them. Turns out . . . it was for me too. I just didn't know it then."

Sara said nothing, but her stillness told him she understood.

"It was about stepping away long enough to see clearly," he explained. "To realize I'd spent years chasing the wrong things—validation, certainty, approval from others. I was searching for something external, something I thought would give me purpose."

Sara nodded, absorbing his words, her eyes filled with gentle comprehension. "And now?"

"Now," Waldo said firmly, stepping closer as if reinforcing the truth of his words, "it's not about chasing something out there; it's about standing still, learning to live with who I am—flaws and all. To be human. To be uncertain. To be enough as I am."

"That sounds like the man I used to believe in."

"It wasn't an easy road, and I'm still learning. But this—coming home to you, to the kids, feeling genuinely present—this is exactly what I needed."

For a moment, silence enveloped them. Melody slipped from her chair, weaving softly around Waldo's ankles as if sensing the change in the air. As they sat down, he reached his hand across the table, palm up. A gesture without pressure—a hopeful invitation. Sara hesitated, then slid her hand into his. Her grip was light at first, then firm—a silent agreement, as if to say she wanted him there. "I'm glad," she said. Her voice cracked slightly, but her eyes were clear. "I needed to feel this again; being wanted, I mean. Being here with you like this." She drew in a breath, slow and real. "I forgot how much it mattered. And how much I missed it."

"I did too," Waldo said, the words catching in his throat. "I'd forgotten what this could feel like."

They sat like that for a long moment—not fixing, not defining, just holding onto something delicate but newly tangible.

Sara exhaled. "Nathan and Grace will be glad you're home."

Waldo smiled at the thought. "I missed them. And you. All of you."

Sara studied his face, as if seeing it for the first time. "You're different," she said, but not with suspicion, just amazement.

"I'm not running anymore," he said. "I'm finally here."

Their eyes held, silently sharing an understanding that no words could fully convey. They weren't the same two people they had been before he left. But that was exactly the point—maybe now, they could build something deeper, something stronger, from this fresh understanding. *Something more in tune.*

"So, now what?" she asked.

Leaning forward, Waldo pressed his forehead against hers, feeling the strength radiating between them. "I'm here," he whispered, his voice thick with emotion. "I'm ready."

"Then, we both are," she breathed.

The world beyond the kitchen fell away, leaving only the quiet intimacy of this moment—the shared promise, the gentle renewal. Together, grounded in love and a presence hard-won, they were finally ready to face whatever lay ahead. He didn't know what came next, but the dragons had grown quieter. And the seahorse on his keyring? Still steady. Still there. He no longer needed the whole map—just the courage to take the next turn with eyes wide open.

They sat there for a long while, neither speaking, both listening to the hum of the house—a silence no longer filled with distance, but with presence. Not everything was resolved, but something had begun.

Chapter 14
A Life in Focus

The morning light had a different hue now—mellowed and golden. As Waldo moved through the kitchen, he felt as if he were reacquainting himself with his own life. Some time had passed since he'd returned from Gull's Rest, yet something in him still felt newly awakened, like he was seeing the familiar through clearer eyes. It wasn't a dramatic transformation but a subtle shift, like the world had tilted slightly, revealing details he had never noticed before. His routines no longer felt like obligations but quiet acts of engagement— each moment infused with a newfound awareness. Making coffee, folding laundry, feeding Melody—no longer chores but a rhythm he'd finally stopped resisting. There hadn't been many chances for him to practice his new mindset, but the decision held steady within him. The relentless weight of seeking external validation had loosened its grip. He wasn't free of it entirely, but he could feel himself letting go, bit by bit, choosing his own steps instead of waiting for permission to take them.

Waldo sat at the kitchen table, his notebook open—worn and honest. For months, it had caught the fragments he hadn't known how to say aloud. But today, as he flipped to a fresh page, he wasn't there to observe; he was there to shape what came next. He paused—not from doubt but because it mattered. More than he could name. This wasn't about errands or obligations. It was about reclaiming authorship, naming what mattered and moving toward it. He had spent years letting life move him, reacting instead of directing. But now, he was no longer waiting. There had been too many mornings when the days blurred, when intention gave way to inertia. He had stopped noticing. Stopped choosing. But not today.

He wrote the first heading in bold letters:

Reset and Rebuild

Underneath, he let the tasks spill out—not as burdens but as choices. Each action a deliberate step forward, a rhythm, shaping the next chapter:

Restart guitar lessons—no more skipping.
Email Victor—clearly confirm my return date for ten days from now. Set expectations directly.
Follow up with Dr. Benson—follow through, no hesitation.
Declutter the den—clear the space, clear the mind. Let go of what no longer serves.
Tackle yard work—restore what winter has worn away.
Paint the fence—let spring speak through the wood.
Fix cabinet door—begin where neglect once lived.
Daily walks—clear my head, reconnect with myself each day.
Practice mindfulness—just five mindful minutes daily.
Family dinner—plan intentionally, reconnect meaningfully.
Short getaway with Sara—a weekend away to recharge, reset our perspective.

There was much to do.

He tapped his pen, eyes drifting to earlier pages—fragments of a life once half-seen, now starting to make sense. For many months, these memories had felt like isolated moments, snapshots of another version of himself. But now, as he read through them, he saw them differently —not as echoes of the past but as clues. He had been untangling himself for a long time, even before he realized it. Maybe this notebook wasn't just a place to collect the past. Maybe it had been a blueprint for the future all along.

Flipping back to his new page, he saw *Reset and Rebuild* were about more than just cleaning up his life—they were about working to remove the threads of confusion, old fears, and habits that no longer served him. He then turned to another fresh page, wanting to write down lessons he's learned. His hand hovered for a second longer than necessary, an urgency tugging at him. But he caught it. Breathed. *Not this time.* He wasn't here to micromanage clarity; he was here to welcome it. So, without overthinking, he wrote:

Family, Growth, and What Comes Next.

He let the words sit there for a moment before he added a simple note beneath:

No more waiting. Start today.

Keyring of Lessons Worth Keeping:

Movement matters. Like in travel, progress comes from stepping forward—not waiting for certainty.

Let go of the map sometimes. Trust your instincts. Embrace the unexpected—my best decisions have come from that.

Small shifts create momentum. A single note becomes a song, a single brushstroke a painting. Every effort adds up.

Patterns reveal truth. The themes that kept repeating in my notes, in my life, they weren't coincidences. They were signposts.

He went back and underlined the last point. *It's time to apply what I've learned.* For the first time in a long time, Waldo didn't just feel like he was preparing for something. He felt like he was already in motion. He closed the notebook. Not to finish but to begin. He grabbed his coffee mug, finding it had gone cold, but he didn't need warmth in the cup. He had something better—direction.

Sara walked in, hair still damp from her shower, tucking her sweater sleeve over her wrist as she reached for a mug with practiced ease. She paused beside him, her hand brushing his shoulder—a gesture so simple, but it landed with meaning. No words. Just comfort. Waldo looked up, and she met his gaze with a soft smile before moving to the coffee pot. In that quiet moment, something unspoken settled between them—trust beginning to rebuild, not through grand gestures, but through morning rituals shared without effort.

She poured her coffee and raised an eyebrow. "Look at you—already up and thinking."

He nodded. "Yep, thinking. Trying to meet the day before it gets away from me." He glanced down at his notebook. "Feels good to be up with some intention. Center myself . . . instead of catching up from behind like I used to."

She smirked over her mug, the edge of her voice teasing. "We'll see how long that lasts."

Waldo grinned, savoring the spark in her tone. "Bet you a fresh pot I make it to Friday."

Before she could respond, a sudden flurry of footsteps on the stairs signaled Grace's arrival. "Dad!" She practically bounced into the kitchen, her backpack swinging behind her, dropped to the floor. Her hug came quick, tight, her excitement pressing into him before she pulled away just as hastily, her energy already carrying her toward the fridge.

"Hey, kiddo," Waldo said, amused at the blur of movement that was his daughter. "Good to see you too."

Grace grabbed an apple and twisted the cap off a bottle of water before turning back to him with wide eyes. "When did you get back?"

"Late last night," he said. "You were already asleep."

She nodded, glancing at the clock. The momentary pause of excitement broke against the wave of urgency. "Oh, no—Mom, we gotta go," she said, stuffing the apple into her bag and slinging her backpack over one shoulder.

Sara took one last sip of coffee and sighed. "You always remember you're late after breakfast."

Grace leaned in and gave Waldo another quick squeeze. "I wanna hear everything when I get home, okay?"

"Deal," he said warmly.

Sara grabbed the car keys from the hook by the door and looked back. "See you later," she said with a quick wink. "Try not to miss me too much," she teased, hand on the doorknob.

Waldo grinned. "Too late."

And with that, the door swung open, the rush of morning pulling them both out into the world.

With the house momentarily quiet and Nathan still asleep, Waldo rinsed his coffee mug and set it in the sink. He cast one last glance at his notebook—fresh pages waiting for action—then tucked it under his arm and made his way toward the den. At the doorway, he paused, hand resting lightly on the frame. The den—still cluttered, still slightly chaotic—waited without judgment. He'd spent countless hours here: thinking, journaling, trying to sort through the noise. But today, it wasn't just a space to retreat to. It felt like a mirror. Every stack, every unopened book, every half-scribbled note—none of it accusatory, but all of it reminded him of how far he'd come. Of how far he still had to go. It held the echoes of postponed decisions—versions of himself he hadn't yet dared to confront. But instead of the usual tug of hesitation, he felt a quiet resolve. Not a surge. Not certainty. Just willingness.

One small action at a time.

Behind him, he heard the faint patter of paws and turned to see Melody padding into the room, pausing at the threshold as if sensing the energy. Then, without a sound, she leapt onto the nearby chair—the one Waldo always meant to give away but never could. She didn't meow. Didn't ask for anything. She just . . . settled.

Waldo watched her, folding his arms quickly, a private smile forming. "You've got it figured out, don't you?" he whispered. The soft rise and fall of her breath, her curling into herself, undisturbed by clutter or the noise of unfinished things, was a reminder: begin even before you're ready. He stood there a moment longer, something in him softening. Then, he stepped fully into the room and placed the notebook carefully on the desk. For a beat, he let the space speak. Then, he flipped back a few pages to the list that had started it all.

The den had become something of a time capsule—not in the nostalgic, well-preserved sense, but in the way that clutter accumulates when you stop making decisions. A graveyard of deferred intentions. Old files stacked in uneven towers. Books unread. Sticky notes bending at the corners, their reminders no longer relevant. He ran a finger down the list, its lines steadying him. Cleaning the den wasn't just about space. It was about permission. A clearing. A return. A choice. One step at a time.

Waldo took a breath and refocused, organizing his priorities, grounding thought into action.

Restart guitar lessons—no more skipping.
Email Victor—clearly confirm my return date for ten days from now. Set expectations directly.
Follow up with Dr. Benson—follow through, no hesitation.
Declutter the den—clear the space, clear the mind. Let go of what no longer serves.

He pulled his phone from his pocket and scrolled to his guitar instructor's contact. It wasn't easy, but it felt good to be making the call. He'd skipped enough lessons to know it hadn't been habit, but even the few he'd kept had shown him something: he wanted this. Not mastery. Just momentum. He hadn't gone as often as he wanted, but when he did, something clicked. The music had started to feel real—honest. Stepping away had been necessary, but now? Now, he was ready to pick up where he left off. Without hesitation, he hit 'Call.'

His instructor answered after just a few rings, his familiar voice carrying the same casual ease Waldo remembered. "Waldo! Good to hear from you. You ready to get back at it?"

A grin broke across Waldo's face. "Absolutely. When's your next opening?"

"Same slot as before, if you want it."

"Perfect," Waldo exclaimed. "See you next Monday."

"Great. And hey, don't think I'll go easy on you just because you took a break."

Waldo laughed. "Wouldn't expect anything less."

As he hung up, he crossed out the first item off his list:

~~Restart guitar lessons—no more skipping.~~

One Step Forward.

Next, Victor. Pulling up the email app on his phone, it took only a moment—simple, direct, no room for hesitation:

> Hey Victor, I wanted to confirm that I'll be back in a week from next Monday and ready to pick up where we left off. Let me know if there's anything specific that I should prepare for. Looking forward to catching up.

Send.

~~Email Victor—clearly confirm my return date for ten days from now. Set expectations directly.~~

He moved to his desk, yanking open drawers with purpose. Out went the outdated notes, the abandoned projects, the junk that had lingered far past its usefulness. He decided quickly, tossing papers and broken bits of the past into the trash can without second-guessing. The pile grew, and with it, a sense of lightness. And by the time he reached the last drawer, he could feel it—trajectory, space opening up, both around him and within.

He took a break, deciding to contact Dr. Benson. Wiping his hands on his jeans before dialing, a flicker of uncertainty rose within him. Realistically, he knew she would expect to hear from him, but part of him still doubted—not her, but himself. The last time they spoke, he'd been tangled in questions he couldn't answer, unsure if any of her guidance had taken root. He pressed 'Call.'

"Dr. Benson's office," came a receptionist's pleasant voice. "How can I help you?"

"Hi, this is Waldo Turner," he said, clearing his throat gently. "I was hoping to schedule one more session with Dr. Benson—if she has any openings soon."

"One moment, let me check." The soft clicking of keys filled the line, followed by a short pause. "Actually, she's between sessions— would you like for me to connect you now? You can talk about schedules then."

"Sure. Thank you."

There was a *click*, brief ringing, then a familiar voice came through —calm, grounded, unmistakably hers. "Waldo. It's good to hear from you."

He smiled, more than he expected to. "Hi, Dr. Benson. I was wondering if we could schedule one more session. I think I'm . . . on the right track. But I'd like to touch base. Wrap things up."

There was a warm pause—no rush, no judgment. "I'd love to see how you've been." He could hear the faint shuffle of papers on her end before she spoke again. "Let's see . . . We had been meeting on Thursdays. Would that still be good? Or do you need another time?"

Waldo glanced at his list, the ink still fresh from the morning's planning. Thursday. Two days away. Just enough time to keep the momentum going. "That's perfect."

"Great. I'll schedule you for this coming Thursday. Same time as before?"

"Yes, that works. Thanks, Dr. Benson. I appreciate it."

As he hung up, Waldo let out a slow breath. Something had shifted. Not because someone else told him what to do but because he'd reached for it. On his own. And she had scheduled him without hesitation. Her familiar voice hadn't just offered support—it had reaffirmed his new momentum. *Momentum.* That was it. He'd said he wouldn't wait for something to change. And now, he wasn't. He was becoming the change, making it real.

~~Follow up with Dr. Benson—follow through, no hesitation.~~
~~Declutter the den—clear the space, clear the mind. Let go of~~
~~what no longer serves.~~

A creak from the stairs pulled him from his thoughts. Nathan. Waldo glanced toward the doorway just as his son stumbled into view, heading toward the kitchen, fresh out of sleep, his hair a mess and his T-shirt wrinkled from the night before. "Morning," Waldo said, casually following him.

Nathan rubbed a hand over his face, squinting toward the sunlight streaming through the window. Then, as his eyes settled on Waldo, he paused, as if his brain was still catching up to what he was seeing. "Oh. You're . . . home."

Waldo smirked. "I am."

Nathan shuffled toward the fridge, muttering something unintelligible under his breath before pulling out the orange juice. He didn't bother with a glass, just took a long drink straight from the carton.

"Good to see some things never change," Waldo said, amused.

Nathan wiped his mouth with the back of his hand and leaned

against the counter. "Didn't think you'd be back yet."

"I got back late last night," Waldo replied. "Didn't want to wake anyone."

Nathan nodded, then took another swig of juice.

Waldo watched him for a beat, then decided to lean in—just a little. "So, Mom mentioned you've got a second interview coming up?"

Nathan's tone stayed low-key. "Yeah. Middle of next week."

There it was—that same casual vagueness Sara had mentioned. Like it was just another errand. "That's great. What's the position again?"

"Entry-level at Vertex Logistics. Operations Associate."

"Sounds solid. That's e-commerce, right?"

Another brief pause. "Yeah." Nathan said.

Waldo could feel it—the space Nathan left in his words, the way he wasn't filling in the blanks. It was a familiar feeling; one Waldo himself had battled for years. "You excited about it?"

Nathan shrugged, setting the orange juice down on the counter. "Yeah. I mean, I guess. It's a good opportunity."

Waldo tilted his head. "You 'guess'? You don't sound too sure."

Nathan sighed, running a hand through his already-messy hair. "It's not that I'm not sure. It's just . . . I don't know. It's a job, Dad. A good one. I just don't want to make a big deal out of it before it actually happens."

Waldo nodded slowly. "I get that."

Nathan glanced up, a little skeptical. "You do?"

A small smile tugged at the corner of Waldo's mouth. "More than you think."

Nathan didn't say anything, but something in his posture eased. This was new. Different. And maybe, Waldo thought, a step forward for both of them.

Nathan stretched with a groggy yawn, then grabbed a cup from the cabinet, filling it with coffee. "Anyway, I need coffee before I even think about interviews."

Waldo grinned. "Try actually sleeping at night instead of whatever you're doing."

Nathan rolled his eyes but snickered. "Guess I forgot what it's like having you around during actual daylight hours." He took another sip of coffee, then added with a teasing grin, "Kinda nice, actually—even if it comes with bonus lectures."

"I'll try to keep the lectures to a minimum," Waldo said, filled with a strange kind of comfort.

With one more final sip of his coffee, he headed toward the stairs. "I'm gonna shower. Maybe then I'll feel human."

As the sound of his footsteps faded, Waldo turned toward the window, taking in the quiet morning.

Time to move.

He grabbed his jacket off the chair and stepped outside, the crisp air waking him up more than his coffee had. Walking down the front steps, he paused—really looking, for the first time, since being so caught up in sorting himself out, that he hadn't really taken in what he'd returned to. The siding, the shape of the windows, the wear and tear—familiar, yes, but now seen with different eyes. Then, he turned his gaze toward the yard. Patches of overgrown grass, weeds snaking between the walkway cracks, flower beds still asleep from winter. The fence definitely needed fresh paint. The mailbox leaned slightly to the side, another reminder of something he'd meant to fix and never did. Nothing new—just things he'd stopped seeing before. He exhaled, hands in his pockets. It didn't feel like failure. It felt like potential.

His thoughts drifted back to Nathan. A job interview. An actual opportunity. Waldo had meant what he said—he understood where Nathan was coming from. He'd spent so much of his own life waiting for the right moment before moving forward. But he also knew that, sometimes, you had to take a step before you felt ready. Maybe Nathan wasn't convinced yet, but he was on the move. And that was enough for now. Waldo stepped back onto the porch, his list waiting inside. A fresh coat of paint, a bit of elbow grease, a sense of direction. He could work with that.

As he opened the door, he felt the momentum building—not just in tasks checked off but in meaningful progress. He wasn't just cleaning up messes; he was laying a foundation. Each step forward, whether fixing a mailbox or reconnecting with his children, was intentional. It was progress.

The afternoon light slanted through the windows as Grace, a whirlwind of noise and motion, charged through the front door. "Dad! You're still here!" she said, dropping her bag by the door and bounding into the kitchen. "I figured you'd be off doing mysterious dad things by now."

Waldo barely had time to react before she enveloped him in a quick, tight hug. Warmth rippled through him from her enthusiasm and from realizing how much he'd missed these small moments. He lingered an instant longer, savoring the reconnection before letting her go. "I'm here," he said, smiling. "And you look like you have news."

Grace pulled back, her eyes sparkling with excitement. "Guess what? I got into two of my dream schools! I've scheduled campus tours: one for the weekend after graduation and the other for the following week. Can you believe it?"

Waldo exhaled, pride and realization washing over him. His daughter was stepping into the next chapter of her life. "That's incredible, Grace. Which ones?"

"Ithaca and Emerson!" she beamed. "Still waiting to hear from a few others, but I wanted to get these locked in early." She paused, then added with a grin, "Mom said you wanted to weigh in on my graduation dress. Don't worry—I've got options."

Waldo chuckled. "Good, because I plan on giving my very serious, well-thought-out dad opinion."

Grace grinned. "That's exactly what I was counting on." She plopped down at the table. "I've got a theme for my outfit choices."

Waldo raised a brow. "A theme?"

She smiled mischievously. "I'm calling it 'understated elegance with a dash of main-character energy.'"

He chuckled. "So, basically your recital look?"

Grace rolled her eyes playfully but laughed. "Hey, that was a great outfit. And I crushed that solo."

"You did. You really did."

She looked up, surprised by the weight in his tone.

"You had this confidence in you," he continued. "That whole performance—you didn't just play the notes, Grace. You owned the room."

Grace blinked, her smile faltering a little as something deeper flickered across her face. "I wasn't sure if you noticed," she said. "You looked kind of far away that day."

Waldo's expression transformed, regret brushed with gratitude. "I did notice. I just didn't know how to show it then. But now? I see it clearly. You've got something special, Grace. Don't ever hide it."

Grace gave a small, shy smile—the kind that didn't need big words to tell him what she was thinking. "Okay, Dad," she said softly, returning her focus to her notes. "Thanks." She tucked her hair behind her ear, then turned toward the door where she had dropped her bag. With a quick pivot, she walked back, unzipping it to pull out her laptop and notebook. "I was just about to start on my project. You busy?" she asked, motioning for him to follow as she headed toward the dining table, like it was the most natural thing in the world. A small but meaningful switch.

Waldo didn't hesitate for a second. "Nope. What do you need?"

As she laid out her materials, she explained her topic with the rapid enthusiasm only she could manage, pulling Waldo into eager discussions at the dining table. He wasn't just physically present now—he was truly engaged, feeling fully alive in her excitement. It wouldn't come without effort, but Waldo was committed to rebuilding his family. It was all about connections, confidence, and trust. Not starting over but starting forward.

And that, too, felt like progress.

∾

From a distance, just outside the edge of the dining room, Sara watched quietly, noticing the ease in Waldo's smile, the warmth in his attention. He seemed more . . . alive. Like the man who had made her believe in forever. Optimism stirred quietly within her, a delightful idea that perhaps he was really finding his way back to life. To her. To them. Not just physically but emotionally. Grace's eyes mirrored it too, sparkling with a newfound radiance.

Later that night, as they prepared for bed, Sara paused by the bedroom doorway. From this distance, she watched Waldo fold his shirt with deliberate care, noticing details she hadn't appreciated in a long time. Over the past few days, Sara had felt the shift. She had witnessed Waldo attempting to change before—moments where he'd promise to be more present, only for old habits to pull him back into detachment. But this time, it felt like it was more than just a fleeting burst of self-improvement. That he was genuinely enduring transformation. She had watched him in the small, everyday moments; the way he listened without distraction, lingered in conversations instead of rushing through them, how he showed up in ways that mattered. It was even in the care he used in tuning the guitar well before it was needed. It wasn't grand gestures or sweeping declarations of change. It was consistency. And with every minor act, the anxiety that had once shadowed their relationship—the hesitation to trust, the guardedness that had built up over time—faded.

In response, Sara softened. Laughing more. Sharing more. Trusting more. Letting go. The tension that once sat on his shoulders, the restless energy that used to make him feel so far away even when he was standing right in front of her, wasn't there. She remained in the doorway, the words taking shape slowly before she spoke. "I can see your effort, Waldo. The kids too. It's been so wonderful having you back with us. And I mean more than just physically."

Waldo glanced up, his hands stilling for a moment before he placed the shirt neatly on the chair and turned to face her. The silence stretched between them, words not feeling like enough to express his appreciation for her.

Sara stepped closer, resting her hand lightly on the edge of the dresser. "How are you feeling now that you've been home for a few days?"

He sighed in relief, as if releasing a weight that he no longer needed to carry. "I feel so much different than I did before. And not just in one way. It's like everything changed. For too long, I was chasing . . . something—some idea of what my life was supposed to be. And in doing that, I lost sight of what was real, what was right in front of me. You, the kids . . . us."

She searched his face, taking in the sincerity behind his words. "You sound so sure. But you had been sure before. What makes you certain it will stick this time?"

Waldo reached out, his fingers brushing gently against hers. His heart tightened from the newfound awareness—this was vulnerability. Something that had been terrifying before but felt right in this moment. His voice emerged steady, grounded in the sincerity he finally trusted. "Because this isn't just words. I'm feeling it, Sara. Living it. And I don't want to go back—I want to fight for what we have. For you. For Nathan and Grace. For the life we can build, not the one I was afraid I was losing."

"I like that," she said with a small smile. "You seem . . . steady, like you've finally found your footing." Her words carried the weight of her hopes.

Waldo's lips curved into a slow grin. "I think so. For once, I'm not running. I'm ready to face it all—even the dragons."

She took his hand and gave it a gentle squeeze. "Dragons, huh?" she teased, humor flickering in her eyes.

Waldo chuckled—then saw it. A spark. Familiar, yet startling—like a light rediscovered after years of dimming. It was the same raw joy he'd once seen on Grace's face the Christmas morning she unwrapped Melody as a kitten, as if the universe had handed her something perfect. That awe—innocent and unguarded—now lit Sara's expression, and it stirred something in him he hadn't felt in years. The memory of their early days came rushing back—her effortless laugh, the quiet beauty in her eyes that never needed adornment. She had once made him believe in forever. And standing here now, he felt it again. Waldo chuckled, warmth blooming in his chest. "Yeah. They're smaller now—or maybe I've finally learned how to handle them."

They stood in comfortable silence for a moment, just holding hands. This was the man she had always known was there. Sara reached up, fingertips grazing his cheek—a touch light but filled with meaning. "Then let's face them together."

For a brief second, Waldo considered saying everything—the dark nights of doubt, the fear that had followed him like a shadow, the countless moments of wondering if he would ever find his way back. But then, as he looked at Sara, he realized she didn't need to hear all the stories tonight. This time, presence said more than any confession could. "I'm not perfect," he said instead. "And I'm still figuring things out. But I'm here. I'm trying."

"That's all I've ever wanted," she said, her voice soft and filled with longing. "Just for you to be here." She stepped into him, resting her head on his shoulder, letting his presence do the rest. It had seemed like years waiting for him to come back. But now? She wasn't waiting anymore. He is here. Fully, undeniably, here. Sara lifted her head slightly, her lips parting as if to speak, but no words came. She didn't need to say anything.

Waldo saw her lingering doubts, her private fears, but also the unwavering belief that somehow, they would find their way through. It was all there—the weight of their past but also the fragile faith she dared to hold onto. He held her gaze, confident and unflinching, letting her see the man he was striving to become. Although not yet complete, he was no more lost. Slowly, he reached out, his fingers grazing the side of her face. The touch was electric, a quiet declaration of everything he couldn't put into words.

Sara closed the gap between them, leaning in, her lips touching his.

The kiss began tenderly, a gentle rediscovery, hesitant yet sure—like a promise whispered in the dark. But then, it deepened, carrying years of yearning, of unspoken words, of a love that had weathered storms but still endured. Waldo felt her exhale against his, the press of her hands anchoring him in place—as if she needed to be certain he was real. And he was.

Once again, in this moment, two became one. The world outside disappeared, leaving only this—this love, this resilience, this undeniable connection. When they finally pulled back, their foreheads rested together, breaths mingling, neither one moving away. Her eyes sparkled with unshed tears, emotion hovering just on the edge. They didn't need to say more. The kiss, the touch, the look between them—it carried a promise far more enduring than words ever could.

As they climbed into bed, the intimacy between them felt stronger than ever. Their partnership felt timeless, like an anchor—something steady in a world that would always be uncertain. They both knew the path ahead wasn't perfectly clear, but for the first time in a long time, that didn't matter. This was the beginning of something great—a new chapter in their marriage where they both learned to be present, vulnerable, and appreciate the life they had built together. They would walk it together—one step, one breath, one moment at a time. And as a symbol of that, tucked beside him on the nightstand, his notebook sat quietly—no longer a record of searching, but a companion waiting to walk with him into whatever comes next."

Chapter 15
Charting a New Path

The next two days settled into a rhythm, a routine that was both familiar and subtly transformed. Waldo moved through life at home with fresh eyes, noticing details he had long overlooked. Mornings were still a flurry of activities—Grace off to school, Nathan buried in work, Sara balancing a dozen responsibilities. Yet, instead of feeling like a passive observer, Waldo felt present, engaged in the cadence of their shared lives.

He continued refining his to-do list, striking off completed tasks and shifting others into focus. Each cross out made it feel like his life was finally aligning in the way he had always envisioned, especially with carving out time for guitar practice. He let his fingers find their way over the strings, reacquainting himself with the melodies he had once struggled to perfect. There was something grounding in the practice, an almost meditative quality that paralleled the quiet mindfulness sessions he had integrated into his mornings. Mindfulness. Presence. Simplicity. These concepts had once seemed like luxuries, ideas that belonged to someone else's world. But now, they were becoming his.

By late Wednesday afternoon, Waldo finally checked his inbox. One subject line stood out:

. . .

```
Confirmation: Return Date & Project Notes.
```

Victor. He exhaled as he opened it—the email was concise and professional, a verification of his return date, a brief note on upcoming projects, with one warm note:

```
Glad to have you back, Waldo.
```

He smiled. There were no questions, no pressure—just a steady, open-handed welcome. Yes. He was returning. But this time, it was on his terms. Not out of obligation, but with a clearer sense of what mattered —and a quiet spark of curiosity for what it might feel like to do the work differently.

∼

Waldo continued to carry that clarity through the rest of the day and into the next morning. As he slipped on his jacket, a faint trace of salt air still clung to the collar—a ghost of Gull's Rest. He paused for a moment, remembering that first quiet walk along the shoreline, the feeling of space widening inside him. That place had cracked some-thing open. This life he was building now? It began there.

When the time came for his appointment with Dr. Benson, he arrived early, stepping purposefully into the office building. The waiting room was as he remembered—soft lighting, neutral tones, the quiet hum of a small water fountain in the corner. There was even the same lavender scent in the air, yet something in the space felt different. Or maybe he was the one who had changed.

His fingers tapped lightly against the arm of the chair as he waited with a sense of anticipation. When the door opened, Dr. Benson's warm, knowing smile greeted him. "Waldo, come in."

He stepped inside, settling into the chair across from her. In all of his previous sessions, he felt like he was there to search for answers, but now, it felt as if he was there to simply have a conversation.

Dr. Benson took her seat and studied him for a moment before speaking. "You look changed."

Waldo chuckled, rubbing his hands together. "I feel changed."

She leaned in, her curiosity quiet but clear. "Tell me about it."

He took a breath. Where to begin? "I finally figured it out—the maze."

Dr. Benson tilted her head. "The dream?"

He nodded. "Yeah. All this time, I thought I was lost in it, trying to escape. But I wasn't lost. I was chasing something . . . someone. It was me. I was chasing myself."

She smiled. "And what does that mean to you now?"

"It means I don't need to keep running." His voice was steady, certain. "I've spent so much time fighting shadows, trying to fix things that didn't need fixing. But now? I'm here. I'm present. And I'm finally facing the things that matter."

Dr. Benson smiled, her silence encouraging him to continue.

He ran his thumb along the edge of his jeans, considering his next words. "I realized something else, too. About dragons."

She lifted a brow. "Dragons?"

He chuckled. "Yeah. The fears, doubts—all the things that used to haunt me—I realized I don't have to defeat them completely. I just need to keep them small, manageable." He was surprised how much fear still lingered around doing something as simple as showing up fully—not for others but for himself.

"That's a powerful shift, Waldo."

He gave a quiet breath of agreement, then reached into his pocket and pulled out a small object, placing it on the table between them. The seahorse key ring.

She glanced at it, then back at him. "What's this?"

"A reminder," he said. "For me. For Nathan and Grace. I bought one for each of us—because we all have our own dragons to keep small, our own mazes to navigate. It's my way of marking this . . . shift. A symbol that I choose to move forward."

Dr. Benson reached for the key ring. The small seahorse swung freely as she turned it over in her fingers. "That's quite a meaningful token."

He shrugged but exuded happiness. "It seems right." And it felt true.

Dr. Benson turned the seahorse keyring over once more, then looked up, her expression thoughtful. "So, how do you carry this home, Waldo? It's one thing to find clarity in stillness, but what happens when your clarity meets someone else's confusion?"

The question caught him. Not in a harsh way, but like a pebble tossed into a still pond, ripples forming. His mind flashed back to a session from months ago, where he had collapsed into this same chair, jaw clenched, voice low. *"I don't even know what I feel anymore,"* he had said. *"And even if I did, I wouldn't know how to explain it to anyone."* The fear of failing Sara, the heaviness of disappointing Nathan and Grace, the panic of being seen and still not being enough. He remembered her gentle silence then. Her willingness to wait. And now? "I think I finally know the difference," Waldo said slowly. "Clarity doesn't make things easier. It makes them worth facing. Even when it's hard."

She received his words with a contemplative stillness, giving them space to land.

"So, when my clarity meets their confusion," he continued, "I won't try to fix it. I'll stay. I'll listen. I'll show them it's safe to not have all the answers. Because that's what I wish someone had done for me."

Dr. Benson offered a small tilt of her head—a signal to go on.

"You helped me see that it wasn't about searching for answers somewhere else. It was about trusting myself. About finally listening." He paused, his voice steady. "Now, I understand—meaning doesn't arrive from the outside. It grows from how I show up, day after day."

"And how does that feel?" she asked.

"Liberating. But also . . . humbling. It's like standing at the edge of a forest. I can't see the whole path ahead, but I know I need to walk it, step by step. And that's okay. I've learned to be okay with not knowing everything."

Dr. Benson leaned forward. "What's next for you?"

"I've decided to take a different path from the one I'd been walking. I want to be more present in everything I do. A few weeks back, I helped Nathan prep for his interview—not just with advice but by really listening. And Grace? She asked for help on a school project, and instead of brushing it off or half-joining, I sat down and gave it my full attention. No distractions. No clock-watching. Just . . . being with her. I used to think presence was proximity. Now, I know better. It's not loud or flashy; it's just real." He smiled. "It's not about being impressive. It's about being intentional. Showing up with care, not just convenience. And it's not just for them—it's for me too. I'm playing guitar again. And I've started sketching out melodies—nothing polished yet, but I'm creating. I forgot how much that mattered to me."

Dr. Benson picked up her pen, jotting something brief—a note, a marker—as if recording the moment he stepped into clarity. "It sounds like you're not just living—you're engaging."

"Exactly," Waldo said, his voice warm with conviction. "I'm not chasing a finish line anymore. I'm here to build something meaningful. To show Nathan and Grace—through how I live—that life is a process, not a race."

When the session wrapped up a short while later, Waldo stood, slower this time, more grounded. He extended his hand. "Thank you, Dr. Benson. For all of it."

She rose and took his hand with both of hers, her expression soft but proud. "You did the work, Waldo. You didn't run from the hard parts. That's what makes the change real."

He nodded, emotion flickering in his eyes. "I'm not searching for a way out anymore. I'm here. And I'm not going anywhere." He hesitated, then let the next words out in a hush. "For a while, I really didn't think I'd make it back. Not just physically. I mean here." He tapped his chest lightly. "To myself. To them. I thought maybe I'd already missed my chance. But I didn't. And that's what I'm holding onto now."

She smiled. "Then, you're exactly where you need to be. And if you ever need a place to return to—you know where I'll be."

Stepping outside into the crisp afternoon air, a long-remembered song drifted through his mind—"Teach Your Children" by Crosby, Stills, Nash & Young. As he hummed the familiar tune, Waldo's own interpretation of the lyrics became clear—a reflection of his deepest desire: nurture them with your hopes, guide them with your truth. It was a reminder that the greatest legacy isn't what you leave behind but how you inspire those who follow.

The world that had changed for Waldo—his perspective reshaped by everything he had learned. Waldo walked to his car, pondering the part in all of this that he originally didn't consider. But now, he knew his rebirth wasn't just about finding himself; it was about the legacy he would leave behind for Nathan and Grace. They weren't just his children; they were an opportunity to pass on the wisdom he'd gained. The journey he had traveled—it was all preparing him to guide them, to help them navigate their own paths. Waldo smiled, feeling the resonance of that truth. The journey of becoming oneself was not just his greatest gift to embrace—it was the greatest gift he could give.

Later that afternoon, Waldo sat in the car outside a local hardware store, the receipt for a new mailbox tucked beside him on the passenger seat. The old one had leaned just long enough. Even though it was an essential errand, he hadn't rushed through it. In fact, he meandered through the aisles—not searching for anything in particular but feeling oddly grounded by the motion. The smell of lumber, the clatter of tools, the quiet hum of everyday people rebuilding and repairing—it all felt honest, ordinary in the best way. There was something soothing about it, this minor act of restoration. And as he drove home, with the window cracked and cool air slipping in, Waldo let his hand rest loosely on the wheel. No racing thoughts. No pressure to figure anything out. Just movement. Forward.

Back at the house, he set the mailbox on the porch. It wasn't procrastination—just pacing. A quiet belief that not everything had to be urgent to matter. Inside, Melody greeted him with a casual flick of her tail, then returned to her perch by the window. A breeze whispered through the open kitchen door, carrying with it the scent of cut grass and sun-warmed earth. Spring, without fanfare, was giving way to summer—slowly, steadily, like everything else coming into focus.

Standing at the sink, Waldo poured himself a glass of water, watching light dance on the cabinets. He wasn't in a rush to do anything else. Not yet. Stillness came first. There was no need to hold it all. No need to force clarity. It was enough, for now, to just be.

That Thursday evening, Waldo stepped onto the porch, guitar in hand, its familiar presence settling against him like an old friend. It had been his steady companion through his recent travels, always within reach, always waiting. He set it against the porch railing and eased into his chair, watching the sun dip below the horizon. The sky melted into twilight, its golden tones dissolving into dusky blue. The air carried a faint chill—not unpleasant but grounding, as if the world itself was holding him steady. Waldo leaned back, allowing his reflections to sink in. The evening hummed around him—the rustle of leaves, the distant laughter of neighbors, the rhythmic song of crickets tucked away in the grass. His mind drifted back to the beginning when everything felt undefined, when fear made every path seem like a maze with no exit. He thought of the nights spent lost in doubt, the long stretches of silence that felt suffocating. And then, the change—the light breaking through, the realization that clarity wasn't about certainty but about trust. Trusting himself.

Life itself was simple. The chaos came from the layers everyone wrapped around it—expectations, fears, the endless chase for certainty.

He had spent so long searching, running in circles, believing that fulfillment was waiting somewhere beyond him. But the truth was clear now: being present mattered most. Most people weren't ready to hear that. He hadn't been for a long while. They wanted complexity, something grand, something just out of reach, but maybe he didn't have to tell them. Maybe he could just live it and let that be enough.

He reached for the guitar, his fingers drifting over the worn wood before instinctively curling around the neck. It felt like an extension of himself now—a tether to something steady, something true. He exhaled slowly and strummed a chord. He remembered the initial days, how often he'd flung the pick down in frustration. His earliest taste of that frustration had come long before the guitar—at eight years old, seated stiffly at the old upright piano in their living room. His mother had tried, patiently, to teach him scales, gently correcting his fumbling fingers as they stumbled over simple melodies. But Waldo hated the mistakes, hated how foreign the notes felt. And then, there was his father—never malicious, just perpetually irreverent. Mid-practice one day, while Waldo scowled at the keys, his dad strolled past and quipped, "I used to play piano by ear . . . but now I use my hands." At the time, Waldo had groaned, the joke landing like a slap against his effort. But looking back now, he saw the intention. His father hadn't been mocking him; he'd been trying to break the tension. Trying to say it was okay not to be perfect. Waldo hadn't understood that music wasn't about mastery, that it was about feeling. About showing up, even when it wasn't perfect.

Now, years later, guitar across his lap, Waldo let his fingers move not with the aim of mastery but with the ease of memory. Each note felt like a return, not an achievement. He no longer flinched at missed chords. Each misstep was part of the rhythm—not a failure but a layer. A texture. The joy was in showing up.

He began to play instinctively, letting the music come without force. The song that came through his fingers was rough-edged, but honest. Not perfect—just real. Each note carried the shape of his journey: missteps, movement, return. This wasn't music for others. It was music for himself—not performance, but proof that he is still here, alive in the sound, alive in the moment. *Still becoming.* He smiled softly, his fingers telling the story he no longer needed words for. When he glanced down, he noticed Melody sitting nearby, her green eyes locked onto him. She must have followed him out. It wasn't her usual place, but she seemed to have decided the porch was just another part of her domain now. And for the time being, her purpose was simply to be a loyal audience—silent, patient, as if she already knew there would be another song.

With the rhythm from his guitar still reverberating within him, Waldo leaned back, the porch chair groaning softly beneath him as Melody stretched lazily against his hip. He let out a slow breath, letting the hush of night fold around him. As the final notes dissolved into silence, a deep sense of completeness settled over him. He felt fulfilled —not just as a man who played, but as an artist, a musician. It wasn't the precision of his notes or the complexity of the piece that made it so; it was the connection, the way each strum returned a fragment of himself. In music, he had uncovered a voice he hadn't known was there. A small smile rose. The vibrations still hummed in his fingers, reminding him this, too, was part of his journey. Still becoming.

His thoughts drifted back to a moment in his travels—a memory that had once felt fleeting but had resurfaced. He was sitting on a weathered bus-stop bench in the small beach town of Gull's Rest. Unexpectedly, a wiry man with silver hair and an eccentric grin had joined him. The lazy heat of the warm afternoon seemed to slow down time, and with no prompting, the man had begun talking. *"The moon, see, it governs more than the tides. It tells me when to plant, when to rest. It's all a rhythm—Mother Nature's rhythm. If you listen closely, you'll hear it. The trees, they turn up their leaves when rain's coming. The birds go quiet before a storm. Everything's connected, guiding you, if you're paying attention."* Waldo had tipped his head politely then, amused by the man's fixation on the natural world. But now, sitting here, the night air thick with meaning, he understood. The universe had always spoken to him, he realized; through signs, through strangers, through moments he had overlooked. Now, he was finally listening. He had walked, and he had learned, and in doing so, he had unraveled the mystery of Waldo. Neither an ending nor a secret—just a rhythm to share.

Night deepened; the porch quieted even more, the last of the neighborhood sounds fading into stillness. Melody had wandered off earlier, exploring the shadows of the yard like she owned every inch of it. Waldo remained seated, letting the stillness wrap around him, like the subtle space between heartbeats. But eventually, he rose, stretching gently. As he reached for the door, a soft *mrrrrp* rose from the porch steps. Melody sat just below, tail wrapped neatly around her feet, blinking up at him with her usual air of expectant royalty. Waldo chuckled and opened the door. "Come on, boss." She slipped inside without hesitation, brushing past his leg as though allowing him the honor of holding the door.

He set the guitar near the entryway and reached for his bag—the one he'd taken on the road and hadn't fully unpacked yet. It was more habit than purpose, the way he unzipped it, intending only to stow it into the closet so he could pull clothes out as he needed them. But something inside caught his fingers—a small box tucked beneath a sweatshirt. He pulled it out, paused, then opened it. There they were, the two remaining seahorse keyrings, resting against the velvet lining. He ran his thumb across one, the smooth metal cool under his skin. He had bought them for later—a symbolic gift, something to offer when the time felt right. Not now. Not yet. But soon. He imagined Grace clipping it to her lanyard one day as she stepped into her first college apartment. Or Nathan sticking it into his backpack without saying much, but carrying it anyway. Not because they needed a token, but because they'd remember. The dragons don't have to be slayed in one swing. Just named. Acknowledged. Kept in view. Waldo closed the box and placed it on the shelf of the entryway closet, nestled beside some old notebooks and a flashlight that hadn't worked in years. Not forgotten. Just waiting.

From the hallway, Waldo caught the gentle rhythm of home—Grace's laughter spilling from the living room, the sound of Nathan's footsteps overhead, likely grabbing something before heading out, and the soft *clink* of dishes from the kitchen. Sara's quiet humming floated out, grounding the space. They were all here—not gathered, but near. And so was he.

He stood there for a beat longer, then exhaled deeply and turned toward the stairs. He continued to think of Nathan and Grace as he did so—how much they'd grown, how many small moments had passed before his eyes, unnoticed. He wasn't fully in sync with them yet, but he would be, and this time, he wouldn't let the quiet moments slip past. He would be ready when they opened the door. And he'd meet them there—not with answers, but with presence.

He climbed the stairs, carrying the music, the memory, and the presence with him. The house wasn't silent. It was full of life. And for the first time in a long while, so was he.

Chapter 16
Creating a Map for the Journey

Waldo didn't wake with urgency anymore. What stirred him now wasn't adrenaline or anxiety—it was orientation. A quiet sense of outward purpose. Each morning arrived with direction, like his internal compass had finally settled and was now pointing somewhere beyond himself. Now, though, it wasn't gifts or goals he looked forward to—it was the joy of being fully present. That was enough. More than enough.

In just a few days, he'd return to work, reintegrating the inner shift with the outer structure of his days. But for now, he wasn't counting down. He was choosing how to show up—one action, one breath, one string of the guitar at a time.

On Monday, he kept his promise to himself. Guitar lesson. No expectations. No performance. Just practice. "You've stopped overthinking," his instructor said after a few bars, grinning. "It's finally coming from your hands—not your head."

Waldo strummed once more, letting the chord ring out. "You know," he said, chuckling, "I used to white-knuckle my way through these lessons. I'd stop every time I missed a note. Get so frustrated I nearly packed the guitar away for good."

"Most people do," he said, nodding. "Especially the ones trying too hard to get it perfect."

"But now . . ." Waldo looked down at his fingers, relaxed on the fretboard. "Now, I kind of like the missed notes. They remind me I'm still learning." Waldo smiled, strumming another chord.

One afternoon, Nathan stepped in through the back door, his shirt damp from the gym. The sound of running water drifted through the open window as Waldo worked outside, kneeling in the dirt, trimming a stubborn patch of weeds. A moment later, Nathan appeared on the porch, water bottle in hand, letting out an exasperated sigh. "Man, this guy at the gym has no idea what personal space is. Like, just because you lift heavy doesn't mean you have to invade mine."

Waldo smirked, not looking up from his work. "Welcome to the world of self-importance. Let me guess—he grunts loud enough for the whole building to hear?"

Nathan pointed at him with the bottle, frustration forgotten. "Exactly. Thank you. You get it."

Waldo chuckled softly, barely able to contain his happiness —not just because Nathan included him but because he'd almost missed these ordinary conversations entirely. The casual, insignificant details of his children's lives that, in reality, were anything but insignificant. They were the fabric of connection, the details he had overlooked for too long. And he was just in time to wake up, not missing any more milestones, including Grace's graduation, which the countdown for had officially begun. She made sure everyone in the house knew it too. Her excitement was impossible to ignore.

Late one afternoon, Waldo stepped into the kitchen, taking a well-earned coffee break from his work outside. He barely had a chance to take a sip before Grace pounced—swift and determined, much like Melody when she decided his lap was the only acceptable resting place. "Dad, you said you'd weigh in," she declared, appearing in the doorway, arms crossed with exaggerated impatience. "I have three options, and I need an actual opinion."

Waldo set down his coffee cup and gestured toward her laptop. "Alright, show me what I'm choosing between."

Grace grinned as she flipped the screen toward him, her enthusiasm bubbling over. The dresses varied—one classic and elegant, one bold and modern, and one playful with a hint of sparkle. Waldo studied them for a moment before tapping the second one. "This one. It's you—confident, sharp, and a little unexpected."

Grace's eyes lit up. "Really? That's what I was thinking!"

"Well, that settles it," Sara said, passing by. "Your dad, the fashion expert."

He held up his hands. "I just call it like I see it."

As Grace darted down the hall, her laughter echoing, Waldo lingered in the kitchen, fingers still curled loosely around his coffee mug. His eyes drifted to the family photo on the fridge—one taken years ago, Grace missing a tooth, Nathan with a bowl-cut he'd since erased from history. Waldo remembered that summer and how Grace had begged him to read her *The Velveteen Rabbit* night after night until she could recite entire passages from memory. He'd always rushed through it back then—exhausted from work, half-distracted, watching the clock more than the story. And Nathan, he remembered the bike they built together in the garage, how his son's small hands struggled with the wrench. Waldo had been impatient then, eager to finish. He hadn't seen what Nathan had really needed—time, presence, reassurance. But now, he saw it clearly; he couldn't rewrite the past. But he could show up for the present. Time passes so swiftly, he mused, and every moment seemed precious, a fleeting glimpse into this wonderful journey called life. And in moments like this—Grace twirling into adulthood, Nathan building his own path—he was doing just that.

∼

By Thursday evening, Waldo sat in the living room, taking a moment before dinner. He exhaled slowly, contentment settling into him. It was a different exhaustion—one born from genuinely investing in the people he loved.

A soft thump behind him broke the thought. Melody sauntered in, tail high, green eyes steady—that familiar feline air of quiet superiority. Waldo chuckled. "What? You checking to make sure I'm still here?" She didn't answer, of course. She never did. He watched her, arms loosely folded, the smile lingering. To truly live meant to notice. *Perhaps,* Waldo thought, *messengers don't always come with fanfare. Maybe some arrive in fur and silence.*

He got up, passing through the hallway on the way to the dining room, when he caught sight of his notebook—no longer tucked away but resting open on the edge of his desk. A few pages were filled, others left blank. He didn't need to write in it every day anymore. The urgency to capture everything had quieted. But he liked knowing it was there—waiting, steady, a companion in this new rhythm. A space for what comes next.

Dinner had already begun—all they were missing was Nathan, who was out. The air crackled with a different kind of energy—livelier, more engaged. Conversations overlapped, voices carrying a mix of anticipation and evolution. Grace was deep in discussion about which shoes would perfectly match the dress she and Waldo had settled on earlier in the week. She flipped between options on her phone while Sara weighed in with practical considerations. "You need something comfortable since you'll be on your feet for hours," Sara reminded her. "Also, don't forget, we need to complete your gown pickup and the RSVP list by Friday."

There was a momentum in the room, not just from their words but from the subtle shifts—the way everyone seemed to step forward, deciding, preparing for what was next. Waldo, watching the flurry of planning unfold, sipped his coffee in quiet amusement.

Sara glanced at him, arching a brow. "Well? Fashion consultant, any input?"

He smiled, shaking his head. "Nope. I already gave my expert opinion on the dress. I know when to stay in my lane."

Grace laughed, clearly unfazed. "Smart move."

When the front door opened, all heads turned. Nathan stepped inside, brushing off the cool evening air. Waldo was surprised to see him. He hadn't joined them much lately—balancing his part-time job and whatever else he kept busy with. So, dinner at home had become more the exception than the rule. But today, he had taken the day off for a callback interview, and now he hovered in the doorway, shifting his weight as if deciding how to say whatever was on his mind. He scratched the back of his neck, that usual armor of practiced indifference softened—not gone, just no longer airtight. "Hey," he said, his voice casual, but there was something underneath it. Something measured. Nathan exhaled, shoving his hands in his pockets. "I got something to tell you guys." A pause. "I got a full-time job."

Sara blinked. "Wait—what? You got a job? As in, officially? Where?"

Nathan grinned, his usual laid-back demeanor barely masking the significance of his words. "E-commerce company. Operations Associate. They offered me the job right after the second interview today."

Grace nearly knocked over her water glass as she jumped from her seat, excitement radiating from her. She let out a small squeal. "No way! That's awesome!"

A mix of emotions swelled within Waldo; pride, relief, eagerness. Nathan wasn't just getting a job; he was finding his footing. It felt like watching him truly step into adulthood—cautiously but undeniably.

Nathan, ever casual, shrugged. "Figured I should tell you guys."

"So . . . you're working in a warehouse?" Grace asked.

Nathan shook his head as he stepped further into the room, the hesitation fading from his posture. "Nah, I'll be working in their distribution division. Particularly logistics stuff—tracking efficiency, routes, systems performance. It's a solid start." He made his way to the counter, grabbed a plate, and began serving himself from the dishes still warm on the stove. "Didn't think I'd be hungry, but . . ." he trailed off, offering a lopsided grin.

Waldo caught Sara's glance, her eyes softening in that way they did when something mattered.

Nathan returned with his plate and slid into the empty chair beside Grace. "Anyway, since I'm home, I just wanted to share it with you guys first."

Grace gave a slow clap. "Look at you, getting all responsible."

Nathan rolled his eyes but couldn't hide the small smile tugging at his lips.

Waldo nodded, considering. "It sounds like a strong foundation. Logistics is a critical industry—especially in e-commerce. Do you think it's something you'll want to stay in?"

Nathan shrugged. "I don't know yet, but it's a genuine job with real responsibility. It's not just some temp gig—I'll be learning a lot about supply chains, efficiency models, and scalability. And unlike training," he glanced at Waldo with a small grin, "I won't be following in your exact footsteps."

Waldo chuckled. "Fair enough."

Sara's expression lit with pride. "Are you excited?"

Nathan hesitated. It wasn't a dream job, but it was his job. A stepping stone. A chance to prove himself. "Yeah," he said. "I think I am."

Sara leaned back, a sly smile playing at her lips. "So, does this mean we're officially living with a full-time adult now?"

Nathan snorted. "Let's not get carried away."

Grace grinned. "Guess that makes me the last kid standing. So, when do I get your room? Adults don't live at home forever."

Sara beamed. "Well, this calls for a celebratory dinner."

Waldo stood, clapping his son on the back. "Proud of you, Nathan." And he was—not just for the job, but for this moment; a weight he'd carried for so long that it felt like part of him finally gave way. There had been nights he'd wondered if he'd missed the window with Nathan entirely, if silence had stretched too far to cross. But now, across a table set with still-warm pasta, his son had come home, and brought his future with him.

Nathan, now done with the formalities, nodded, relieved to receive his family's acceptance. He ate quickly and headed upstairs, already pulling out his phone—likely making plans to meet up with friends.

The conversation at the table eased back into its natural rhythm, picking up right where it had left off. Reaching for the serving spoon, Sara absentmindedly stirred the remaining meal while glancing toward the staircase. "Well, that was very . . . Nathan," she mused with a small shake of her head. "Big news, minimal delivery."

Simultaneously, Grace and Waldo snorted before saying, "Classic." They looked at each other, a momentary expression of shock etching their faces, and then they laughed even harder. There was no denying he had rubbed off on his children, and it surprised him when he felt proud of this fact for once.

As dinner ended, Waldo carried the warmth of the evening with him. Tomorrow, the quiet would shift—emails, deadlines, decisions. But as he rose from the table, watching Grace and Sara clear the plates, he reminded himself: stillness didn't depend on silence. It came from orientation, from the compass inside him, steady at last. Waldo no longer needed a map—he already knew the way.

Chapter 17
Adventure in a New Quest

O n his first day back at the office, his footsteps echoed softly on polished floors as he returned to his desk. Settling into his chair, the computer screen came alive, a familiar routine without the old sense of pressure. He turned his focus to the stack of project updates waiting on his desk. He exhaled, straightening the first file. *Time to reengage my work brain.* As he flipped through the reports, he traced the threads of progress that had continued in his absence. Some initiatives had advanced, some had stalled, and a few had taken an unexpected turn.

Interesting.

What decisions had been made? What still needed input? It was like stepping back into a game already in progress—not trying to control the board, just taking notes to understand the new lay of the land. The old Waldo might have felt the need to prove himself, to reassert control, but now? He was catching up, taking it all in.

The gray monotony of office life hadn't vanished, but it no longer drained him. He approached each task methodically, finding small pockets of satisfaction in completing them. Before, it had always felt like an uphill climb, a battle to stay ahead. Now, it was naturally a pattern—one he had learned to move with instead of against. He wasn't consumed by the question of whether his job was meaningful. Instead, he directly did the work.

After settling in, Waldo pulled up his calendar. Tomorrow morning, he had a meeting scheduled with Victor—a quick debrief to get up to speed. Deciding to be as proactive as possible, he fired off a quick message:

```
Hey Victor, glad to be back. Let me know if you
want to meet sooner—I'm ready to hit the ground
running.
```

The response came quicker than expected:

```
Welcome back, Waldo. Let's stick with tomorrow—
gives you time to go through emails and project
updates first. Catch up, and then we can go right
away. Looking forward to it.
```

He appreciated the practicality. It was exactly what he needed—time to reacquaint himself before diving in. Turning back to his inbox, he braced himself. Hundreds of unread messages. A few flagged as important. The usual flood. He simply rolled up his sleeves, and got to work.

As the morning unfolded, Waldo's return didn't go unnoticed. Colleagues stopped by his desk, offering casual nods and easy smiles.

"Good to have you back, Waldo," someone said in passing.

"Office felt quieter without you," another added.

Even members of his team, who once came to him only when necessary, seemed to genuinely acknowledge his presence. Waldo felt like he truly belonged—something he rarely felt. Not just because others seemed happy to see him, but because he is here, engaged, and ready to step forward. During a coffee break, he listened to others' stories—not just nodding absently or waiting for his turn to speak, but actually listening. A coworker chatted about their weekend, a hiking trip gone laughably wrong, and Waldo chuckled because he truly enjoyed the story; not just to be polite.

The work itself had changed, too. Not in structure, not in expectations, but in how he saw it. He no longer felt like he was battling to prove something to himself. He wasn't waiting for validation, searching for some grand sense of purpose. He is here, doing what needed to be done. And that was enough. Even as he shut down his computer and grabbed his jacket, he felt a sense of satisfactory closure to the day—not the usual exhaustion or the lingering weight of unfinished tasks.

He stepped out into the evening air, the remnants of daylight casting a soft glow over the parking lot. He got into his car, looking forward to the drive home. By the time he merged onto the highway, the steady rhythm of tires against pavement punctuated the quiet hum of the city winding down for the night. Before, this drive had been nothing more than another obligation—twenty-five minutes of stop-and-go frustration, a dull transition between the demands of work and home. But tonight, he let himself notice; the way the fading daylight stretched golden streaks across the overpasses, casting long, fleeting shadows that flickered and disappeared. The way the streetlights blinked awake, one by one, as dusk settled in. He spotted people at crosswalks, weaving between cars, some moving with urgency, others pausing for a moment—checking their phones, glancing up at the sky. It was all so beautifully ordinary. *How had I missed this before?* A couple at a bus stop stood closely together, their laughter barely visible in the way their shoulders shook or how their heads tilted inward toward each other. Even the wind, threading through the trees lining the boulevard, felt like something more than just weather. It was movement. Change. A reminder that everything—even this drive, even him—was constantly shifting.

As the highway stretched ahead of him, his thoughts drifted back to his hockey days, but not with regret or longing. It was nothing short of appreciation. Back then, every game had been a strategy, every move a deliberate act toward a goal. That same energy, that same sense of purpose, now coursed through him, but in a broader, deeper way. Life itself had become the arena, and he was learning to play. Not to win. Not to prove anything. But to fully experience every moment.

As he neared his turnoff, he caught sight of a runner pacing steadily along the sidewalk, earbuds in, lost in their own world. Maybe that had been him, once—head down, lost in the motion, unaware of the surrounding details. But now? Now, he lifted his foot off the gas just slightly, allowing himself to take in one last stretch of the road home, making it a journey, not just a drive.

As they settled into dinner, the absence of Nathan was noticeable but not unusual. He was still finishing his last shift before starting his new job, and his place at the table—though empty—was still very much a part of the conversation.

"So," Sara said, glancing between Waldo and Grace. "I was thinking we should do something special this weekend."

Waldo lifted a brow, setting his fork down. "Special how?"

"A dinner to celebrate Nathan starting his new job, and Grace, since graduation is practically here."

Grace, mid-bite, perked up instantly. "Wait, does this mean I get to pick the menu?"

Sara smirked. "It means we'll discuss it as a family."

Grace groaned dramatically. "Which means we'll be eating something boring."

Waldo chuckled. "You know, most people don't think of grilled salmon and roasted vegetables as boring."

Grace pointed her fork at him. "And those people are wrong."

Sara shook her head, clearly used to this battle. "Fine. We'll compromise. But before we worry about food, let's make sure everyone's actually free. Nathan's schedule is still packed until Friday, and you, Grace, have that music showcase Saturday night with your friends."

Waldo nodded. "Sunday works for me."

Grace gave a thumbs-up. "Sunday sounds good." Then, narrowing her eyes, she added, "As long as there's cake."

Sara sighed. "We'll have cake."

Grace grinned. "Then, I'm in."

Waldo glanced between them, a love so profound filling his heart.

Later that night, Grace yawned, said her goodnights and disappeared into her room, already thinking about the next day's schedule. Upstairs, she paused in the hallway, her hand resting on the banister. She could hear her father humming faintly from the kitchen. For months, she had held her breath around the silence between her parents, reading the quiet like a weather forecast. But now, she felt like she could breathe again. She didn't say anything. Didn't need to. She simply closed her bedroom door behind her and smiled—a quiet, almost imperceptible thing. But real.

Sara, after a long day of juggling responsibilities, headed upstairs for a leisurely bath next, craving some personal time before bed. With the house settling into its own nighttime rhythm, Waldo found himself naturally retreating to the porch. Once, the porch had been nothing more than an escape—a refuge from the daily drain of life. But now it had transformed. Now, it was a sacred space, a place for lucidity, reflection, and renewal. It was deliberate. A touchstone for grounding himself in the present. The weight that had once pressed on him, the misinformed expectation to be someone he wasn't, had lifted.

He smiled to himself, aware of what was happening. The tangled web of falsehoods he had lived under—that his worth was tied to his productivity, that being needed was the same as being seen, that fulfillment came from chasing goals instead of living truthfully—was finally unraveling. The dragons? Shrinking. And with them, the self-imposed limits that had kept him stuck for so long. He wasn't chasing anything anymore. He wasn't lost. He was finally home within himself.

Waldo settled into his chair as the first drops of rain gently tapped the roof—soft, tentative, like the opening notes of a conversation. Soon, the steady rhythm picked up, enveloping the porch in a soothing melody. The occasional low rumble of thunder in the distance and the growing pools of water in the yard replaced the usual evening sounds, encircling the porch in a cocoon of rain-soaked serenity; not unlike a quiet guitar line, fingerpicked, patient, each drop echoing the kind of music Waldo had come to love most: honest, unhurried, and full of presence. Each drop seemed to cleanse not only the air but also any lingering heaviness that had once clouded his mind.

Now, learning to inhabit the moment—observing the world rather than rushing past it—he allowed his thoughts to flow freely, like the rain gathering along the porch railing, each droplet starting slowly, tiny points of clarity, before falling in its own time, unhurried and sure— steady, like the way Sara had started to look at him again: not with doubt, but with belief. He exhaled deeply, his breath mingling with the cool, damp air, feeling gratitude for the peace and insight he had reclaimed.

As he sat in the peaceful hush of the rain, his thoughts drifted back to the car ride after leaving Dr. Benson's office. He had been thinking about Nathan and Grace, about the tools he would pass down to them. *I know I need to pass this understanding on to them, but how? How can I help them start their own journeys without being burdened by expectations or fear? What could he give them that had taken him so long to find?*

Thinking of the past conversation with Nathan, he recalled the question about finding the right path. Back then, Waldo had fumbled for an answer, unsure of what to say. But now, as he replayed that moment in his mind, he knew exactly what he would tell him. *"Nathan, it's not about being on the 'right' path. What matters is that you start walking. The path will reveal itself as you go. Trust in the journey, even when it feels uncertain."* Not long ago, the idea of offering advice had panicked him, made him feel unfit to be their compass. What if he failed them? What if he said the wrong thing? But now, his role felt clearer and not because it had changed, but because he had. His children would walk their own paths, face their own uncertainties, and ask the kinds of questions he'd once been afraid to voice. But he had finally learned: they didn't need him to have all the answers—they needed him to walk beside them.

The lessons he'd gathered weren't a doctrine. They were seeds, lived truths, ready to be planted. Not as instructions, but as invitations. Insight, he now understood, wasn't for keeping. It was meant to be passed on as courage, replacing any uncertainty that remained.

He rose, his mind already preparing for the days ahead. Tomorrow, the routine would resume—work, family, familiar rhythms. But now, each step carried purpose. These things were meant to continue. To be passed on. And he knew, without a doubt, that tomorrow wouldn't be a return. It would be the beginning of a legacy he was finally ready to live out.

Chapter 18
The Man in the Glass

The rain from the night before had left a crispness in the air, a lingering freshness that made everything feel just a little more alive. The light outside was still dim, the horizon teasing the arrival of a beautiful sunrise. The sky carried the last traces of the storm, but the world itself felt renewed—and so did he. Waldo stepped into the kitchen, moving with energy as he brewed his coffee, savoring the warmth between his palms. Today wasn't just another day. Today was about preparing his children for the paths they would one day walk on their own. He had spent so long trying to untangle his own knots, chasing clarity, learning stillness, slowly relearning how to show up with intention, but now, the questions that once circled him like smoke had settled. He could feel the ground beneath him again.

The house stood—steady and unshaken—holding the weight of everything they'd built. Sara was still asleep, and he had seen Grace off to school, her being in the final stretch of her senior year—that in-between place where classes still ran, but the next chapter was about to begin. Then, as Waldo stood in the kitchen, with his coffee in hand as he watched early light stretch across the floor like a whisper, he heard the soft *creak* of stairs. Nathan appeared, already dressed—tie slightly crooked, hair still damp from the shower.

"You're up early," Waldo said, not surprised but moved at his son's effort.

Nathan gave a half-nod. "Didn't sleep much. Just . . . felt like I should get moving."

Waldo glanced at the time. Nathan still had a bit before he needed to leave—enough for a short walk. He gestured to the door. "Walk with me?"

They stepped out into the cool morning, shoes quiet on the pavement. The street was hushed—birds in the distance, the low hum of a world slowly waking. They didn't speak right away, but the silence between them wasn't emptiness; it was sacred, a thread of quiet understanding. After a while, Waldo said, "First days are strange."

Nathan gave a small laugh. "I don't even know if I'm nervous or just tired."

"That feeling doesn't go away," Waldo said. "But you learn to keep moving anyway."

Nathan glanced over. "Is that what you've been learning all this time?"

Waldo considered it, his breath clouding in the air. "I used to wait for clarity—like it had to come first. But I've learned it doesn't wait for you or seek you out. You walk, and it meets you on the road."

They turned the corner. Sunlight brushed the rooftops gold. Waldo looked at Nathan—*really* looked—and saw not just his son but a young man stepping into a future of his own making. Two lives, once entangled, now unfolding in quiet parallel. It wasn't just a father witnessing his son grow. It was two men intentionally walking into new roles.

At the end of the block, Nathan checked his watch. "I should get going."

Waldo nodded. "You ready?"

Nathan gave a slight shrug. "I'm moving. Guess that counts."

"It counts more than you know."

Nathan smiled faintly, a silent thank-you in his eyes, then turned back toward the house to grab his car, his shoulders square, his stride confident.

Waldo stood a moment longer, watching him disappear—the way one watches a ship leave harbor: proud, hopeful, slightly undone. *Your job isn't to shape them—it's to trust they'll shape themselves*, Waldo repeated in his mind.

Upstairs, in the bathroom, Waldo adjusted his tie—an old motion, made new. Then, he caught his reflection. For a moment, it didn't just stare back—it *changed*. Not drastically but enough for him to recognize his own story as well as the stories of those who had shaped him. And in his eyes, he saw her; his mother. Her presence was steady. Warm. Knowing. Waldo's breath caught from the recognition. The past had never left. And the future had just walked out the door. He closed his eyes and let the moment make a home within him. He could still picture the way she'd smiled on a particular day—gentle, as if she saw a version of him that he hadn't grown into yet. She once handed him a small, carefully wrapped box with no explanation. Inside, nestled beneath soft tissue, was a framed poem: *The Man in the Glass.*

At the time, he'd unwrapped it with a teenager's distracted curiosity—grateful but missing the point. Seeing the confusion in his eyes, she'd rested a hand on his shoulder, her voice low and even as she said, *"There'll be times when the world feels harsh, Waldo—when you won't know which way to turn. And when I'm not around, I want you to remember this: The man in the mirror is the only one you ever truly need to answer to."* He had nodded then, appreciating the sentiment but failing to grasp the depth of her words. At that age, he had been consumed with expectations, goals, and outside pressures, so the poem had meant little—just another well-intentioned lesson from a mother offering insight he hadn't yet grown into. But now, he felt the substance of it.

The framed gift had long been lost. Maybe it had been forgotten during a hurried move, left behind in the disorder of packing boxes and fresh starts. Perhaps he had thrown it away during one of his many attempts at decluttering. Or maybe it had simply been lost to time—another casualty of growing up, of moving on. But no matter which one it was, the words may have faded but not the feeling. Because now, bathed in the pale morning light, he didn't need the frame to remember. He needed the truth it held.

Struggling to recall the lines, he left the bathroom and made his way downstairs to the den. At his desk, he opened his laptop, fingers steady as he typed: *The Man in the Glass poem*. And there it was; Dale Wimbrow, author. The words flickered onto the screen like something sacred returning. As his eyes scanned the words, his heart swelled with an old, familiar warmth. It wasn't the poem itself that undid him but what it represented. It was as if his mother were standing right beside him, smiling softly, welcoming him home after a long, tiring journey. She had always known that life would test him. That he would fall. That he would question himself. His mother had given him something that would outlive her voice—not instruction, but insight. And all these years later, he had finally received it.

A long breath filled his chest, inhabiting this moment fully. He heard her voice again, remembered in truth: *"The man in the mirror is the only one you truly need to answer to."* Not the critics. Not the clocks. Not the ever-moving horizon of accomplishment. Just this. This presence. This integrity. This becoming. He no longer mistook clarity for completeness, and he didn't need a map to walk forward. What he needed—and finally had—was alignment.

The laptop screen dimmed, and in the darkened glass, his reflection surfaced, as if it had been waiting for him all along. He didn't look away, either. This time, he met his own gaze and held it. The reflection didn't just show the man he had become; it held echoes of all he had survived to get here. The man in the reflection was no longer a stranger.

Turning from the computer, he smiled. He didn't need permission to live fully anymore. He didn't need applause. No longer would he measure his worth by anything other than the mirror—and the man it reflected. His path wasn't a question anymore. It was a choice—and he'd already made it.

Chapter 19
Taming Dragons Together

The drive to work was smooth, the rhythm of traffic predictable. Unlike before, he felt prepared for what the day would hold. He'd reviewed his notes at home, then once more before heading into his meeting with Victor. He had done his homework—read every project update, tracked the progress made in his absence, and prepared himself to re-engage.

And it paid off.

Victor, predictably pragmatic, was pleased. The conversation was smooth and efficient, and Waldo was able to answer the questions with confidence, offering insights without hesitation. There was no fumbling, no scrambling to keep up. He was back in full force, and Victor saw it. "It's like you never left," Victor said as they wrapped up.

Waldo smiled. "I can't lie, it feels good to be back."

And it did. Not because he was returning to the same place but because he was bringing something new into it. However, as smooth as the meeting was, Waldo recognized the challenge beneath it. This wasn't just a performance. It was his first real test—to face the dragons of self-doubt and prove, mostly to himself, that he wasn't the man who'd missed the deadline. Not anymore. Instead, he was a man holding steady to the two most important elements in life: family and career.

Back at his desk, he moved easily through the familiar: emails, meetings, project updates. He checked tasks off his list, re-engaged with colleagues, and let the steady hum of office life carry him forward. But when he considered his family, his mind racing with ideas, a few guiding thoughts began to crystallize. Between reports, he reached for his notebook, scribbling fragments—loose, instinctive, like anchors, forming in real time, taking shape. He didn't even notice what he was building at first. Only that the thoughts wouldn't wait.

Courage over certainty.
Trust the questions.
Small steps matter.

Each note felt like a thread—not a conclusion but a piece of something larger. He didn't have all the answers yet, but the framework was beginning to take shape. *How can I prepare my children for their own paths?* he asked himself again. *How can I pass on the wisdom I have gained —not as rules but as tools?* These questions fueled him, the thoughts already swirling in his mind.

Around midday, an email arrived marked **"URGENT"**. The old reflex to panic—to avoid, delay, deflect—clawed at his chest. But this time, he paused, inhaled slowly, and opened it. No spiral. No narrative. Just presence. One dragon kept small. He remembered how easily this kind of message used to undo him, but not today. Today, he showed up anyway. That was the shift being put into practice. The application wasn't perfect or even fearless, but he held the commitment to stay engaged—even when the outcome wasn't clear. He thought of it as meeting the dragons on steadier ground.

The dragons were no longer strangers: the spiral, the perfectionism, the ache of never enough. He didn't banish them—he just didn't bow to them. They were no longer mythical, just old habits, shrinking in the light of presence.

The workday wound down with a final flurry of emails and a few loose ends tied up before Waldo finally shut down his computer. As he gathered his things and stepped out of the office, the transition from work to home felt seamless—not a jarring shift between two separate worlds, but a natural flow, one feeding into the other. And when Waldo stepped through the front door, the evening welcomed him the way only familiarity could; the scent of garlic and herbs in the air, the shuffle of feet against tile, Grace's music spilling faintly from her earbuds.

"Dinner in five," Sara called over her shoulder, elbow-deep in a mixing bowl.

He grinned, reaching to taste from the pot.

She caught him mid-reach and nudged his hand away with the back of her wrist. "Don't get cocky. You're still on table duty."

He gave a mock salute and grabbed the plates.

After dinner, Grace stood and made a beeline for the pantry. "If I'm going to dig through years of embarrassing childhood photos, I need backup snacks."

Sara smirked, rinsing a plate. "That's not a nutrition plan—that's a cry for help."

Waldo raised a brow. "Wait—photos?"

Grace's voice floated back from the pantry. "Class slideshow. Pictures from elementary through now. It's going to be a disaster." She returned with pretzels and a cookie in hand, unfazed. "Oh, and by the way, I still use the color-coded calendar and disciplined study blocks. I just eat my feelings around them."

Waldo chuckled. "Advanced multitasking."

She flopped back into her seat, bit into the cookie, and exhaled like a survivor. "And someone's totally going to dig up that picture of me with missing teeth and spaghetti on my head."

Sara grinned. "That was adorable."

"Adorable? It was a war crime," Grace deadpanned, already heading for the stairs. "I'm going to see what blackmail-worthy photos I can find before someone else does."

Waldo shook his head, smiling after her.

As Sara passed by Waldo, she brushed something from his shoulder —flour, maybe, or nothing at all. "Go," she said softly. "You've got that look."

He didn't ask what she meant. He just nodded. As he reached the porch door, a plate slipped—the sharp clatter of ceramic against metal snapping the hush of the evening. No one called out. No panic. Just the subdued shuffle of cleanup resuming. The screen door clicked softly shut behind him as he settled into his chair, notebook balanced loosely in his hands. Now outside, the night opened around him—crisp, unhurried, alive. The porch light hummed behind him, low and steady. Waldo leaned back, letting his thoughts unfurl—not with purpose but with space. Just as he uncapped his pen, his hand paused, hovering above the page, the sound of that fallen plate still faint in his chest. And then the memory came: clear, somber, and formative.

He had been eleven, maybe twelve, when he was showing off with a borrowed baseball one summer afternoon, trying to impress a friend, when the ball sailed wild and cracked the neighbor's side window. For a full hour, he sat in the garage pretending to sort his dad's tools, palms sweating, heart pounding with guilt.

When his father finally found him, he didn't raise his voice. Didn't scold. He just sat down beside him, wiped sawdust from his hands, and said, "You know, Waldo . . . some people think being good means not messing up. I think it's about telling the truth, even when it costs you something."

Later that evening, Waldo walked with him to the neighbor's door. It was Waldo who had to speak—voice shaking, eyes down—and his father who quietly offered to pay for the repair. But it wasn't about the window. It was about the kind of person you chose to be in the moment things broke. That memory had faded for years, but tonight, with Nathan and Grace on his mind, it returned like an old compass drawn from the back of a drawer. He remembered the faint cross etched on its back—something he'd noticed as a boy but only now began to understand. A reminder: direction wasn't always about maps. Sometimes, it lived in what you carried close—and chose to return to.

He didn't want to teach them how to be perfect.

He wanted to teach them how to stand back up. Not just with integrity, but with presence. With moral courage. With faith, not in the outcome but in the walk itself. In others. In becoming who they were meant to be.

Flipping to a fresh page in his notebook, Waldo let the pen move before the words were ready. Some came as questions. Others as loose fragments—not quite a list, not yet a structure. Just pieces, jotted quickly, as if he were catching fireflies before they slipped away.

Start walking—clarity comes later.
Be honest. Even when it's easier not to.
Courage matters more than certainty.
Faith = showing up.
Ask what matters. Then ask again.
Mistakes? Let them teach you.
Show up. Especially when it's hard.
Don't wait to feel ready. Move anyway.
Small steps count.

The map's yours. Make it.
Trust the questions.

He paused, reading over what he'd written before adding:

Victory: letting go of the need to be complete in favor of being
present.

Waldo sat back, closing his notebook, embracing the feeling of anticipation.

Sara stood just inside the porch door, wrapped in a sweater with two mugs of hot cocoa cradled in her hands. She watched Waldo for a moment as he gazed into the night—the set of his shoulders, the quiet steadiness of his posture. Sara rarely joined him here, the space more his than hers, but tonight, she seemed drawn to an unusual syncopated presence of the evening and her thoughts. The screen door creaked softly as she eased it open, the gentle sound breaking the hush. She crossed the threshold onto the porch, a warm mug extended as a small token of acknowledgement for her interruption. "Mind some company?" she asked, her voice gentle.

Waldo glanced up, his smile easy, warm. "I never mind your company." He took the cocoa, their fingers brushing briefly.

She sat beside him, their movements unhurried, as if this moment had been waiting for them all along. For a while, they simply sat—no rush, no need for words—just the comforting cadence of crickets in the distance and the occasional hoot of an owl standing sentry in the trees. Sara turned to him, breaking the silence. "Your involvement with the kids goes further than just being present. There's something more, isn't there?"

Waldo chuckled softly, taking a sip before meeting her eyes. "You always see through me." He smiled slightly. "Yeah. There is. It's something I've been sitting with a lot lately, my role with them. I used to think being a father meant guiding them toward a certain outcome, making sure they took the 'right' steps. But that's not it at all. Nathan and Grace don't need me to tell them what to do. They need me to show them how to think, how to question, how to trust themselves. It's not about teaching. It's about guiding."

"That sounds . . . different. Like you've found something solid to hold on to."

"I have," he said. "And it's not just about them. It's about us. I want to be present—not just as their father but as their guide while I still can. If I can give them what they need now, they'll have the foundation to carry forward long after we're gone."

She set her mug on the porch rail, fingers curling around its warmth. "That's beautiful, Waldo, but I hope you know . . . you don't have to carry this alone. The kids need both of us." She hesitated, then added, "I need you too."

Waldo reached for her hand. "I know. And I'm not doing this alone. I've just finally figured out how to show up. How to be the father and husband I always wanted to be." He exhaled, his voice steady. "It is about us. About Nathan and Grace. About what we leave behind."

Sara's gaze softened. "What we leave behind?"

He nodded, smiling. "Someday, we'll just be memories to them. That's the reality of life. And that's not a bad thing—it's just made me think. What kind of memories do I want to leave? What kind of foundation are we building for them now? Not just advice or rules, but the example we set—in how we live, how we love, how we handle life's challenges."

"That's a big thought. Important but big. How do we even begin something like that?"

"We already have," he said, a whisper of certainty in his voice. "Every interaction, every moment, every decision we make—it's already shaping them. Whether or not we realize it, we're showing them how to handle life. It's not about getting it perfect. It's about being intentional. We can't script every moment, but we can make sure the ones we have count." He turned toward her, a teasing glint in his eyes. "I want them to see us face the hard questions, fight the dragons, not just hear the answers we try to give."

A coy expression illuminated her face, and as she suppressed a smile, she said, "So, what you're saying is . . . we're in the dragon-taming business now?" Her smile was soft, but there was a strength behind it—a woman who had wrestled her own quiet dragons in the dark and now stood ready to teach beside him.

Waldo let out a hearty laugh, the sound rolling into the night air. "Exactly." With playful exaggeration, he mimed drawing an invisible sword, as if he were nine years old again. "Training them to face the dragons," he declared. "To fight the fears and challenges life throws at them. And maybe even to tame a few along the way."

Sara watched his antics, warmth and amusement mingling in her expression. "You're ridiculous."

"And you love it," he countered, grinning.

"I do," she admitted, laughing and reaching for his hand once more. "And I see what you're trying to do. It's beautiful, Waldo. If we can give them the tools to shape their own lives, then . . . that's the best legacy we could ever leave. But . . . what if we fail? What if we think we're teaching them something valuable, and it doesn't stick?"

"That's the thing, Sara. It's not about controlling the outcome. It's about planting the seeds. We might not see them grow the way we imagined, but that doesn't mean they won't take root. What matters is that we try. That we show them what it looks like to love, to learn, to face challenges, and to grow." Waldo let a memory surface, his mother's wisdom nudging him forward. He tightened his grip on Sara's hand, his voice steady. "The best time to plant a tree was twenty years ago. The second-best time is now."

Sara blinked, then let out a breath that sounded almost like a laugh. "That's . . . fantastic."

He squeezed her hand. "We can do this. Together."

Sara studied him for a long moment before nodding. "That's all I've ever wanted." She placed her cocoa mug down on the porch rail, then shifted forward, resting her hands over his. A quiet agreement. A promise. The night air cocooned around them as they sat in silence. He remembered a night like this once, long ago, before life complicated everything. But this time, the stillness wasn't filled with potential. It was filled with presence. Eventually, Sara stood, stretching, the day's weight catching up to her. "I'm heading to bed." She collected her mug and brushed a soft kiss against his cheek. "Don't stay out here too long."

"I won't," Waldo promised, watching as she disappeared inside, the screen door tapping shut behind her.

Tonight, the hush of the porch, usually a familiar blanket, carried something more—joint commitment, a sense of promise, of possibility. The moments he had shared with Sara that evening, the strength of their connectedness, had ignited a spark of excitement and anticipation, a sense of adventure that reminded him of the rush he used to feel as a child turning the pages of *Where's Waldo?*, eagerly searching for the next challenge. He exhaled deeply, gazing out at the darkened yard, each passing minute reinforcing the shift within him.

Not just hope. Not just love.

Forward motion, made visible.

He thought of Sara again, now resting inside, and resolved that the future they envisioned together wouldn't just be about his newfound clarity. Their shared dedication to creating something enduring, something that would guide their children and, perhaps one day, their grandchildren, would form the foundation of their future. Not through lectures but through shared reflections. Not with answers but with stories.

He imagined Nathan, already asleep after another long shift. For Nathan, the creed wouldn't be a checklist or an emotional map. It would be the quiet confidence to trust his instincts when the world gave him no clear answers. Grace would wear it like a bright thread through her day—curious, bold, and questioning. She'd reshape it into something uniquely hers. That was the beauty of it. The same truths, held in different hands. That was enough. That was the start.

When Waldo crawled into bed shortly after Sara, he turned toward her sleeping form, his heart steady, a single thought resonating deep within him. *"Whether you think you can, or think you can't—you're right."* It wasn't about blind optimism but about the private confidence that comes from trusting yourself enough to take that first step. Belief wasn't the destination—it was the compass. He wanted Nathan and Grace to understand the power of belief. Not as something to clutch blindly, but as something subtle, enduring—an assurance that could guide them through uncertainty.

Chapter 20
The Creed Begins at Home

The next day, Waldo decided to leave work early, feeling drawn toward Cooper's Café—a place he hadn't visited since returning from his time away. The ease of the day's flow had left him with some unexpected free time, and rather than rushing home, he adjusted. It felt natural to pass his car, walking the few blocks to the café; a quiet pivot, a subtle choice to engage rather than retreat.

Long shadows stretched across the sidewalk as he drew near, the late afternoon sun painting everything gold, and the comforting aroma of roasting coffee beans preceded him into the shop. The chime above the door rang as he entered, and almost immediately, a few familiar faces turned in his direction. "Well, look who it is!" a barista said from behind the counter, her smile warm and welcoming.

Waldo returned the smile sheepishly as he nodded in greeting. It was a simple acknowledgment but one that carried a warmth he hadn't expected. The welcoming atmosphere of the café wrapped around him, a greeting that went beyond words. He stepped further inside, scanning the room, letting the subtle words of conversation and the clink of ceramic cups settle into his senses. His usual booth by the window was unoccupied—as if waiting for him. Sliding into the seat, he set his bag beside him and exhaled, letting his muscles relax into the well-worn leather. As he walked to his seat, a few regulars glanced up, some offering a quick nod, others giving small waves. *Not invisible, after all.*

"Good to see you back, Waldo," another barista called, wiping down the counter. "Thought we lost you."

Waldo smiled again, relaxing into the familiar banter. "I'm afraid not. You're stuck with me." The last time he'd been here, he'd been a different man. Restless, searching. His mind was a tangled mess of questions without answers. Today, though, he wasn't seeking escape. He was simply here. Present.

A steaming cup of black coffee was placed in front of him without a word. He looked up to see the barista smirking. "Didn't even have to ask," she said.

"Guess I'm predictable," Waldo mused.

"Or just well-known," she countered. "Did you want anything else?"

He considered her question for moment before saying, "Just coffee, thanks." As she moved onto the next customer, he glanced around the café again. Had he always belonged here without realizing it? He pulled out his notebook and flipped it open. The pen rested between his fingers as he absently traced the edge of the notebook, using it as a pointer while reviewing the notes from the day before. Thoughts. Ideas. Fragments of something larger. It was easier now—letting the ideas take form, without forcing them. He underlined three phrases carefully:

Courage over certainty.
Trust the questions.
Small steps count.

Simple phrases, yet each vital. They weren't just words; they were principles—pieces of the foundation he hoped to pass on. They weren't rules, not exactly. Just reminders. A language he was still learning to trust.

As Waldo took a sip of coffee, letting the bitterness ground him, a familiar thought tugged at him, persistent and unyielding. His well-intentioned advice to Nathan—*"You'll figure it out"*—had felt incomplete even as he said it. He'd known it then too. The addition of *"Sometimes . . . it just takes time,"* hadn't helped; it had rung hollow, a placeholder for something deeper he couldn't articulate in the moment. He paused thoughtfully. The advice he'd struggled to give Nathan hadn't been just about time revealing answers. It was about something deeper. It was about action, finding the courage to break free from the web of hesitation. Sitting here, in this small café, with the familiar world moving around him, Waldo realized what had been missing. He wrote and circled one last phrase in his notebook. The most profound realization was this:

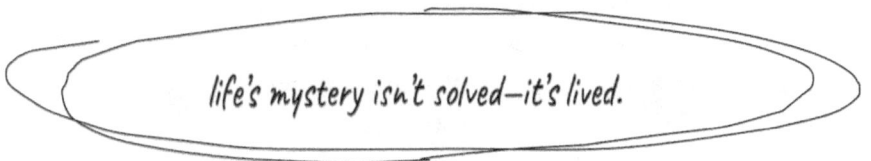

life's mystery isn't solved—it's lived.

A movement in his periphery caught his eye. The barista was sliding his bill onto the table, but before she left, she gave him a knowing look. "See you tomorrow morning?"

Waldo hesitated, then smiled—not at her, but at the thought of returning. 'Yeah. I think you will."

As Waldo finished his third cup of coffee, staying a while longer than he had planned, he closed his notebook with a satisfying *snap*. The café had given him more than just a brief escape—it had become a place of clarity, a quiet corner where his thoughts could breathe and take shape. He slid his notebook into his bag and pulled out his wallet to pay for the check. As he moved toward the door, he took one last glance around the café, a few familiar faces nodding in passing, reinforcing the acknowledgment of his presence. Maybe he hadn't been as invisible as he once thought after all.

Walking back to get his car, Waldo paused at a crosswalk at the end of the block, noticing an elderly man leaning patiently on his cane. The man's stillness captivated him, emitting a peacefulness in his tranquility that stood in stark distinction to the hurried people around him. The contrast was remarkable, and Waldo couldn't help but gaze at the man. It wasn't just his physical stillness—it was something in the way he carried himself, in the way he savored the time while waiting for the light. The world hadn't captured his pace; instead, he had mastered the art of "seeing"—being thoroughly present in the space between moments.

As Waldo watched him, he could almost hear his grandfather's voice again, warm with wisdom: *"Boy, do it now . . . It's later than you think."* The words wrapped around him like a familiar grandpa hug he always loved as a kid, urging Waldo to pause and actually notice the world around him. Waldo shook himself free of the moment as the light turned green, but the image of the elderly man stayed with him, a beacon of the calm he had been seeking.

Back in his car, he took a deep breath, the seahorse keyring gently swaying in the ignition. The moment he just experienced would be another lesson he'd share with Nathan, Grace, and all aspiring explorers. Prepare your mind, stay curious, keep moving, believe—learn to take a moment, slowing down and savoring life. *Because it's later than you think.* The greatest adventures, he realized, weren't out there; they were waiting inside, ready to unfold.

He arrived home, a bit later than normal, the edge of twilight softening the streets. Inside, the rhythmic hum of Sara moving about the kitchen drew him closer, and as he leaned against the doorway, he smelled vanilla. "Cake?" he asked with a playful smile.

Sara looked up, returning his smile lovingly. "I promised Grace something special. It's been a long time since I baked this cake. Mom's recipe. She always baked it on special occasions. Seemed right for Sunday."

Waldo walked further into the room and inhaled. "Smells like memories."

She nodded. "Grace is thrilled. Nathan too, though he'd never admit it. Celebrating this job means a lot to him."

"Means a lot to all of us," Waldo said faintly. "Ever wonder how we got here?"

"Constantly," she chuckled, lightly mixing batter. "It's not what we imagined, but it feels right."

"Funny," he said, resting his elbows on the counter. "I spent years chasing clarity, thinking the answer was somewhere ahead. But now, what's clear is that faith means trusting the journey without knowing exactly where it leads. Action, that's what moves me forward, even through doubt."

Sara's gaze softened. "You're different, Waldo. Grounded. I haven't seen this in you for years."

"I feel different too," he admitted. "Simpler."

A comfortable silence settled between them, broken when Waldo mischievously dipped a spoon into the batter, swiftly tasting it.

"Waldo!" Sara swatted his arm, laughing.

"It tastes perfect," he declared.

She rolled her eyes. "You're impossible."

"In a good way," he teased.

With a flirtatious smile and a wink, she added, "This is you. The man I fell for all those years ago."

His face fell into a clandestine expression, one of gratitude, love, and a touch of roguishness only she could decipher. It was their private language, unspoken but unmistakable. "I'll set the table," he said, pushing away from the counter. "You focus on making sure I don't eat half of that before it makes it to Sunday."

Her laughter filled the room as he moved away. This wasn't just about Sunday's dinner. It was about everything they were rebuilding, one moment at a time.

Chapter 21
The Ripple of Becoming

Later that evening, as Waldo volunteered to clean up the kitchen after dinner, the house settling into a comfortable stillness, Waldo felt the rhythm of belonging—stronger and clearer than ever. Melody watched from her perch by the sink, her usual feline scrutiny occasionally breaking his concentration with gentle meows. When her sounds grew more insistent, Waldo paused, checked her food dish, and found it full. "What's up, Melody?" he asked, genuinely curious.

She blinked slowly, her expression clear: *You should know.*

Smiling, Waldo finished the dishes, flicked off the kitchen light, and was just turning away when Melody suddenly leapt from the counter. He barely had time to step aside as she streaked past him, bolting toward the back door, pausing just long enough to glance back, expectant—waiting, maybe even insisting that he follow.

Startled, he laughed. "Ah, so this was the plan all along." With a final glance around the room, his eyes landed on the guitar by the bookshelf—tonight, it didn't just beckon. It felt necessary. He picked it up and carried it with him as he opened the back door, following Melody outside. Above, stars scattered across the sky, tiny remnants of forgotten stories. Waldo settled into his chair, drawing a breath that reached all the way down. The guitar rested in his lap like an old friend, the strings ready beneath his fingertips. It belonged here, just as he did.

Melody circled once at the porch's edge before curling into her spot. As Waldo adjusted his grip, she let out a long, contented *purr*, and the sound stirred something in him—not the casual affection of a pet but something older. More sentimental.

His mother.

Just her presence—the way she moved through the house with quiet rhythm. Not performative. Simply there. Steady. Constant. He hadn't recognized it like this before—not until now, mirrored in Melody's breath-like purring that came across as a current. It was the same current threaded through Grace's music. The same stillness he'd spent a lifetime outrunning. Perhaps music had always been the thread, strong enough to tether him back to what mattered. To who he truly was.

Melody took her usual spot at the porch's edge, her gaze patient, expectant. Her soft meow pulled Waldo from his thoughts, making him chuckle. "Alright," he whispered, fingers brushing the strings. The first few chords came unhurried, exploratory, before shifting into something deeper, a conversation without words. And then, the music came alive. The notes carried whispers of his journey—the longing, the gratitude, the laughter, and the lessons that shaped him. And as he played, it hit him; teachable moments. He had lived them. He remembered the artist in the park: *"Pay attention. The world is always speaking—you just need to listen."* The woman at the gallery: *"Step back from chaos; meaning reveals itself."* The man at the bus stop: *"Nature never rushes; find your rhythm."* Each encounter had offered wisdom, but he had been too distracted to understand the depth of that wisdom at the time.

The idea he once held—that he was invisible, unnoticed—had been another deception, spun from fear. But now, the knots were loosening, the falsehoods unraveling. Wisdom hadn't come in declarations. It had come in glimpses. Experiences. In the pauses between what he thought he needed and what he already had. No lecture, no instruction—just occasions, experiences, pieces of a larger puzzle waiting to be assembled. That was how he'd pass it to Nathan and Grace—not by dictating their paths but by being present, allowing them to discover what they need to. That was the genuine gift—the ability to see, to interpret, their own connections, their own truths. *Teach when the moments arrive.* He plucked the strings again, softer now.

Melody purred louder, her eyes half-lidded all the way until the last note. A soft meow replaced his playing and Melody continued to watch him, tail flicking once before she raised a paw and swiped it gently across her face.

"So, I've finally impressed you, Melody?" he teased.

She blinked slowly, unimpressed as ever.

Waldo stood, ready for sleep, but before going inside, he paused, looking skyward, as if the stars might hum back. He wasn't reaching anymore, not chasing distant answers. He'd found it. *What's your thing?* The question drifted back like a leaf on the wind—Nathan's voice, curious and innocent, from that morning at Cooper's Café so long ago. *"Dad, other than work, what's your thing?"* Back then, the question had hung in the air, unsettling him, stirring a restlessness that sent him searching. Now, in the stillness of this moment, Waldo felt no restlessness at all—only understanding. He let the memory of that day wash through him and noticed how gently it settled into who he had become. The truth of who he was—clear and constant—had been here all along, growing quietly with each step of the journey. And finally, he knew in his heart what his "thing" was. It wasn't a hobby, a project, or some far-off dream. It was right here, woven into the life he'd embraced—the late-night talks and early-morning pancakes, the music and shared laughter, the quiet steadiness he offered Sara, the wide-eyed wonder he mirrored in Grace, the tender moments with his son, and the quiet minutes with himself. His thing was being present in every breath he took and every bit of love he gave. And maybe, just maybe, that was what Nathan had been asking all along.

Not what he did.

But who he is.

Life is less about having all the answers and more about being open to asking the right questions—to embracing the journey, twists and turns and all. His father's words echoed: *"The two most important days of your life are the day you are born and the day you find out why."*

Waldo listened to the silence for a moment longer, feeling peace settle in his chest—born of gratitude and belonging.

He needed no other answer.

He was simply just living in the truth of the man, partner, and father he had become. He knew his "why" and now, it was his turn to walk the path and help his children find theirs.

After breakfast Sunday morning, Waldo stood by the kitchen window, watching sunlight spill over the backyard—the lawn still neat from yesterday's work. Sara joined him, taking a sip from her mug before glancing at him. "You've been thinking about tonight."

Waldo nodded. "I have." He turned toward her. "This dinner should be more than just a celebration. Something they'll carry with them," he said. "Even if they don't realize it yet, like a touchstone they don't know they're holding."

"Like the keychains?"

He smiled. "Eventually. Right now . . . they're still finding their footing. This isn't about handing them a message. It's about planting a moment."

She tilted her head thoughtfully. "So, tonight is just about planting seeds."

"Exactly." He leaned against the counter. "They'll carry these moments with them, even if they don't know it yet. When the time comes—when life presses in—maybe something will surface. Not an answer. A direction."

Sara nodded, her eyes on him. "You've already started writing it, haven't you?"

"No, but last night, a thought came to me, and I think I'm ready to write it down." He crossed the room, where his notebook lay open on the table, a few dog-eared pages curled at the edges. He flipped to a clean page and let the pen move.

Sara followed and leaned on the back of the chair across from him, her coffee cradled between her palms. She stood close, eyes on the page. He could feel her presence beside him like a steady current. "You're turning this into a list?" she asked, brow raised, more curious than skeptical. "Didn't think you were a bullet-points kind of guy."

Waldo glanced up briefly. "Not exactly. More like . . . fragments. Things I want to give them without handing them a script." He let his gaze drift for a moment, then returned to the page. "As I picture them, I don't see myself as a teacher anymore. Not in the way I used to be, anyway. I'm not trying to give them answers. Just a way to navigate without one."

Sara nodded with a kind of strength you didn't have to announce—only carry.

"Life doesn't follow a fixed map," he continued, voice softer now, more to her than to the page. "Their paths will bend and break in ways we'll never predict. I want them to shape their own way forward, but I also want them to know they're not alone, that I'll walk beside them when I can, and that even when I'm not there, something of me still is."

Sara took the seat across from him, her eyes on him. "Not advice," she said, "but presence."

His lips tugged into a slow smile. "That's the idea." He thought of Nathan, steady, searching, burdened sometimes by the need to get it right. And Grace, curious, bold, untamable in the best ways. They would each need different kinds of guidance, and none of it could be prescriptive. "I'm not giving them a roadmap," he said. "Just tools. Anchors. Little truths they can carry with them, like mental snacks. My dad used to do the same thing. A line that made no sense at the time . . . until it did."

Sara tilted her head. "'Mental snacks?'"

He grinned. "Something small but nourishing. Like what my dad used to say, little lines that might not make sense until years from now, but when they do, they'll land just right." Turning serious, he said, "There are fears too. The quiet dragons—the fear I haven't done enough . . . that I might not be here when they need me." These weren't just gentle truths— they were dragon armor. Quiet tools for loud moments, meant to protect and empower. Not to shield his kids from every storm but to show them how to walk into one and still stand tall. What he was crafting wasn't a lecture. It was something far more personal—an enduring Creed for the Journey. When the dragons whisper doubt, it would be there. Waiting. A quiet invitation to move. "But I don't want to lead with fear. I want to lead with presence." With one more stroke of his pen he wrote:

Action.

Sara reached across the table and placed her hand over his. "You are."

They stayed like that for a beat. Then, Waldo gently turned back to the page. His hand moved slowly, the ink a kind of breath, marking the beginning of something lasting. These weren't instructions. They were offerings.

The Creed for the Journey
(Notes for Nathan and Grace—written, not yet shared)

Start walking. Clarity follows.
Courage over certainty.
Trust the questions—even when they don't come with answers.
Mistakes teach. Let them.
Show up, especially when it's hard.
Be honest, even when it costs you.
Faith isn't knowing—it's continuing.
Small steps count.
Ask what matters. Ask again.

Your map is yours to make.
Don't wait to feel ready. Move anyway.
Kindness is strength.
Curiosity is survival.
Integrity is showing up.
You don't need the whole map. Just the next step.

Waldo read the list through once, then passed the notebook to her. "Would you . . . read it to me? I want to hear how it sounds."

Sara took the notebook, her fingers trailing the margin as she read each line aloud—slow, steady, like a litany. When she finished, her thumb lingered on the edge of the page, tracing it lightly, as if grounding herself in the weight of what he'd written. She smiled, her thumb still resting on the corner of the page. "Your little mental snacks," she said softly. "That's what they'll reach for. Like the compass your dad gave you—not to tell them where to go, but to remind them they'll find their way." Then, she carefully closed the notebook, almost reverently, as if sealing something sacred.

Waldo glanced at her, a half-smile curving. "And maybe even tame a few dragons."

"You mean we're still in the dragon-taming business?"

He laughed—not loudly but with warmth. "Until the very end."

Sara smiled. "This will stay with them," she said, her hand resting on the closed notebook. "Not because it's perfect but because it came from you."

Waldo reached for her hand. "Tonight is the beginning," he said, the words slow, certain. "Not a lecture—let's set it in motion. Memories we'll want them to carry."

Sara placed a hand on his arm, anchoring him. "Then, let's make tonight count."

He nodded. "Not just for us. For them."

The plan was set.

~

By the time the afternoon rolled around, the house buzzed with energy. The rich aroma of garlic mingled with the warmth of freshly baked bread, while Sara's famous herb-crusted chicken roasted to perfection. Laughter wove through the air, mingling with the occasional clinking of glasses, setting the perfect tone for an evening meant to be more than just a meal. Then, once at the dining table, conversation continued to flow, a mix of playful banter and genuine excitement. It was a true celebration of milestones and the unwritten future waiting for each of them.

Nathan, settling into his chair, took a bite of his meal and grinned. "Okay, so there's this guy in my department who takes 'coffee break' to a whole new level. I swear, I've seen him work maybe four hours in an eight-hour shift."

Grace, sipping her iced tea, raised an eyebrow. "So, basically, he's living my dream?"

Nathan rolled his eyes. "Yeah, except his 'dream' means everyone else picks up the slack."

Waldo chuckled. "Ah, welcome to the joys of professional responsibility."

"So, what's the verdict? Do you like it?" Sara said.

Nathan paused, considering. "Honestly? Yeah. It's not what I picture myself doing forever, but I like the challenge. Every day brings something new, and I'm getting the hang of everything." He hesitated, as if choosing his words carefully. "Like, I'm actually doing something real."

Waldo nodded, recognizing the shift in his son's voice—the subtle change from uncertainty to something firmer, more assured.

Grace let out an exaggerated sigh, dramatically flopping back in her chair. "Meanwhile, I'm over here trying to figure out how I'm supposed to pick a major and a career and not completely lose my mind in the process."

Sara shot her a knowing look. "That's why we need to have this conversation now, so you don't procrastinate until August."

Grace groaned. "I don't procrastinate. I just . . . take a more scenic route."

"Yeah, straight off a cliff." Nathan winked at Grace.

Grace stuck her tongue out at Nathan before reaching for the bread-basket. "Hey, at least I don't spend all day thinking about logistics."

"I mean, I did just get hired for a job that requires me to think about it every day."

"Still waiting to see if that means you'll start optimizing things around here," Sara said. "Maybe figure out how to get the dishes from the sink into the dishwasher? Or, better yet, design a system to stop your sister from monopolizing the bathroom every morning."

Grace gasped in mock offense, setting down her drink. "Excuse me, self-care is essential. Some of us have standards."

Nathan snorted. "Some of us also have places to be."

Grace waved a dismissive hand. "Then, wake up earlier. Problem solved."

Waldo chuckled as Sara shook her head, amused. "Well, there you go, Nathan. No need for optimization—just sacrifice more sleep."

Nathan groaned. "Mom, I promise, my career does not extend to household efficiency."

"Shame," Sara said, trying her best to hide her smile. She passed the butter. "Real missed opportunity."

Grace grinned. "I think we should take it up with his manager."

Waldo leaned back, taking in the moment. These small exchanges—the heart of their family—were the very moments he'd once overlooked. No longer. He glanced at Nathan. "Hey, Nathan, remember when you asked me how you're suppose to know when you're on the right path?"

The room quieted, the switch in tone subtle but immediate. Nathan's fork hovered over his plate as he looked up. "Yeah," he said slowly. "I remember."

Waldo exhaled, choosing his words carefully. "I realize now I didn't give you a very good answer back then." He paused, letting the moment breathe before continuing. "You don't."

Nathan's brow furrowed. "What do you mean?"

"That's the trick. It's not about knowing if you're on the right path. It's about taking the first step and letting the path reveal itself as you move forward."

Nathan's expression was thoughtful, his fingers drumming lightly on the table. It was a familiar look—one Waldo had seen in himself many times before. The moment of wrestling with an idea that hadn't quite clicked yet. But Waldo didn't expect him to understand it fully, not right away. He knew he was planting a seed.

Across the table, Grace, ever perceptive, scanned her father's face as though searching for the deeper meaning behind his words. Waldo could see her wheels turning, wondering how this lesson might one day apply to her own life. She, too, would face moments of doubt and uncertainty. And when that time came, he wanted her to have these tools—the ability to trust herself, to embrace uncertainty, to find joy in the process of becoming.

Waldo leaned forward. "The adventure starts the moment you stop waiting for perfection and simply take that first step."

Sara, adding a question to help the kids understand better, asked, "So, what you're saying is . . . we're not handed maps?"

Waldo shook his head. "Nope. But we don't need them. The journey itself, figuring it out, embracing the twists and turns—that's the reward."

"Yeah. I guess that makes sense," Nathan admitted. "I just . . . I don't know. Sometimes, I wish I had a clearer picture."

Waldo nodded in understanding. "We all do. But think about this, you didn't know exactly what this job would be like when you took it, right?"

Nathan shrugged. "Not really."

"But you took it, anyway. And now you're figuring it out."

Nathan considered this, then smirked. "So, I should expect my entire life to be one big 'figure it out as you go' situation?"

Waldo laughed. "Pretty much."

"Oh, great. So, we're just winging life?" Grace said.

Sara chuckled. "More like learning as we go."

"Fine. Scenic route it is."

As Waldo looked around the table, he felt an overwhelming sense of gratitude—not just for tonight but for every moment that had led them here. This wasn't just his journey. It was theirs. But even then, Waldo knew that his impact wouldn't stop with Nathan and Grace. He hadn't yet extended this shift beyond his family—not to his community, his friendships, or the lives of strangers in those quiet, unseen ways, but he knew he would. The transformation he had undergone wasn't meant to stay confined within the walls of his home. That was how his legacy would take shape, a legacy in motion. Nathan and Grace were only the beginning.

Waldo leaned back in his chair, watching as his children processed the conversation. He had done what he set out to do—planting seeds, not forcing understanding but offering them something to hold onto. He wouldn't be there for every choice they faced, not every crossroads, not every storm. But maybe, somewhere down the line, Nathan would pause before a leap he couldn't quite name and remember the steadiness in his father's voice. Or Grace, standing on the edge of something wildly uncertain, would feel the pull of fear, and then the deeper pull of curiosity. And in that breath, before the decision, not a memory, not a quote, but a felt knowing, they'd hear it: "*Start walking. The path will meet you.*"

He caught Sara's eye, and she gave him a small smile before rising from her seat. "Well, I think it's time to bring out the real star guest of the evening."

Grace perked up immediately. "Wait—cake?"

"You sound way too excited about that." Nathan said, failing to hide his own excitement for dessert.

Grace shot him a look. "It's cake. Homemade. It deserves enthusiasm."

Sara returned from the kitchen, carrying a beautifully frosted cake, setting it in the center of the table with a flourish. "Now, let's see if we can make it through dessert without a full-on negotiation over who gets the biggest piece."

Nathan rolled his shoulders. "No need for negotiations—I obviously get the biggest slice. I mean, this entire dinner was for me, wasn't it? New job, new perks."

Grace scoffed, folding her arms. "Oh, please. I'm about to graduate. Do you know how much stress I've been under?"

Nathan raised an eyebrow. "Yes, actually. I live here."

"Then, you should know this dinner wasn't just about you and your new job. It's also about me and my upcoming graduation. So, by that logic, I should get the biggest piece."

Waldo chuckled, exchanging an amused glance with Sara. Some things, it seemed, would never change. And maybe that was a good thing.

Eventually, Sara reached a fair distribution—mostly because she handled the slicing with diplomatic precision, ensuring no one left the table feeling cheated. Laughter and conversation stretched into the evening, but as the plates emptied, and the yawns started, the night wound down.

Nathan stretched and stood, ruffling Grace's hair as he passed. "Alright, I'm crashing. I have to be up early."

Grace swatted at his hand but grinned. "Fine. Just don't hog the bathroom in the morning."

"No promises," he called over his shoulder.

Sara began collecting the dishes as Grace sighed, finally pushing away from the table after a moment's hesitation. "I'm gonna head up too. Big day tomorrow—college decision stuff."

Waldo reached out, squeezing her hand as she left the dining room. "We'll figure it all out, kid."

Grace nodded, offering him a sleepy smile. "Night, Dad. Night, Mom."

As the footsteps faded upstairs, Waldo turned to Sara, who was stacking plates in the dishwasher with a contented hum. He exhaled deeply. "That was good."

Sara glanced at him, her eyes twinkling. "Yeah. It was."

When everything was tidied up, Waldo followed Sara upstairs, certain that tonight would be more important than it appeared one day in the future.

Monday morning pulled Waldo back into its usual cadence—or so he thought. It was a normal day until a sudden phone call shattered Waldo's work routine. A customer's system had crashed, stalling production. Every tech was already out, so Waldo jumped in, no longer his usual role, but there was no time for hesitation. He grabbed his keys and headed out, shooting a quick text to cancel his guitar lesson before pulling out of the parking lot:

> Got called out on a work emergency. Going to have to reschedule. Let me know what times are open later in the week.

By mid-afternoon, after a meticulous process of troubleshooting, patching, and recalibrating, Waldo had the system back up and running. The relief on the client's face made the effort worthwhile. Although fieldwork was no longer his job, solving a tangible problem still brought deep satisfaction. Still, as he walked out of the client's building, the length of the day settled over him. The unexpected disruption had stretched him thin, and the idea of diving back into more work felt draining. He checked his watch—barely an hour and a half left in the workday. By the time he drove back to the office, settled in, and tried to refocus, it would almost be quitting time. Returning to squeeze productivity from the remaining hour seemed pointless. What he needed now was breathing room. The work could wait until tomorrow.

With that thought, he pulled out his phone and called the office.

"Hey, it's Waldo. Everything's handled here, but it doesn't make much sense for me to come back this late in the day. I'm heading home."

The admin on the other end barely hesitated. "Got it. See you in the morning."

Waldo stood by his decision. He had spent years letting work dictate every moment, pushing himself even when it wasn't necessary. But today? Today, he was choosing differently. Sliding back into the driver's seat, he realized he wasn't quite ready to go straight home either. What he really wanted—what he needed—was a peaceful moment alone.

As he navigated the unfamiliar side of town, his eyes landed on a small café nestled between a bookstore and a row of boutique shops. Something about the idea of a peaceful cup of coffee before returning to the house sounded like a necessary reprieve. The café was unassuming yet inviting, a place that had likely been there for years, unnoticed by those who weren't looking. Drawn by its quiet charm, Waldo pulled into a nearby parking spot, recognizing an opportunity to pause, reflect, and reset.

Although not his usual haunt, Cooper's Cafe, this place had the same welcoming atmosphere. The warm glow of its interior and the rich aroma of coffee centered Waldo in the present moment as he opened the door. Soft conversations and the gentle *clink* of mugs created a comforting backdrop, easing the fatigue from his day.

He placed his order before scanning the café—shelves lined with books, a cork-board by the counter covered in flyers for local events, a barista who greeted regulars by name. It was the kind of place that had history, a lived-in feeling that existed for people who needed a quiet corner to think.

When he had his coffee in hand, he found a table in the corner—secluded enough to give him space, yet still connected to the café's steady cadence. He settled in, relishing the warmth of his cup in his hands, and took a slow sip. The tension of the day's earlier chaos had faded. His gaze drifted across the room, quietly observing the lives unfolding around him: a young couple leaning in closely, laughter bubbling between them; a man typing furiously on his laptop, his brow furrowed in deep focus; an older woman turning the pages of a well-loved book, her fingers lingering on the worn edges as if revisiting an old memory. Then, amidst the familiar bustle, something unexpected caught his eye. A few tables away, staring pensively into his cup, sat an old friend. They had once been close—late-night talks, road trip debates, half-formed dreams over beers neither of them could afford. Life had pulled them in different directions, but the recognition was instant. Waldo rose, a current of curiosity pushing him forward. "Dan? Is that really you?"

Dan looked up, startled, but then his face lit with familiar warmth. "Waldo? Man, I haven't seen you since . . . what? The year of your epic beard experiment?"

Waldo chuckled. "Yeah, I've repressed that one. You doing okay?"

"Define okay," Dan said, gesturing to the half-drunk coffee and open laptop beside him. "Still climbing ladders I'm not sure I even leaned against the right wall."

Waldo nodded toward his own table. "Come sit. I've got time."

Dan joined him, letting out a breath that seemed older than he was. "Work's steady. Family's good. But I don't know, man . . . I wake up some days and wonder how I ended up here—like I took all the right steps to the wrong place."

Waldo listened quietly. A few months ago, he might've answered with something safe—a platitude dressed up as wisdom. *"It'll all make sense someday."* But not now. He'd lived the confusion. He'd learned better. Instead, he said, "I used to chase answers. Waited until I felt ready. Certain. But I've realized . . . clarity doesn't come before the step. It comes *because* of it."

Dan looked up from his coffee. "So, you just act without knowing?"

"You act with *intent*," Waldo clarified. "Even if you're not sure where it's leading. You don't wait to feel ready. You trust that motion creates meaning."

Dan leaned back in his chair, mulling that over. "That's scary. Kind of freeing, though."

"Both," Waldo said. "But freeing wins."

"You know," Dan said, after a beat, "I almost stayed home. I could never have guessed I'd run into you today."

"Funny how the right moments don't need our permission," Waldo said, smiling.

They clinked coffee mugs like old friends still learning how to be new men. And as they parted, Dan looked lighter—not transformed but *open*. Waldo recognized the look—he'd felt it himself. Like a stone dropped into still water, the ripple had started. Waldo wasn't just passing on lessons or advice. He was leaving echoes—small truths offered gently, meant to take root when the time was right.

Stepping outside, the crisp evening air met him, cool against his skin. He hadn't expected to find himself here today, hadn't planned for any of this. But maybe that was the point. Perhaps, as he'd told Dan, the path had gradually revealed itself. Waldo turned the ignition, the car's engine humming to life. He sat there for a breath longer, hands still on the wheel, staring ahead. His sense of direction faltered for just a moment—not because he was lost but because the day had pulled him sideways, stretching the boundaries of who he thought he was. As if his inner compass had been recalibrated by conversation, memory, and a brush with the past. He eased the car into gear and turned out of the lot, choosing a route home he couldn't remember ever taking—unfamiliar, quiet, winding.

The road curved gently beneath the golden blush of sunset. Long shadows spilled across the dashboard like echoes of all the versions of himself he had once been—the seeker, the skeptic, the silent one. He didn't resist them. He simply let them pass. Then, rising ahead like a memory made manifest, he saw the old inn. He hadn't come here by design, and yet, it felt inevitable. The sign, the porch, the garden gate . . . unchanged. Waldo pulled into the small parking lot and turned off the engine. For a long moment, he didn't move, just breathed. He had come here once in turmoil, chasing answers, haunted by questions that refused to form words. But tonight, he felt no urgency. Just stillness. Just peace.

By the gate stood a young couple, their bodies leaning toward each other in quiet tension—uncertain, hesitant, teetering on the edge of decision. The weight of "what if" and the ache of not yet knowing was clear as day as they spoke. It was a familiar dance, one he had lived. He thought, briefly, about approaching them and offering some insight, some comfort, some roadmap, but instead, he simply smiled—not with superiority, but solidarity. Theirs was a journey they had to take on their own. Just as he had.

Turning the key once more, Waldo guided the car away from the inn and onto the open road. The night deepened around him, but his vision remained clear. He hadn't found answers he once sought, but he no longer needed them. He had found the courage to keep walking. Life, he now knew, wasn't about perfect clarity or final chapters. It was about turning the next page with intention. It was about holding space for mystery, for transformation, and for love. What started as a ripple within had become something more—an enduring current of presence, purpose, and love, stretching beyond the shoreline. He might never see where they reached, but he no longer needed to.

The tires whirred over the uneven asphalt, each rise and dip in the road a steady rhythm beneath him. Street lamps flickered to life in the distance, their glow pooling across the pavement like faint echoes of day. On either side, the trees streaking by in a whisk of late-spring green—tall, familiar, blurring into outlines—were being softened by dusk. The rearview mirror caught his reflection in the fading light, and he saw he was older now, more grounded, but not lost. Months ago, he couldn't meet that gaze. Now, it felt like second nature. The man looking back didn't carry answers, but he carried something steadier— the will to show up and to keep going. Faith isn't knowing—it's continuing. The final word he'd written in the Creed surfaced in his mind: *Action.*

There were still dragons. Still unknowns. But they were no longer bigger than the presence he now chose to live by. As Ralph Waldo Emerson once wrote, *"What lies behind us and what lies before us are tiny matters compared to what lies within us."* He hadn't just discovered what lay within—he had chosen to live from it, and with every step, to leave a ripple behind.

"Finding Waldo" had never been about becoming someone different. It was about returning inward, reclaiming the presence, the purpose, and the quiet strength that had been there all along. And he no longer needed to be seen to know he mattered. Somewhere in the dark, ripples moved beyond the shoreline, carrying pieces of him into stories he'd never hear, lives he'd never touch directly, but they would still matter. They already did.

By the time the final tassel turned and the spring air carried echoes of names called at graduation, something in their home had shifted too —not all at once, but like the seasons: slow, steady, inevitable. Waldo took a breath and in that sacred stillness, he knew without a doubt that he had finally found peace.

$\sim$

A Final Note from Me to You

~

Waldo's story may have reached its final page, but for me, this journey lives far beyond the ending.

Finding Waldo Within began as something personal—a way to make sense of the questions I've carried for years. Questions without easy answers. But somewhere along the way, it stopped being just about me. It became something more: a reflection of the quiet, the often unspoken longing many of us carry, and the search for meaning, for connection, for peace.

If you've made it this far, my hope isn't that you've walked away with answers. It's that you feel a little more willing to sit with the questions. To stay curious. To keep listening. To trust the unfolding of your own story. Like Waldo, I've faced dragons. Detours. Moments of silence so loud they left me rattled. But I've also been held together by music, by laughter, and by people who showed up at just the right time—sometimes, only briefly, and sometimes, for good.

If something in these pages stirred something in you—a memory, a feeling, a moment of pause—then maybe a ripple has begun. That's all I can ever hope for.

Thank you for walking this part of the path with me. And remember, you don't need the whole map. Just the next step. Wherever your journey leads, may you walk it with faith, with courage, and with enough wonder to keep going.

Warmly,

S. Bobby

There is a path beneath the noise, beneath the waiting.
It does not demand answers—only your willingness to walk.
You were never lost.
Only learning to trust the thread you already held in your hand.

The journey behind *Finding Waldo Within* was shaped by more than just plotlines and character arcs—it was built on a foundation of insight, reflection, and the lived and shared experiences that continue to guide those in search of deeper meaning. While much of this novel emerged from personal reflection, it was also deeply informed by stories entrusted to me over the years—conversations with friends, family, and readers who have navigated their own turning points. Their quiet bravery, honest questions, and moments of uncertainty helped me write more truthfully than I ever could alone.

What follows is a curated list of the key works, ideas, and creative influences that helped form the emotional and intellectual architecture of this novel. Spanning philosophy, literature, psychology, music, and lived experiences, each entry represents a thread in the fabric of Waldo's unfolding.

These authors, thinkers, artists, and songs didn't just inform the story—they helped shape the space from which it was written. From quiet porch moments to turning points in the maze, their presence can be felt throughout the story's heartbeat—sometimes, in a quote, sometimes in a mood, and often in the subtle, teachable moments that echo long after the final page.

And now, if something stayed with you—if a thread caught, or a question stirred—I'd love to hear what echoed forward.

What Stayed With You?

~

Some stories stay with us—not because they answered something,
 but because they named what we hadn't yet spoken.

If *Finding Waldo Within* stirred something in you—a memory, a
question, a quiet shift—I'd be honored to hear what echoed forward.

You don't need perfect words. Just your voice, in whatever shape it
takes.

This isn't about response—it's about resonance. It's how we recognize the threads that connect us, and the signals that guide us quietly
home.

Scan the QR code
or visit:
https://sbobbyalexander.com/reflections/share-reflection-waldo/

https://sbobbyalexander.com/reflections/share-reflection-waldo/

A space to speak back to the story — now, or whenever you're ready.

Ways to Share

Choose what feels right for you:
- Share a private reflection (via the form)
- Offer a short testimonial (for the Reader Reflections wall)
- Leave your line—a single sentence that stayed with you
- You may remain anonymous, if you prefer—the story still hears you

Because sometimes, writing it down is how we remember what mattered.

And sharing it is how we pass it on—one truth, one step, one echo at a time.

With gratitude,

S. Bobby

∾

Inspiration Behind the Journey

~

I. Foundational Works & Guiding Voices

Ralph Waldo Emerson – *Self-Reliance*

Emerson's reflections on authenticity, individualism, and inner truth form the philosophical core of the novel. His call to "trust thyself" reverberates through Waldo's gradual reawakening.

Friedrich Nietzsche – *Thus Spoke Zarathustra*

Nietzsche's embrace of becoming—not despite struggle but through it—shapes Waldo's deeper reckoning with adversity and the idea that suffering may be essential to growth.

Marcus Aurelius – *Meditations*

The stoic lens of acceptance, resilience, and control of the inner self offered grounding throughout Waldo's reflections—and echoes in Nathan's emotional restraint.

Aristotle – *Metaphysics*

The novel's core question, what does it mean to live the good life?, draws from Aristotle's exploration of purpose, fulfillment, and the journey toward potential.

Stephen R. Covey – *The 7 Habits of Highly Effective People*

Covey's call to lead with intention and to prioritize what matters most, helped shape Waldo's shift from survival to meaning. His presence lingers in the narrative's quiet questions: what are you building? Who are you becoming?

Joseph Campbell – *The Hero with a Thousand Faces*

The arc of Waldo's journey borrows from Campbell's classic Hero's Journey structure: the call, the mentors, the descent, the gift, and the return. Except here, the dragons are internal.

Kahlil Gibran – *The Prophet*

The poetic, spiritual intimacy of Gibran's work informed the emotional texture between Waldo and Sara and his desire to pass on something meaningful to his children without forcing answers.

James Hollis – *Finding Meaning in the Second Half of Life*

This piece echoes Waldo's questioning of inherited definitions of success, identity, and masculinity.

Viktor E. Frankl – *Man's Search for Meaning*

Frankl's belief that suffering, when met with purpose, can become a gateway to transformation, deeply shapes the novel's exploration of resilience. His insight—that meaning can be found even in the face of pain—is demonstrated through Waldo's gradual reframing of his own struggles.

Pema Chödrön – *When Things Fall Apart*

Chödrön's compassionate guidance on embracing groundlessness helped inform the emotional tone of surrender that runs through Waldo's arc. Her call to lean into discomfort, rather than resist it, becomes a quiet undercurrent in Waldo's journey toward inner steadiness.

II. Therapeutic & Psychological Frameworks

Carl Jung – Collected Works
Jung's ideas of the shadow self and integration deeply inform the maze metaphor. Waldo's dreams and internal wanderings mirror Jung's belief that, to meet the true self, we must first face what we fear.

Brené Brown – *Daring Greatly* and *The Gifts of Imperfection*
The themes of vulnerability, courage, and emotional transparency are cornerstones of Waldo's healing.

Tara Brach – *Radical Acceptance*
Brach's insight into presence and self-compassion informs Waldo's journey toward wholeness. Her teachings help reframe acceptance— not as surrender but as a quiet path to freedom from false striving.

Matt Haig – *The Midnight Library*
This piece explores themes of regret, second chances, and finding meaning in life's different possibilities, similar to Waldo's quest for fulfillment and imagined lives unlived.

Gail Honeyman – *Eleanor Oliphant is Completely Fine*
This novel focuses on a woman's journey of self-discovery and connection, echoing Waldo's search for belonging, healing, and authenticity beneath a carefully maintained exterior.

III. Personal Dialogues & Everyday Wisdom

The voices of family, mentors, strangers, and small-town rhythms were instrumental in shaping the heart of the story. Much of Waldo's awakening is less about answers and more about echoes—echoes of his father's quiet truths, his mother's music, Sara's strength, and the questions posed by a park bench stranger.

IV. Cultural Echoes & Lived Wisdom

Mark Twain

"The two most important days in your life are the day you are born and the day you find out why." This frames Waldo's quest not for success but for rooted purpose.

Henry Ford

"Whether you think you can, or you think you can't—you're right." This sentiment reflects Nathan's self-doubt and his growth into believing in his own voice.

Mahatma Gandhi

"Be the change you wish to see in the world." Both Waldo's evolution and Sara's steady presence stem from this principle—transformation that begins at home.

Wayne Gretzky

"You miss 100% of the shots you don't take." This one threads itself into Nathan's leap toward independence and Waldo's overdue courage to risk rediscovery.

Albert Einstein

Einstein's respect for curiosity and imagination influenced Waldo's shift away from rigid certainty and toward wonder and presence.

Mother Teresa

Her life as an embodiment of presence and compassion ripples through the nurturing legacy passed from Waldo's mother to Sara to Grace.

Paulo Coelho – *The Alchemist*

A fable about following one's dreams and uncovering one's "personal legend" mirrors Waldo's internal pilgrimage toward purpose, clarity, and home within the self.

Mitch Albom – *Tuesdays with Morrie*

A touching exploration of life's deeper lessons through candid conversations about love, meaning, and mortality, resonating with Waldo's awakening to legacy and presence.

Fredrik Backman – *A Man Called Ove*

A piece that centers on a solitary man learning to reconnect and heal through unexpected relationships, paralleling Waldo's emotional thaw and rediscovery of quiet meaning.

V. Creative and Poetic Resonance

Robert Frost – "The Road Not Taken"

Waldo's journey is less about choosing the obvious path and more about realizing which trail he's been afraid to follow.

J.R.R. Tolkien – *The Fellowship of the Ring*

Themes of inner strength, quiet courage, and finding purpose through connection echo throughout the Turner family's emotional bonds.

Vincent van Gogh

"Great things are done by a series of small things brought together." Grace embodies this spirit—beauty in everyday moments, the unnoticed gifts of presence.

Martin Handford – *Where's Waldo?*

The title is more than playful. Like his namesake, Waldo Turner has always been there, hiding in plain sight, waiting to be seen—even by himself.

Parker J. Palmer – *Let Your Life Speak*

Palmer's reflections on vocation and authenticity resonate with Waldo's shift from external obligation to inner alignment. His call to "listen to your life" mirrors Waldo's quiet turn inward, from noise to knowing.

David Whyte – Poetry & Essays

Whyte's meditations on courage, presence, and the emotional terrain of transformation echo in Waldo's interior tone. His poetry helped shape the novel's rhythm—slow, questioning, and quietly bold.

Mary Oliver – "The Journey," "Wild Geese," & Other Poems

Oliver's reverence for nature and her gentle insistence on self-trust breathe through Waldo's moments of stillness. Her invitation to belong to oneself, "No matter how lonely," is a quiet thread in his becoming.

Anne Lamott – *Traveling Mercies & Bird by Bird*

Lamott's voice—candid, wry, and quietly reverent—helped shape the tone of Waldo's narration. Her belief that grace lives inside the mess offered permission for both humor and humility.

Clarissa Pinkola Estés – *Women Who Run with the Wolves*

Estés' mythic approach to storytelling and her reverence for intuition helped shape the novel's symbolic layers—especially the inner maze, the dragon metaphors, and the quiet return to instinct. Her work echoes in Waldo's journey toward wholeness through reconnection with his deeper, often hidden, self.

bell hooks – *All About Love* **& Other Works**

hooks' reflections on love as an active, conscious choice resonate throughout Waldo's evolving relationships with Sara, with his children, and with himself. Her belief that love requires honesty, presence, and accountability helped frame the emotional undercurrent of reconnection in the second half of the novel.

Brené Brown – *The Gifts of Imperfection*

This piece encourages embracing vulnerability and wholehearted living—aligning with Waldo's evolution through self-compassion, courage, and letting go of performance.

M. Scott Peck – *The Road Less Traveled*

A spiritual and psychological guide to growth, discipline, and love—echoing Waldo's struggle with resistance, discomfort, and the slow work of inner transformation.

Dale Wimbrow – "The Man in the Glass"

A poetic reminder that self-respect and truth begin with the reflection in the mirror, underscoring Waldo's eventual reckoning with the man behind the mask.

VI. Musical Undercurrents

Music in *Finding Waldo Within* isn't just a backdrop—it's a companion to the soul, a way of expressing what Waldo often couldn't articulate. In key scenes, melodies stand in for memory, for longing, and for truth. These songs and composers shaped the emotional resonance of the novel, capturing everything from quiet despair to flickers of hope.

Pink Floyd – "Comfortably Numb" & "Another Brick in the Wall"

These tracks capture the early layers of Waldo's emotional detachment—the walls he built, the numbness he mistook for stability. Their echo lingers as he begins to confront the hollowness behind his façade.

Ludovico Einaudi – "Nuvole Bianche"

A delicate, aching piano piece that reflects Waldo's quiet porch moments—filled with reflection, melancholy, and the slow unfurling of something more hopeful.

Nick Drake – "Place to Be"

Introspective and tender, this track resonates with Waldo's inner ache, his quiet search for a place where he feels truly at home within himself.

Simon & Garfunkel – "The Sound of Silence"

A haunting anthem for emotional disconnection. This song underlines the distance between Waldo and Sara during their unspoken struggles—silence louder than words.

George Winston – *Autumn*

Winston's solo piano offers a meditative calm, an echo of the small, grounded beauty Waldo begins to rediscover through presence, family, and stillness.

Sara Bareilles – "Uncharted"

This song speaks to venturing into the unknown without a clear map—a lyrical twin to Waldo's shift from needing answers to simply embracing the process of becoming.

Jordin Sparks – "One Step at a Time"

A heartbeat of encouragement that quietly underscores Waldo's arc —the reminder that healing, change, and meaning don't arrive all at once. They come, one honest step at a time.

Tommy Emmanuel & Andy McKee – Instrumentals

Their acoustic guitar work—intricate, expressive, and wordless— mirrors Waldo's emotional honesty. It's the music he might play when words fall short, when emotion speaks louder than language.

Crosby, Stills, Nash & Young – "Teach Your Children"

This is a long-remembered tune that drifts through Waldo's reflections. The message lingers as a quiet guide—not to pass down perfection, but presence. To be an example, not an answer.

VII. Spiritual & Reflective Touchpoints

Lao Tzu – *Tao Te Ching*

Its quiet wisdom shapes the novel's rhythm and tone, urging surrender over control, flow over force. Waldo's path echoes its central truth: the way forward often begins by letting go.

Thich Nhat Hanh – *Peace Is Every Step*

His gentle teachings on mindfulness and presence inform Waldo's shift from reaction to awareness. The call to, "Wash the dishes to wash the dishes," echoes in Waldo's embrace of everyday rituals as acts of intention and peace.

Shunryu Suzuki – *Zen Mind, Beginner's Mind*

Suzuki's insight—that true understanding comes from openness, not expertise—parallels Waldo's journey from certainty to curiosity. The beginner's mind becomes his quiet companion as he learns to meet life freshly, moment by moment.

Rumi – Spiritual Insight Through Paradox and Presence

Rumi's poetry hums in the emotional undercurrent of *Finding Waldo Within*—not as quotation, but as quiet philosophy. His work reminds us that longing, uncertainty, and inner ache are not flaws in the journey, but signals of depth. That what feels broken may, in time, become a doorway.

Waldo's path echoes Rumi's enduring belief: that healing doesn't arrive despite our wounds, but often through them. That we must lean into the silence, the ache, the unraveling—because it's there that the light first begins to seep in.

Rather than lifting direct lines, this novel is shaped by the spirit of Rumi—the way his words invite us not to solve life's mysteries, but to live them. In that way, his presence lingers—not in a stanza, but in the spaces between them.

Jon Kabat-Zinn – Mindfulness-Based Stress Reduction (MBSR)

This inspired the rhythm and internal stillness explored during Waldo's retreat.

Christian Mysticism – *The Cloud of Unknowing*

This classic text shapes Waldo's quiet return to faith—not as belief in answers, but as trust in presence. Its core message, that love, not knowledge, leads to truth, echoes in his journey toward grace, stillness, and surrender.

These titles and thinkers offered handholds and lanterns—not definitive answers but invitations. They shaped not only Waldo's growth, but the space I created to write him into being. So, if Waldo's journey stirred something within you, these titles may deepen your own exploration, offering insight long after the final page.

What if clarity isn't something we find—but something we remember?

∾

About the Author

~

S. Bobby Alexander is a devoted husband, father of three, and recently retired professional whose life has been shaped by over five decades of experience in sales, consulting, entrepreneurship, teaching, and the arts. A lifelong storyteller at heart, Bobby has worn many hats—business owner, mentor, collector of art, and now, author.

His journey through personal and professional setbacks, fatherhood, reinvention, and self-discovery forms the soul of his writing. With a style that is authentic, heartfelt, and insightfully relatable, his stories are shaped by a lifetime of lived experience—the very ground from which his hard-earned insights have grown. These are the pearls of wisdom he's passed on to his children over the years—not as rules, but as anchors. Simple, quiet truths meant to guide—not instruct.

Finding Waldo Within marks Bobby's debut as a writer—another reinvention in a life filled with purpose. What began as a personal reflection evolved into a gift of guidance, written not just to tell a story, but to pass something meaningful on. His approach to writing is an extension of the way he's always led: by example, with warmth and perspective, always keeping what truly matters—family, connection, and presence—at the center.

He lives on the East Coast, where he enjoys collecting art, listening to music, savoring great movies and musicals, reading, cooking, and drinking a well-made cup of coffee. His ongoing passion? Pursuing one's true calling—and helping others find theirs.

Legacy is rarely loud.

Sometimes it arrives in the form of a quiet phrase, passed hand to hand—from grandfather to father, from father to son—waiting until we're ready to understand it.

"What they gave me wasn't advice—it was experience, folded gently into words, so I might walk farther with fewer wounds. They didn't give me answers. They gave me nourishment—small, steady truths that stayed with me long after they were gone."
— **S. Bobby Alexander**

Live your best life—it's later than you think.

~

Disclaimer and Acknowledgments:

Disclaimer and Acknowledgments:

The artwork, graphics, writing and story development presented in **Finding Waldo Within** *were created with the assistance of artificial intelligence tools. While every effort has been made to ensure the authenticity and originality of the content, AI-assisted technology played a role in the creative process.*

All ultimate decisions, narrative direction, and thematic elements are the sole responsibility of the author, **S. Bobby Alexander***, and any interpretations or attributions made are based on that collaboration.*

Special thanks to the communities and individuals who shared their experiences with me, shaping the insights that I tried to convey through Waldo's story. Each of you played a role in helping me explore the human spirit, resilience, and the idea of personal growth.

To my readers, thank you for trusting me with your time and emotions as you journeyed with Waldo through his quest for meaning and self-discovery. Your engagement is the heartbeat of this book.

Finally, to the philosophers, writers, and thinkers whose works I've referenced and drawn inspiration from, your words lit the path for me in moments when I needed wisdom.

∾

www.ingramcontent.com/pod-product-compliance
Lightning Source LLC
Chambersburg PA
CBHW050021120726
47903CB00006B/1865